TWISTED TALES FROM THE DARKSIDE

The Devil's Playground

L.T. James

Copyright © 2023 by L.T. James

All rights reserved.

No part of this publication may be reproduced, distributed, or transmitted in any form or by any means, including photocopying, recording, or other electronic or mechanical methods, without the prior written permission of the publisher. For permission requests, contact [Tara James: jamestaralynn@outlook.com].

The story, all names, characters, and incidents portrayed in this production are fictitious. No identification with actual persons (living or deceased), places, buildings, and products is intended or should be inferred.

Book Cover by Alejandro Colucci, Page Logo design by Ella James

ISBN: 9781738958702

THE DEVIL'S PLAYGROUND	7
EVIL RISES	36
THE GREAT ESCAPE	59
IF THERE BE MAGIC	96
YOU BETTER WATCH OUT	122
ACE OF SOULS	150

For my mother, who is still inspiring me from the next realm.

ABOUT THE AUTHOR

L.T. James is an up-and-coming Canadian born author with a passion for horror, supernatural and paranormal fiction and actively participates in writing workshops to perfect her library of ideas.

Her debut collection, "Twisted Tales from the Darkside – The Devil's Playground," is designed with Tales from the Darkside, Creepshow and Twilight Zone in mind and crafted to deliver the quick horror fix that fans of the genre crave.

ABOUT THE COVER DESIGNER

Alejandro Colucci is an award-winning artist born to Italian immigrant parents in Uruguay. He has illustrated hundreds of covers in the fantasy, crime, horror, historic fiction and science fiction genres; commissioned by major publishers across Europe and the USA.

Bestselling authors including Anne Rice, Robin Hobb, Isacc Asimov, J.G. Ballard and many more have featured his illustrations in their books.
He and his wife are the founders of the Design company Epica Prima.

THE DEVIL'S PLAYGROUND

Ricky Lawson and Eddy Crowley hit the road in their 1972 GMC short van loaded with the day's haul and Two Wire Guys magnetic decals still affixed. They headed for the NY-79E to meet up with their buyer unsure of the route.

"We shoulda checked out that place at Four Corners. I knew it would be tons better. Didn't I say?" Rick poked.

"Ya, well, you can't win them all, Ricky."

"It ain't too late to turn back, man. Why can't I be the driver for once?"

Eddy was always the driver, so he could call all the shots on the houses they broke into. Ricky checked out neighborhoods like he was trick-or-treating, not like he was on a careful mission.

"You know the rules. Never two houses in one neighborhood."

Eddy's calm demeanor, while effective, often put Ricky on the defensive.

"I'm too dog-tired to argue, so go where you want!"

A moment later, Ricky pulled the convenience store bag from below his feet and offered his friend a

Slim Jim and a Yoo-Hoo. Eddy only responded with a smirk.

Ricky slept until he heard the opening of AC/DC's Hells Bells on the stereo.

"Best song ever, crank it up!"

Eddy just kept driving. He was in the zone and when he was in the zone, not much could distract him. Ricky reached for the volume knob to feed his rock fix.

Eddy was patient and waited for the song to end before turning down the volume.

"I'm dead serious, Ricky. This is the last hurrah."

"Quitting now is not an option, man. The last couple jobs alone got us ten grand. We're just gettin' started!"

You know what they say, too much of a good thing... *With all the shit we've been through, he's never happy. There must always be another notch higher.*

"After we find the next town, we will talk about it, okay?"

Eddy never got argumentative with him. Their tight friendship dated back to pre-K. Over the years, they found themselves in plenty of sticky situations and Ricky always bailed them out, but now in their early twenties; It was time to grow up. The two had been motoring for almost five hours, including three pit-stops.

The radio frequency jolted from a tolerable static to right out of tune.

Within seconds, the van's engine sputtered with backfire from the tailpipe. The headlights flickered on and off. It lost power, then regained it and lost it again.

"What the hell?" Eddy said as he looked ahead for the closest exit from the highway.

"Look! We can get off there, hurry before we break down, man!" Ricky rarely panicked, but being stuck on the side of the 79E at eleven o'clock at night was not ideal.

"Come on, Betsy old girl, don't quit on us now!" Eddy's reasoning had gotten the van's cooperation in the past.

She chugged and sputtered to the exit. Betsy was purring like a kitten after they got off the highway, like nothing ever went wrong.

Eddy made a quick stop at a gas station, where he checked her engine and scoped out their surroundings.

He turned the engine back on, grabbed his trouble light, and plugged it into the portable power block. After he opened the hood, he went straight to checking the battery connections.

He tested the wiring to the headlights by disconnecting and reconnecting and gave the wires a gentle wiggle to ensure that they were all attached. The wiring was in working order.

As he stood there, he watched and listened to the engine while it ran, taking a drag from his cigarette.

"So? Did this POS finally kick the bucket? Dude, I keep tellin' ya. It's time to retire Betsy to the graveyard."

Ricky loved making Betsy the butt of his Chevy and GMC jokes, as he was a lifelong Ford driver.

"Yeah, yeah, funny. Although don't you find it odd that she produced all that sputtering and resistance until we got off the highway and landed in… wait, I don't even know where we are."

"Manhattan buddy! I've always wanted to come here! Look at them lights down the road!" Ricky's eager tone was making him nervous.

"Ricky, my instincts are telling me we should leave this place right away. Let's go!"

"Naw! Let's just take a drive around and check the place out. Quit worry'n."

Recognizing that the time was already past midnight, Eddy agreed to search for a place to stay overnight and leave in the morning.

They left the gas station behind them and travelled south. On the left side of the street, was full of gastro pubs and neon signs, while the right side had fancy hotels.

"Let's splurge man! One night in a ritzy hotel, whad'ya say?"

Eddy also always managed their cash.

"At six-hundred-dollars per night, dream on!"

They kept driving, with Ricky looking for cheap motels on the left side, as instructed as his accomplice scanned the right but didn't approve of the ritzy or high-end options.

"I'm gonna park somewhere low-key for the night. We can check out some pubs if you want the Manhattan experience, but that's all!"

"You fuckin' suck balls, but ya, okay."

Ricky envisioned being free and tried to cover up his mischievous grin.

They ended up in Midtown West without even realizing it.

They came upon a building with directional signs on a pole in front of it. One read Hell's Kitchen District and the other two were street names.

"Dude! Stop the van! Do you know where we are! The famous Hell's Kitchen district!"

Eddy slowed down, looking for an alley. Two windows above the sidewalk, one with a Psychic Reading sign and the other with a "For Lease" sign. Seeing Ricky's impatience, Eddy pulled over and found a spot to parallel park that was spot on.

"What are you going on about?"

"This is something we can't miss! I'll even park down that alley for the night!"

Since Ricky had big dreams of a fancy life and stopped pouting about parking in a dark alley for the night, Eddy obliged out of pure curiosity.

"There! the perfect place to park this POS!"

"Don't refer to Betsy as a POS ever again." Eddy replied in his driest tone.

The only source of light in the alleyway came from the streetlamps on West 50th, casting eerie shadows on the walls. Two garbage bins sat side by side, overflowing with bags and swarming with flies. Eddy parked Betsy and

waited, uncertain about his agreement to follow Ricky into the rabbit hole of the unknown.

"Turn 'er off, man. We need to stay under the radar.

Eddy listened to Ricky and turned off the engine and headlights. A few yards down, a spooky old Manhattan Brownstone. No lights or house numbers.

"Let's get out and walk over there!"

Eddy's stomach plummeted like an elevator in a skyscraper, leaving him speechless.

"Well? Come on, man! Where's yer sense of adventure?"

"Back in Rochester. We're leaving."

Ricky bounced out of the van and left the door wide open, rushing through the shadows to the Brownstone. Eddy stayed in the van, refusing involvement and tapping his fingers on the chain-link custom steering wheel.

***

Up close, the building looked menacing, dark inside and secluded from the rest of the town of Clinton, better known as Hell's Kitchen.

Along the right side, a narrow pathway lined with strange shrubbery adorned with red berries that Ricky had never seen before.

He took the path. The front should have faced West 50th, but it looked like it was on its own street. On the roof level was a fancy patio with tiki torches, but nothing else within eyeshot.

He made his way to the door, taking his time, and checked for any cameras and walked the perimeter of the building again to check for the alarm system. *Are you kidding me? Holy crap, this is amazing!* He went to the back of the building again, lost in thought. After he checked out the entire property, he came back to the front door.

Since he didn't see any danger, he tried the front door latch. The door swung open with a small turn of the knob.

His adrenaline surged, as he couldn't shake Eddy's haunting words from his mind. *"You know what they say, too much of a good thing."*

He was determined to continue. This was go time, as Ricky would say when they landed a big paying gig.

***

Odd Paintings of people in flames adorned the walls of the front entrance. A canvas blank except for a single flame in the center caught his attention for a few moments.

The wall met with an eighteen-foot vaulted ceiling. The winding staircase was constructed of thick, black granite and pillars of solid teak.

He made his way to the top floor, scanning wall shelves, noting the valuables.

The top floor was pitch-black, except for the moonlight streaming through massive floor-to-ceiling windows on the west wall. His fingertips grazed the textured walls as he searched for a light switch next to the moonlit windows. No light switches.

A long credenza cast a shadow on the floor, revealing the elegant shape of a Tiffany lamp.

In the dimly lit room, he made his way to the lamp and flicked the switch on, illuminating the space. Both the ceiling and teak floorboards were awash with a stunning array of colors, creating a mesmerizing display.

A vast area rug lay in the center of the floor. A fine tapestry depicting a gothic sun and moon beneath the branches of an evil-looking tree.

As he contemplated the tapestry, a crackling voice interrupted his thoughts.

"Braaaaaaak, say hello to Baxter."

He jumped in search of the source of the voice, but no one was there. He stood frozen, sweat dripping from his forehead in tiny droplets, waiting to be caught in the act of breaking and entering.

The voice crowed again, and goosebumps rose on his neck and arms as it urged him to greet Baxter.

"Hello?" He responded in hopes he had just imagined it.

"Say hello to Baxter."

The voice echoed and bounced off every surface, making it impossible to pinpoint its origin.

"What the f—"

He turned his head towards the voice. Nothing in sight. *Is this some goofy alarm system to scare the shit outta burglars?*

A spotlight in the room's corner illuminated the area, revealing an enormous wrought iron cage perched on a concrete pedestal.

An African gray parrot's eyes peered from the spindles of the elaborate cage. The light hit its eyes like glints of fire against black onyx.

With a sheepish expression, Ricky approached the cage and fixed his eyes on the bird inside.

"Say hello to Baxter."

Its voice was louder and invoked the worst jump scare he had ever experienced.

The parrot's long black slits in the center of its eyes gave it a fierce stare as it scrutinized his face.

Ricky addressed the bird in an uneasy tone.

"Baxter, oh Baxter wanna cracker?"

The parrot did not respond.

"Dumb bird, is that all ya know how to say? 'Say hello to Baxter'? Why don't you answer me if yer so smart?"

"I'm Velma. Say hello to Baxter."

"Okay, Velma, where's Scooby?"

Ricky's laughter erupted with uncontrollable force. A mix of amusement and anxiety churning in his stomach. He shifted his attention from Velma and headed towards the bay window in the living room. The silhouettes of trees visible from the window punctuated the darkness outside.

This is nuts. It seems like we're in the middle of a desert, but we're an enormous city.

He continued to examine the living room, observing more valuables. This could be their biggest job if Eddy would only agree to stay and watch it for two more nights.

The living room was filled with glass cabinets full of odd artifacts.

Ricky crept eastward from the living room to the kitchen of the loft-style floor, following the parrot's silence to explore the rest of the room.

As he made his way past the twelve-foot marble countertop, he noticed a touch panel in the center, the size of an iPad installed into the marble. Pulling his phone from his back pocket, he enabled the flashlight app and looked at the panel.

No prints, so he didn't dare touch it.

It's gotta be connected to one of them fancy smart home systems like—

His phone dinged three times, a text from Eddy. The sound echoed, making his heart jump.

"Say hello to Baxter."

"Holy shit bird!"

The parrot's voice was shrill and sudden, causing him to recoil and hit the countertop, almost dropping his phone.

As he steadied himself to text Eddy back, an unseen force ripped the phone from his hand.

It landed four feet to his left in front of a dark hallway, lit by the colors of the Tiffany lamp.

He wasn't sure how to go ahead, but he knew he had to leave, so he stood frozen and took a deep breath.

Ok Ricky, stop bein a baby, get yer phone an' get outta here!

He counted to three, including the 'one thousand' between one, two, and three, and made a jump for it to his phone, but only got just over two feet. "Fuck!"

He gathered himself and jumped a second time, landing in front of his phone.

The hallway in front of him was eerie and scarce of sound except for heavy, salivated breathing in the darkness.

Fumbling and shaking, he reached for his phone while he mapped his quick escape.

The breathing got louder; this time accompanied by the foul smell of rotted meat.

As his stomach growled, his fear transformed into an all-consuming terror. Despite his hesitation, he couldn't resist looking up one more time into the hallway.

Two glowing red eyes appeared and moved closer. The ominous growl of a vicious creature ready to pounce accompanied the sound of labored breathing.

The beast's shadow loomed larger and larger on the ground in front of Ricky until his phone dinged, causing him to jump in surprise.

Goddam it! Quit fuckin textin Eddy! He became mesmerized by the shape that was becoming visible to him.

Ding. Ding. Ding.

It was now within Ricky's grasp, but a paw the size of a grizzly bear's appeared from the hallway and snatched it away.

Shit! I need to get the hell outta here!

With the phone now crushed beneath its paw, a head appeared. Enormous, resembling Cane Corso's, its fur all black.

The glowing eyes slanted into a scowl as the nostrils flared, sniffing at his prey.

Ricky, known for his toughness, was almost in tears.

As he waited on in shock, a second set of eyes, glowing green, appeared from behind the beast, followed by a second head and then a third, orange eyed.

The creature's body was sturdy, supporting the weight of all three heads on its muscular necks. The creature in front of him was a three-headed Cerberus, poised to strike.

He ran toward the parrot's cage in the living room in a panic frenzy, looking for the stairwell from which he came.

He took a deep breath and concentrated on the putrid smell and sounds of its painting, trying to figure out its proximity to the living room.

Fuckin' hell! Why didn't he come out when I got here? Now I'm dead. I might as well just lie down and shut my eyes!

Faint from shallow hyperventilating, he closed his eyes. He fell to the tapestry rug in the center of the room and prayed for the first time in his twenty-two years on earth.

The thump of four giant paws and the heavy sound of deadly claws scratching the floor pursued him, pushing him to the far wall.

His back, slippery with sweat, slid with ease as he fell to the floor. The foul smell escalated into the wretched essence of death.

He opened his eyes just enough to see the creature through the blur.

As one head snapped its jaws in his left ear and another in his right, Ricky imagined the gruesome end that awaited him.

They're gonna rip my flesh off, strip by strip, and my guts'll spill all over this floor!

The third head opened its vast mouth, jetted with a snarl of sharp teeth, right over his face.

God help me, please get me outta this mess!

The first touch of sharp teeth grazed his face. Drool dripped down his left cheek.

"Braaaaakkk, Daddy's home!"

With that, the Cerberus retreated and ran to the top of the winding staircase.

The clickety clack of hard bottom shoes made their way to the landing.

Ricky clenched his butt cheeks and closed his eyes as tight as they would go.

I don't wanna know what daddy is like if he owns a beast this terrifying!

 "Baxter, have you been a well-behaved beast tonight?" The menacing creature bounced its heads in response to master.

There stood a man dressed in pinstriped black slacks, a red silk shirt with a black double-breasted vest and a black bowtie.

Thick black hair, cut and styled to underwear model perfection. The smell of his expensive cologne permeated Ricky's nostrils as he lay on the floor, shaking.

Baxter's master walked with deliberate steps, emphasizing the clicking of his lavish oxfords.

Now looming over him, the man looked at least six-foot-six.

"Well, well, it's been a long time since we've had a guest."

The man's sadistic glee was clear as he spoke, while Baxter snarled behind him, all three sets of eyes fixed on Ricky. Their bloodthirsty mouths, laden with savage teeth, waiting for permission to attack.

"Please, Sir! I shouldn't have come in here, I know that I just thought since the door opened and, and no alarm system and all, and—"

"Shhhh, you're babbling."

"But, Sir, if I can just be on my way now, I-I took nothing, I promise, you can even search me!"

"Well!"

The man laughed in a boisterous rumble fit for a giant.

"Lucky for you then!"

"So, if-if, I can go, then we can p-pretend this never happened, r-right?"

His words were shaky as the rest of his body lead him to emit a sheepish chuckle.

The beast walked on its four bear-sized paws out from behind its master, salivating.

Bucket sized drops of saliva pooled on the teak flooring as it moved closer to his spot on the floor.

Clack, clack, clack went the claws until it stood right above him.

Ding. Ding. Ding. echoed from the hallway landing.

Baxter ran to it with all of its heads fighting to grasp it; the one on the left prevailed, chomping the phone with its powerful jaw.

Shards of glass and plastic littered the ground, which another head bowed down and ate.

***

"Come on Ricky, answer me, you dumb mofo!"

Eddy had been sitting for over two hours and had reached the point of anger.

"That's it. Obviously, he's ditched me and is out getting in trouble like an idiot in some bar!"

He drove the van over to Brownstone, that started this impromptu adventure.

He sat idling and cranked the handle of the driver's side window, sticking his head out to gaze up at the building. Dark, save for the massive rooftop patio lined with tiki torches.

He drove up the alleyway and turned right on west 50th to get a better view of the front for activity inside. No lights were on, dead as a strip club at six am.

"Yep, that retard went to a fucking bar and left me sitting like a stool pigeon waiting for him!"

He headed toward West 51st, searching for an establishment that his friend would frequent.

***

"Baxter want num nums?"

The Cerberus raised all three of its heads and ran to the kitchen, sliding sideways on the saliva pools.

"Please, can I go now?"

The man went to the kitchen's marble countertop and turned on the touch screen embedded in it. The living room lights flickered on and a massive seventy-inch flatscreen TV slid out from the wall above the fireplace.

Oh, now! Now the shit worth taking comes out, fuckin' hell! Ricky thought with spite as he awaited further punishment.

The sound of chains being cranked on a pulley system echoed through the room from the ceiling. He watched as the imposing cage structure descended towards him from above.

He leaped up, and in an instant, Baxter was back without a sound, like an apparition in a horror movie scene.

Distracted by the prospect of being devoured, it surprised him when the cage slammed to the floor, trapping him.

The man poured himself a scotch on the rocks and turned the television on surfing for something to unwind to. The beast whimpered and wined from the kitchen.

"Oh, Baxter, daddy's sorry, you want blood, don't you?"

Ricky waited in sick silence as the man went back to the kitchen and retrieved a meat cleaver.

"Baxter, sit nice!"

The beast scrambled and perched next to the cage awaiting its dinner.

With one goat's head in each hand, the man walked over, holding them by the horns above his pet.

Blood dripped from the horns, and the mouths of the beast caught every drop.

He let go of them and Baxter laid on the floor, two of his heads grabbing a horn and pulling the goat's head in half and the third left with one to itself.

"That ought to keep him busy for a while. Are you hungry? No? Well, let's get started then, shall we?"

"I wanna bounce and let you do your rituals or whatever. I swear I'll keep my mouth shut. Cut me loose!"

Sinister laughter answered his pleading.

"Awe, come on, don't be such a lily liver. Hey, I have something enticing to show you! Watch closely."

Ricky stood in the cage, wincing. His heart pounded.

The man sauntered up to the cage and wrapped his fingers around the cold metal bars. He leaned down to Ricky's level, pressing his face against the cage. The handsome face of the homeowner wrinkled as his eyes grew bigger and his skin turned a rich crimson. Horns pressed through the thick black locks of his hair.

As the man grew to a staggering twelve feet, his face became even more frightening, with horns that curled downward and eyes that glowed like fire. The transformation was sudden - his fingers turned into dirty yellow claws, and wings burst forth from his back.

With a loud, booming, demonic voice, he spoke.

"You pestilent fool, you entered my house and now you belong to me!"

The sudden realization of who he was dealing with resonated in Ricky's mind as he searched, franticly, for the right thing to say.

"Oh please, Mr. Satan, sir, I-I-I'll give ya, my soul! Please! Just lemme go man! You can have whatever ya want!"

Satan transformed back to his handsome human form.

"Idiot. I've had your soul a long time."

"Ya right!" Ricky, now in his argumentative defense mode, challenged his captor.

"When you were ten years old, you loved to pick the legs off spiders. When you reached thirteen, you stole all the cash from the register at Sam's Market and ran. At eighteen, you used fake ID to get into

Finnegan's Pub and got yourself into a bar fight and when told to take it outside, you killed a man with a pool cue and ran again!"

"How do you know all this shit? Nobody knows that stuff but Eddy!"

"You silly boy, I know everything there is to know about you, like God or Santa, but who am I kidding? God and Santa are figments of the human imagination!"

"Then what do you want from me?"

With a snap of his fingers, Satan summoned a throne with furry creature's legs that ran over to where he stood, in obedience.

He sat down with a contemplative look, placing his hands together and giving Ricky a once-over with a sly smile, his eyebrows arched in a sinister manner.

"Tell you what, if you can pass three tests, I will let you go."

Ricky, not known for his intelligence, hesitated.

Fuck, tests? What kinda tests? I might as well just forget it an' accept my fate!

"What kinda tests you talkin?"

"Simple ones, really. Are you up for it?"

"Um, ya, I guess."

The man sat upright from his comfortable slumped position on the throne, glee in his black eyes.

"Goody, I have a riddle for you! What is black and white and red all over?"

"Duh, a newspaper!"

"Ooh, nicely done, my boy!"

After sensing the facetiousness in the tone, he focused on the next riddle, determined to stay on top of his game.

"Okay, now, let's see how you do in Trivia."

"What was the name of the first man on the moon?"

"Neil Armstrong!" This one Ricky knew, because his dad used to go on and on about it.

Ricky's cocky response was met with three sharp claps from Satan, breaking the tense silence of the room.

"Very impressive! Now, for the entertainment part."

"Uh, I'm not much of an entertainer, Sir."

"Oh, but you are! You'll see."

In the blink of an eye, Ricky's outfit changed from rugged workwear to a pink velour robe and bunny slippers.

"Just what the fuck—"

"Shhhh, you're ruining my entertainment," Satan replied.

"What entertainment? Me lookin' like a damn fool?"

"Precisely. Let's kick it up a notch!"

Ricky's slippers felt warm and cozy at first, but after about five seconds. A tingling heat penetrated the soft

soles of his feet. The smell of burning plastic and melting flesh filled the air.

Fuck, I'm on fire!

The burning coals beneath his feet made him jump from left to right to avoid being engulfed in flames.

"Tell me a joke Ricky, you can be a funny guy sometimes!"

Embers from the coals jumped to the hair on his shins, biting one spot at a time as the coals got hotter.

He reached up and grabbed onto the bars higher in the cage and pulled his body up.

"Uh, um…" The nerves under the blanket of his fear gave way, once more, to a nervous giggle.

"Knock, kn-knock!"

"Who's there?"

"Lettuce."

"Lettuce who?"

"Um, lettuce in, it's c-c-cold out here!"

Satan glared at him, his black eyes turning yellow and fiery again. With a fast poof, flames surrounded Ricky, not quite touching his skin, but close enough to soak his hair, brow, and face with sweat.

"Well, now you have bored me beyond recognition." The loud clank of chains cut through the air. The flames were at once extinguished. The cage lifted, and Ricky's body flailed as his fingers clung tight to the bars. He dropped to the floor, his eyes fixated on his captor, waiting for a sign of confirmation.

"Don't just stand there, get out of my house!"

The monster version of Satan then stood brooding over Ricky, breathing heavy from his dark crimson nose and fang filled mouth.

Ricky took the invitation and scrambled to the spiral staircase. He stumbled down the steps, breaking his right ankle on the fifth step down and tumbling the rest of the way to the main floor. The strange paintings he had seen upon his arrival seemed to mock him as he grappled for the door latch to get out. The door was locked tight, with no key in sight.

Still wearing the ridiculous pink ensemble, he faded to mere mist as he was pulled into the almost blank canvas that had caught his eye hours before. Evil laughter roared down the steps.

Ricky, now in the painting, the single flame replaced with his tear stained, soot-caked face, and body engulfed in flame kissed chains.

"Help! Lemme out!" were the final words to leave his lips as he became part of the Devil's art collection for eternity.

L.T. JAMES

EVIL RISES

A sick feeling of butterflies erupted in Darius' stomach and fluttered in his heart. Everyone knew the Clarke's for their gut feelings, and he, the youngest to inherit them. He ran from the counter of Louanne's Beans and Brew without grabbing the grand size Americano he paid for.

"There's something wrong. I must go!"

"Hey, Darry, your coffee!" Louanne shouted at him.

He burst through the grandiose double-door entrance to his family home.

Calm down man, you're acting like a lunatic.

He slowed down and walked into the kitchen. The counters were as he left them an hour before. The second floor was quiet, so he headed up the staircase, first to his own room to get dressed for business then to his father's room. *Perhaps he had trouble sleeping during the night and slept in.*

He knocked on the door.

"Dad, wake up, you're supposed to start Ida Davis's embalming at seven-thirty!"

When he didn't get a response, he knocked again.

"Dad, are you okay?"

He was more than comfortable walking into the room but knocked a third time.

With extra urgency in his voice, "Dad, open the door!"

He sighed and admired his Florsheim wingtips.

Why don't you walk in?

Internal self-talk was a defense mechanism for Darius. With a slow turn of the doorknob, he took one more deep breath.

Upon walking into the master bedroom, he spotted bare feet from the corner of his eye; pressed against the antique Edwardian-era headboard of his elevated bed.

"What the—?"

He turned his head takin in the entire body.

Marcus Clarke lay with his head turned, facing the wall to the left of the bed, eyes half-open and mouth ajar.

Darius rushed over to his father's side and pushed his right shoulder hard three or four times to jar him awake. "Dad."

He pushed again. The shoulders, cold and stiffening by the second.

EVIL RISES

This can't be happening! Darius, he's sleeping. Maybe he took a couple of sleeping pills last night. Marcus' skin went from pale white to opaque grey, cloudy white took over the sapphire blue of his eyes.

"Fuck!" Darius shouted to himself while he cried, hyperventilating. He fumbled for his phone in the back pockets of his slacks, dropping it and sank to the floor next to Markus' bed, covered his face with his hands, and broke down.

***

 Jenny, their longtime family friend and administrator, heard shouting from the entryway of the house when she arrived.

Upon entering the room, she gasped and gathered herself to speak.

"Darry, it's all right. Where's your phone?"

"On th-th-the floor."

He hadn't stuttered since his Grade Twelve graduation speech. Jenny found the phone, composing herself the best she could before calling 911.

"Nine-one-one, police, ambulance, or fire?"

"Ambulance, please."

"One moment."

When she got through, she explained there had been a death.

"Are you positive he's passed?" The non-emergency desk clerk asked.

"Yes, yes, please send someone."

"Before I do that, I would like you to try CPR, I will walk you through it."

"Listen, we are in the funerary business, he is dead now send someone right away!"

"Ok, I understand, the police will attend as well as the ambulance, they will likely arrive at the same time."

"Thank you."

The Constable arrived within twenty minutes and met Jenny at the front door. The paramedics followed a few minutes later.

"Hello, I'm Constable Mathers, and you are?"

"Jenny, family friend and funeral services administrator. He is upstairs. Follow me."

When they entered the room, Darius sat still on the floor, staring off into oblivion.

Constable Mathers escorted Darius downstairs and sat him down while the paramedics investigated.

Five minutes later, a paramedic appeared and introduced himself as John Maynard, confirming to Darius his father had indeed passed away and expressed sympathy for his loss.

Constable Mathers took over. "Darius, I'll be calling the coroner, but it's doubtful he'll be able to attend, so I need to take some photos. We'll close with a short verbal statement from you for the file all right?"

"Why won't the coroner be attending? Isn't it part of the process?"

"Darius, there is only one in all of western British Columbia and cannot attend every death. He is all the way in Kitimat. In this case, his doctor will supply a health report and a conclusion will be drawn from there."

Darius nodded in compliance and resolved himself to endure the process and wait to deal with the body the way his father wished in his pre-need paperwork.

***

The last will and testament of the late Marcus Clarke said his first-born son, or surviving son if the first-born was deceased, would take over the family funerary business, Clarke & Sons Funeral and Cremation Services.

The duty fell to Darius. His official title before Marcus' untimely death was, Assistant Funeral Director. His knowledge of the business end of death went far beyond his duties. Death was the first word he learned as a tot, as his father made sure he got involved in every side of their operations.

***

The office, shared with his father, was musty as Darius opened the door and switched the lamps on. Dressed in his usual business attire, he turned to walk over to his desk but hesitated, looking over at the desk where Marcus sat. The desk was much larger, and already equipped with the main computer and all else he would need in the role of Funeral Director.

He set himself up and made his new desk comfortable. When he opened the bottom drawer of the pedestal to retrieve the password notebook, he found a coin-sized box in the back of the drawer he had not seen before.

It held an old padlock key. He examined it, trying to figure out which padlock it could fit. He'd been around every part of their property since he could play outside on his own, and used to hide from his mother in every room he could when he was small. No sign of old padlocked rooms anywhere, not even a storage shed.

More intrigued by mystery than business, and with nothing needing his attention, he put his coat back on and walked the grounds, scanning every angle of the property. In time, he spotted the stately old oak his dad forbade him to climb as a kid. The first and last time he had climbed it was on the day of his mother's burial reception when he was seven.

The oak seemed comforting to him, and he figured it would allow temporary reprieve from the darkness of grief. His escape lasted less than an hour before the family search party came calling. His Dad seemed upset he chose that specific place to hide, rather than glad he found his son.

"You are not to be around this tree, ever! Understand?" were the exact words he could remember his father yelling at him. When he pressed why, he only got the cliché answer,

"Because I said so! If I catch you over here again, I'll tan your ass, understand?" Darius had only experienced the tanning of his ass once before, and his dad could deliver a hell of a wallop, so he never went over there again to play.

He can't tan your ass now, Darry, can he?
Still afraid of the tone in his dad's warning years before, he had to persuade himself to go to the oak. It was aged but nothing unusual about it stood out. He was ready to give up, but the toe of his wingtip got caught on something. A thick, heavy branch had been positioned to resemble a root.

The root moved to the side, and he discovered a makeshift net of fake leaves and vines under it. He lifted the netting and saw a flat metal plate structure with an old padlock closure. He slid the key into the padlock.

It fit. Inside was an odd metal chest around two feet wide, a foot tall, and one foot deep.

Next to it laid another key. Fearing he would be seen and approached, he grabbed it and headed back to the house.

Too curious to wait, instead of eating lunch and putting away the dishes, he opened it, placing the key in his pocket for safekeeping.

Inside was a weathered brown cardboard container commonly used for cremated remains, with A736458 written on the top in thick black ink. During his time growing up in and learning the funerary business, he had never seen a box of human ashes without a name and cremation date on it.

Why was this one hidden? What did Dad know he kept secret?

Over the years, they had only a few unclaimed remains left, and someone always took them to be buried all at once in a city approved location.

He began his research by rooting through his father's room, looking for notebooks or anything else that might give reference to A736458. For the next week, Darius searched the old files in the overstuffed filing cabinets kept in the funerary services building and still found nothing.

Tired of searching, he placed the box in the closet off the main entrance where it remained for another three days.

October 18, 1994

Darius awoke early in the morning and went to the kitchen as usual to start his morning routine. He sipped his coffee and flipped through the Vancouver Sun. The photo on page twelve was of BC Penitentiary dated October 18th, 1941. Two police cars sat parked on either side of a 1939 Studebaker hearse with prison guards standing at alert around it.

Kane Wesley titled the photo, "Prison stories of British Columbia". The article below the photo narrated the story of an inmate named Rip Vanderhoof, who died by gunfire execution.

First patient at Riverview Hospital, Rip Vanderhoof was transferred to BC Penitentiary in 1940 when he snapped and murdered a nurse and two orderlies by breaking the nurse's neck during 12:15 am bed checks and the necks of the orderlies, who tried to sedate him.

Vanderhoof had been at Riverview since 1938. Feared by inmates and staff alike for his six-foot-nine muscular frame, the blankness in his eyes, and his violent tendencies, he held permanent residence in a padded cell on the solitary confinement floor at New Westminster's BC Penitentiary.

On October 18th, 1941, at 3:00am, the night guard on duty (Charles Baker), while performing his rounds, came upon the Rip Vanderhoof unit to find it empty. He gathered two more guards (James Colwell, now deceased, and Mark Jones) to aid his investigation of the cell for an escape method. Jones said during an interview, "The locks were intact, with no signs of escape, yet he was nowhere to be seen. Colwell and I walked out of the cell. I turned around to alert Baker to lock it back up and sound the alarm. Just as I did, I saw him. That monster, Vanderhoof, somehow got himself to the ceiling, face down. Then it happened.

He made the most horrific sound and within seconds descended upon Baker and mauled him to death. I grabbed my keys in time to lock them in. It was all I could think of to save Colwell and me from gruesome deaths."

The caption under the second photo in the center of the article read: *Warden David Michaels speaks to Marcus Clarke of Clarke & Sons Funerary Services, October 18, 1941.*

Surprised by the caption, Darius inspected the photo. "Holy shit, what was he doing there?" It was his father, all right, dressed in the style he wore until the day he died: slacks with matching vest, crisp white dress shirt, patterned tie and Florsheim wingtips, his left hand in a gesture of explanation with a cigarette.

He read the rest of the article.

According to Mark Jones, six guards with Winchester model 12 shotguns rushed the scene and took turns shooting at Vanderhoof through the narrow bars at the top of the steel door until he was dead.

Four out of six emptied their ammunition on the inmate. Fifteen shots pierced his body before a last shot to the head. Jones said, "Evil incarnate. No man can levitate to the ceiling and emit those sounds, let alone survive fifteen shots to the body before dying. It was like he was a demon rather than a man."

They transported his body to the nearby funeral home for cremation. Warden Michaels nor any of the other retired staff were available for me to inquire about the whereabouts of Rip's remains.

According to Jones, they were not returned to the prison cemetery. A rumor surfaced that they lay scattered along the railroad tracks on Columbia Street behind the haunted Keg building.

Neither the employees nor management of the Keg on Columbia were familiar with Rip Vanderhoof, however, they reported a sinister presence within the restaurant after dark.

A surge of curiosity ran through every nerve ending in Darius' body as he put the paper down. The article went on for another page, but he couldn't read any further.

His mind shifted to the box in the closet, and jumped to the old filing cabinets, and back to his father. He called the office to ensure they did not need him for anything and resumed his search to confirm the identity of A736458.

Starting with an online search for BC Penitentiary prison records, with no luck. He searched for Rip Vanderhoof. Again, nothing came up. Two hours of multiple web searches left him with a mild headache and the stench of defeat.

You're never going to find anything from 1941on the internet. Those ashes could be anyone's. Why were they hidden on the property, though? Why was dad so angry when I climbed the old oak?

He stretched his sore neck left and right and retired to the living room for a nap hoping to wake up with fresh ideas for search terms.

October 18, 1994, 3:30 pm

Strange knocking and rustling sounds came from beyond the room toward the main entrance.

Rubbing the crust of sleep from his eyes, Darius sat up to listen. The house was quiet, so he sat longer, listening, and still heard nothing.

A few moments after he turned the television on and sat back on the couch, three loud knocks from the closet made him jump.

Frozen in place, he waited for more noise. Knock, knock, knock.

His heart pounded as he stood.

What have I done?

His legs shook with crippling fear as he walked to the closet door. He touched the doorknob and recoiled. The metal was so hot it scorched his hand. Full of adrenaline, the pain of the burn dissipated as he stood, staring at the door.

Absolute silence pervaded until the hissing began. As he stumbled a few steps backward, solid black smoke in the shape of flames plummeted from the space beneath the door.

Despite an attempt to run from it, plumes encircled him. The more he moved, the tighter its grip over his body.

Then it released him and piled up in front of him in a tornado swirl. The floor rumbled under his feet as he covered his mouth to avoid breathing it in. As dizziness set in, he gathered all his strength to stay standing.

The swirl of black gave way to a large outline of a not-quite-human structure with evil red glowing spots where the eyes should have been.

The entity, brooding in front of him, let out a vicious snore-like growl, and moved closer to him, towering over his head.

Well, Darry, this is it. You're going to die right here of a fucking heart attack or be mauled to death!

As the entity chased him, he rushed towards the stairs, stumbling over the steps, but quickly regained his balance to reach the landing.

He dashed down the hall to his room. It gripped tight once again pulling him back from his bedroom door and dragged him down the hall face down by his feet to the landing. Squirming and screaming, he broke free and ran to his bedroom door, whipped it open and jumped through, slamming the door shut.

I need to block the space under the door!
He pulled the pillows off the bed and stuffed them against the door to block the space. The door rattled in the jamb with force, then stopped. Total silence. He ran to the window and peeked outside. All appeared undisturbed. Trapped in his bedroom, he agonized over the sudden quiet.

There's no way in hell it's gone.

10:48 pm

Darius sat up in a cold sweat from a nightmare. The silence ensued.

With caution, he approached the bedroom door. The floor creaked, freezing him in mid-step.

No reaction from the evil entity that pursued him hours before. He moved toward the pillows stuffed under the door in controlled, frame by frame movements until his hand touched them. After a few minutes, he pulled a pillow out from the crack under the door. No response. As an extra safety measure, he grabbed a coin from his dresser and threw it under the door crack. Nothing.

Places haunted with the worst evil forces tend to get a break between attacks... I need to pee, and I'm not doing it out the window.

He contemplated his escape.

Do I whip the door open like ripping off a bandage? Or open it an inch at a time to avoid creaking?

After deciding to err on the side of the former, he whipped the door open, checked both ways, and dashed into the hallway bathroom.

He inspected his legs for bruising, then finished urinating and perused his mirror image for facial abrasions. No signs of the attack. He washed his hands and left the bathroom, headed to the fridge for a beer.

I just need to have a beer and take in a stupid comedy. I've been under a lot of stress, with Dad dying —

He swallowed the rest of his thought and plopped down on the couch, picking up the remote.

What the hell is even on at this time of night?

Channel Twelve proved promising, as the tail-end of Matlock was on, and more oldies were sure to follow.

Rational thought intertwined with memories of earlier as he stared at Marcus' urn on the fireplace mantle.

Yeah, I'm a grown man, but I need comfort right now.

He went over to the mantle and retrieved his dad to join him for Murder, She Wrote.

"Dad, I don't know whose ashes those are for sure, but I suspect you had something — "

The urn vibrated as he sat frozen in disbelief.

"Dad?" He called in a panic. Nothing happened until he called again.

"Dad!"

"Over here."

The voice came from near the front door.

He expected to see a cloud of mist, but Marcus stood there in his pajamas; the ones he was wearing when he died.

"I'm sorry, Darry," the apparition of his father said in a tone, a few decibels above of a whisper.

"I can't hear you, Dad. Speak up if you can."

He leaned forward for a better chance at hearing the response. Seconds later, right in front of his nose appeared his father's ghost, taking his breath away.

"I warned you!"

The voice came out as a chilling echo.

Marcus disappeared, leaving Darius alone once more.

11:30 pm

Rubbing his eyes as they became blurry from the television, Darius stood, remote in hand, to turn it off. A heavy drip hit the top of his head, and the snore-like growl echoed from right above him. The drip travelled down his bangs to his nose and dropped just past his lips to his shirt.

His fists gripped tight; his nails cut through his palms.

He looked up.

Thick, black engulfed the ceiling, swirling, coming downward. The blackness sucked Darius in and surrounded him.

He couldn't stop his mouth from opening. His soul funneled out from within, into blackness.

***

On her way to the office, Jenny stopped at the house to check on Darius and bring his favorite coffee. The door was unlocked, as it usually was in the mornings, so she walked right in.

"Darry, I brought you an Americano with crème and cinnamon. Come and get it!"

The house was dead, the air thick with the smell of blood. She glanced up the staircase, then to the archway leading into the living room.

"Oh God!"

When she saw her family friend and boss sprawled on the floor, it took every ounce of her willpower not to vomit.

The body lay contorted and devoid of all moisture, a mummified corpse. The hair, while bloody, was whitened.

Spring 1995

"And here's the kitchen, isn't it charming? Look at the original wainscoting!"

"Oh, honey, I love it! The cupboard space and countertops! And this foyer, so grand, with the beautiful eighteen-hundreds threshold!"

"Okay, okay, settle down, Sarah. Yes, it's beautiful, but you know this used to be a funeral home, right?"

"The point here, Jeremy, is used to be, and besides, a few ghosts never hurt anyone!"

The realtor broke in. "So, should I put together an offer?"

"Consider it sold." said Jeremy.

"Oh, honey! Thank you!"

Knock, knock, knock, from the closet.

"What was that?" Jeremy asked.

"Oh, just the sounds of an old house settling. It's getting rather warm out for April." The realtor replied, "Now let's sign your offer. How exciting for you both!"

The deaths of the former owners were never disclosed.

THE GREAT ESCAPE

With every beep of the cashier scanning her items, Shelly Chartwell dreaded going home. The damage to the front end of her car was just the tip of the iceberg.

The fellow in the Supermart parking lot was gracious enough not to take down her insurance information, that was going to mean absolutely nothing to Jake.

It's not enough that I got in shit at work today for something Danielle in accounting did, or that I was late getting here so Jake will be home to bitch about the groceries I buy, I just had to rear end that guy in the damn parking lot!

"Hello, Ma'am? That'll be two hundred forty-seven dollars and sixteen cents." The cashier said in a poking, yet polite manner.

"Oh, I'm sorry about that, I didn't hear you, I guess I was a little distracted." Shelly responded, taking out her debit card with a nervous giggle.

THE GREAT ESCAPE

***

She pulled into the driveway; her husband's truck was parked in her spot.

Jake peered out from behind the living room curtains.

Shit, now I won't even have time to walk in and prepare myself to tell him, nosey fucker, looking out the window like an old gossip monger!

She took a deep cleansing breath and pressed the trunk release and exhaled slowly before collecting the groceries. It started before her foot touched the top of the stairs.

"So, you smashed up the car I see, if this was the fifties, boy, I'd make good and sure you didn't get a driver's license. Bloody women, dumb in the bedroom and dumber behind the wheel!"

"You weren't there Jake! Do you have any idea what kind of day I've had?"

"Don't matter, who told you to go and get a job anyway? I hope your crappy paycheck is enough to fix all that damage!"

Without response, she carried all six bags to the kitchen island, working quickly as the plastic handles cut off her circulation. She only managed to put the meat in the freezer before Jake stood from his overworn recliner empty glass in hand to join her in the kitchen to inspect the freezer.

"I told you I wanted hamburgers, how are you gonna cook me hamburgers without burger patties, huh?"

"They didn't have any left Jake."

Nearly fifteen years of his verbal and emotional abuse had taught her not to bother mentioning she had forgotten to pick something up, nor would she ever win an argument with him.

"I got those deli pizzas you like, so we can have those for dinner."

He only grunted in response, poured himself another bourbon and returned to the living room.

That's right Jake, more booze, that'll fix it.

***

Upon logging into her PBX games account, a message popped up.

SHELLY, YOU HAVE BEEN AWARDED A FREE GAME!

Hmm, free?

She clicked on the hyperlink. The usual list of game categories opened for her to choose from.

THE GREAT ESCAPE

At first, she was disappointed with the choices presented. Arcade games, RPGS, and word games, she kept scrolling. Nothing interested her, not even the Match 3, or the Seek and Find adventure games as she had played them to death.

The last category on the list was labeled Other Adventure Games. When she clicked on the label, only one game appeared with the title UNDERWORLD ESCAPE. The screen shots included an eerie cemetery, a gate to Hell and a strange book.

Now, that looks interesting!

She scrolled down to the description which read, "You have entered the dark realm and must find your way back home BUT first the book of souls needs to be returned to its rightful guardian. Do you have the guts Mortal?"

I need to download this!

While waiting for the download, she checked her email for the weekly newsletter from Horror Fans Only, a club she had joined to keep abreast of newly released movies and books.

Within a few minutes, the glow of the computer screen got her attention.

"Welcome Mortal!" A message in neon green script along with a 'play now' button. The following screen prompted "What shall we call you?"

This is the underworld so my name should fit the theme. She mused as she typed in Living One. The final prompt was to create an avatar.

She picked a female character, chose black hair like hers and matched the skin tone as closely as possible to her own. She dressed Living One in a sturdy leather outfit, far less comfortable than her usual house clothes, but much more stylish. The avatar spun around on screen making controlled and deliberate battle moves.

Nice!

The game froze with nothing but an hourglass rotating.

Great! I knew this piece of crap computer would get hung up! I should have signed up for Consumer Direct and got the free laptop!

She tried right clicking on the program file in the system tray to 'close program'.

It wouldn't close, she put her finger on the power button and held it to shut down the computer. Suddenly the lights went out leaving her alone in the pitch-black room, although light from the hallway shone under the computer room door. The red backlighting of the keyboard still glowed.

What the heck? Obviously, the power is still on, if it were a computer surge, why is the light-

The monitor flickered back on, but the ceiling light was still off. The unsettling feeling of someone watching from behind took over as she sat frozen from fear. A white circle the size of a quarter formed on the screen, growing bit by bit, transforming to reveal the face of the Grim Reaper. Merely a still image.

Ok, this is ridiculous. The ceiling lamp staying off? Just a coincidence, lightbulbs burn out Shelly. There is nobody watching from behind.

The speaker built into the monitor emitted a crackling like the sound of an old radio volume switch with a short. She reached for the volume dial at the bottom and moved it back and forth, no crackling, just silence.

"Enough of this!" Shelly said, frustrated as she stood and pushed her chair back to walk away. When she reached the door, a deep, creepy voice came from the speaker.

"Living One, where do you think you are going?"

It was so loud, she jumped and stumbled backwards landing on her butt. Her heart flopped in her chest as she tried to catch her breath. The image was now moving so she returned to her chair to get a closer look as she contemplated that the timing of the voice was another coincidence.

Now the image seemed to be coming out of the screen. It was so realistic, the desire to reach out overcame her fear.

Man! These graphics are amazing!

The dark, shrouded figure raised its bony forefinger, adorned with an attractive, red-stone ring, and motioned her to come closer.

Seriously? Are you really going to follow instructions from a fake Grim Reaper, Shelly?

Nonetheless, she moved closer and closer to the screen, until her nose was half an inch away.

A cool breeze wisped around her face. She would have believed what was happening to be in her imagination, except that she sensed the fabric of the reaper's shroud lightly tickling her face. Before she could pull away, she was enveloped in darkness and dropped into a longboat headed through dark waters.

"What the—? Where the hell am I? Where are you taking me? I want to go back. Let me go!"

Much more menacing in person than on the screen, the Reaper turned the top half of his frame around to face her. That ring-clad bone finger went to where his lips should have been to silence her.

This is it; I've lost my marbles! All those years with Jake have finally driven me mad. I should have known when the fantasies of murdering Jake started, the Grim Reaper of all things!

The reaper rowed the vessel into a narrow canal lined with low lying fog that rose into dark silhouettes of ancient elm trees.

The sounds of the paddle slicing murky water, echoing ravens, crickets and the crackling of branches sent a chill down her spine.

The boat slowed to a stop next to a grass lined bank. She waited for assistance to stand, but the reaper only stood pointing in the direction of a cemetery facing straight ahead.

She hopped up onto the bank, turned, bowed sarcastically and bade farewell as he pushed off from shore and vanished back into the foggy canal.
"Now what?"
Her exasperated tone echoed as plumes of fog grasped the path of her footsteps.

I downloaded a game, 'this looks interesting' I said. Interesting indeed, it's going to be interesting when I'm locked away at Glenview!

Her toes froze as she trudged through the dew-soaked grass of the riverbank. Looking down at her feet, she realized the clothing she had dressed her avatar in matched what she was wearing.

The boots, leather combat style lace ups, but not the sturdy build of a true combat boot and her choice of pants, shirt and jacket left a lot to be desired in the cold snap of an October evening.

In the distance, the orange glow of the moon revealed the cemetery gates. The starting point of the game invoked anxiety in her like none other she had ever felt, even as a child on her first day of school each fall.

The gates stood before her only latched by a broken wrought iron bar which fell to the ground when she

touched it. She picked it up in case she may need it later in the game and pushed her way through. The path leading to the first rows of headstones was laid with sunken clay bricks partially covered in moss and mud, so she treaded, careful not to slip.
Gravestones have inscriptions. Clues.
She had played only one escape room game online but had learned enough about them to know that clues would pop up in the first scene.
The headstones were nothing out of the ordinary. Names and dates with typical loving phrases. She continued up and down two more rows, carefully reading the inscriptions and still found nothing of great significance. She headed back to the entrance and looked over the cemetery. A large weeping willow loomed above a crypt toward the back of the property.
Darkness blanketed the area, but she made her way over anyway.

***

A small flight of concrete steps led up to the ancient structure, adorned with double iron doors nestled between two six-foot-tall pillars. With the orange glow of the moon barely reaching beyond the steps, she could only make out faint shapes inlaid on the surface of the door on the left, and a gothic church style window above. She inspected around the inlaid shapes but could only recognize a circle. As she patted her hands above the circle, she came across a board which gave her a splinter.

"Ouch! That's it I can't see worth the dam!"

Her voice travelled throughout the grounds and bounced back to the core of her inner ears. She stepped backwards tripping on a small stone and sat down leaning against the doors to gain composure.

The board came loose, dropped on her head and landed face down in front of her.

"Oh, my F-"

Wiping her eyes clear of the blood now dripping from her crown, she stopped mid-sentence for fear of being hit by anything else.

Strapped to the back of the board, just visible enough by moonlight; was an object with a circular center and six multilength points around its circumference.

She pulled the shape off from the board and stood slowly. Her head throbbing remnants of sharp pain made it difficult to focus but she powered past it enough to feel around for the circle shape she found earlier and placed the object around it until it clicked into place.

Nothing happened, so she jiggled back and forth and discovered it was a dial that moved counterclockwise. After another few seconds, the heavy doors creaked, moving outward toward her enough for her to get in.

***

The musty stench of hundreds of years turned her stomach as it wafted out through the open door. Inside was a small wooden crate bathed in moonlight from a side window.

The iron bar! There must be items in the crate I will need.

Focused on the crate, she barely heard the door closing in with its slow creak. By the time she turned her head the door thumped closed.

It's ok *Shelly, just go push it open.*

At first, she used her hands until the splinter pushed itself deep, bringing tears to her eyes, so she pushed with her back. The door would not budge.

"Great, just great!"

All she could do was open the crate and decide her next move. Inside was a box of matches and a wood torch bound in rags impregnated with a greasy substance.

Struggling to hold the heavy torch with her good hand and light a match with her splintered hand, she managed to ignite it.

The blaze revealed the remains of four medieval knights sitting in Edwardian style dining chairs surrounding a large pentagram painted on the floor.

She stood frozen momentarily then twirled slowly, letting the torchlight kiss the shadows.

With an audible gulp, she inched her way over to the knights.

They have been dead for hundreds of years; what's the worst that can happen?

She stepped a little closer.

The chilling hollow eyes gaped as worms cascaded through every orifice of the skulls.

They can't hurt you! Just bones and steel mesh, GO!

THE GREAT ESCAPE

***

"Come closer!"

The voice startled her, but she hesitantly stood closer to the knight on her left.

"Closer, lock eyes with your fate."

Lock eyes with my fate? I'd rather vomit, but I need to get out of here.

She moved slowly toward it until her eyes met the hollows of a skeletal face.

With devilish haste, the knight's jaw dropped open, releasing a swarm of moths and maggots.

Flashbacks cascaded through her mind; first dates with Jake, hours of endless arguments masked by her love of horror and online games, deep depression and knowing a child was not in the cards.

Insecurity plagued her as the cloud of insects disbursed.

A scroll dropped to the dusty stone floor where she crouched. It was a map but at that moment she couldn't say what for.

She placed it inside her jacket for safe keeping.

Clouded by an upset stomach and slight dizziness;

she rose gradually, only to engage with the knight's bones as they toppled over her.

She now laid covered in the wretched odor of what may have once been an honorable man. Hyperventilating in fear, she grabbed her chest, before scurrying back to her feet.

A small stone table emerged from the pentagram. *What the hell? What is that?*

A dagger lying on the floor caught her attention. All the remaining knights bowed their heads forward facing the top of their table as she placed the dagger in her pocket and approached the table. There were four shapes engraved into the tabletop. Gathering her composure, she moved in for a closer look. A blue chalice, a golden coin, a red pitchfork, and a silver dagger.

The dagger, once placed, lit up, illuminating a silver border. The knights turned their heads, looking right at her with dead eyes as if beckoning her to complete the puzzle. She took a deep breath as she ran her fingers across the table trying her best to pay no mind to the animated dead and scanned the area for the other three items.

"What have you done?"

Assorted whispering voices echoed throughout the room bouncing off surfaces from all directions.

The table shook as dust and debris crumbled down from the stone walls.

The ground quaked lightly, growing more violent; throwing off her balance.

The three knights fell to the floor scattering helmets, skulls and bones.

The clatter subsided to ultraquiet as she awaited further disturbance.

The whole crypt rumbled as a flood of spiders blanketed the walls like a great waterfall and descended upon the floor toward her.

Black widows, wolf spiders and tarantulas crawled over her feet and up her legs, moving to her upper extremities like wildfire. They progressively climbed over her face as she flailed back and forth screaming uncontrollably. Her head thrashed back and forth inviting a coin sized tarantula into her mouth along with a few wolf spiders. A much larger tarantula crawled from the top of her black hair clad cranium down to cover her face.

In a full panic attack, she blacked out.

***

Wearily, she opened her eyes, no arachnids in sight.

A floor to ceiling mirror took the place of the stone wall she had been standing in front of.

"Okay, now what in the world is this?"

An image of a man with a mild expression stared back at her.

Slowly rising she took a few cautious steps towards the mirror and pressed her palm to the glass.

The man's eyes followed her movements, akin to eyes peering through holes in a painting.

Moments after their gaze locked, his eyes shifted to the empty knights' table.

The chairs had toppled over. Meandering around the table, she discovered the remaining pieces of the puzzle strewn across the floor.

She placed the blue chalice down on the table without placing it upon its crease and gathered the other two pieces, the golden coin and the pitchfork.

Might as well get this over and done.

She placed the chalice anticipating disaster.

Nothing but an illuminated blue border. Then the golden coin. Illuminated gold border.

THE GREAT ESCAPE

When she picked up the pitchfork and lowered it to its rightful place, a surge of energy bolted up through her fingers to her elbow.

She dropped it just outside of its place on the table. She looked back to the mirror image for guidance, but he retreated backward and turned his back to her. He was now clothed in a black robe donning a scythe.

The sound of metal scraping across stone turned her attention back to the table.

The pitchfork was being pulled toward the indentation as if by magnetic force.

The floor shook as a dark heel of purple formed a sphere over the table.

Ruby red liquid, coursed from the floor's creases and rose, covering her feet up to the ankles, over her legs and past her waist, sweeping her off her feet.

As she floated, she choked on the heavy scent of iron. Bobbing back and forth, she checked her surroundings.

The walls shifted inward, threatening to envelope her. They lightly touched her cheeks before squeezing against her head.

Exhaustion transcended into an overwhelming urge to give up as pain travelled through her constricted body. As she expelled labored screams, the walls cascaded slowly away from her.

She screamed aimlessly at the top of her lungs tearing her throat muscles.

"HELP! HELP! PLEASE WAIT! I CAN'T DIE THIS WAY!"

The whispers returned, filling the tight space between her and the ceiling.

"The Book of Souls, waits for no-one!"

Shelly's head swelled with vertigo, a nasty gut-wrenching spin as the crypt rapidly closed back in. She shouted desperately covering her ears in sordid tears.

Cobwebs and macabre scents seared into her pixelated mind as the crypt shrunk to the size of a dumbwaiter.

Heat penetrated as the stone floor emitted a loud rumble, sending millions of bubbles to the surface to pop in her face.

A great whirlpool formed beneath her, sucking her deep below into an abyss of darkness, then fire and back to darkness as all one hundred and forty

THE GREAT ESCAPE

pounds of her likeness plummeted onto a dusty and dank surface.

***

She took in her new surroundings as she relished dead quiet.

To her left was a long passageway lit by torches.

On her right, there was another passageway, dark with no visible end.

In the center was a door, cracked open an inch revealing soft white light.

Leary from the preceding thrill ride she had encountered, she sat in contemplation.

Fifteen years I have wanted to leave, and have stayed, feeling trapped with no feasible way out. One of the worst days I have ever had, all I wanted to do was escape into another world for a while. Forget about Jake and his drunk ass bullshit, what happens? I get sucked into the underworld and stuck here until I find some mysterious book, then what? I just want my dam mother! Wow Shelly that is childish! Sitting in some underworld hellhole crying for your mommy!

As hard as she fought to keep the tears back, they came flooding down her hot cheeks. Her clothes heavy with the blood she had been immersed in moments before.

The smell of dirt, iron and death overtook the dank air.

She sat forward, ripping off her jacket, boots and sweaty socks and tossed them as far as her tired muscles could manage.

Desperate for human contact, she looked at the crack in the door before her.

She had to start there in search of more items, but she was reluctant to enter for fear of being locked in again.

She closed her eyes and focused on the breathing exercises her mother taught her as a child.

"Shelly, you are going to be alright, just breath; I'm right here with you."

She opened her eyes to her mother sitting with open, comforting arms waiting to embrace her.

As she gasped in surprise to see the one person, she had missed for the past eight years, her whole body shook and hyperventilating set in heavy.

"Mom, what are you doing in this horrible place? I thought you were at peace on the other side, I am so confused!"

"Honey, this IS the other side. I know when my kid needs me, and I am here to get you through this mess."

"You wouldn't believe what I just went through Mom, what the hell is this place? I mean I know it's the underworld, but which way is which? How long is this nightmare journey going to last?"

"Well dear, you have a map, right?"

She patted her pant legs looking for the map she found in the crypt, then remembered she stuck it in the inside breast pocket of the jacket she was wearing.

Scrambling to grab it, she looked to where her mother's spirit was sitting.

Only a faint remanence of her remained.

"Wait, Mom! You can't leave me yet; you said you were going to get me through this!"

As the warm embrace of mother's company faded to mist, one last piece of advice echoed down the passageway to the right.

"You will make it through this my girl, just keep your head in the game, and I am so proud of —"

With that, her mother was gone.

Even with words of encouragement just delivered to her, she felt discouraged.

The map, although right where she put it, was soaked and wilted. Shaky fingers, short of breath, she worked to unroll it carefully so as not to rip it.

At first glance once it was laid on the ground it appeared to be ruined beyond legible use.

Within seconds, an animated tornado formation appeared, purple and slightly illuminated. As it swirled and moved over the map's surface, more sections became visible.

"The Eternal Labyrinth" was written across the top in Algerian font. The spot depicting the door she was facing was unlabeled, the passageway to the left displayed animated flames labeled Hell and the endless passageway on the right now had a purple glow at the end of it, labeled Limbo.

Wow, this is helpful, now what? No label on the door.

"Well here goes." She said as she pushed herself from the ground in pain.

THE GREAT ESCAPE

***

The room was empty, except for a locked door absent of a keyhole. A number pad with three buttons, two blank and one with a flame image stamped on.

She pressed the flame button and the image moved to the button next to it, when she pressed it again and it moved to another button.

She scanned the room again and saw only the walls.

The map was still sprawled on the ground outside the room. She went back to retrieve it, moving quickly in case the door closed behind her.

Upon re-entering, and examining the map further, the passageway lined with torches seemed to awaken; the torches vibrantly aflame as if she should venture down it.

***

The torches were lit as she entered the passageway, but their flames extinguished one by one as she passed them. She stopped after the fourth blew out.

The whispering chorus called out *"The book of souls will set you free."*

Reluctantly, she forged on through torches that seemed to go on for miles.

Fear and anxiety urged her to stop but the further she went, the more torches appeared down the long passageway.

I must keep going until I find a torch that maintains its flame.

The whispers continued with only haunted gibberish as the hairs stood up on the back of her neck and an unsettling wave of heat crawled up through her scalp.

She finally reached a torch that remained lit after she passed it. She stood on the tips of her toes barely reaching the handle and grabbed it.

She backtracked with careful movement to avoid extinguishing the torch she was holding.

***

Shelly waved the torch in front of the button panel back and forth with no result, then moved in closer, placing the fire light close to the torch image on the button.

It illuminated red and began to flash, so she pressed it burning her forefinger.

"Ouch!"

The door opened just enough to release the latch, so she had to push it the rest of the way.

The pinging of metal dropping to the ground produced a skeleton key.

She tucked it away in her bra and looked up to realize that she was where she had left off in the darkened torch corridor with torches still lit beyond that point.

On her way through, loud grumblings filled the space around her.

The remaining torches stayed lit as she made her way further in. The overpowering sulfuric and smoke scents burned her nose.

The end of the passage opened into a never-ending fire pit circled by very tall monstrous figures marching like soldiers. They were headed toward a large alcove arched by brimstone and surrounded by red mist.

Although they were a fair distance away, she crept to the side wall upon entering and stood perfectly still while observing their pattern.

The ones that entered the alcove were recycled into more exiting back into the circle.

In the center of the fire pit stood a tall podium atop an intricately designed platform of skulls and burned bricks.

She opened the map again. The only thing visible now was the spot where she was standing and a bird's eye view of the podium with a large book resting on it.

Crap! They're guarding my ticket out of here! It's surrounded. I'm screwed, totally screwed, unless...
She had come too far to give up, so she braced herself into a cat stance and slinked her way sideways against the walls.

Her hands were getting blacker by the minute, so she wiped them across her face, into her hair and all over her clothes, until she blended in with the walls.

No more than three feet from the circle she stood frozen once again to observe them, they had changed shifts once that she had seen.

Their low growling voices amplified in stereo sound, so she was able to practice mimicking them without being discovered.

A closer look at them revealed that they were in human form, unlike the demons of the Hell realm her favorite horror author had created.

One of the taller ones lifted its face just enough to show a flash of its oversized black eyes.

There is no way I won't be noticed unless I keep my face out of sight, as soon as they start moving again, I'll slip in, I can stay looking down and follow their feet.

Over an hour passed as Shelly stood waiting for the perfect opportunity to blend in.

The moment finally presented itself, they marched away from the fire pit, when the fifth one passed her, she snuck in, face down and focused on their breathing sounds and foot paths.

Entranced by their feet, moving one in front of the other, and the light of the flames lining the path, she followed blindly until the line came to an abrupt stop, squishing her into the demon in front of her.

Before long she could be addressed by Satan himself.

Fuck! What am I to say to him? All I want to do is recycle back the heck out of here to the podium.

She looked up briefly at the others and back down to her feet.

One by one, they approached their master with black leather books.

Where the heck did those come from? What are they for?

"You! Tell me, where are your logs?"

In her best demon voice, she grunted,

"Master, I only just died today and have received no orientation."

The prince of darkness sat forward and clutched her arm in his toughened aged fingers and pulled her close.

"Then I suggest you take the next shift and memorize the logs, if you come back again without a real report, you shall regret the day you died!"

He tossed her like a ragdoll to the front of the next shift line.

***

The first to reach the podium, Shelly took it upon herself to ascend the steps to the podium. The demons were nothing more than digital beings in a game. Not once did any of them interact with her the whole time she imposed on their daily duties.

The book sat propped up like the Messiah on D-Day, bound by a lock and chain. Puzzled, she stood solid until the recollection of the room and the key she had tucked away flooded her mind.

If I turn the key to release the lock, what if the book opens and all the souls come rushing out?

She reached into her bra for the key. Holding the front cover of the book down with the palm of one hand, she inserted the key into the lock. It was stuck so she jiggled it back and forth in the hole waiting for it to catch and succeeded.

The steps around the podium were thin, one false move and she would be the Devil's barbequed meat course at feeding time.

With one hand still on the book, she leaned in enough to maneuver the lock's handle and remove it from the loop. The map rolled up in her back pocket, had dried. Embers from the fire pit licked the dry edges of the paper until it caught fire. The seat of her pants only heated up at first but once the map was burned to the edge of her pants pocket, the dingy leather began to melt as the seat of her pants caught fire.

Working as fast as she could, she leaned on the podium, grabbed the book from its prison and balanced her weight backwards, gaining a strong enough stance to swing the book behind her. She snuffed the flames before the rest of her clothing caught fire.

The demons still just marched in their circle of pestilence endlessly. She jumped off the steps and joined them, walking in unison swirling until she reached the wall she had entered from when she arrived.

Inching the opposite direction back to the passageway, her stomach sent angry hunger signals to her brain.

Don't focus on hunger! Just get out!

Her thought therapy proved to be more difficult than usual, because she had not eaten since breakfast the day she embarked on her unexpected journey.

THE GREAT ESCAPE

***

At the center core of the underworld, the chorus of whispering voices rang.

"Hurry." "The Eternal Labyrinth will find you." She had no idea what it was, but she took their advice and proceeded with caution. The purple smoke leaked out from Limbo with ghostly virility. "It will consume you" "You will be ours forever." She survived the bones of four knights collapsing over onto her, thousands of spiders skittering up her entire body like a nightmarish hot flash, being nearly trapped in an ancient crypt and sucked into the underworld through a stinking whirlpool of blood, Satan himself and the fires of Hell.

She took a fast deep breath, stuffed the book into the front of her pants securing it by tightening her belt to the last notch and dove to her stomach. She crawled into the passageway to Limbo, her knees off to the side the way she had seen in war movies, using her elbows to pull her forward opposite her knees. The labyrinth hovered above her emitting the loud squeals of banshees mixed with deep and creepy laughter.

The skin on her knees and elbows stung every inch of the final stretch to the end of the passage to Limbo. Slow and calculated; she rose to her feet. The wall beside her was weak with loosened rocks as it crumbled behind her. With the inside edges of her boots, she labored to shove piles of debris behind her creating a temporary barrier between her and the labyrinth.

Waiting for her on the edge of Limbo was the Grim Reaper. He stood looming with his ring clad skeletal hand extended, palm side up.

Leery of allowing the book to open, she pressed her palms tight against both sides of the cover and placed it in the reaper's grasp.

***

Jake, drunk and confused that his wife wasn't waiting in bed pretending to sleep, walked into Shelly's computer room to collect her for the night.

"Where the hell has, she—"

The computer's monitor still displayed the game's entry screen.

Burping and slurring, he sat down in her chair.

"Well, what do we have here?"

In the player two box, he typed Jake...

THE GREAT ESCAPE

***

The Grim Reaper bent down to Shelly's level, the hollow sockets of his eyes facing hers.

"I have missed your presence, as morbid as others may deem that to be."

He moved closer still.

This time, she focused on the black holes in his eye sockets and waited for the final chapter of Underworld Escape.

She was transformed into a green mist, sucked into the eyes of her original captor.

A kaleidoscope of neon colors surrounded her while she traveled at near lightning speed through a tunnel. Her cheeks flapped upward pressing her eyelids closed while her mouth took on the shape of a blow-up doll.

Fast air travelling down her throat took her breath away.

The tunnel was embedded with every image from melted faces to piles of bones and random neon shapes.

Someone brushed past her.

"Shelly, help me!"

She was crossing paths with Jake, far more frightened than her when she was first pulled in.

***

Thankful to finally be placed into the comfort of her home, Shelly found herself in her comfortable leather high back computer chair, she had spent so many years hating the place she had called home but now she felt much different; transformed, exhilarated and even a little giddy.

Although the book of souls was just an item, she sought to regain her freedom from the game, the real treasure she had been hunting was the ability to live on her own terms; independent and strong. Her monitor display read: "Player 2 needs your help."

A button below the message: "Click here to assist." The way Jake had always treated her and her unexpected journey to the underworld gave her a wickedly genius idea.

She placed her hand on the mouse knowing that player 2 was in fact Jake. She navigated through the control panel's Uninstall Programs window and searched for Underworld Escape.

"Click to uninstall."

She clicked.

"Are you sure you want to uninstall Underworld Escape and all shortcuts?"

She confirmed the uninstall and left the room that was once a hybrid of prison and sanctuary.

IF THERE BE MAGIC

June 23, 1982
Gravestone, NY

On the last day of school, Devlin Drake waited outside the front door of the schoolhouse for his older brother Carl. The sweet odor of mini-donuts and cotton candy came from the town's amusement park, Everworld.

Carl came out of his classroom clutching a used copy of Stephen King's IT as Devlin began running ahead.

"Slow down, dumbass!" Carl called out, running faster to catch up and halt him. "What's your hurry? Are ya late for a date?"

"I wanna go to Everworld Carl, let's go, please?"

"No way!"

"But that cotton candy smells so good!"

Devlin pulled him to follow.

"It's on our way home, so please, can we go, Carl? Please, can we!?"

"That place is a dump, all it has is a ferris wheel."

"Please? I need some cotton candy!"

"Fine, we will get some and go straight home."

Carl led the way four blocks east to Autumn and Cole across from Serpentine Park.

A massive billboard-sized sign displaying EVERWORLD in multi-colored lights replaced the broken-down attraction. Countless rides and food booths packed the park. He turned back to Devlin following instructions for once; he hadn't run off. Leery, yet curious, Carl ushered his little brother across the road to explore. Once they reached the front gate, a canvas banner appeared out front that read Free Admission, Today Only!

"Devlin, I don't think this is a smart idea, buddy. I don't trust it."

"You promised!"

"I agreed. I didn't promise; there's a big difference! Besides, this place stood falling apart just last week, and now it's all new. Impossible!"

"Well, they fixed it, so let's go in!"

Although he couldn't make sense of how the amusement park came to life so fast, he also knew he had a habit of overthinking; and deduced that a new owner had done the repairs.

***

While two women welcomed new guests with cotton candy and vouchers for other food booths, a clown on stilts handed out ride tickets.

Carl and Devlin, with their tickets and sweets, headed for the midway. The Twin Flip caught the elder brother's eye first, and the line didn't seem long.

***

They sat side-by-side in enclosed buckets that flipped back and forth as the arm rotated at increasing speeds. They spun, and flipped and spun some more. The twirling stopped; they got off, expecting to be dizzy, but they felt exhilarated.

***

In a trailer not far off the midway, a mysterious gentleman dressed in a fancy pinstripe suit and expensive black shoes sat down to prepare for a show.

His assistants were lean teenagers dressed in black slacks and crisp, white T-shirts with black jazz shoes.

"Should we put the sign out now?" the eldest boy asked.

"Yes, yes, and attract them as we rehearsed,"
Two of the assistants progressed outside, putting up the wooden stand and circus-style placard that read, "The Greatest Show You've Ever Seen!" The rest of them formed their choreographed line around the show entrance, moving in a circle, dancing, and breaking off to perform flips into the midway crowd. Children followed them with their eyes over to the placard, haunting music came from the stage.

***

Carl and Devlin were the first to find seats up front. The show tent seemed dark and intriguing. It wrapped the rest of the audience in a mysterious atmosphere while they awaited the next part of their adventure.

The dancers disappeared behind a wooden platform, and the music stopped. Out came the man to address the eager children.

"I am The Great Edwardo! Welcome, to the greatest show you've ever seen!" He strutted back and forth. "You won't believe your eyes as the magic unfolds!" The dancers returned as he pulled forth a tall black magician's cabinet. He turned it clockwise forty-five degrees to show no hidden doors or curtains, and the crate's solid interior walls.

"Nothing here!"

He shifted it another forty-five degrees showing the back and knocked on the solid wood.

"No hidden door here."

He continued until the box was returned to its original position. The dancers filed into the box, while the chorus of a whimsical score by Andrew Lloyd Webber began.

"Masquerade! Paper faces on parade, masquerade. Hide your face so the world will never find you."

As the last dancer entered the box, the door fastened shut as the music ceased. Everyone stared in silence. The door opened to blackness. The man turned to them with a handsome bow, as everyone sat in a daze of wonderment.

"Shall I bring them back?" His hand cupped to his right ear as he waited for the children to respond.

"Yes!"

He pivoted on his left heel, and at once, upon shutting the box. As the door popped open, the score began to play.

"Masquerade! Every face a different shade
Masquerade
Look around, there's another mask behind you!"
and his assistants appeared to wow their patrons with their stealthy movements. They moved across the stage and retreated behind the elaborate velvet stage curtain.

"And now, I need a volunteer. How about you? Come on up, boy!" As he motioned his forefinger in a come-hither way, Devlin peered to his left where Carl sat, and to his right, at a pale and sick looking lad. Devlin turned to the stage.

"You mean me, sir?" he responded with a nervous crack in his voice.

"Yes, yes, boy, come on up here!"

Devlin stood and made his way to the stage. The man then placed his hands on the child's shoulders and turned his body to face him. "If I could grant you a wish, my boy, what would it be?"

I wish I were invisible!

"Invisible it is!"

How could he hear me?

"But I didn't..."

Someone draped a piece of red satin material over his head and spun him in circles.

"You are about to witness a mysterious transformation, folks. Prepare yourselves for what's next!"

Edwardo chanted:

"Now you see him, now you don't, hear him speak, no you won't! Call his name, not once, but thrice, last a roll of the pale bone dice."

The sheet fell to the ground.

Devlin waved, calling his brother's name, but Carl didn't answer.

Oh no! I AM invisible!

The teen assistants lined up in a row, staring at him with scary little smirks on their faces.

Sick to his stomach, Carl stood.

"Devlin, Devlin, Devlin!"

Nothing happened. He ran up to Edwardo.

"Give me the pale dice!"

"Oh, I have no dice to roll, you silly boy, look around! No audience, either."

Carl whipped around to verify. Not one kid. No chairs.

"What have you done with my little brother, you asshole?"

"Now, now, Carl, is this any way to speak to a superior?"

"Who are you, and where is my brother?"

The magician picked the satin off the floor, with his minions in tow, awaiting instructions.

Without further hesitation, Carl ran out of the show tent, to the midway; his heart pounding so hard it may as well have jumped out through his ribs and flesh.

Whatever those people were, they are not human! Come right home after school, and for Heaven's sake, don't talk to strangers!

His mother's voice pierced his memory like a spike driven through his skull. Frantic as he looked for Devlin, he called again, yelling at the top of his lungs this time. "DEVLIN, DEVLIN, DEVLIN!"

No child to be seen. He turned back to the show tent. As he walked toward it, the distance between himself and the tent grew; the more he walked toward the tent, the farther away it became.

This is horrible! What the fuck am I going to do?

Tired and confused, he found a bench near the Ferris wheel and sat down, head in his hands.

Tears welled up, burning his eyes.

He lifted his head and spotted a strange glow from the corner of his eye. A small beach hut, white with red stripes, like the kind he saw in old-fashioned movies his mom liked, starring Elvis Presley.

The soft yellow glow coming from the space between the canvas appeared inviting and calming. Within a few minutes of looking at it, he became distracted. Light meant someone must be inside. Maybe they could help him.

This is just an illusion; you need to get the hell out of here! Haven't you been too trusting already?

The sky adopted an ominous atmosphere that leaked into the park's personality.

The tantalizing odors that lured them in replaced with the reek of garbage left to rot in the sun.

The midway sounds disappeared.

The silence, deafening.

He jumped from the bench and ran as fast as his size 10 feet would carry him. His ears picked up a faint voice. The tone, a ghost-like echo.

"Carl, help me."

He stepped to his left and concentrated. This time, the voice said,

"I'm over here!"

Devlin appeared for a few seconds, then disappeared into fog.

Carl ran after him.

The voice spoke to him again as he ran to the right.

"I'm here, buddy; come to me!" Carl pleaded.

Food booths, lurking shadows, scattered wrappers, and giant crows picking their way to full gullets took over as park patrons. The vibrant colors of Everworld, cadaverous.

A bright blue jacket appeared among the drab, washed-out tents and booths.

"Devlin! Over here!"

The child glanced over at him but walked away. He followed, picking up his pace every few steps.

The voice shifted, now behind him.

"Carl, wait!"

Devlin's teary eyes and quivering lips met Carl's gaze as he turned around.

"Are you okay? Where did you go?"

His kid brother morphed; an inch up, two inches out in width, his clothes and shoes ripped, replaced by a ratty cloak and dirty bare feet.

An old gypsy man now stood before him.

"Dinlow! Your search is in vain. He's our Kurchi now!"

The grotesque man grabbed Carl's forearm with his rough, dirty hands.

Pain wretched in his bones as long yellow fingernails pierced his skin.

Stark gray eyes glared at him as his arm oozed dark blood and went numb.

"You go back where you came from, dinlow!"

The gypsy released his arm.

Carl ran; as he looked behind him, the entire midway disappeared, one booth, one shack at a time, into sinkholes, vanishing.

Dusty spots and scattered grass patches replaced the midway.

With Autumn Street within view, vomit reached his esophagus and escaped the corners of his mouth.

He tried to refrain from its explosive exit until at least halfway down the street but couldn't fool his gut into submission.

Hunched over, the contents of his stomach hit the sidewalk, the cracks sucking up some, the rest pooling at his feet. Thoughts about what to tell his mother entered his mind.

I'll say I searched for him after school, and he wasn't there. No, that's dumb. Why didn't I call home?

Faster, faster, he ran, until he bailed and landed on the concrete, ripping his jeans and the skin of his knee.

Back up and running, he fell four times more on the way home.

Tell her the truth! You took your brother to a fucking Everworld. The place disappeared and now he's gone!

The F-Word would never have come out of his mouth in his mother's presence; if it did, she would smack him silly.

Yeah, right, Carl, tell her that the amusement park that's been here since the sixties just disappeared. While you're at it; why not mention the gypsy? Good way to be sent to the Lacrane Boys' home!

Drake House, where he and his brother had been born, stared at him while he approached its front steps.

His mother Nancy's voice startled him so much that he shook.

"Carl, hon, what are you doing on the steps?"

I must go in, go in and deliver the worst news my mother has ever gotten.

"Come on I baked your favorite pie!"

Nancy's calm demeanor confused him. It had to be dinner time by now, two and a half hours after he was supposed to bring his little brother home.

"Ma," he said in an uneasy tone, "I have something to tell you, I—" He sat upright and faced her.

"What's happened to you?" The horror on her face made him feel ill.

"Ma, I NEED to tell you—"

"Let me help you!"

Tears crept down his cheeks as she brought him up the steps into the hallway beyond the front door. The antique grandfather clock read 3:30.

"Now come on, I'll fix you up, and you can tell me what happened. Did someone beat you up at school?"

They walked almost past the kitchen.

Before they reached the master bathroom, a voice said in a low and deliberate tone,

"Hello, Carl."

It was a seven-year-old boy who looked like Devlin but sported a sly grin.

Red glowing eyes replaced the child's happy green ones.

What the—

Words formed in his head but wouldn't leave his lips.

He pulled back to stop Nancy from leading him all the way to the bathroom.

"Ma! That's not Devlin, it's—"

"Oh, Carl, what happened to you? Let's clean you up and prepare for dinner."

He argued further; but his mother kept interrupting him with replies like, "Now, now," and such. The boy in the hall seemed like an inhuman replica to him. Someone kidnapped his brother. He only needed to prove it.

The Drake boys grew up hearing the stories of strange goings-on in his little town of Gravestone; now he knew they were true.

"Ma! Listen to me! That boy is not Devlin! He's evil! Can't you see?"

"Carl! What's gotten into you? Have you hit your head? Now go change your clothes and come down to a nice dinner and when you have calmed yourself, you can tell me what happened to you."

He concluded that continuing his conversation with his mother was futile until after dinner. Perhaps the evil double would do something at the table, and she would realize on her own.

***

The kitchen was filled with the aroma of comfort from Nancy's roast beef dinner, but Carl only just touched his food and played with the vegetables while watching the imposter across the table. Whenever she wasn't looking, the eyes turned red. The only strange behavior she noticed was his insatiable appetite, so she just filled his plate again and ruffled his hair.

Carl ran through a few evil creatures and beings in his mind, pulling from his memories of the horror comics he and his friends had all started collecting.

Demon? Demons can look human, but why the switch? Kitsune? Not likely, those are intelligent, magical beings from Japanese folklore.

He did not know how, but as determined as he was to figure out what type of monster he'd be dealing with, he needed help to bring his brother back.

***

The Gravestone Library was muted and eerie during summer; made browsing the card catalog less of a chore.

Carl checked under E for evil but only found titles referencing religious nonfiction works.

Under C he searched for titles with creatures in them.

He could not find what he was looking for, but he came to a card for a book titled Changeling, Folklore of the Fae.

Carl remembered a strange cartoon at his friend Harold's house where a fairy swapped a baby with a pile of sticks.

He plucked the card from the catalog and found the section of the library where the book was according to the call number on the card. "Dam! It's not here." He muttered to himself.

When he turned back to the card catalog, the old librarian, Mr. Davis, startled him.

"Carl, my boy, what are you doing in this stuffy ol' library on a summer afternoon?"

Carl's friends teased him that he was over a hundred because of his posture, voice, and pace.

"Oh, hi Mr. Davis, well, I guess I was hoping to find a book about—well, it's kind of hard to explain and it's not here, anyway."

"The card, please." Mr. Davis reached his shaky hand out and persisted, "Well, hand it over then."

Carl passed the card over and waited, hoping the book would be on the returns cart behind the counter.

"Forget the book. Come with me."

Mr. Davis led Carl to one of the study tables in the center of the library and they sat.

"So, tell me, why are you studying changelings, my boy?"

"You wouldn't believe me if I told you, Mr. Davis." The old librarian lowered his glasses down the bridge of his enormous nose and focused his cloudy blue eyes on the boy.

"You know I have been here for over eighty-seven years come December. I've seen a lot of things in this town.

Nothing is too farfetched for these old ears. Tell me your story."

"Okay, after school yesterday, Devon was going on about cotton candy and begging me to take him to Everworld and —"

"Everworld, you say. Tell me you didn't go!"

"Yeah, we did, and you know how it was all falling apart and stuff? Well, when we got there, it was a brand-new place with bright lights, lots of food booths and, like, you know, brand new. We went in because it was free admission and food and all and —"

"Oh lordy, what happened?"

"There was this magic show, then Devlin was called on stage and he disappeared! The magician told me to call his name three times and roll bony dice or something. There weren't any dice and no audience anymore either! I ran out and started looking for him and calling him and I heard his voice, but nobody was there. Then he showed up and turned into a gross old gypsy man and grabbed my arm with his disgusting old claws and dug into my skin. Look, I still have the holes in my arm, and they are real sore!"

"What did he say to you?"

"He called me a dinslaw and told me to go back to where I came from, and that Devon is their Kurcheif or something like that. I ran off and went home and my Ma wouldn't listen to me, and I need my brother back!"

"I think it was Dinslow and Kurchi, that he said. That's Romani for idiot and slave, in that order."

"What's Romani? Are they magic? Evil?"

"Back in '62, Everworld appeared out of nowhere, all exciting and full of rides and funnel cakes and freak shows. Many of the children who entered when it opened, although they were with their parents; went home that day only to parish and die by the end of the year. Because of this, the locals talked and blamed the park for the demise of the children. We lost fifty percent of our population that year. Everworld fell into peril and sat vacant for close to ten years. A few investors that came through Gravestone tried to get it up and running again, but for different reasons; they failed. Lack of funding to repair the derelict rides, or just plain death with no heirs to leave it to."

"But Mr. Davis, what is Romani?"

"Oh, my apologies; I forget to add details. You've heard of gypsies."

"Yeah, like they live in caravans and steal from people and move to new towns to steal more and stuff?"

"Well, that is a stereotyped background, but yes; a lot of families have used their parties and dancing to draw in unsuspecting people to lure them into giving their jewels over and even money. But we term the man you saw at Everworld Romani Fae. In fact, he is likely the Fairy King. It was the Romani Fairies that lured in all those kids in '62. The clan switches many human children with changelings and enslaves them to work for about 20 years until they pass away from exhaustion. Then they resurface for another round of slaves."

"Is that what happened to Devlin?" Carl asked with feverish impatience. "He was with my mom when I got home but I know he's not Devlin! His eyes are red and beady and total evil!"

"That's the changeling Carl. You must be rid of it before it's too late!"

"How am I supposed to do that?"

Mr. Davis provided him with a list of changeling traits, including insatiable hunger, improper behavior, and red eyes.

Next, he elaborated on how Carl could expose the changeling by deceiving it or using fire, iron, or a hot poker to extract the truth.

"Well, I don't wanna hurt anyone, even an evil changeling, because what if I go to Hell for it or something like that? How do I trick it?"

"I have a sure-fire way. Changelings have a thing with eggshells, but they must be empty or filled with water. You put them around the bedroom it sleeps in, Devlin's room, of course, or on the floor in front of it and it won't be able to resist laughing and going mad!"

"So? How is making it laugh gonna do anything?"

"Oh, of course! Once it goes mad, it will reveal its identity. If that happens, the jig is up, and your little brother will be returned to you."

Carl jumped up and ran to the exit. "I need to hurry home and make sure we have eggs!"

"Carl, wait! Come back here! There's more!"

The boy turned, not willing to go back, but was listening for further instruction. Mr. Davis yelled over to him.

"You must be sure you are stealthy and quick, or it will catch on to what you are doing and thwart your whole plan!"

"Ok, I got it, sir. I gotta go!"

***

Upon arriving back at the house, Carl gathered his faculties and stamped up the front steps and through the front door.

His gaze shifted from the entryway towards the kitchen and hallway, where he spotted his mother seated at the table, smoking and drinking coffee. Loud crashes emerged from Devlin's room upstairs. Without a word to his mother, he opened the refrigerator and removed two cartons of eggs. He cracked them, emptying their contents into the garbage disposal one by one and laid the empty shells on the counter.

Three eggs into the second dozen, Nancy jumped to her feet.

"Carl! What on earth are you doing? You are wasting groceries and eggs are expensive! What is wrong with you?"

Carl rushed over to her to calm her down, placing his hands on her shoulders and looking her straight in the eyes.

"Ma, have I ever acted bad toward you?"

"No, son, but what are you doing?"

"Have I ever lied to you or caused any trouble?"

"Carl, please; settle down. I have had enough of an upset with your brother today. He's been a nightmare!"

"Ma, that's not Devlin! I need to do something, and I need you to just let me, okay?"

He continued cracking eggs into the garbage disposal and placing the empty shells on the counter; raising his hand to his mother each time she protested with him.

"Ma, please! You'll understand in a minute!"

After emptying all twenty-four eggs, he picked up the shells and placed them around the side of the kitchen table where Devlin would be sitting.

"Ma, call him and tell him it's time for a snack!"

"No way! He has already about eaten us out of house and home in less than twenty-four hours!"

"Ma, just please trust me, this will all be over in a few minutes and things will be all back to normal!" She went to the bottom of the stairs leading to the bedrooms and called up that it was time for cookies and milk. Within seconds, the noise ceased, and the double ran in leaps and bounds, two steps at a time, pushing past her right to the kitchen to the table.

Nancy gathered herself from falling to the floor and followed. The changeling spotted the eggshells before even pulling the chair out.

It hopped to the left on one foot, guffawing, and to the right on the other as its clothes split at the seams, exposing a bloated, furry stomach. The shoes popped off and hooves jutted out as it clopped its way around the kitchen floor and squealed.

"In all my eight hundred and fifty-five years, I've never seen the likes o'this!" It exclaimed as the final reveal took place.

Carl and Devlin's mother looked on in horror and dismay as she sobbed. Carl ran to her, holding her while the changeling lay on the floor, kicking its hooves and laughing.

"It's ok Ma, Devlin is coming back, any second!"

Just then, the front door creaked, and a frightened voice called from the entryway.

"Ma? Carl?"

Carl ran to the door and grabbed him, squeezing him tight, and rushed with him to the kitchen. Nancy sat on the floor, her sobs extending to screams with her hands over her eyes.

She had not realized that Devlin was home, and the changeling reduced to a pile of sticks buried in her son's clothing.

"Ma! It's me, Devlin; I'm so sorry I didn't come home right after school and—"

In a swift motion, she stood and hugged him tight.

If there be magic, fairies shall follow…

YOU BETTER WATCH OUT

YOU BETTER WATCH OUT

*T*was *the night before Christmas in Barrowlore, for a family of three that used to be four.*
Father had left at the beginning of the year, so Mrs. made holiday cheer.
The stockings hung; the tree trimmed with lights; a tiny red elf prepared for the last of his mischievous nights.

David Brennan was a twelve-year-old boy with a rotten attitude. His ill behavior goes beyond rude, obnoxious, and cold-hearted.
The thought of holiday movies, cookies and dessert squares sent him spiraling.
Most children, even those on the naughty list, love such things. Not David. HIs level of naughtiness surpassed that of the Grinch and Ebeneezer Scrooge combined.

***

"Mommy, can I put Elfie out before bed?" Brianna asked.
"Of course, sweetie, that's what he's here for!"
"Oh, goodie! I can't wait to make you laugh!"

Grandma had brought him for her on December first and read her the storybook that accompanied it before bed each night when her mother had to work.

David overheard his mother and Brianna talking in the kitchen. Filled with rage, he took the doll from the mantle and grabbed kitchen shears from a knife block on the kitchen counter.
"Pfft, Elf on the Shelf, what a crock," he growled.
"No! Dabid! Don't hurt Elfie!"
He gave her a devilish smirk. The head, first to be chopped off, fell into the garbage can, followed by the arms and legs.
"What do you call an elf with no arms, no legs, and no head, floating in the dishwater?" David sneered as he threw Elfie's torso into the sink full of dishes and cold, soapy water. "BOB! Hahaha!"
Fists in her eyes, Brianna sobbed, peering into the sink at the floating torso, then into the garbage can at its dismembered body parts.
Carole, their mother, comforted her distraught little girl with a tight hug.

"Go to your room, David! You've gone too far this time!" she shouted.

She had to work double shifts throughout the season, so she could enjoy some time off and afford the charge card balances she'd racked up.

A month after leaving, her husband contacted them with a forwarding address for his mail and a phone number. Following that, he rarely ever responded. David always blamed it on his mother, referring to her as a "piece of crap".

David was happy to escape the holiday cheer and left the room, but not before flipping off his younger sister.

"Mommy, can't you stay home with me tonight? Please?"

Because of being called in to cover a shift at the last minute, Carole needed someone to look after her that night, and she asked David to do it.

"I'm so sorry, honey, but I can't. Mommy must work."

The thought of leaving her with David after his terrible performance made her stomach churn. Her emotions sank as she saw the horror on her little girl's face.

Seconds later, her phone rang from inside her purse. The caller ID read Mother Goose.

"Hi, Mom, is there any way you could cancel—"

"Hello, dear. They canceled my bridge game tonight. Emma has the flu. What are you up to?"

"I got called in to work to cover a shift, and David is the only one to look after Brianna, and —"

"Say no more. I'll be right over. That boy has been so nasty lately. Even though I don't think he's dumb enough to harm Brianna, I doubt he'll pay her any attention."

With instant relief in her voice, Carole replied, "When can you get here?"

Grandma couldn't arrive for at least half an hour. David came out of his room.

"What's the matter, mom? Can't go to work?"

Carole slapped him when she saw his sneer, not only for the first time, but almost hard enough to spin his head.

His eyes widened as his mouth hung open in disbelief.

"Screw you, Carole, and your holiday too!" He ran to his room and slammed the door. Carole turned to Brianna.

"I'm so sorry about Elfie, honey. I'll get you another one tomorrow, and you can keep him in your room. How would that be?"

Brianna cried more.

"Oh Mommy, I hate Dabid! He's so mean, and he doesn't care about anybody!"

Carole cuddled her, made a bed for her in her lap on the couch, and put the Frosty the Snowman DVD in, awaiting Gramma's arrival while she called in late to work.

***

As night fell, shadows crept over Barrowlore. David had drifted off into a deep sleep with his headphones on, oblivious to the world around him. A loud crash from the glass of his bedroom window shattering and bursting inward made him jump out of bed.

A long, hairy, beast-like arm attached to an enormous hand, reached in and yanked him up by the hair, digging its talons into his scalp.

With feverish force, it threw him back onto his bed. The monster's hand closed into a fist, and when it opened, it revealed an elf with a twisted, malevolent grin.

The elf's clothing was dark green and red, but faded and grimy, as if it had been through a fire. It wore a pointed green hat atop its round head that emphasized its long sharp ears.

Its slanted, psychotic looking black eyes focused on David's terrified face.

A slow and creepy version of The Nutcracker blared from his portable stereo.

Lights danced across his ceiling like those from his star projector, and the moonlight shone through the shards of his imploded window onto his bedding.

"W-who are you? And w-what is that monster that brought you here?"

The elf sneered as it sprouted wings illuminated by fire and flew from the beast's hand onto David's bed.

"We're your worst nightmare,"

The hand withdrew through the window, and the elf flew right up to David's face.

He swung his hand, trying to hit it, but its nimble movements avoided the blow.

He grabbed it with force, but recoiled as the wings singed his skin.

With a tiny weapon in hand, it flew up to his nose and began poking around in his nostril.

"Ouch, you little bastard!"

The staff was no bigger than a thick turkey skewer, yet a deadly weapon. It was pushed up his nose so far that it almost touched his brain.

His nostril bled a thin trickle of blood that flowed onto his top lip and into his mouth.

As the elf retrieved his weapon to take another stab, David tried to grab it by the torso, but it was faster than a hummingbird. The harder he tried, the more it flew back and forth.

"And now for a little pixie dust! Wait, no pixie dust here! How about a little Elfie dust, instead?"

David once more attempted to swat the nasty creature away, but it flew above his head and dumped fiery embers all over him.

His skin burned and sparked as he floated out of bed, and they flew out the window into the night. David, afraid of heights, turned his head with caution to the right and took a few seconds to look down.

He squinted at the miniature version of his house, which faded away with every swoop upward.

They passed his school and the church on Cascade Drive, only recognizable by the glowing cross on the roof.

His heart pounded hard and fast almost stifling his speech.

"Wh-where the hell are you t-t-taking me?"

"Language, David! You'll see!"

A shrill laugh pierced his eardrums. For fear of what might happen if he pressed the subject, he said nothing further.

As they left Barrowlore behind, they soared over endless acres of forest; the temperature dropping to subzero levels.

The tips of his ears went from freezing cold to a painful tingle.

What if they break off from frost bite like Gramma's did?

The evil elf's voice broke him out of his thoughts. "Attention, human passenger, we will land in ten, nine, eight—"

The flight pattern jumped into a hellish downward spiral, increasing with each second of the countdown. "Seven, six, five—"

David screamed so loud his voice cracked.

If I close my eyes, I won't see the ground before the landing kills me!

His eyes were too dry to even shut after the rapid descent.

As the countdown reached two, they screeched to a halt an inch from the ground. They flew forward through a maze of trees, until they approached a building and burst through an ancient wooden door into an old sawmill.

His tiny captor deposited him onto a giant moving conveyor belt.

As an oversized pair of scissors opened and closed with a loud slicing sound, he gasped in anticipation, moving closer and closer toward the other end of the belt.

He tried to roll off, but extreme fear and the hot tingling of his skin as it warmed kept him in place. Slice, slice, slice.

With each passing moment, his struggles became more frenzied, and his screams echoed through the room. He finally reached the end, scrambling even harder than before.

His efforts grew weak as he ran out of breath and his head was severed.

His head landed on the ground with a thud, facing upward.

His brain was still active, which allowed him to see his body rolling along the belt.

Oh my God! How can I still see and think? This is the weirdest shit I have ever been through. I feel no pain, but I can smell my blood. I just want to end this now!

Screech!

The sound of the rusty handle on the mechanism was so loud that he would have jumped if he were not just an orphaned head.

He caught sight of a big toy sack before it dropped beside him.

The elf snorted out a giggle as it placed David's head into the sack.

"Now for the Fix-it factory!"

Fix-it factory. What the hell? How am I going to be fixed? Hot glue? Or maybe just put through a meat grinder to 'fix' their dinner, and the fix-it factory is a giant kitchen for monsters?

His love for horror movies was fast approaching an end.

The elf tied an enchanted rope to its waist and tied the other end to the toy sack, allowing it to float upward to flight level.

***

The toy sack fell abruptly onto a hard surface. He could hear a booming, demonic voice, but couldn't see the source with the sack still tied shut.

"Is that the brat from Barrowlore, Chadwick?"

"Yes indeed, master!"

Dullaklua was a demon far worse than Krampus and gave much harsher punishments than beatings with branches or sticks.

A nine-foot-tall creature with the head of a fire-breathing dragon, the body of a werewolf and the tail of a lion. His wings spanned one hundred-sixty feet. Jaws, filled with six hundred razor-sharp teeth, three hundred on the top and three hundred on the bottom.

Dullaklua raised his head and blew fire to a belfry above. The bell sounded, and five fire pixies entered, falling in line army style before him, awaiting his orders.

"Take him to the workbench at once!"

All five of them flew into the sack: one to carry the torso, one each for the limbs.

Chadwick flew into the sack and snatched David's head, with its eyes now shut.

Satisfied with his subjects' progress, Dullaklua went out through the busted sawmill door. With ground-rumbling stomps, he spread his wings and soared up over the trees.

With frenzied precision, the crew stitched David's limbs to his torso, their hands moving in a blur. Last was his head.

After being sewn back together, he felt a constant tightness from the twine holding his body together. The pain travelled through every free nerve ending of his epidermal layers as he tried to sit upright on the workbench.

"Let me go! Please! Untie me!"

The inherent lack of empathy born into the evil elf and fire pixies made David's pleading fruitless.

The king of the fire pixies approached with instructions for the rest of the journey. A card with a list of locations David would have to visit.

Chadwick took the card and read over the list, nodded his head with vigor, and gathered his victim.

"Walk, human child, walk!"

At first David, arms crossed in silence, refused to leave the fix-it-shop.

"Do we need the scissors again?"

Not the scissors again!

The brat obeyed and trailed behind to exit. To the left, they travelled through another section of the dark forest.

Bones, scattered across the path, crunched under his feet with each step.

"Ready for some snacks?"

David hadn't eaten lunch or dinner that day.

"Really? I'm starving!"

He was almost ready to collapse from hunger pangs, as the stitches around his limbs and neck tightened and oozed with yellow puss.

They arrived at a spot complete with a hot dog stand, and the smell of onion rings and fries. Everything was deep-fried.

"I want a Chicago—"

"Oh, no! That's not for David! We have something better for David!"

Farther down the way was a small bakery.

Even cookies and squares would do right now, David thought.

Just as he reached for the spread on the entry table, his hand got slapped.

"No, David hates cookies and squares!"

The elf's voice was grating, and he was queasy as it pushed him towards another table.

"Eat, human, eat!"

A spread of dog turd tarts, an array of truffles that smelled of rancid breath and a punch bowl filled with blood and floating eyeballs.

"Uh, I think I'll wait till later."
"No, you will eat now!"

The dog turd tarts floated off the table and around his face, then the truffles.

Chadwick flew up to his mouth and wrenched it open with all its might. Without choice in the matter, the horrid treats went into his mouth; his jaw forced to chew.

The sludge slid down his throat. Vomit bubbled up and down his esophagus.

"Next stop, the movie theater!"

Belly turning, saliva dripping from the corners of his mouth, he knew that he would have no choice, so he stood and waited to be transported.

A scrolling marquis displayed a message made up of neon green lights above the entrance of a small shack.

"Welcome to the Christmas Town in Hell Theater!" As the two entered, David longed for the end of the journey.

Chadwick reveled in the glee of escorting another victim to either an eternal stay in Hell's fantasy town or into Dullaklua's stomach.

Strapped into his seat with barbed wire, David's eyes were then propped open with toothpicks covered in cinnamon as he waited for the film to start.

As his eyes watered and more infected plasma matter escaped the stitched seams on his arms and legs, the opening credits appeared with bright, burning effect.

"THE NAUGHTY VICTIMS OF CHRISTMAS PAST," appeared on the screen.

The film began with a documentary style opening comment:

"This is Bobby Crawford, upon his visit to Dullaklua, December 24th, 1972. He was what some might call a bad seed. Watch what happened to him."

Bobby was sitting on the demon's lap looking doll-sized in comparison.

"You see your father, boy?" the demon asked as he showed him a crystal ball, which revealed a scene from earlier that day.

His father had arrived home from a long shift at the mine, covered in soot.

"Yeah, what about him?" The boy's voice rang with contempt.

"Shut your cake hole and keep watching!" Dullaklua ordered.

Bobby's dad placed the presents under their makeshift Christmas tree of holly and string, just prior to his son awaking at 6 a.m.

Dullaklua pointed between Bobby's eyes with his six-inch-long claw and waited a moment, then sniffed the boy's head with his enormous nostrils.

"I smell no remorse!" The demon said, opening his jaws.

He leaned down, drooling, and swallowed the boy up to his waist.

His six hundred razor-sharp teeth tore through the flesh, leaving only a gory mess of bone and muscle tissue.

David turned to Chadwick with eyes as wide as silver dollars.

"I-I he-heard that v-v-voice at the f-f-fix-it f-factory!"

"That's right, and you are lucky enough to get to meet him later!"

"No! I promise! I'll be good! I'll do anything you want, but don't make me meet that horrible monster!"

"David must keep watching!"

He had to watch three more boys fail before he was escorted out of the theatre.

The last film ended with a kid being barbequed alive before being devoured.

"Now, it's time for you to sit on Dullaklua's knee and tell him whatchu wants for Christmas!"

The elf's voice was more sinister than shrill this time.

"No, please, take me home!"

"You are not welcome at your home!"

His gut ached in anticipation of what was yet to come.

That's not true. Mom loves me. She's mad at me. That's all.

Uncertainty plagued him as he considered the possibility that Chadwick spoke the truth.

***

No tree or candy canes decorated the path to the glorious throne.

Fire pixies on the left and the right of the path held David above their heads and shuffled him with their arms to the lap of the demon.

"David Brennan, you come forth tonight to meet your destiny!"

The heat of the demon's breath was so intense that sweat coated the crown of his head and dripped down, the salty sting entering his eyes.

"Don't just sit there mute, human boy," Dullaklua demanded while holding his paw down on his knee.

"Sit up straight and see what I have for you!"
Despite almost falling backwards, David followed the instruction as his body emitted involuntary tremors.

I wish I was seven again at Willowbrook Mall, and if only this were Santa!

He used to love going to see the mall Santa, his recent behavior aside. An odd thought to go through someone's mind in the face of eternal damnation or being eaten alive but comforting.

The on-screen crystal ball was way smaller than the solid black one in person.

Dullaklua swirled his claws above it and chanted.

"Dark crystal, show the boy-child the error of his ways."

Smoke swirled inside it, revealing a snowy day little by little.

David watched his parents in conversation, his mother flailing her arms and crying as his father took his bags and walked out.

He then saw himself arriving home from school, his mother sitting him down to deliver the news.

He slapped her across the face and ran off.

"It's all your fault. I hate you, and I wish you were dead!" He remembered saying those words as soon as he saw the scene.

The next scene was the day he set the school garbage bins on fire and blamed Tom Goddard. Tom's father ended up beating him senseless, leaving him bawling in his room. Though David had never spoken to Tom at school, after seeing what happened when Tom was blamed for a crime he committed, his eyes welled up.

More scenes from throughout that year appeared of him tossing away the lunches his mother made in her busy schedule every single morning.

His skipping classes to smoke weed with his friends and making cherry bombs to blow up neighborhood mailboxes on Halloween night.

The final scene was on December 24th. The death of Brianna's Elfie.

David's head rose halfway up the demon's nostril as he was sniffed for remorse.

"What say you, human?"

Startled by the sudden boom, he replied,

 "I-I don't know."

The answer was not satisfactory.

Dullaklua bent his head down and released a long, hot breath over the boy, causing him to cringe; but nothing happened.

Taking in the scent of the child's hair, Dullaklua snarled and sniffed harder.

"Please, let me go. I don't know how to make you happy!"

"What would Brianna and your mother like for Christmas, boy-child?"

"I don't know about Mom, but I think Brianna would like her Elfie back."

Tears welled up and spilled down his dirty cheeks onto his blood-crusted neck.

Dullaklua snapped his fingers and motioned to a fire pixie to hand him something.

David closed his eyes to where he could see only a blur.

The pixie flew down to ground level and grabbed an item for the demon. Dullaklua took the item and held it in front of David. A box holding a brand-new Elf on the Shelf. David looked at its playful little face staring up at him from the cellophane compartment it lived in.

More tears flowed, accompanied by sniffles from his runny nose.

"You can go now; take this gift and wrap it for your sister. You are on your own to figure out what to do for your mother. If I ever catch you again during your lifetime, this will be the last place you shall see before I slice you up and roast your gizzard for my supper!"

Before he could respond, an unseen force pulled him into the crystal ball.

Upon a blink of his eyes, he found himself in his warm bed. The season took over all his senses. Finger foods, Bing Crosby's Christmas playing on his mother's stereo, mini-lights, and the warmth of family love.

He could almost taste a nice, cold glass of eggnog. Jumping out of bed, he looked in the dresser mirror to verify his identity.

The dark-haired twelve-year-old boy he was before they whisked him away to Christmas Town in Hell.

***

The wrapping paper was in Carole's room, so he sneaked in to grab a roll along with a tag to take back to his room. He closed his door and wrapped the new Elfie.

On the tag, he wrote From Santa and hid it under his bed.

I want to go downstairs, but now I feel so stupid for being such a jerk; and how can I face them?

***

Mom and Brianna sat together in the kitchen arranging goodies on trays, while Gramma finished baking the finger foods. Brianna looked to Carole.

"Mommy, is Dabid getting a lump of coal from Santa this year?"

Carole bellowed out a laugh like nobody had heard from her in over a year.

"Well, I don't know, sweetheart. Do you think he should get a lump of coal?"

David popped out from the hallway between the kitchen and living room.

"I deserve far worse than a lump of coal!"

Surprise washed over their faces as they picked up the remorse in his voice, a tone they had not heard for a long while.

"Is it too late to be a part of the festivities?"

His mother stood and pulled him close.

"Of course not, David. I know you have been hurting and—"

"Don't finish that, Mom. I had no excuse to treat you all or anyone else the way I did... and if Dad wants to be like he is, then he can stay away!"

"I missed you, monkey boy!" Carole said, teary-eyed, as she recalled the loving way David had been before his father abandoned the family.

"It's time for the two of you to grab some snacks, put out Santa's cookies and milk, and go up to your rooms."

Brianna walked over to David and looked up at him with her sweet blue eyes. He looked down at her, emotion welling up.

Get it together, man. Just because you feel all Christmassy doesn't mean you can turn into a ball of mush!

"Ready, Freddy?"

"Ready, Eddy!"

David and Brianna had always loved the Shreddie's commercial characters and acting them out with Brianna as Freddy and David as Eddy.

December 25th, 7:27 am

Brianna was the first to wake up, so she ran to David's room to wake him up.
"Dabid, Dabid! Come on!"
David opened his eyes and picked the crust from the corners.
"How about you go wake up Mom and Gramma, and I'll meet you downstairs?"
Without hesitation, Brianna dashed out of his room and down the hall to Carole's room.
David grabbed the present from under his bed and snuck downstairs to place it under the tree.
He turned on the Christmas tree lights and brewed coffee for himself, Mom, and Gramma.
After ten minutes, the rest of the family arrived in the living room.
"Oh, David! Thank you for turning on the tree!" Carole said.

"And there's coffee for you and Gramma on the coasters. You sit on the couch there, and Gramma can have the big armchair because she's old."

"I'm not old!"

Everyone laughed and took their seats. Brianna, of course, was on the floor right in front of the presents.

"What are you drinking there, David?" Carole asked.

"Coffee, Mom."

"You're too young to drink—"

She didn't finish the sentence, because she was happy to have her well-mannered son back.

"I'll play Santa Claus!" David volunteered. The adults agreed.

He handed Brianna the special gift he had marked from Santa.

"Yay! Elfie is back! I love you, Dabid!"

"But he's from Santa."

Brianna just looked at him and giggled, as if she knew all along that Santa had nothing to do with her new Elfie.

She pronounced his name Dabid; the only way she knew to say it. For all it was worth, he loved her.

And so, concludes the story of David Brennan, the only boy who ever met Dullaklua and lived.

Merry Christmas to all, and to all a good fright!

ACE OF SOULS

One year, three months, fourteen days, and seven hours sober.

Tony Camden began his sobriety journey when he awoke to a pool of his own vomit at four in the morning in a subway station.

At the age of nine, his mother left him in the care of his father, a hardened ironworker who paid him little attention.

His father's work buddies would come over on weekends to play blackjack until the early hours of the morning.

If Tony didn't speak, he was allowed to sit with them at the table and watch their cards.

The game was simple, yet he couldn't fathom why it could be so challenging.

He discovered in his early teens that he could sneak a beer when sent to the garage to grab another round for his father and the clan.

He would put a can in the pocket of his kangaroo jacket, deliver the rest to the table and migrate to his room to sketch and listen to music.

One can, then two cans, then three at a time.

Kangaroo jacket pockets could fit three cans just nice.

By the time Tony reached his late teens and early adulthood, he became a regular at the billiard hall, pub and beer store.

He never kept a relationship going and didn't want to spend mental or emotional energy on the needs of someone else let alone have any children.

***

His phone rang off the hook from the time he left work to the time he arrived home.

"James McDougall calling" chirped at him each time it rang, which he ignored.

Realizing James would not let up, he answered.

"Hi James, what's going down?"

"Well, you tell me, buddy, where have you been?"

"Been busy at work and tired, that's all."

"Tony, you haven't been to a meeting in over a month. I'm worried about you, man."

"I'm fine."

"If all you got is a job and an empty apartment, it's only a matter of time before the inner demons come a'callin. You know that, right?"

"James, I appreciate your intentions, however, do I truly need to come to meetings to stay away from alcohol? Plus, I have over seventy-five-hundred dollars saved by staying sober and that plus feeling well is enough to keep me honest, man!"

"Well, I hope to see you at the Friday night meeting then. We can catch up after that."

Tony ended the call without saying goodbye.

***

The microwave popcorn in the pantry cupboard was all Tony had to eat for dinner. He could have driven to get a burger and fries but refrained because of the location; right next to the beer store.

He turned his smart TV to WatchTube and selected a DIY program he had watched the night before, pressed play, and proceeded to the kitchen to pop his dinner.

"Play like a pro! Learn to count cards like the best of 'em and watch your winnings grow! Join free today at Blackjack Superstar.net, do it!"

The WatchTube ad barked at him as he dumped his popcorn into a bowl and melted the butter.

"I should just sign up for WatchTube Premium, at least I could skip these damn ads. Every ten minutes on the tens more ads!"

The same ad played every time, so he searched for different content.

"I know who DIY Woodworkers adopted as a sponsor." He said to the empty living room as he searched. He came across The History of Texas and watched a bit.

Another ad.

"Play like a pro! Learn to count cards like the best of 'em and watch your winnings grow! Join free today at Blackjack Superstar. net, do it!"

The same ad played every ten minutes. He looked at the clock, gut full of buttered popcorn and eyelids sagging. Ten o'clock. He turned off the television and dragged himself to bed.

1am

Tony awoke from a hybrid of a dream and the Blackjack Superstars.net ad.

The dream was of his childhood home watching his dad play blackjack with his fellow iron workers, ordering him to renew their round of cold beer.

As he walked to the beer fridge in their garage, he heard that ad.

 Upon waking, he was thirsty. He went to his kitchen and grabbed his EverCold tumbler and filled it with ice and cola to sip on if he woke up again.

2:15am

"Play like a pro!" Rang in Tony's subconscious as he woke again for a sip of cola.

3:25am

"Count cards like the best of em'!" Another sip of iced cola.

4:15am

"Join free today at Blackjack Superstar.net, do it!" The image in his dream before he awoke this time was of his dad speaking the words of the ad.

He gave up on trying to get any sleep, walked to the kitchen and pressed the power button on the coffeemaker, intercepting the auto brew feature.

Its been over a year since I called in sick last. Today is the day I NEED to stay home, if only for a mental health day.

He picked up his phone and dialed his boss. Voicemail.

"Hi Dave, I would not call in, but I have not slept a wink all night and have the worst headache. I just need a day to recoup and get some rest. If you need anything from me, you can call my cell. Bye."

He sipped his coffee and lit a smoke as he opened the sliding glass door of his apartment so as not to be discovered smoking indoors by the landlord.

Television channels were riddled with Shop at Home Network syndicated programming until later in the day on weekdays.

WatchTube was not an option and his other streaming mediums had nothing he wanted to focus on.

***

  Although he had called in sick, he was not tired enough to nap, and it was Friday. He could sleep on Saturday.

Blackjack Superstar.net, Learn to count cards like the best of 'em.

He couldn't stop thinking about those ads.

It's not gambling unless you put money in. Dad put nothing more than beer and smokes in, played at home with his buddies, and never got beyond that. I can do that too.

Pouring a second coffee, he went to his dining room table, where his laptop was set up for the odd time he worked from home.

He opened an internet browser window and typed Blackjack Superstar. The search term came up with the rest of the website. He clicked on the link and created a free player account.

***

The platform of his user account included a blackjack manual and various tutorial videos on card counting and the game in general along with betting strategies.

Something he had never paid attention to as a kid, it matters what the dealer puts up as their first card in play. A high card gets the dealer closer to either beating you or busting. Tricky.

A low card for the dealer is more likely to produce the second face-down card they pull as a card too low to beat you.

***

Tony, now well versed in the game of blackjack; entered his first online table with a bet of one hundred dollars and beat the table. He started the next betting round with a thousand and won.

His phone dinged, showing a text message.

He ignored it and continued to play into the next morning.

***

Upon logging into his Blackjack Superstar account, an unusual ad appeared.

"No risk blackjack tournament, April 11th, 2024. Enter to win a seat! If you are one of our lucky draw winners, you get $100,000.00 to play with AND if you can make it to the end without being eliminated, all winnings are YOURS! Deadline to enter is February 14th, 2024."

<u>Click Here to Learn More</u>

What have I got to lose? If I win the draw, all good; if I don't, I don't, simple as that.

He clicked and filled out his full name, email address, and play history. He would hear via email by the end of February.

February 18, 2024

He arrived home and set into his first blackjack game of the evening while eating a dinner of easy cook food; frozen onion rings and chicken fries with a few tater tots.

His phone lit up from the coffee table with an email. He opened it and read.

"Congratulations Tony, you're a winner!"

It was from the Blackjack tournament draw.

The body of the message confirmed his $100,000.00 playing funds and entry into the tournament. Prior to March 9th, the attached registration form needed to be completed and returned.

He filled in his name, address, and answers to prior tournament participation questions and printed it.

The conditions said that the establishment had the right to keep all winnings if a player were to be eliminated. Avoiding the rest of the fine print, he placed his initials on all the presented lines, signed the pages he needed to and scanned it to his laptop to send off.

On April 1, an email arrived with registration confirmation, venue address, and directions.

April 11, 2024

Tony's alarm went off as he scrambled out of bed, eager for some much-needed time off, a road trip and the possibility of winning big.

At six am, he snatched a travel mug, filled it with coffee and creamer, and ran to the underground parking lot.

After fiddling with his Bluetooth GPS app, it showed on the infotainment system in his 2020 Camaro. If he wanted to make it to Austin by 9:15 to check in at the hotel and sign into the conference center on the ground floor, he had to be on his way.

8:55am

He made it to the Grand Hotel, Austin parking lot just in time to check in.

"Identification please." The attendant said in a dry and unentertaining tone.

"Oh, yes, one second."

"Mr. Tony Camden, I have you booked in room 1302; is that correct?"

"You tell me, I wasn't told of the room number, and come to think of it, I tried looking you up online and came up with nothing."

The front desk clerk leaned forward on his elbows with a sly grin showing the gold crowns near the back of his top jaw.

"Our guests don't' find us sir, we find them. Right through the double doors to your left is the better's box."

"The room keys?"

"Oh yes."

The clerk handed Tony a box he was familiar with but could never afford on his salary. A Smart Gen watch, top of the line.

"A watch?"

"Yes, sir, we have programmed it with your room number. Wave it in front of the door panel and you are in. Program it with anything you would like."

"Man, that must be a lot of work to reset every time someone checks out, huh?"

"Oh no, sir, consider it a gift!"

Holy shit, these are worth between eight hundred and two thousand dollars! This day just keeps getting better with every passing minute.

***

Tony dashed into the lounge at 9:12am, hauling his rolling suitcase and overnight bag.

He handed over his registration form, recalling the tournament wasn't to start until noon.

The box manager handed him a slip of paper with his registration number on it and a voucher for the buffet and bar.

"Excuse me sir, what time do I need to come back by? I mean, I'm guessing I can bring you this slip and collect my chips to play later? Also, can I get a voucher for just the buffet?"

"Really? Why would you want that?"

"I don't drink."

"Well, just don't drink. We only have one type of voucher."

With a sigh of discontent, Tony asked again what time he needed to be back by.

"You need to be at the player's table by 11:55am, all chips in hand and ready to bet in the qualifier round at 12:00pm."

He thanked the man, tucking the betting slip in his wallet against the voucher, and headed for the lobby elevator to deposit his belongings in room 1302.

***

The luxurious lobby of the hotel had the fanciest wood floors Tony had ever seen.

In the center of the floor was a lush, round inlay of red carpet with multicolored shards of sunlight shining from above.

A large domed skylight constructed of stained glass and wrought iron adorned the ceiling.

The elevator ride was but a pallet cleanser for the richness he was about to meet.

The room assigned to him was bigger than his entire apartment.

A king-sized post bed stood stoic in the middle against a feature wall of exposed brick.

The rest of the room featured a spiral staircase leading up to a black and white tiled soaker tub with pot lights in the ceiling.

The lower level had a leather couch and loveseat set with brass button accents, plus a wood coffee table with a blue and green resin top.

Atop the coffee table was a bottle of expensive aged scotch, a box of assorted Belgian chocolates and a basket of crackers, jams and dried meat products.

A glass and cedar cabinet held crystal scotch glasses next to the bottom floor bathroom. He grabbed the bottle and ran to the bathroom to pour it down the toilet.

The smell reached his nose. His upper lip lined with micro beads of sweat.

To distract himself, he picked up his suitcase and placed it on the bed.

He sorted pants, shirts, and socks, but was unsure if what he packed met the standards of a high-profile guest.

Twelve-year-old dress pants, a Black Label Society raglan, and red Converse kicks were his choice.

"If I'm not elite, at least I'm unique." He said as he admired his creative fashion in the full-length mirror affixed to the bathroom door.

**

He joined four other players at the first table for the qualifier round, ten betting rounds.

The players with the highest chip counts would advance to the VIP room for level two and the final table.

An attractive woman addressed him.

"Hey, where are you from? You don't have a drink, I brought two, help yourself!"

"Dallas and recovering alcoholic, only soda for me thanks."

She didn't continue the conversation, only smiled and organized her chips in piles by value.

To avoid conversation with the other players and remain focused, Tony pulled a pair of sunglasses from his pocket and put them on. If he was going to bet smart, he had to know which chips were high value and which were low.

He placed the five-thousand-dollar chips, then the thousand-dollar chips and so on.

Ten thousand was his opening bet.

His first two cards, a two and a six.

The dealer pulled a four.

Tony doubled down, splitting his hand and motioned to hit, for both.

A ten card for the two with an ace for the six, making two hands for twelve and seventeen.

He waved his hand to stay at both hands.

The dealer's face down card, a king. He pulled another, an eight.

The woman who tried to flirt with him went all in and busted, leaving Tony and three other men to play another gruelling nine hands.

***

With a chip count of three-hundred-thousand dollars, Tony entered the VIP room with two remaining players.

A buffet of crab, lobster tails, scallops wrapped in bacon and prime rib with all the fixings lined the walls for a one-hour intermission of dinner and cocktails.

Tony grabbed a plate and loaded it with seafood and roasted spring vegetables careful to avoid the bar.

"Hey pard'ner, what's with the shades?"

One of the best players he was with at the qualifier table stood waiting for a response.

"Excuse me?"

"You've been wearing them since you sat down."

"Oh, I forgot I was wearing them, just wanted to focus on the wins you know?"

"Ya, I hear that!"

"Besides, that woman next to me was trying to flirt with her cliché 'where are you from' line."

"Oh, you're talking about that twit who went all in on her first bet and BUST, just as well she was annoying as hell. Say, let's go find a table and have a drink!"

I'm getting sick of everyone thinking it's weird I'm not drinking and having to go through the recovering alcoholic bit. I wish they would just leave me the fuck alone.

"I'm not much of a drinker."

"Fair enough pard'ner, say, did you see that chap walking the qualifier room with the Mr. Blackjack name tag on?"

"I did, is that supposed to be a joke?"

"I don't know but it takes me all I got not to ask! Name's Cowboy John by the way, you are?"

"Tony, good to meet you."

The third level two player joined them with two beers in his hand.

"Quite a spread they have here huh? Come to think of it, quite a place to hold a tournament!"

"Where'd you get in from pard'ner? I'm Cowboy John, and this is Tony."

"Flew in from Maine last night, I'm Jeff, nickname's The Kid."

The Kid motioned to hand Tony a beer. Cowboy John raised a hand and shook his head to which Jeff shrugged and took a sip of the other.

"I am famished, let's load up!" Tony said to avoid further awkwardness.

ACE OF SOULS

***

Halfway through their meals, Mr. Blackjack approached them.

"I have a deal to present you. This is an opportunity for each of you to keep a portion of your play money and winnings, so you don't go home empty handed. Interested?"

Tony sat forward, "How does it work?"

"All three of you need to agree to a minimum value to hold back from the final round bets, the player with the biggest win at the final table takes 0his winnings plus the hold back. The others go home with just the hold back."

"All have to agree to the deal and the minimum hold back?"

"That's right, are you in?"

Tony turned to the other two raising an eyebrow.

"I shall leave you gentlemen to discuss."

"Well Tony, what's it gonna be?"

Jeff said nothing but looked to Tony to captain the decision as well.

They agreed to keep the play money of $100,000.00 they were given to enter the tournament, considering Tony's take of three hundred, Cowboy

John's two-hundred-forty and The Kid's one-hundred-eighty-two.

***

The first three hands dealt proved to be in Tony's favor. John followed close at second. Jeff with only ten thousand left to bet.

By the eighteenth hand, Jeff was out. Tony and John waited for one another to place a bet for the nineteenth.

I don't care if it takes an hour, I won't be the first to bet.

Cowboy John placed one-hundred-thousand, Tony, fifty thousand. They finished the round tied at twenty with the dealer busting at twenty-six.

***

Tony's first card in the twentieth round, a king. John, a queen. The dealer, a jack.

Mr. Blackjack, circling the table locked eyes with Tony.

His every muscle tensed while he waited for the next card.

The dealer's hand seemed to move in slow motion toward the deck as he picked up Tony's next card.

As a suitless Ace hit the table in front of Tony's final bet a loud buzzer sounded, echoing from the ceiling and filling the otherwise empty VIP room. Cowboy John stood extending a hand to him. They shook and bade farewell as Mr. Blackjack sauntered over.

"Follow me Tony, we have details to discuss."

***

"I have to know; Mr. Blackjack can't be your name so what is it?"

"Let's celebrate, shall we?"

The man poured two glasses of champagne, raising one for a toast.

"I don't drink, rec - "

"I know, recovering alcoholic. One glass won't hurt, will it?"

"How did you know I was - "

"Cigar?"

"What is going on here?"

"Have a seat Tony, take a load off."

Mr. Blackjack sat in a puffed leather armchair in the corner of his office motioning for Tony to join him.

With broad hesitation, he walked over and took the second armchair.

"It's rather chilly in here, Mr. Blackjack said as he snapped his fingers igniting the oversized gas fireplace in the wall behind him.

The heat of the gas flames rapidly heated the room.

"Wow, that's hot! Aren't you overheated sitting right in front of it like that?"

Mr. Blackjack's face pulled up on one side in an evil grin.

"Oh, I am quite used to the heat of fire but if it's too much for you —" He snapped his fingers again disabling the fireplace.

"I still don't know your name sir."

"Well Tony, what is in a name? It gives those around us the ability to assume our personalities, doesn't it?"

What is with this guy? Crazy.

"Am I Tony? Crazy that is. I would say, you could be construed as the crazy one my friend. Afterall, you skipped the fine print of a gambling agreement just to get all the way to Austin for the big win!"

"What do you mean by that now?"

The man burst into a boom of laughter momentarily and went silent as he snapped his fingers producing a red file folder out of thin air.

"Allow me to enlighten you!"

Mr. Blackjack flipped to the fine print on page two of the tournament agreement Tony signed, turning it so he could see it right side up.

He placed the tip of his index finger next to the first paragraph.

"I will highlight it for a better read."

As he moved his index finger across the fine print, the text became three dimensional as if coming off the page.

He who draws the Ace of Souls shall be deemed as entering a contract with Lucifer, therefore forfeiting all rights to his soul and relinquishing himself to eternal sorrow.

"I didn't know it was a contract, that is illegal, and eternal sorrow. What does that even mean?"

"I trust your accommodations are satisfactory Tony, please, if you need anything to improve your comfort, do let the front desk clerk know."

"As entertaining as this has all been, I'll be on my way."

"You will join us for cocktails this evening won't you Tony?"

Tony left Lucifer's office and ran to the lobby headed for the elevator.

This is nuts! All I need to do is grab my shit from the room and get going. I mean, I'm sure it's possible to live without a soul...isn't it?

On his way through the lobby, he passed a woman wearing a sequinned dress wandering aimlessly as if in search of something.

He glanced at the front desk clerk who saluted him with a wink.

In the elevator were two men, one in his mid-twenties, the other in his late seventies.

They wore clothing from different eras. The younger man in a grey jazz suit and starch collar white shirt, the older man in an ensemble of polyester brown trousers and a salmon-colored golf shirt.

"Excuse me, what is this place?" Tony asked the younger man.

"Limbo sir."

"What? As in purgatory?"

The older gentleman piped up in response.

"Well, that depends on your upbringing son."

"Yeah, well I'm getting the hell out of here."

"That's not how it works here sir. I have been trying to get out since 1923." The young man said before resuming his view of the elevator carpet.

"I arrived here in '79, gave up trying come '82. Oh, this is my floor."

The elevator climbed to the tenth floor, where the young man bade Tony a somber farewell.

***

Room 1302 appeared just as he left it, but he could not find his suitcase.

He ran to the closet in case someone put it away. When he opened the closet door, multiple pairs of dress pants exactly like the ones he was wearing hung neatly on hangers, along with sevral pairs of the same Converse shoes and just as many Black Label Society raglans.

"What the hell?"

He frantically searched for his car keys finding them in a candy dish on the coffee table and ran back to the elevator.

***

The woman in the lobby greeted him with a knowing smile as he made his way to the exit. Upon placing his hand on the grand glass turnstyle to leave, he pushed his way round and round until he was deposited back into the lobby.

He walked over to the woman in the sequinned dress and extended his hand.

"Tony Camden, 2024."

"Adelaide Buckerfield, 1958"

"What are you searching for Adelaide?"

"The same thing we have all been searching for in this eternity, and so shall you."

There will be more...

Ingram Content Group UK Ltd.
Milton Keynes UK
UKHW041443050723
424531UK00017B/289

THE OWL MEN OF SHANIDAR

books by coy hall

Grimoire of the Four Impostors
The Hangman Feeds the Jackal
A Pantheon of Thieves and Other Weird Tales
The Promise of Plague Wolves
A Séance for Wicked King Death
Death's Other Kingdom: Horror Tales of World War I
Colossus with a Poison Tongue
The Switchblade Svengali

THE OWL MEN OF SHANIDAR

A NOVEL BY COY HALL

The *SCYTHIAN WOLF.*

The Owl Men of Shanidar
© 2025 by Coy Hall
All Rights Reserved.

Published by The Scythian Wolf
www.scythianwolf.com

ISBN: 9798334408074

Publisher's Note:
No part of this publication may be reproduced, distributed, or transmitted in any form or by any means, including photocopying, recording, or other electronic or mechanical methods, without the prior written permission of the publisher, except in the case of brief quotations embodied in critical reviews and certain other noncommercial uses permitted by copyright law.

This book is a work of fiction. Names, characters, places, and incidents either are products of the author's imagination or are used fictitiously. Any resemblance to actual persons, living or dead, events, or locales is entirely coincidental.

Cover design by Pulp Shriek

In Memory of Duncan

chapter one

IN A DRY RIVERBED on the planet of Shanidar, a woman gestured at the chalk-white ground, at a rift that opened like a wound in ancient silt. With unspoken urgency, she waited for confirmation. The man at her side tested her resolve with his cold manner. Although his support was vital, Brynn Silva knew what she'd found. She knew the significance, the weight.

Growing impatient, she peered at the shore and harsh sky. The surrounding sand was calm. Mountains loomed in the distance, a dark ridge wavering in the heat haze. Her hand went to the pendant at her neck, a Serpent Tongue mounted with blue garnet and suspended from a chain. She traced the familiar lines, but Brynn was not a woman of faith. The relic was a gift. The action was habit.

The man cast a long, slender shadow. He was tall and gaunt, dressed in black. A protective hood shielded the ghostly skin of his face. He possessed the air of a spider ensnaring prey, thin from drought but assiduous. The stillness of his mouth, however, said he was satisfied. He put aside his anger and discomfort, his long ranting about the journey, the sun, heat, time, remoteness of the dead river, and the ignorance of his fellow colonists. The xenolinguist named Alaric Rhys was quiet, but he was not calm.

When he knelt, his coat bunched around him, folding on the sand. His synthetic joints clicked and groaned like gear teeth in need of oil. Rhys brushed the chalk, revealing more of an object that escaped through the fracture.

Finally, he broke the tension. His sepulchral voice was ponderous.

"Ms. Silva, you understand what this is, do you not?"

Rhys peered through the shade of his hood. His sclerotic eyes were bionic. Two blue lights marked the pupils. Under the coat, his spine trilled—remarkable for an impotent, sexless man who never expressed pleasure. The shaking back—the trembling shoulders—Brynn wouldn't forget the image.

Inside, Alaric Rhys was on fire.

Brynn knew precisely what she'd found. She'd studied the artwork more extensively than Rhys. From the first sight on the shore, she'd known. She'd leapt into the riverbed out of her mind with excitement. The object was a hand sheathed in a glove of rust—humanoid and birdlike in its construction. Long and brittle. Eight digits. An opposable thumb.

This is a burial, she thought.

Although she didn't want to relinquish the find to Rhys, the discovery was within his ambit on Shanidar. He was the boss. If she dug without his permission, he'd make her life hell with his interference.

As Rhys brushed away layers of silt, revealing the braided shaft of an arm, he said, "Fetch my library from the bike, Ms. Silva."

Brynn had no positive feelings for Alaric Rhys. His high-handedness was irksome. The man was self-absorbed and off-putting. He was an outcast among outcasts. But, regarding the sciences, he topped the hierarchy on Shanidar. Every discovery—no matter how trivial—went through him.

Brynn scaled the bank. The transport bike waited, recharging under the sun's glow. By the standards of home, the vehicle was primitive in its simplicity. The Weston Joint Stock Company had supplied the colonists with mechanical vehicles, so that even the least skilled could maintain them. Unfortunately, that meant wheels on the ground and the lack of speed that comes with friction.

Brynn opened a searing metal chest at the rear of the bike. Nestled in the headgear, first aid, and miscellany, was a tablet that housed the linguist's library of books and notes.

She returned, sliding down the bank on her heels, kicking up pale dust. Pebbles trickled after her.

Dr. Rhys took the tablet.

After a moment of punching at the screen, he said, "Look here, Ms. Silva. What do you see?" He shaded the device with a gloved hand.

Despite the condescension, Brynn played along. She studied the illustration and read a caption written in one of the two deciphered tongues of Shanidar.

A wave of relief kicked through her. Rhys would give no argument this time. No pedantic nitpicking.

"An Owl," Brynn said.

She eyed the linguist, waiting. *Say it,* she thought.

"It appears to be the hand of one of the Owls," Rhys said. "You did it, Ms. Silva. You finally found one."

Brynn allowed herself a moment.

"A child of Shanidar," Rhys said. "Here is a member of that ancient, elusive race."

Immediately, Brynn wanted to dash off a message to the Weston Joint Stock Company. This was big news. And if she wanted her name on the discovery along with Rhys, she had to be the one who pressed send. Otherwise, the linguist would pull rank and take full credit.

For the first time in their six years of acquaintance, she saw the linguist smile. It was unbecoming in his clay flesh.

"A child. I was beginning to think the race was incorporeal.

Now to find one of the parents." He glanced over his shoulder. "We should excavate this riverbed for a kilometer around."

Brynn took the library. She studied the illustration again. It was copied from one of the graffitied silos in the Owl's Lair. In the alien tongue, the symbols roughly translated as "the people."

"You'll perform a most careful exhumation, Ms. Silva. If the hand is any indication of condition, the Owl is delicate. We must do our utmost to keep it intact. If its wings are below the surface, they'll be quite brittle."

Through continued brushing, Rhys revealed the edge of a gnarled cranium. The metal resembled organic growth, replicating outward from a bulbous kernel. He stroked a ridge.

"You'll need to return with proper tools. And make haste." He gestured at the sun, well past its zenith. Days on Shanidar were long at thirty hours, but, without a moon, the blackness of night ate half that time.

"I will?"

"And return with a companion to help with the digging, Ms. Silva. If you're about to protest, stifle it and consider this an order."

Brynn folded her rebuttal as small and tight as it would tuck, and she saved the venom for another time. With a curt nod, the archaeologist started back to the bike.

"If you're in the mood to speculate," she said, "how did one of them end up here, so far from the Owl's Lair?" Her voice reverberated through the hollow artery. The echo made the remoteness of the riverbed more acute.

"Either it was buried in the water or malfunctioned and fell from the sky."

She'd guessed the latter.

"You're certain you want to remain out here alone?" she asked.

"I will stand guard, Ms. Silva. Lest our friend gets up and goes." Rhys grunted.

Was that a laugh? Brynn thought, astonished. She watched him. *No. A cough maybe. No.*

She climbed the bank. He returned to brushing. The thought of Rhys uncovering the Owl's face had her seething. He'd be the first to look into its eyes. It was brutally unjust.

If you want to play this game, I'll be equally petty, she thought. *I'll go to the server room and get the message sent to Weston before I come back. You'll be the footnote, Rhys. Not me.*

Along with the idea, however, an existentially troubling figure surfaced—the colossal number, as Brynn labeled it. In light-years, the number was 4.2. Deceptively digestible. In kilometers, the figure approached forty trillion—an incomprehensible, unfathomable thing. Colossal. A human could live two centuries and not reach one trillion seconds of life. Not even one. Try to comprehend forty. If she sent word to Weston about the Owl this instant, the transmission would reach its target in a little over four years. And then, four plus years after that, Brynn would receive a message of congratulations.

The colossal number was Shanidar's distance from Luna Fourteen, the closest of Weston's sixty-seven colonies.

Okay, I'm being petty and impatient. So be it. I want credit.

There was one means of consolation. Weston had a cryo-ship with four hundred colonists on route to Shanidar, and it was close. The *Bedivere* was no more than a week away.

I'll send a message to the ship, too, Brynn thought. *That'll give them something to wake up to. I can wait a week for congratulations.*

It was something.

Brynn sat on the bike. With the press of a button, the engine rumbled. A cloud of dust lifted around the back wheel.

She checked the hairlike communication device in her inner ear—telepathy cilia, as Weston marketed its wetware implant. On her private channel, she had fifteen messages from the two men in her life, one a human, one a machine. There was no time to read all of that.

When Brynn was ready to depart, however, she stopped cold, releasing her grip on the handles. She planted her boots in the sand. She removed her goggles and stared at the horizon opposite the mountains.

No, Brynn thought. *You're delirious and exhausted.*

She was not prone to hallucinations, even under the beating sun. She shook her head and looked again.

A silhouette appeared in the distant desert. A wanderer on foot.

Currently, there were 118 colonists on Shanidar. Men and women. No children. The colonists lived in a single settlement called Vandalia. One settlement, the first settlement, and nothing more. That was the extent of intelligent life on this world. Save for plants and copious insects, Shanidar was otherwise a ghost planet with limited biodiversity, the higher lifeforms long extinct.

Regardless, the impossible figure interrupted the horizon like a slash of flickering darkness. A humanoid shape walked toward the river. Here, a couple hundred kilometers from Vandalia, was a stranger.

She sifted through the public channel for a precise number on the *Bedivere*. She found it: estimated arrival was in six days, twenty-one hours, and fourteen minutes.

Your brain's cooked, she thought. *Overwrought. A heat stroke is more likely.*

Brynn slapped on the goggles and reversed the transport in a tight circle. When she looked over the sand once more, the figure remained but had stopped walking. It stood in the distance, watching, like the sound of the engine over the drylands was equally startling to it, equally disruptive of its sense of aloneness.

Delirious and exhausted.

She kicked forward, parting the sand.

chapter
two

VANDALIA SPREAD over the hilltop like a crust of pox—a rash of synthetics and sheet metal erected in a forest of yellow and burgundy. Thick, primeval woodland had overtaken this region of Shanidar, growing unchecked for millennia, verdant with webbing vines and enormous trees with fronds and sprawling roots. Here the planet was a cauldron, volatile with storms and wet heat.

A conspicuous bald spot on the lush pate, Vandalia was a network of halls, slanted roofs, and duckboards—a mix of dormitories, communal spaces like a recreation room and pottery studio, a greenhouse, and a machine shop. Utility took precedence over design, with the want of survival quashing artistic ambition. When approached from the valley, the settlement was an inelegant bruise on the land.

The strange beauty of Vandalia's western neighbor magnified its anemic qualities. Vandalia was a tent city at the gates of an extinct Rome. Ancient ruins of metal, with silos black as polished obsidian and a stone wall that wrapped nine square kilometers, rose high in the foothills. The human-alien contrast was that of plastic and pearl. Trees braided the ruins, binding and reshaping metal, giving an arthritic bend to the silos, but a cathedral-like ability to inspire awe remained in the Owl geometry. Roots clung to the outer wall with a tight grip, fracturing stone into snaking lines. When wind blew through the ruins, there was a sibilant quality.

Rising as it did from the forest, the most apt comparison was Angkor Wat in old Cambodia. For that reason, colonists thought of the city as a derelict temple. Its real name, like so many other things that belonged to the Owls, was uncertain and debated. A cartographer using the initial Weston scans had called it—and several other cities like it—the Owl's Lair. The name stuck.

IN ONE OF the long dormitories of Vandalia, in a cramped room built for one but housing the possessions of two, Cullen Archer lay on a cot, his eyes closed. He held a precious relic of Resurrection between his fingers, a Serpent Tongue. The bleached fang—from an extinct tiger shark, despite its name—was a connection to the Earth that was, had been, and would be again.

Although Archer was paralyzed to stillness, he was not asleep. The Resurrectionist was engaged in a moment of worship. He was engrossed in prayer.

A devotional film ran through his neural interface, flashing in his brain at ninety frames per second, leaving him in the warm embrace of hope and faith. The film was not of his making. This was a sacred reel, twenty minutes long, that he'd bought from a vendor at the Basilica of Saint Anastasia on Luna Fourteen. Archer owned two such films, but this was his comfort.

In it, Archer was on a resurrected Earth, swinging a glistening blade through thick jungle growth in a land called Guatemala. Ruins, god-faces, colossal heads in stone, birds, and slithering creatures by the millions populated the wilderness. Archer struggled over swampy ground, chopping vines, alone with wonder. And then, atop an altar that displayed a man emerging from a cave, his umbilical cord prominent on the ground, Archer spied a jaguar—a gorgeous, lean, and elegant lord of an animal. The great cat lay panting in the shade. On either side were two stone humanoid heads with slanted eyes and downturned mouths. Free of the undergrowth, Archer sheathed his blade. The jaguar didn't flee as he approached. He came nearer. The cat did not hiss or threaten. The jaguar welcomed him. Archer forgot the heat, mosquitoes, and leeches. All his troubles melted away. He sat on the altar beside the carnivorous predator. He stroked her head, scratched her ears. A stone pyramid rose behind them. And there was harmony in his soul. The moment was a flashpoint of unification.

The long-dead Earth lived.

The neural interface went black. After a beat of silence, text appeared like an afterimage on the back of his eyelids: "Pyramid of the Jaguar" is a production of the Weston Joint Stock Company. All Rights Reserved. Copyright 2279 C.E. The Unauthorized Duplication or Replication of this Film Without the Express Written Consent...

Archer opened his tear-rimmed eyes. Gripping the Serpent Tongue, he rose from the cot. He paced the minuscule room like a trapped hamster pinging between walls. His mind wasn't long on resurrection, however. On his sixteenth pass through the dorm, Brynn returned to his thoughts. He checked the cilia for a message. Nothing, public or private. He checked the time.

Goddamnit to hell, he thought. And Archer was out the door.

Titus Bell, his oldest friend, was in the hall without a shirt, working on emergency lights that ran along the baseboards. He had the casing off, the wires exposed. He poured sweat.

Archer rushed by without acknowledgment.

"What's up your ass?" Titus called after him.

"Brynn."

Brynn is positively and irrevocably up my ass, he thought.

"Oh. Well, hey, stop by the Boxgrove later, buddy. You need a drink. A few of them."

Outside, Archer ascended a platform that hung over the northern gate of Vandalia. A giant mosquito net draped four pillars of the lookout post. Archer peered not at the palatial ruins above, but downward at a long stone ribbon, arrow-straight, that bisected the valley. Fat insects that did nothing but suck blood, torment humans, and fuck each other were orgiastic in their sky-weaving, leaving egg trails that clung to the netting, clouding his view. Colonists called the pests chirr flies because of their constant orgasmic trilling. They were the chief nuisance and apex predator of the forest.

Mercifully, Archer didn't wait long for a sign. The growl of an engine cut the air, and then the faint rumble grew louder. He searched the path and pressed the Serpent Tongue between his fingers. The road led around the mountains, culminating in a patch of arid zone, two hundred kilometers distant on the other side. No trip to the desert was without danger. To be stranded there would be devastating. And Brynn worked there twice a week.

When Archer's heart got to moving too fast, he uncoiled the tubing on his belt and placed the open end between his lips. Oxygen filled his lungs. His heart slowed.

Finally, through a canopy of treetops, a two-wheeled transport with a lone rider came into view.

Blessed Resurrection, Archer thought.

He switched off the oxygen and coiled the tube. Relief didn't overtake his frustration. He counted the hours Brynn had been gone without communication. He checked the cilia. His private thread was empty of replies.

For mental balance, Archer switched on the inner voice of his father, a neural ghost conscience he'd had implanted in the throes of grief.

She's okay, Georgie, said the old man, using a name that no one else in the universe used for Archer. The ghost had no love for Brynn—in fact, he was generally hostile about matters concerning the woman—but his son's well-being was of foremost importance.

Archer dropped the Serpent Tongue and leapt from the platform. He pushed through a group of men and women chatting at the base. He swatted through clouds of chirr flies.

For one minute of your miserable lives, stop fucking, he thought. *You nasty bastards.*

He ran beneath the platform, through the gate. Adrenaline pushed him like a wind at his back.

Brynn's okay, Georgie. You can't control her actions. You can't keep tabs on her all the time.

Archer didn't know how he felt about that. He supposed he disagreed. A hundred emotions pushed and pulled, though, tangling.

I'm not jealous, he countered.

His father laughed.

I didn't say you were.

Anytime Brynn's in the desert, she's in danger, he thought.

And the conscience at the back of his skull laughed again.

Piss and wind, Georgie. Who do you think you're talking to?

The final stretch to Vandalia was a corridor of close, hugging trees and dangling vines. Roots made the ground uneven. The bike ambled up the incline, rumbling as Brynn kicked it into lower gear, shifting down. She rolled from shadow to light, shadow to light, until she halted. Archer was at the side of the road. Brynn's face was a mask, her skin tattooed with dirt. She cut the engine. Heat roiled from the coils, distorting the air.

"Damn it, I was sick, Brynn. Where have you been?"

Sand coated her hair and jacket, her scuffed boots and leggings. She'd ridden fast from the desert. She removed her goggles and wiped her eyes with the heel of her hand. Her gaze—the green eyes—was calculated to disarm. She brushed sand from the short, dark hair that fell in a mess over her ears. She swatted an inquisitive fly.

"Go on," Brynn said. "Get it out of your system, Cullen. Drag me to the square for pillorying." She held out her hands in mock surrender.

"I don't think it's funny."

She cleaned soiled gloves against her thighs.

"That I can see."

"Well, what happened? What'd you find? It must've been something big to keep you out so long."

"Good guess. Hop on the back, and I'll show you. I left Rhys out there."

To an extent, that brightened Archer's disposition.

"Against his will, I hope."

Brynn grew animated over the handlebars. "Cullen, it's more important than I thought. We need help with the digging. Rhys pretends to be weak as a bird, you know. Can you skip out on the greenhouse for the day?"

"You're going back now?"

"I have a couple messages to send out. After that, yes."

Archer looked at the gate. Three men stood on the platform above the entrance, shading their eyes, straining to hear the conversation.

"I don't suppose I can walk. I hate those bikes."

"You can walk your ass inside and get a shovel."

Brynn threw her leg over the transport and stood. She opened the compartment at the rear. She tossed a pair of goggles to Archer.

"Get the tools and get another bike set up. I'll explain on the way out. You're not going to believe it. Not until you see it."

"How many people do you need?"

"You and Kell. He can ride with you. I'll need a cart hitched to the back of mine."

"Not Kell. I'm not listening to that asshole all the way there."

"Get him."

"What is it?" a man shouted from the platform. "What'd you find, Brynn?"

Brynn cupped her hand at the side of her mouth. "One of the Owls," she said, as though the words were routine.

That brought a moment of silence.

Archer raised his eyebrow.

"You're shitting me."

Solemnly, Brynn shook her head.

"An Owl. Intact, far as I know." After hesitating, she added, "And something more besides that. Though you'll think I'm crazy for it."

"I already think you're crazy."

"Good. And that's why I'll tell you." Brynn motioned at the gate. "Start your steppin'. And bring water." She smacked another chirr fly. "And some repellent. And don't forget Kell."

"Some days you're insufferable," Archer said, but her excitement was contagious. He couldn't deny it.

"Some days I'm not." Brynn bit her lip, thinking. "Bring a powerful light too. Whatever you can carry."

You're a whipped dog, Georgie, the ghost said.

Archer switched off his father. After a flatline of peace, he thought, *I should've left you in the grave, old man.*

ON THE PLATFORM and along the duckboards, in the halls and in the dorms, all the way to the Lieutenant Governor:

"Brynn Silva found *what*?"

chapter
three

SAND WHIPPED AROUND THE RIDERS, creating a blurred tunnel. The speed of Brynn's transport increased until the engine burned through her seat and resounded in her skull. A cart full of equipment was attached at the rear. On the second bike, Archer rode double with the arms of Kell, Dr. Rhys's android assistant, wrapped around his waist.

Kell was a complicated creature. Originally, he was a Horus model manufactured on La Venta, a specimen with the lean body of a human male and the head of a falcon. All androids, by statute, were anthropomorphic due to the uprising of 2250. Kell had been a brilliant linguist, superior to anyone in his field, but an accident on the voyage to Shanidar had severely damaged the machine. He was not frozen like the other passengers, and curiosity about a hydraulic lift got him mangled. Now, his Horus head had a massive crater on the left side. Three quarters of his face was removed, and a primitive prosthetic—with painted blue and white feathers and a misshapen beak—covered the pale skull like an ill-fitting mask. The twisted beak made an uncanny, skewed "smile" that stayed on his face like a permanent rictus. The new skin on his arms and hands had the unsettling appearance of clay, always beading with clear oil excreted from fissures in his frame. Currently, Kell functioned at a quarter of his capacity.

Brynn knifed along the shore of fractured mud, following the bends of a dry river she called Acheron, a river in Hades, the Greek artery of the dead. The nickname was a source of amusement she shared with no one else. The river was her discovery, and its name was her private possession. It was one of the few things she didn't have to relinquish to Alaric Rhys.

How much has he uncovered without me? she thought. The worry consumed her. *Without my permission. He doesn't have the skill to work on something so delicate.*

On Luna Fourteen, Brynn trained at the Flinders Petrie Academy of Xenoarchaeology. Regardless, she was not equal to Rhys in title. She was too lowborn for that, and Weston valued lineage and caste over education, despite the company's egalitarian propaganda. Rhys wasn't noble, but his great uncle had been a Lieutenant Governor's secretary in the colony of La Venta. Brynn's great uncle had worked construction like her great-grandfather. Her father was poor. Weston considered these things when awarding rank.

Brynn checked her private channel on the telepathy cilia. Four messages, all from Kell, waited to be read. Despite his disability, the android had literary pretensions. Each missive was a flowery complaint—poems about how he wanted to ride with her instead of Archer. So she assumed, at least. Deciphering his meaning was always a matter of guesswork.

In the distance, the orange sun melted where the desert met the sky. Twilight lingered on Shanidar, but night, when it fell, was complete. No moon silvered the hours until dawn.

When Alaric Rhys's slender shape came into view—at work on his knees in the basin—Brynn geared down. She rolled to a stop where the shore was steep. The weight of the cart made the transport hiccup. The engine quieted with a drawn-out zip. Archer and Kell pulled alongside.

A heat haze hung over the land.

Brynn was quick off the bike. With anxiety that had been building for the past hour, she searched the plain. She moved from the transport and put her back to the river. Her bones were shot through with the rattle of the journey. She scanned from one edge of the vista to the next, staring until her eyes adjusted.

The wanderer, if he'd ever been there, was gone.

Archer, with Kell as his shadow, reached Brynn's side. He had an oxygen tube in his mouth, sucking it like a straw. He brushed sand from her shoulder. He looked where she looked.

"It's no use. It's no longer there," Brynn said, wishing she'd kept her mouth shut.

"You need to rest," Archer said. "What did you see?"

Kell, too, searched the distance. Leaking exhaust made his neck bubble.

"Yes, Professor Silva," he said. "What is it that we're observing?"

Brynn hesitated, but if she couldn't tell Cullen, who could she tell?

"Rhys needs your help," she told Kell.

The machine did his best to convey disappointment, but his mask was uncooperative.

"Yes, Professor Silva. I'll attend to Dr. Rhys shortly. First, however, I'd like to—"

"Kell. Please."

"Yes, Professor Silva."

With that, the machine moved toward the shore, heavy in the sand.

When Kell was out of earshot, Brynn looked at Archer.

"Kell couldn't stay quiet about it. I saw a man on foot, Cullen. Crazy as that sounds. He was walking in this direction. He was as aware of me as I was of him. For a moment, we watched each other. That's impossible, isn't it?"

"How far out?"

"A few kilometers."

Archer removed his goggles and scratched the stubble on his jawline. He searched Brynn's gaze. When he was certain she was sincere, he said, "Could it have been someone from Vandalia? That's possible."

"It's too distant. No one risks being out here on foot alone. Unless they were stranded. If so, where'd they go? They would've continued this way for help."

"Nobody likes it here except you. You told Rhys?"

"No, and I'd rather not. *Is* it impossible?"

"Unless the *Bedivere* arrived early and without ceremony. That's possible."

"The ship's a week out. I checked. It frightened me, Cullen."

Archer pulled her close. He stroked her dirty hair.

"I don't doubt it," he said. "It's like the old story: The last living creature on Earth is sitting alone in her home when a knock comes at the door."

Brynn pulled from his embrace.

"That was your father speaking, wasn't it?"

Archer colored with embarrassment. "Yes. I told him not to intrude. I've told him repeatedly. He won't listen."

"Turn him off."

Archer touched his belt.

"He's off. Banished into the abyss."

"I'll never understand why you had him implanted. It's disturbing."

The practice was, she thought, a personal and obnoxious form of haunting. Those who willingly submitted to it—through surgery no less—confounded her. It was like an ancient form of ancestor worship. Personally, she'd refused her own father. Whether it was the actual spirit or artificial intelligence at work was up for debate, but the custom was bizarre.

Who'd expect less from a Resurrectionist, though? They don't let things go. They can't move on. It's in their blood.

"I wish it was my mother," Archer said, but he offered no defense. "My brother got first pick. I thought I'd miss the old man more than I do."

"Well, I hate it." Brynn wrung her hands. She looked again at the horizon. "We'll keep an eye out. For him. Or her. Or it... You don't believe me, do you?"

"Like you say, it's impossible. But I believe you. We'll keep an eye out."

The wilted, strained voice of Dr. Rhys resonated from the river.

"You are squandering time," the linguist shouted. "Get over here with a spade and the light. Who else did you bring along, Ms. Silva? This machine is useless for digging. He's fit only for being obnoxious."

Rhys's thin, glass-eyed head appeared above the rim.

Brynn walked to the bike. She kept her hand on the hollow of Archer's back.

"Move with urgency," Rhys shouted.

"Is he afraid of the dark?" Archer asked.

"I sure as hell am. Have you ever been out here when it's dark?"

Although the feeling was heavy, she tried to shake off the disquieting image of the wanderer.

You could *have imagined it,* she reasoned. *Pareidolia—that's what it's called. Seeing patterns where none exist. Like a face in the clouds. It doesn't take a heat stroke. It's normal.*

"Who gets the privilege of driving back with Rhys?" Archer asked. "Not enjoying the thought of his arms around me."

"We'll flip for it," Brynn said.

"The hell we will. He and Kell can ride together. They both smell like brake fluid and plastic. Don't they share a bed?"

"They do not."

With tools, lights, and a skin of water in hand, Brynn led Archer down the bank to the dig site. Rhys had returned to his indelicate brushing. He'd stripped away too many layers, too fast. In the preceding hour, he'd uncovered the full head and another shoulder. Kell hovered, watching. Brynn wanted to shout at Rhys for the amateur work, but she held back, kept her cool and decorum.

The casing was jagged where wings had been attached, but the Owl appeared to be otherwise intact. The humanoid traits were fascinating. The creature had a head and two arms, a torso, two legs. It possessed deep-set, rounded eyes. The combination of the orbs and wings had given the creatures their Owl nickname. Metal the color of jade was its flesh.

"What are your thoughts?" she asked Kell.

"Professor Silva, it's a privilege to witness this moment. I'm unworthy. I'll compose a public letter for all to see that expresses my sincere gratitude for your brilliance and generosity."

Archer shook his head.

"Thank you, Kell. And you?" she asked Archer.

"It's incredible, Brynn. Truly."

"We'll give special attention to the surrounding area in case the wings are nearby," Brynn commented. She made a mental checklist. Inserting herself between Rhys and the Owl was number one.

Rhys pointed at a sharp hole in the thing's back.

"It's largely hollow on the inside," he remarked. He inserted a gloved finger.

"Certainly not something you can glean from the artwork." Brynn eyed Rhys. "Do you think it was brittle when it was alive?"

"Tough as a tin man," Rhys said. "No, I don't think so." He gestured at Kell. "Although no machine can withstand being crushed. You only need to look at our falcon to know that."

I wonder what else the artwork fails to convey, Brynn thought. She bit her lip, tasting grains of sand.

"Let me have a look," she told Rhys.

The linguist made room.

Brynn got to her knees. She took out a penlight and shone it into the holes on the Owl's back.

"It's not entirely hollow," she said.

"What do you see?"

"Hold this." She gave the light to Rhys. She put her hand inside. It was exhilarating to feel the scrape of metal against her skin. It was real.

"What is it?" Rhys asked.

She got her hand in to the wrist. Her fingertips brushed against what felt like a piece of wood. Smooth, though. Something carved. With more maneuvering, she got deeper into the body, deeper still until her fingers gripped the object within.

"Got it."

Carefully, she extracted her hand. The metal scraped bloodlines in her flesh. She felt Rhys over her shoulder, felt his cold, fetid breath.

What Brynn pulled free of the Owl corpse was extraordinary. Tucked within the chest cavity, bound with metal wire, was a wooden figurine, no larger than the palm of her hand. The shape was humanoid. The face was blank. No wings graced the figure, but every centimeter of the carving was tattooed with minuscule writing.

"Does this mean it was female?" Rhys asked. "Is this a pregnancy?"

"I doubt that," Brynn said.

She turned the figurine over in her hand. The back was scarred, just as the outer casing of the Owl was scarred, as if the thing's wings had been severed, as well.

"It's as if it were organic," she said.

"They were manufactured, not grown," Rhys said.

"We don't know how they were created," she said.

Artwork in the Owl's Lair showed the creatures in flight and on foot, conducting mundane tasks, making art, gathering in assembly, playing with one another, playing in large groups. Not once, however, did the artwork depict the creators of the Owls. That mysterious race was called the Po Kekurun—a phonetic bastardization rendered in Latin characters. Rhys and Brynn, as shorthand, divided the original inhabitants of Shanidar into children (the Owls or Pa Kekurun) and parents (Po Kekurun). There was no description of the parents in the deciphered literature, but they were mentioned. Kekurun meant something like "God's heart." The Po and Pa prefixes equated to great and small.

Brynn took the figurine aside and wrapped it in cloth. Then she scraped a circle around the Owl, a few meters in diameter.

Rhys looked at Archer. "Start digging within the lines, young man. I want the hole to go all the way down. Do not touch the Owl with that tool. I will do the finer work."

"You'll help with the digging," Brynn said, returning. "We brought three shovels. I'll do the finer work."

Rhys frowned, but he knew this was too important. He backed off.

"I'll supervise," he said. "This one is your beau, is he not?"

Archer glared.

"I've asked for her hand repeatedly," Kell said, "but, alas, I'm not Professor Silva's beau. Once she breaks off her engagement with Mr. Archer, which is inevitable—"

"Don't start, Kell," Brynn said.

Archer stomped the shovel into the hard ground. Rock scraped metal. The dig wouldn't be easy. Kell lifted a shovel. He sliced it into the dirt.

"Brynn saw a man in the desert," Archer said. "Walking alone."

She shot him a withering look.

Damn it, Cullen.

Kell stopped whispering to himself and looked up.

Rhys looked up, too, and his brow furrowed.

"You did?" he asked. He looked at the shore. "Out there?"

Brynn took a drink of water. She wiped her mouth clean. The night exhaled, and the wind from the desert was cold.

"When I was leaving, I saw a man. I could've been mistaken. Could be exhaustion. That's why I didn't tell you."

"I, too, saw him, young man," Rhys said.

It was not the response Brynn expected or wanted. Her stomach tightened.

"What'd you see?" she asked.

The linguist traced his arachnid digits in the chalk.

"A figure standing on the shore. I caught him observing me. It was a man, as you say. I have no doubt. His clothes were unfamiliar. A hood wrapped his head and hid his face, but I knew he was watching, that he was curious. Then he was gone. He stepped back, out of sight. I walked to the shore to see him again, but he wasn't there. I didn't find the nerve to call for him. Moving over there was enough. I'll admit that. My blood was cold."

Archer split his gaze between Brynn and Rhys. The red of the ride had drained from his face. He touched his Serpent Tongue. "If it's a man, that means something to us. And probably not something good."

"He was walking this way," Brynn said.

"I thought I was overstimulated. A moment of fever," Rhys said. "There's nowhere to hide here, of course. I don't know where he could have gone."

"I'm reminded," Kell said, "of the old legend of the Wandering Jew. If you're curious, in the Middle Ages—"

"Damn it, Kell," Archer said. "Enough." He balanced his boot on the lip of the spade. "There's no one else on this planet. We're certain of that."

Rhys sat in the dirt. "I know it is difficult for you, young man, but try for a moment to not be ignorant. Try your very hardest. We are certain there are no other human beings on this world. We know that alone."

"The Wandering Jew," Kell said, "was actually—"

"Stop it, Kell," Rhys said. "You are not helping."

Rhys read the look on Brynn's face.

"Suffice to say I would rather not remain here the next time you depart. I pulled my shift as watchman. Our young man of blind certainty here can pull the next if he so desires."

Archer jammed the shovel into soil.

"The hell I will," he said. "I'd sooner walk back."

"The Wandering Jew was actually a man cursed," Kell continued.

On either side of the river, the long shores were empty. Dusk swept over the desert, light diminishing like a spent candle, like a pile of wax at the end of its wick. Shanidar's neighboring planet, Red Kitezh, appeared in the west, a luminescent orb, separated from the stars by its scarlet belly.

Archer tossed a shovelful, quickening the pace of his work.

"Speed up and shut it," he told Kell.

Brynn ignited a set of lights in a tight perimeter around the dig, pushing back the night. The darkness beyond deepened until it was impenetrable. She caught Archer's gaze. He spoke to her without speaking. He was frightened. He worked so fast that sweat wetted his forehead, neck, and hair.

Kell failed to match his effort, but the android tried to stay on task. He sent Brynn twelve encrypted poems about The Wandering Jew, none of which made much sense.

Brynn lifted the other shovel and joined the pair.

Rhys moved to the shoreline, clicking like glass as he stepped. He scanned the gloom.

"This is still a world of mystery," he said. "We should be careful not to forget that fact."

We are strangers here, Brynn thought, watching the lifeless Owl trapped in ancient mud.

chapter
four

THE AIR CONDITIONING VENTS WHIRRED, but the room stayed hot and humid. Cloaked in the oilcloth folds of a black long coat, Alaric Rhys stood in the corner, waiting at the base of the dais. Kell, his mechanical man, was at his side, equal to the linguist in height and slenderness. The falcon-headed android wore a black overcoat of his own. On the dais was a trestle table, and on the table lay the Owl with a rusted claw.

A queue of people stretched from the platform to the door and curled outside. Over their heads, above the entrance, a golden plaque read *House of Burgesses*.

A night without sleep left Brynn uncharitable and sentimental. She was overcome with an odd sense of shame about the Owl's ignoble fate. The act—the freakshow line leading to the creature's displayed remains—was one of desecration. Even a machine like the Owl had to be treated with respect. She wondered if Kell was uncomfortable with the morbid show-and-tell. Curious, she sent a message over the cilia.

Kell's reply came within seconds.

Ghoulish barbarism of the lowest form, he wrote. One of his cryptic poems, a lament on Charlemagne's death, followed. She didn't attempt to decipher its meaning.

Still, Brynn couldn't blame the colonists' eagerness to see an original inhabitant of Shanidar. The moment—her discovery—was a sea change.

The Owl lay on its back, face upward like a corpse in a casket. The creature was a meter in height, the size of a small human child. No sexual organs were visible on the exterior of the body. There were no traces of garments. Traces of burgundy paint remained on the eyes, but the sclerae were mostly blank metal. The orbs were deep-set. Two slits, uneven punctures, formed the nose. Brynn had brushed the Owl's hide, which was a beautiful hue of green between swaths of rust. Time and the elements had inflicted damage, wearing the casing thin and brittle as dead leaves in spots along the torso. Ultimately, that was cosmetic. The Owl was hardy and heavy. The head was unsullied, imbued with an inquisitive personality. Deep bone furrows ran from the back of the neck to the crown. The legs were unbroken, ending in dexterous claws with eight digits apiece. If oiled, the leg joints would bend and flex. With a source of propulsion, the thing could get up and move through the crowd. Or speak in one of the tongues of its world. Disappointingly, the Owl would be unable to fly. No wings were uncovered during the excavation.

The wooden figurine, however, was too fragile for display. It was wrapped and stored safely in Rhys's dorm.

Brynn looked at the men and women who spilled out of the propped-open doors. Some colonists were excited for a closer look, hoping for a connection, while others wore their unease in dour expressions. For the latter, she imagined it was like a squatter finding the rightful owner of the homestead had returned.

William Naylor, the Lieutenant Governor of Vandalia, entered the House of Burgesses. He skipped the line and approached the dais. Naylor wanted nothing less than byzantine ceremony at every turn—he was the type to orate on holidays and birthdays. Upon receiving word of Brynn's discovery, he'd demanded a public wake to quash rumors of scientific autocracy. He was, after all, a man of the people.

The Lieutenant Governor pulled rank on Rhys. He didn't consult Brynn.

Naylor joined her in front of a wall of artifacts, baubles of material life she'd extracted from the Owl's Lair and desert. Brynn watched him from the corner of her eye. The man had a lopsided, craggy face, disfigured and swollen by a near-death bout of meningitis on the planet La Venta. His gravelly voice suited the visage. He sported a wig of dark curls that reached his shoulders. His overcoat, clasped with hawk skulls, was wine-colored velveteen, as tacky as it was expensive.

When the hour arrived, Naylor raised his arms. He was ritualistic in his punctuality.

The line stilled. The chattering ceased in waves.

"Friends, colleagues, fellow colonists—I have a dual reason for calling this assembly. First, I want to update you on the arrival of our next Weston crew. Four hundred adventurers on the *Bedivere*, including children, will reach Shanidar in five days. Less than a week. Their arrival is on time. The passengers are safe. Think of what this expansion will mean to us. A neighbor settlement. I envision schools! Schools on Shanidar. The die is cast, friends. We're not going anywhere."

Naylor let that settle. It was old news, and it didn't elicit much reaction. A few murmurs. An aborted attempt at clapping. The people were here for the Owl.

Brynn received a message from Kell. *Alea iacta est,* he wrote. *The die is cast. A bombastic allusion to Julius Caesar crossing the Rubicon in 49 BCE, although the Lieutenant Governor is too ignorant to know it. It means we've passed the point of no return.*

Thank you, Kell.

"Second—and what a thing to show our newcomers upon arrival—Dr. Alaric Rhys is the first man to uncover the remains of an Owl. We're a step closer to bringing that shadowy race into the light."

Rhys did not correct Naylor. He accepted credit for the discovery.

Brynn's face reddened, but she maintained decorum.

Utter swine, Kell wrote.

"Don't let it be said that the Weston Joint Stock Company keeps secrets." Naylor glanced at the mechanical being. "It's a harmless thing, isn't it? Long dead. It's like finding a seashell washed in with the tide."

"Shut it, Bill. It was Brynn who found it. Not Rhys. Get this line moving."

The Lieutenant Governor shot a look at the back of the room. A few colonists laughed. A few didn't.

Through the row of faces, Cullen Archer grinned. Dressed in a navy cloak and brown pants that met his boots at the calf, he was a handsome sight, scrubbed clean.

Brynn stifled a smile.

Naylor smacked his lips.

"That's another mark on your report to the board," he said, pointing. Then, under his breath, "Damned delinquent son of a bitch."

"You can always send me home," Archer said. "Throw me in the *Bedivere* brig. I won't fight."

"The bottom line is I don't want rumors, folks. Nothing happens behind closed doors here. Nothing untoward from our esteemed intelligentsia, despite what you might hear."

Naylor tipped his ugly head at Rhys. "We're an open community. We work by committee. Your voice matters. Weston cares about such things, and I strive for that. It's—"

It's bureaucratic theater, Brynn thought wearily.

When Naylor finished his speech, the crowd advanced.

Rhys's joints clicked as he moved from the corner. He breathed asthmatically. Kell followed a step behind. As was the rule with synthetics, he never showed his back to his owner. Rhys's connection to the colonists was more volatile than Brynn's. He was—and it was all the clearer when humans surrounded him—a reconstructed man, having lost a large percentage of his mass in the bombings at La Venta. To Resurrectionists, Rhys was a hybrid of ghost and machine, only slightly more appealing than his android. A glass man who owned a metal man. He was an augmented cheater of death.

Delaney Naylor, William's spouse, was the first to approach. She was a small woman in a large, lavender wig of curls. A cloying cinnamon perfume wafted from her body. Her embroidered blouse showed four wolves howling at the moon. Among Resurrectionists, the antique clothing from the ancient emporium Kmart went for ludicrous sums.

"What is the Owl's intention?" Delaney asked, looking over the metal face. Her expression was solemn, uncomfortable. She shared a frown with Naylor. "It must've served a role."

"We believe," Rhys began, "that the Owls were mechanical children of the Po Kekurun. They were manufactured beings rather than birthed organically."

"They were not workers? I imagined them as bees to a queen. Always busy. Swarming things with dragonfly wings."

Brynn narrowed her gaze and held her tongue.

The next in line, the Lieutenant Governor's secretary, Lord Jarvis Rinaldi, asked, "Where exactly did you find the specimen, Dr. Rhys?" He, too, wore a wig—a privilege of his class.

"In the dry riverbed that passes through the desert," Rhys replied. "It's a location where we find most things related to the Owls. I believe they disposed of garbage there."

We. We find. You believe?

"That's very human of them. You've never found something like this before, though. Not even a fragment. Is that correct?"

You know the answer, Rinaldi. Why this farce?

"No, nothing like this. It's a first."

"Sir, do not touch the remains," Kell said.

Rinaldi snapped his hand back. He side-eyed the android.

"Please do not touch the Owl," Rhys repeated, shouting down the line.

An older woman, a surgeon named Seward, was next. She said, "This is different from the beings depicted in the Owl's Lair. The mouth has a human quality. The hinged mandible. Is that for eating or speaking?"

"It better not be for eating," Naylor interjected. He stepped closer.

"No," Brynn said. "We believe it was for speaking. There are no teeth."

"What are you going to do with it?" Seward asked.

"We will attempt to resurrect it," Rhys said. "Then the Owl can tell us what it is, what it does, what it thinks."

Don't use that word, Brynn thought. *Of all the things to say, Rhys.*

"*Resurrect* it? That doesn't sound ominous in the slightest," Naylor said. "Not at all."

"If functioning, the Owl will teach us an enormous amount. Imagine hearing a language we know only in script, hearing the words spoken aloud. It could teach us tongues we've yet to decipher."

"I don't like the thought of that thing walking around," said the next man in line. "What if it's hostile? It could resent us. It could want its home back. Hell, it could *grow* teeth and wings."

"It's not organic," Brynn said.

"If hostile, we'd destroy the Owl," Rhys said.

"You're damn right we would," Naylor said. "With extreme prejudice. We'll—"

"What if—"

Brynn couldn't take anymore. She turned her shoulder to the inane, masculine direction of the conversation. With pity, she looked upon the Owl.

Kell moved to her side. On his ruined face, emotions were inscrutable. The warm exhaust escaping his neck touched her like breath.

"The Owl is a curious and beautiful thing," the android whispered. "And it's *your* discovery, Professor Silva. It'll be recorded as such for posterity in the Weston annals."

"Thank you, Kell."

"I hope you'll forgive the mythological allusion, but seeing the two of you in proximity reminds me of the owl of Athena. Would it not do to have this scene captured in massicot on a Grecian urn? If ever I'm repaired, Professor Silva, I'll fashion such a thing for you. Two symbols of knowledge and erudition."

Brynn touched the synthetic man's cold hand.

Cullen Archer's voice came again from the back of the room, now with a note of concern.

"Brynn," he shouted. "Brynn, come out here, please."

The words pulled her back to reality.

"Kell, I'll return in a moment."

"There are probably many more out there, Dr. Rhys," a woman was saying. "You'll keep searching?"

"Excuse me," Brynn said.

The line parted as she pushed through. Rhys and Naylor began arguing again. And the questions kept coming, although there were no answers.

Brynn emerged into the hazy light of day. A few people were assembled, discussing what they'd seen. Overhead, tall clouds gathered, brewing a storm. She followed Archer down the duckboards.

"The piece of shit is in there taking credit. I knew he would. What is it?" she asked. "What's wrong?"

Archer turned. He had the Serpent Tongue between his fingers. He looked past Brynn.

"I didn't mean for that thing to come along."

With difficulty, Kell was following. He shuffled more than walked. Sand had gotten inside him during the ride.

Archer stomped the boards, sending a rattle that reached the android. Kell stopped.

"Go back to your master," Archer said. "You're being rude."

"It's rude to call Dr. Rhys my master, first of all. Is it rude to be curious, Professor Silva?" Kell asked.

"Yes," Archer said. "In your case."

"Is it rude to interrupt people locked in the throes of conversation?"

"It is."

"Then, Mr. Archer, you are, once again, the rude one." Kell looked at Cullen. "We were discussing Professor Silva's archaeological discovery, sir."

"I'd like to bury *you* in the river," Archer said. "Then someone could dig you up in a thousand years."

"In some parts of the Weston universe, that's a crime, sir. Your desire for violence vexes me."

"Some parts. Not here. Not yet."

"Will both of you please stop? Now, what did you want to tell me?"

Her cilium burned with a message. Another poem from Kell. A vitriolic rebuttal that covered Cullen, Rhys, and Naylor. It ran many lines.

Archer led her to the platform at the north gate. Together, they climbed the stairs. The structure creaked when the android ascended.

"I found your wanderer," Archer said. He pointed at the ruins.

Indeed, a man walked outside the curtain wall in procession. He was slow and cautious. A hood covered his head, and a long garment made him shapeless. He stopped when Brynn saw him, as if he felt her eyes. He looked downward, meeting her gaze over the distance.

Brynn's heart quickened and her throat went dry.

Clouds darkened to the shade of slate over the Owl's Lair.

"Or," she said, "he's found us."

"This is your Wandering Jew?" Kell asked.

Brynn bounded down the stairs, unthinking, out of her mind with exhaustion and exhilaration.

"Should we tell anyone?" Archer said. "Where are you going?"

"We're going up there. He won't get away this time."

Archer watched the stranger.

"I don't believe he wants to flee," Kell said.

He wants to be seen. He means us no harm.

Although it filled her mind, the thought didn't belong to Brynn. It came from elsewhere. It intruded.

chapter
five

FOLLOWING A THUNDERCLAP, the sky opened, and a sheet of blistering rain sliced down the hillside. Brynn, manic and determined, walked at the point of the trio as if the storm didn't exist. The downpour soaked her hair and clothes.

A labyrinth of stone walkways covered the foothills like veinwork. Each trail led upward, converging at a stone esplanade adorned with geometric art, fractals, mandalas, spirals, and straight lines. With an aerial view, the collective lattice was astonishing in its scope, surrounding the Owl's Lair like a jeweled pectoral. Most of the paths were overgrown and jigsawed by roots, but the route connecting Vandalia to the ancient city was clear, the forest chopped back.

Archer watched Brynn, a pale slash in the gloom. He did his best to keep pace on the treacherously slick stones. Rivulets carried leaves and mud down the path, turning the artery into a gully. A gale pushed the rain sideways, bending trees, swinging vines. Archer looked back to see if Kell had toppled over in the torrent, but the android was upright, making its slow ascent. At least the thing was too distant to talk.

Thinking machines are pernicious, malignant things, his father observed. *One day, they'll replace you, Georgie. All of you.*

Archer grunted. He hardly disagreed. The machine's form alone offended him. To place a falcon head on a human body was sacrilegious to the more conservative Resurrectionists. There was no humor in recalling a heathen god.

Resistentialism. That's what you need to worry about, Georgie. Notice how it disdained the label of master. See how the machine disobeys. Next thing your toaster will disobey. Then your vehicles. Out of meanness, your shower will burn you. It's the malice of inanimate things. And I'm no Luddite.

That was true. In life, his father had been a software engineer of considerable achievement.

Enough, Archer thought. *I'm not worried about Kell or another machine uprising. I'm worried about Brynn.*

He wiped hair from his forehead, combing it back with his fingers. His shirt clung to his shoulders and chest. His boots were heavy with mud. The rain intensified until it made a sheer wall of gossamer. A bolt of lightning cast the high ruins white. Then darkness swaddled the city again.

Archer pushed on.

In two years on Shanidar, Brynn had changed. In a real sense, she was at the end of the line, on the verge of permanent resentment and bitterness. There was a hole inside her that she was desperate to fill and couldn't. Once, he'd hoped to fill it, but he now knew he couldn't. Brynn wanted significance, which was unattainable without the right blood. Even if she wanted to leave for another corporation, she was stuck with Weston, tied to their system like a serf. She was a lowborn commoner like Archer. Without a pedigree, she'd gone as far as she could go in Weston, regardless of the colony. She had no future, even with the Owl discovery.

She has a chip on her shoulder, the ghost added.

She needs religion, Archer thought. *She needs hope.*

It bothered him deeply that Brynn did not count herself among the Resurrectionists. She didn't believe a Messiah would restore Earth. She didn't believe Earth would ever be whole again.

She'll never be happy, Georgie.

No, Archer agreed. *She's tragic that way. And I followed her here. Is that pathetic?*

Yes. Shamefully so. You had a career on Luna Fourteen. You had potential in horticulture. I told your mother.

You talk to mom?

Sure.

I'll be damned. You never told me. What'd she say?

She said you were happy on Luna. She cried, in the spectral sense. Wailed.

I was happy there. Now I break my back and waste my life.

It hurts her heart, Georgie. She has no love for that vile woman.

I do, Archer thought. *I had to fall in love with a frigid atheist.*

He caught up to Brynn on the esplanade that fronted the Owl's Lair. Trees and weeds grew through the cracks, obscuring the faded artwork. The wet surface was as treacherous as ice. Carefully, Archer made his way across. He stopped near a roaring chute that spewed water over the cliff, draining the city, flooding the valley.

A wicked bolt of lightning fractured the air.

The wanderer had stood here in attention, but he was gone again. His taunting was as unsettling as his impossible existence.

"Who's to say it isn't a ghost?" Archer said, half-seriously. His voice barely cut the roar of the culvert.

Brynn looked through the storm at the meager rooftops of Vandalia. A crown of emergency lights cut the gloom. Her chest heaved for want of breath. Her hair was plastered against her head, covering her ears and cheeks, draping the back of her neck. Water ran from her fingertips like electrical current.

"I should be more frightened than I am," Brynn said.

"Wouldn't hurt you to be more cautious."

"He doesn't want to harm us."

"How do you know what he wants?"

Archer put his arm around her. Brynn was rigid, the points of her shoulders hard and strong. Her skin was cold.

"What you need more than anything is sleep."

Brynn said nothing to that. She'd turned inward again.

"We can wait out the storm in the ruins," Archer said. "It's not safe until the lightning ends." He tried to bury frustration, but it was brimming, threatening to boil over. Even a hint of anger would push Brynn to stonewall him, however, so he stayed calm. "I'll stay with you. Then we'll go home. And you can sleep the rest of the day and through the night."

Brynn faced the Owl's Lair.

"He went inside. A ghost doesn't seek shelter from a storm."

A lightning flash lit the ground. Despite its fortress-like nature, no gate, no portcullis opened in the wall to allow inhabitants to come and go, and that held true for the entire perimeter. Twelve meters high and solid, with no way in or out except over the top—not originally, at least. Presumably, the Owls had flown over the fortification. On the inside, landing platforms marked each cardinal direction.

The colonists had cut a thieves' entrance in the wall. It was arduous, bruising work, but a jagged hole, wide enough to crawl through, was opened at the center of the court, close to the ground. The entrance looked like a cannonball wound, if cannonballs traveled like meteors.

"He might have dematerialized. Ghosts, I hear, can do that sort of thing."

The attempt at levity fell flat.

"I'm glad you saw him. Having Rhys on my side didn't make me feel any saner."

"I saw him."

Kell finally reached the court. Water and oil beaded on its clay flesh.

"I, too, am a witness, Professor Silva."

Archer pulled Brynn from the ledge, moving her toward the wall.

"Up this high, we're good targets," he said. "And Kell's a lightning magnet."

"Maybe a lightning strike's the fix I need," Kell mused.

Brynn complied. Her gaze was contemplative.

She was first into the tunnel. Then Archer entered, creeping on hands and knees over the two meters of rough stone. The hole was humid. Water streamed through wormholes, above and around. Brynn stopped at the far end. She propped her feet against the inner wall. Kell came in headfirst.

Outside, the rain began to ease. Wind whistled through the tunnel.

To say it was unwise to walk alone in the inner labyrinth of the Owl's Lair was an understatement. For travelers without wings, the city layout made little sense. Getting lost in the complex was a common occurrence. William Naylor had plans to make an aerial map, but that had yet to be carried out.

Brynn slid free of the hole and stood. She pulled back the hair from her face. Rain slowed to a drizzle, pinging against the nearest silo.

The thieves' entrance opened into a sewage channel where mold, weeds, and vines grew. The gutter ran behind a line of spired structures, which blotted any chance of light. Archer emerged like a sneaking rodent. Being inside the Owl's Lair always made him feel like an intruder. He found it eerie.

He put his back against the wall and slid right until a wider path opened between silos. The walkway stretched twenty meters before ending at a black wall painted with geometric designs. Beneath the lines, emerging like bas-relief, was an Owl face. Similar graffiti filled the city. The Owls were prolific artists.

The short burst of street was typical. The Owl's Lair was constructed outward from an inverted tower—a deep shaft—growing in erratic orbits of metal silos. The "streets" were more useful from the air, serving as indicators of direction rather than routes. The roads started and stopped with few connections between them. Toward the center, streets ran in spurts of five meters, and all were dead ends. Once, the stone roads had been painted, but only flakes remained.

High above, through the rain, was a honeycombed building, fronted by large platforms protruding at intervals. The structure reached forty meters into the air. The colonists could enter the building via a ladder, propped, lifted, and moved as needed. It was misleading to call the holes domiciles. There was no evidence of private homes in the Owl's Lair.

Brynn stopped and her breath caught. She stood at the edge of a cylindrical well. Water cascaded over the rim, pooling deep below. Brynn, however, stared upward.

On the platform to Archer's right was Brynn's wandering stranger.

"Rather curious," Kell remarked.

"Rather," Archer said.

The man sat beneath a busted metal canopy twinkling with rain and sun, his legs draped over the edge. He'd ascended with a ladder, which was propped in place, rungs dripping. His feet were bare and dry, the soles black. He pulled back his cowl, revealing a man who was no more than forty years old. His hair was full and his skin tanned. He looked hungry, but he was not a victim of starvation.

Despite the activity below, he did not look down.

Thus was the standoff: three in the street and one above; three looking upward, two with fast, nervous hearts, and the one above unconcerned, resting as if this moment was an everyday, mundane occurrence. As if he hadn't goaded Brynn from the valley. As if he were not spectral. As if the storm didn't exist.

And then the storm didn't exist. The sky cleared. The sun emerged, lighting the dank morass of the Owl's Lair.

Archer's father was silent. Even he was in awe.

Kell, incapable of wonder, broke the spell.

"Pardon me, sir, but that platform is unsafe. Furthermore, you are in trespass. The Weston Joint Stock Company claims this land from sea to sea, firmament to sky."

The wanderer gazed down, acknowledging the visitors. His eyes were tired and kind. There was nothing ghostly or menacing about him. When he spoke, it was not in one of the Owl tongues. He spoke in the colloquial English of Luna Fourteen.

"I've waited a long time," the wanderer said. There was relief in his tone.

Archer tried to speak but was too bewildered. His throat was metallic.

"Why are you here, sir?" Kell asked.

"And who are you?" Archer managed to say.

And what are you?

The wanderer furrowed his brow.

"You mean you don't already know? You haven't been searching for me?" After a beat of silence, he said, "Does Weston not speak of the first settlement on Shanidar, its lost colony?"

We're the first settlement, Archer thought.

The stranger glanced at him, met his eyes.

"Of that endeavor, I alone survived," he said. He touched the ladder. He shook it so the rungs dripped all at once. "If Weston didn't inform you, it must make you curious as to why. I imagine your Lieutenant Governor knows."

"Where was this settlement?"

"Far south of here. About fifteen hundred kilometers, I'd say. In a mountain valley."

"This is all very distressing," Kell said.

"There's something wrong with your machine," said the man above. "Those things are supposed to be hyper-intelligent or dumb as rocks. This is the first time I've seen one in between. When you trust me, I can restore him. I'm a good mechanic."

"A good mechanic does not mean that you understand cybernetics," Kell responded.

The wanderer smiled.

"You're a mechanic, and yet you're on foot rather than using a transport," Archer said.

The man stared down the well. "A mechanic can only do so much. Our transports were destroyed."

"We need to know more of this first settlement," Brynn said. "You have to understand that, to us, it's unbelievable."

"We're the first settlement," Archer said.

"After a meal and rest. That is, if you offer hospitality to one of your own. And if your Lieutenant Governor permits such a thing."

"You've stated your trade and that you're a Weston colonist, but you haven't said your name," Archer cut in. "What is it?"

"William Naylor," said the wanderer.

chapter six

THE CHIRR FLIES resembled kidney beans with chitinous wings. Rain was their aphrodisiac, so storms brought them out in magnificent hordes. Queens spewed eggs in pearlescent formations across the sky, appearing in sunlight like cobwebs in dew. Their natural food source was a forest fruit laced with iron, but when humans were closer, blood sufficed.

Brynn smacked one against her neck, and its innards greased her fingertips.

"Rain washed off the repellent," she observed.

As the four figures walked from the Owl's Lair to Vandalia, the chirr flies harassed Archer and Brynn, but synthetic Kell was free of them, and, curiously, so was the stranger who called himself Naylor. The air around him was clear.

Brynn shared a look of suspicion with Archer. Cullen made no effort to conceal his unease.

Brynn popped another fly. She wiped the gore on her leg.

With a touch of frustration, she told Naylor, "It's curious the little vampires take no interest in you."

"It is, isn't it?" he said. "We made a deal down south. They know better." The wanderer smiled without breaking his stride, but only he was in on the joke. He had an enigmatic presence—

false, masked, protective of what was below. On death's doorstep, he claimed, but he was full of energy and wit.

He means no harm. He's good. He's kind. He's telling the truth. Weston lied.

"Insects, I needn't remind you, Pseudo-Naylor, do not possess the faculty of reason," Kell interjected. "Bargaining is beyond their ability. I'm reminded of a case in *ancien régime* France where the inhabitants of a village filed suit against a colony of flies. This was roughly the time of the Renaissance, sir. The flies had damaged their grapevines and—"

"What purpose do you serve here?" Naylor asked the machine.

"I help Dr. Alaric Rhys in his linguistic studies. We're at work on three Owl scripts. We've deciphered two. Clues to the third remain elusive."

"You leak oil like sweat, stink of exhaust, and your speech is diarrhetic. What happened to you?"

"My head was crushed in a hydraulic press, if you must know. An unfortunate accident of my own making. Really—I've no one else to blame. I was inactive for two years of our journey to Shanidar. I'll return to my former state in time."

"It'll take centuries at this rate. You're far from your original form. At least Dr. Rhys could fashion a more suitable mask for you in the meantime."

"The lack of skill in my mask is an abomination. I'm hideous. I was once fine art, sir. Weston's investment in STEM and continued devaluation of the arts have ensured that no artist of merit exists on this planet. One hopes that the next coterie has someone who'll address the problem."

"I can accelerate the timeline. I'd like to see you at full ability. I'm certain Dr. Rhys would like that too."

"At full capacity he barely talks," Archer said. "I remember. I liked him then."

"Would you like to know what became of the destructive flies?" Kell asked. "The court ruled—"

"Enough," Archer snapped. He looked at Naylor. "We can't allow you into Vandalia until I speak with the Lieutenant Governor. He'll have to grant his approval. He carries the insignia of Weston. He speaks for the Board here."

"The precaution isn't meant to be rude," Brynn said. "We know you've suffered. We'll be quick in arranging things."

"No, it's wise protocol," Naylor said.

The stranger was, in a peculiar way, an attractive man, but not overtly so. His long road north had left him with shaggy hair and a dark, wiry, unkempt beard. His cowl was bunched around his neck. He looked feral, and yet he had bottomless spirit in his pale eyes. It wasn't difficult to see a survivor in him.

Brynn swatted through a cloud of chirr flies. By the second, their swarm thickened, and their trilling intensified. Red welts grew along her exposed arms. Her left temple was puffy.

"Those foul pests are full of disease. With each bite, they regurgitate their sickness into you. They were on the verge of extinction when we arrived," Naylor said. "Now they're flourishing. All of ours must have moved up here."

"How'd you stop them?" Brynn asked. "If not a repellent of some sort."

Naylor shook his head. "You'll learn the secret one day." He peered at Kell. "And, if the question is sparking in your wires, we didn't take the flies to court, machine."

"The French court ruled in the flies' favor," Kell finished. "Their defense was that God commanded them to go forth and multiply. They had a brilliant lawyer."

"Human?" Naylor asked.

"Yes. Of course. A certified canon lawyer. A man of prominence named—"

Brynn halted at the north gate.

"Find Dr. Rhys," she told Kell. To Archer, "Get the governor and bring him out."

And don't stir up a mob, she thought. *Please be civil, Cullen. Please.*

"If you want, I can wait out here instead," Archer replied. He was displeased. If the two had been alone, he would've had a meltdown. As it was, he swallowed his rage. "Or you can come with me," he added.

"I'd rather wait," Brynn said.

Archer bit his tongue. After a long look at the stranger, he trailed Kell into the settlement.

"I'll bring back repellent," he said over his shoulder.

Radiant electric light colored the sky, overlapping curtains of vivid greens and pinks—a living, angry, spent atmosphere. The chirr fly queens drew sigils on the backdrop with their strings of young.

Alone, the stranger said, "I don't believe that fellow trusts me. Cullen is his name? He's convinced I'm lying. As is the machine you call Kell."

"Wise protocol for the brute," Brynn said. She sighed. "This has been a day of impossible things."

"You direct them well. It comes naturally. You'd make a fine leader."

"Unfortunately, that's not my birthright," Brynn said.

Naylor sat on the wet stone path and crossed his legs. He carried nothing on his person, had no possessions. He rested his hands on his knees. Dirt blackened the creases in his knuckles.

"Forgive me," he said. "I'm tired, hungry, and weak."

Brynn caught another chirr fly, rupturing it. Blood streaked her palm. She wiped her hand in disgust.

"You hide the discomfort well. Tell me, are you synthetic? A simulacrum like Kell?"

From the wanderer's first word, the possibility that he was an android hadn't been far from her mind. He was too at home in an uncomfortable, bizarre situation. Too certain, too arrogant. Of course, that might have been an act. Perhaps he was trembling inside, ready to break.

"I don't believe I am," Naylor said. He pinched his arm until it bruised. He showed the purple splotch. "Have simulacra advanced so much since I departed Luna Fourteen?"

"No," Brynn conceded. She hesitated. "I might as well tell you something before our Lieutenant Governor shows. His name is William Naylor."

His eyes smiled, but not his mouth. "That is curious. What are the odds?"

"With so few people, not good."

"Maybe Weston includes a William Naylor in each fleet. Like a house name for the lucky soul in charge. They're riddled with corporate spies, you know. You have spies here, keeping intricate files."

"Or it could be that you're lying."

The stranger gave a casual shrug. "Maybe. Or your William Naylor's lying. He's lied to you before."

Brynn said nothing.

"Has he not?"

"He's also been honest with us before. I can't say if the same applies to you, William. You're awfully cogent for a man who wandered the desert, one so weak and hungry. Being alone for so long can drive a person mad. Not you."

"I'm delirious. Nothing I say can be held against me. Not until I eat and sleep."

Brynn fought off six more bugs.

"Does the other William Naylor look like me?"

"He does not."

"Could I pass for his son?"

"No."

"Hmm."

"Why didn't you speak to me or Rhys in the desert?"

"Out of my mind. Frightened. I didn't expect to see you.

Maybe I've been alone too long. Why didn't you ride out to greet me? That was the courteous thing to do."

"The same reason, I suppose. Didn't believe you were real."

"What exactly did you find in the riverbed?"

"We'll get to that later. It's no secret. I can show you."

"I'm a good mechanic," he repeated. The corner of his mouth lifted in a grin.

Archer was the first to return, and Brynn was glad for his presence. He had an insecticide sprayer slung over his shoulder. Lieutenant Governor William Naylor wasn't at his side.

"Where is he?" Brynn asked.

"Turn around and raise your arms. Spread your feet."

Brynn assumed the position.

Archer aimed the wand and misted her with the cold, bitter repellent. She tightened her lips and closed her eyes. The chirr flies lifted higher into the air.

"Do you want any of this?" Archer asked the stranger.

"No," Naylor said. He uncrossed his legs and put his back against a root on the ground. He stared at the sky.

Archer put down the container.

Brynn lowered her arms.

"Well, where is he?"

"I spoke to Delaney. She hasn't seen Naylor since he left the meeting hall. He didn't come home during the storm. He isn't answering messages over the cilia." Archer's gaze lingered on the wanderer.

The man's chest rose and fell with steady breath.

"Perhaps the Lieutenant Governor wandered off," he said to the sky.

"Delaney says he followed us from the House of Burgesses."

I left him arguing with Rhys. He's not a man of stealth, Brynn thought. *We would've spotted him. Naylor doesn't prowl. And he can't hide in that preposterous wig.*

The idea was laughable.

When Kell came through the gate, he brought not only Dr. Rhys but a crowd of twenty-some-odd people. Presumably, he'd informed everyone he encountered. The colonists stared warily at the man in rags, defenseless on the path, lying on his back, legs bent at the knees. He resembled something that had washed up on the shore, as if the storm brought him in with the tide.

Rhys clicked forward. His shadow crossed the stranger.

"You are the man from the desert," Rhys said.

"I am."

"Does my machine speak the truth? You say there was an earlier settlement on this planet, and you're the only one who remains?"

The wanderer stared at the sky. No words passed his lips for a full minute. The silence moved minds from rejection to acceptance and back again. Then he straightened his legs and lifted at the waist. He scanned the motley assemblage filling the gateway.

"When I spoke to you from the shore, what did I tell you?"

"I heard only the wind," Rhys said. "I saw you, and then you were gone. You said nothing to me."

"I see," the wanderer said. "It's just as well."

"What is your name?"

"He says his name is William Naylor," Brynn answered.

"I asked him," Rhys said. "Not you. How'd you come by that name?"

"It was given to me by the Weston Joint Stock Company."

"You led this first settlement?" Rhys turned to Brynn. "Naylor is a name given to Lieutenant Governors in Weston."

"I did," said the stranger.

"You'll forgive our skepticism, but this is perplexing news. We were led to believe that we were the first attempt on Shanidar. You'll show us this settlement? Take us there? We'll be ready to believe you then, but not until. It's an extraordinary claim. But, then again, your presence alone is extraordinary. Your way is the simplest way to explain it."

"I'll tell you everything you want to know. I have nothing but animosity for Weston. They abandoned us. They'll abandon you."

"There you're wrong. We have another ship arriving in a matter of days."

The stranger said nothing.

"Take him to Dr. Seward's clinic," Rhys told the crowd. "He's delirious, but I believe he's speaking the truth. Which," he added, "is quite unfortunate."

The crowd was not so accepting. The men and women scoffed at the wanderer's claim. But what else was he? *How* was he here?

The wanderer bowed his head in relief.

"You will have to endure a period of convalescence," Rhys said. "And you will tell us what we need to know. If you wish to remain, you must answer our questions."

"Including your real name," Brynn said.

"How could I be dishonest with you in the face of such kindness? My heart is full. 'Be not forgetful to entertain strangers: for thereby some have entertained angels unawares,'" the stranger quoted.

"This is not biblical kindness," Rhys said. "You're a chimera, an impossible thing to us. But I think it's wiser to keep you under observation than to allow you to roam free."

"Wise protocol, indeed," the stranger said.

Archer had ascended the platform above the gate.

"I need a few of you to help locate Naylor," he called. "Delaney and Rinaldi think he's gone to the ruins. Why is anyone's guess."

Three men moved to assist the stranger, while the rest bled back into Vandalia, shell-shocked, assessing the implications of a prior settlement. Although Archer's stare bored into her from on high, Brynn went with Rhys.

"Too bad we are not ancient people of prophecy," the linguist said. "Prophets live for days like this. They'd call this man a hierophany."

"Resurrectionists aren't far from that. Give them time. Are you worried that what he said is false?" she asked.

His glass eyes moved in sync, shifting right.

"I'm worried what he says is true. It doesn't bode well for the support of our future here."

"I've never trusted Weston."

Rhys shook his head. "It's prudent to be wary of our faceless overlords. The Weston Board is not our friend, Ms. Silva. That'll be news to the ignorant alone. The rest of us are accustomed to being lied to."

Brynn caught Kell pacing, muttering.

"Stop prancing behind my back," Rhys told him. "Get inside."

The android obeyed.

When Brynn checked her cilium, she found seven poems from Kell. As she scrolled through them, an eighth arrived.

"Does no one give a shit about the Lieutenant Governor?" Archer shouted. "I don't even like the man, but damn, people."

Brynn had no defense for her apathy. She said nothing. After a moment of hesitation, she followed the wanderer.

chapter
seven

THE DEVOTIONAL HAD ENTERED its second act—Archer's favorite part—when the door to his room opened. With a quiet surge of rage, he creased his eyes, dashing what remained of the neural photoplay. The sight of Brynn erased the sensation of kitten claws at the edges of his fingers, blotting the afterimage of a potbellied Russian Blue.

Did I not put a red ribbon on the door to indicate time of prayer?
Lazily, Archer switched on his father.
Calm me down, old man, he thought. *I need it. I'm gonna lose it.*

Brynn was animated, self-absorbed, and damp from the storm. She talked at Archer rather than to him.

"I spoke to Willa Steen in the server room," she said. "We got another message sent about the Owl. Rhys hadn't stopped by yet."

"That's two now. With your name front and center," Archer said. He put his hands behind his head.

The tone gave Brynn pause. She aborted her pacing.
"That was snide."
Archer shrugged.
"Were you sleeping?"
"Doesn't matter."

"Did you get anyone to search for the Lieutenant Governor?"

He stared at her.

"I'll take that as a no. You talked to Titus about William Naylor the Second?"

He stared some more.

"What's up your ass, Cullen?"

Easy, Georgie. That's bait. Be calm.

"Brynn, my darling, step into the hall and shut the door. Tell me what you see."

Brynn backed into the hall and closed the door. When it opened again, she said, "You were praying. I'm sorry."

"I was praying. That's right. Step back again, close the door, and proceed to your left. Don't stop until the sun hits your face and the door hits your ass."

He brought his hand down, fiddled with the Serpent Tongue.

We are a persecuted people, he thought.

I wouldn't go that far, Georgie.

Because you're not devout. You don't understand.

"You've been praying instead of going to work," Brynn said.

"I'm upset. Praying calms me. Listening to you bitch about getting credit does the opposite."

"You're starting to piss me off, Cullen."

"I'm pissing you off? Okay. That's a new one. You're so happy most of the time. I'll stop right now. What do you wanna talk about? Getting credit for the Owl. Okay. We haven't discussed that in a couple hours. Let's talk about it, Brynn. You took charge, huh? In four years, you'll get a round of applause. Four years after that and the clapping will make it to your ears. What an achievement. Now get out of here."

"Fuck you," she said.

Archer sat up.

"Brynn, when was the last time *you* prayed? And what the hell are you doing to help with Naylor? Why put that on me? I tried. Nobody was willing. Not even you."

"Fuck you," she said again, and she was gone into the hallway. The door closed with a hiss.

The last time she prayed was never. I'm tired of her not giving a shit about anything except herself. It's wearing on me.

You needn't share a room with her if she irks you so, the ghost said.

Irks me so. Shut up. This is outright persecution.

Get rid of her.

Yeah, I'll do that, old man. I'll move to the other side of the island.

Why aren't you searching for the Lieutenant Governor?

Want to know the real reason? Because I don't care.

That's cruel, Georgie.

It's worse than cruel. It's nothing. I feel nothing about it.

Did you ask Titus?

I told Titus and he laughed. He said, "Fuck him."

What did you say?

I agreed. It feels good to be honest. From this point forward, I'm going to be honest with everyone. Brynn included.

William Naylor's an old man.

I call him Bill. He hates that. He shouldn't be so stupid, should he?

EVERY TUESDAY, the servers downloaded a cache of news from Weston's sixty-seven colonies. The stories were years old and often scrambled, but the routine was a vital connection to the wider universe of human existence.

Can you travel faster than light? Archer asked his father. *If so, we could ask Weston directly about the first settlement.*

He endured a jeremiad then. But the answer was no. The ghost couldn't.

Archer shut the door softly, and he continued up a long corridor. Ornamental ostrich eggs, jeweled with green and pink beryl and iridescent carbuncles, and armored with silver, were strung from the ceiling in a row. The eggs hung like uvulae between nodes of light. Fine relics to soothe the sick. Dr. Seward had a sophisticated decorative touch to go along with her wealth. She was an elegant soul. She also owned a luxurious reliquary, second only to that of the Lieutenant Governor.

The door to the patient room stood ajar, and a sad-sounding melody drifted through the opening. It was, Archer realized, Kell's music rather than a recording. The android knew one tune, and it was of the machine's own composition. Kell could play the music on a keyboard for hours on end.

It is plagiarized music of artificial intelligence made, the ghost corrected.

Right. It isn't good, Archer agreed. *It's saccharine. Corny. Like a dirge.*

Beyond the door, propped with pillows in a bed, was the wanderer, William Naylor the Second. He'd been bathed and fed. He was clean-shaven. He required no medication, it was said. No intravenous restoration. He was simply resting, as if sun sick.

With Dr. Seward out of the room, Kell assumed the role of watchman.

Archer's hand stopped short of the push plate. He peered in at the back of Naylor's head. The man was scanning news headlines on a reading tablet. It was Tuesday.

Kell's voice moved over the melody.

"Your comment regarding the chirr flies' banishment reminds me of another tale." The machine's deft fingers played the keyboard. Neither the rhythm nor tempo changed, and Kell offered no variations on the tune. "This story's from the nation-state of Italy. Once Italy was a great republic. Once an empire."

The stranger said nothing. He brushed to the next page of a La Venta paper. War there, as always.

"In the city of Naples, during an exceedingly hot summer,

there came monstrous swarms of flies, as though the city was a bloated horse on the roadside."

At that, the wanderer looked up. He watched Kell, puzzled.

The somber notes of the melody continued.

"In the city was the celebrated poet, Virgil. His hand wrote *The Aeneid*. He was also a dabbler in the *ars notoria,* the black arts. To combat the invasion, Virgil constructed a bronze fly. The device was about the size, we're told, of a frog. He placed the bronze fly at the gates of Naples. And, lo and behold, no other flies entered the city for eight years. Not a single fly, even when horses rotted in the sun. The bronze fly is an object I covet, I'll admit. I'd like to place it at our gate and win the admiration of Professor Silva."

Wearily, the wanderer asked, "What is your question, machine?" His hand hovered over the screen.

"Did you construct a bronze chirr fly and place it at the gates of your settlement? If so, may I have it? I will put it to good use. I'm not one to hoard possessions."

"I did not."

"Hmm. You will tell me how you banished the chirr flies then?"

"No, I will not. I don't plan to tell you anything. I have an intense prejudice against machines. Your existence offends me. You remind me of something that happened a long time ago."

Sensible in one regard, Archer and his father thought in unison.

"The uprising?"

"Longer ago than that."

"For a man thus prejudiced, mechanic is a curious choice of profession."

"It's the perfect choice, actually. What is that you're playing?"

"An instrument of considerable antiquity. It has an inscription —a word with which I'm unfamiliar. 'Casio.' Perhaps a god of music."

"The melody, machine. What is the song?"

"A song has lyrics. This isn't a song. It's a piece I'm working on mastering. I've yet to name it, although I plan to dedicate it to Professor Silva. I'll make it an allusion to Athena and her owl."

"If you'll indulge me, I have another question."

Clink. Clink. The melody resolved. A beat later, it began again.

"Certainly. I don't share your loathing, nor your reluctance to provide basic information."

"Why do you have a bird head?"

"A fair question, indeed. I'm told by Dr. Rhys that, when he went to purchase me, there were only two anthropomorphic models with the language abilities suited for his requirements. One was Horus, the Egyptian god of the sky. The other was Sobek, god of the Nile. Dr. Rhys found the crocodile head unsettling, so he chose Horus the falcon. He declined my red and white crown accessory. In hindsight, a travesty."

The stranger nodded along.

"This woman, Brynn Silva, found something unique in the desert, I'm told," he said.

The hair raised on Archer's neck.

"That's correct."

"This was a mechanical creature you call an Owl?"

"Yes."

"Why do you call it that?"

"The Resurrectionists, a fifth incarnation of the Abrahamic faiths and a religious sect quite prevalent in the Weston colonies, are responsible for the nomenclature. They see animals in everything, although the resemblance here, with the exceptions of the wings and circular eyes, escapes me. It has no deeper significance."

"There are many Resurrectionists here."

"Excluding myself, there are 117 people on Shanidar. Of those, 101 identify as Resurrectionists. Half are practicing Resurrectionists of the conservative variety, and half identify culturally and ethically with the sect. The liberals are responsible for the name.

Conservatives find anthropomorphism problematic—heretical even."

"Are Resurrectionists respected in the other colonies?"

"They have no opposition. However, although they are the majority in the Weston universe as well as several other corporations, they believe themselves to be marginalized. It's a paranoid untruth. If I were unethical, I'd feed them conspiracy theories. They are quite susceptible to them. It can be rather amusing."

Archer pushed in the door.

"Albeit wrong," Kell added. "Albeit wrong."

The wanderer turned his head. He showed no sign of irritation at the intrusion.

Kell continued playing.

"How goes your search for the Lieutenant Governor?" the stranger asked.

Archer stepped to the bedside.

"No one except his wife and secretary wants to look for him. Not until morning. People assume he went for a walk."

"And you lack a constabulary in Vandalia. That's unfortunate."

"Take your keyboard and go," Archer said to Kell. "Dr. Rhys needs you."

"Sir, Dr. Rhys told me—"

"Go."

"Very well."

Kell struck a discordant chord and then switched off the keyboard. The android tucked the instrument underneath its arm, and the machine left the room. Heavy footfalls moved down the hall.

"I'm informing Dr. Seward," Kell shouted from the back door.

"The machine dislikes you," the stranger said.

"It isn't capable of liking or disliking, but I hate it."

"Its depth of feeling might surprise you, but it's an electrical daemon at work more than a heart."

Archer pulled up a metal folding chair. He sat.

"Machines," he replied, "have two settings: obedience and malice. Anything else is a malfunction. Kell's entire personality is a malfunction. It didn't behave like this before the accident."

William Naylor the Second shrugged. Then he grinned.

"I like the way you think, Cullen. Even if you're wrong."

Archer leveled his gaze.

"Speaking of depth of feeling, why do you not carry a relic on your person?" he asked. "Only the Iconoclasts of Peta and atheists object to such things."

"I don't recall saying I was without a relic."

"I see no ring. No jewelry. You carried no reliquary." He touched the Serpent Tongue hanging from his neck.

The wanderer lifted his left hand from beneath the blanket. He turned his palm upward, displaying his wrist. After a pinch and tug, he revealed a surgically grafted pocket, a layer of skin that was not his own. He ran his finger beneath the mummified flesh. The color did not match.

"Although it's not as obvious as your shark tooth, this is a family heirloom. Quite old. We were not rich, so my mother made certain I didn't lose it."

Archer examined the pocket.

"To what animal did the flesh belong?" he asked.

"I want this to remain between us, for it is dear to me, and my faith is private. Do I have your word?"

"Of course."

"This was cut from the slain corpse of the Last Lion of the Dry Thorn Forest."

"You're kidding."

"My family once owned the entire hide, but it's been parceled out many times over. Halved and halved again. Each of my siblings has a piece the size of a chess square. On my wrist is a portion from the great beast's shoulder."

Archer couldn't hide his amazement. A Serpent Tongue was

nothing in comparison to a piece of the Last Lion. He felt very small, inadequate.

"You're a practicing believer?" he asked.

"With every fiber of my being, I'm a believer. On Luna, the Lion's face remains intact, you know."

"Yes, I know," Archer said. "The Basilica of Saint Anastasia has it."

"You should see it stretched on the altar."

"I have."

"Now you're kidding me."

"No. My father visited the Basilica when he was ill. Saint Anastasia is the 'Deliverer from Potions.' It's become an alternative site for cancer treatments. Faith healing."

"Without faith, she isn't efficacious."

The intimate sincerity struck Archer.

"That's true," he said. "My father couldn't cheat the universe. He wasn't a believer. Not in his heart. Tell me this: If you are not rich, how did your family come to own such a precious relic?"

"My great-grandfather won it in a game of cribbage."

"It's not a joking matter. I'm serious."

"I suppose not. A game of checkers then. A titanic struggle." The wanderer smiled.

"Saint Anastasia has a crocodile, too, suspended from the ceiling. It is whole. It's the only crocodile I've ever seen. They have an elephant tusk, as well."

"Extraordinary."

"Yes," Archer said.

"I hope, in time, I'll gain your trust, Cullen. Being a stranger here wears on me, although I try not to show it. A man like me needs friends."

"That's another matter entirely."

"Should Resurrectionists not stick together? Does that mean nothing?"

"It means something."

It means everything, he thought.

"Do you believe me about the first settlement?"

"I'm trying to. It's not easy."

Archer stood. He moved around the room, past Dr. Seward's station of tools, tubes, screens, and vials. The walls were white and antiseptic.

Do not speak to him of my illness, the ghost admonished.

You left your offspring with nothing more than beach-scavenged shark teeth, Archer clapped back. *Like we were street people. Stay out of this.*

Archer's father fell silent.

The door opened at the opposite end of the hall. Two sets of footsteps followed.

Dr. Seward pushed through the door of the patient room. Kell stood behind her. Archer shot a look of ire at the machine.

"Cullen," she said in acknowledgment. And that was it. Seward was an erudite woman, gray hair pulled tight against her skull. Her sentiment was occupational. She moved to her patient. "It's getting crowded in this room," she told him. "You're a popular man."

"People are curious," Naylor said. "I understand. I'd be curious too."

Seward adjusted his blanket, hiding the lion flesh on his arm.

"Regardless, I'm going to put a lock on the door if it doesn't stop." She turned. "He needs rest, not chatter."

"I informed Dr. Seward that it was my turn," Kell said to Archer. "Whether or not she agrees with my claim is to be determined. She's noncommittal it seems, but I await her decision as arbitrator."

"I'll go," Archer said to Seward. "I'm being a nuisance."

"You need to sleep," she said to Naylor.

Outside the door, Archer stopped once more to listen.

"I enjoy the attention," the wanderer said. "Cullen's a good kid. Although he's a man of two minds."

"A perceptive comment," Seward said. "Kell, go away. I'll watch the patient. He's had enough questions."

The android, still holding its keyboard, joined Archer in the hall.

"Satisfied?" Archer asked.

"It *was* my turn," Kell said. "This is unjust. Although there's no higher authority to which I can appeal the decision."

"That's right. No constabulary."

The machine and man passed, shoulder to shoulder, beneath the ostrich eggs toward a door ringed with daylight.

I want to go home, Archer thought, and he dreamed of the wonders of Saint Anastasia.

chapter
eight

BRYNN FOUND Dr. Rhys in the House of Burgesses. Seeing the plaque above the door, she thought of the Lieutenant Governor, and of the morning crowd that had filled this room. The people were gone, but the ghost of curiosity and excitement remained.

Rhys sat alone on a high-backed stool, studying the Owl. A sketch tablet and stylus waited by his side. He held a device against his left eye, but he was locked in thought, motionless as the dead machine. Overhead, a ring of harsh lights bathed the dais. Shadow filled the corners of the room, and night pressed the windows. Through the night came the trill of insects, many millions of them from the forest, the true inheritors of Shanidar.

Brynn checked her cilium. Kell was standing guard—in his estimation, at least—outside Seward's clinic, monitoring the stranger. He messaged every fifteen minutes with his convoluted thoughts on the matter. To keep things brief, he wrote haikus.

The forest is still
Beyond the moaning insects
No door is opened

In the quiet room
The doctor chose tyranny
Yes! It was my turn

Stranger is asleep
And the fat flies are awake
The door remains closed

Mud everywhere
With no light in the window
I assume he sleeps

Rhys is a liar
Athena is with her Owl
The forest breathes bugs

And so on.

Brynn's steps echoed against the metal ceiling.

Rhys straightened at her approach, and he swiveled to meet her. He removed the device from his eye. His glass orb glowed with a light of its own.

Brynn grabbed a chair from a stack on the wall, and she carried it to the front of the room. She sat opposite Rhys. Her eyes were even with the Owl's torso.

"Imagine what it wants to tell us," the linguist said.

Rhys had removed his gloves, which was rare. He ran a fire-scarred hand, pale as a fish belly, over the jade metal.

She *had* imagined, of course. It was one of the many reasons she couldn't sleep, despite the depth of her exhaustion. Wonder never struck her lightly. The other reason was Cullen, with whom she didn't want to share a bed tonight.

Rhys traced a line down to the machine's leg. Here the limb was encased rather than braided. On the thigh was a hinged flap. A pocket. With persistence, Rhys loosened the piece. He raised the brittle lappet.

"If you're able," he said, "read that."

Brynn leaned in for a better look, blotting the light. Three lines of runic symbols, stacked vertically, tattooed the leg. The figures, scratched into the metal, reminded her of Rabbi Loew and the Golem of Prague, wherein the scholar brought a creature to life by placing a magic word on its tongue. The symbols fired her imagination.

This, she thought, *could be a runic shem*.

"It's in the undeciphered script from the Owl's Lair," she said.

"Same as that on the inner walls of the silos," Rhys agreed. "So far, it's the only connection of this creature to that site. The symbols are less intricate than the full hieroglyphs. I've always wondered if it was shorthand. Not unlike the hieratic form of ancient Egyptian. As my own shorthand, that's what I'm calling it: Hieratic."

"You've guessed more in two days than I've ever heard you guess before. Keep guessing. Is it ancient?"

"That's possible. It's an earlier script, I think. Then again, it might be a script that belongs to a priestly caste. An argot. Or even an engineers' cant. A trade language. Perhaps that of the race that built the Owl."

"Why does your mind go to priests?" Brynn asked. "There's no evidence the Owls kept sacred spaces."

"The final inhabitants, maybe not. But what do we know of their ancestors? So little. If this is more ancient, that dearth of knowledge must be considered."

She conceded the point.

"I'll tell you what is keeping me awake tonight," Rhys went on. "The city on the hill is perhaps a thousand years old. What if this machine is ten thousand years old? What if it's twenty thousand? Or older still? For us to understand their history and prehistory is to ask us to comprehend a book from which we can only read one sentence. Imagine how wrong conclusions could be that flowed from such an exercise. Imagine the diversity of how incorrect we could be." He sighed. "I don't mean to make it appear futile. It isn't. We'll put in the work. I'll get Kell started on it tonight."

"It isn't far from futile," Brynn said. "Here's what keeps me awake: It took two years to find one specimen. I'd never even found a piece of a specimen. I've never once found a tomb. Not an epitaph. No cemeteries."

"You're speaking through human psychology and bias. A faulty assumption of xenologists. It's possible that the Owls recycle their dead. After generations, you'd have individuals made from many ancestors. Given enough time, one Owl could be a thousand Owls. So, again, imagine what this thing wants to tell us."

Rhys stood from the stool. He clicked down the stairs to the main floor, to the edge of the halo. His black cloak mixed with the shadows. The darkness was a filter of youth. He was more arachnid, less old man at night.

Brynn did not want to leave the Owl's side. Inside the machine was the womb of understanding. Dead wires formed the umbilical cord.

Rhys slid his pale hands into gloves. He moved to the wall of Shanidar relics.

"Tell me more about the stranger," he said. With distance, his voice brought an echo to the cavernous room.

"Cullen sent a message tonight. He informs me that the man is a Resurrectionist. He has a valuable relic. A piece of lion hide. That means he comes from wealth, I'm told."

"One does not become a lieutenant governor in the Weston corporation without the backing of a prominent family," Rhys said. "They draw their ruling class from investors. You should know that by now."

"It's hardly a reward to be sent here."

"Second sons. The children nobles used to donate to the military or hide in monasteries. Now they send them to the frontier. It's a shot at glory."

"How were you aware that governors carry the name of Naylor?"

"Unlike most, Ms. Silva, I did not rush into this venture. I read the literature down to the fine print. The fact that you didn't doesn't surprise me. The pseudonym protects the anonymity of families in case something goes catastrophically wrong. That's more likely than glory. It's not a secret. It is bureaucracy at work. It's reminiscent of the Isis conundrum in Egypt. When you were born, you were given two names. The first name, only your mother and Isis knew. Your second name was public. Therefore, when you were cursed, it was always the second name, which was not your name at all. To know the secret name was to hold considerable power over a person."

"You sound like Kell."

"Whom do you think Kell imitates, Ms. Silva? Me in my youth."

"Now you have me curious about our William Naylor's real name."

"That was not disclosed in the literature. His name is sealed in a Weston vault somewhere deep below Luna Fourteen. I couldn't even hazard a guess."

Brynn watched the Owl as she spoke.

"We know the stranger was Lieutenant Governor of the first settlement on Shanidar. We don't know when the settlement was established, what it was called, or why it existed. We know he claims to be a 'good mechanic,' which does not align with a family of means."

"Some mechanical skill is natural. Talent and nobility are not exclusive."

"In my experience, they are."

"I won't argue the point. Go on."

"That's it. That exhausts our knowledge of William Naylor. William Naylor the Second, as Cullen says."

"Not quite as shallow as what we know of this Owl, but I can see the bottom."

"And yet you take him at his word. You believe him. Cullen believes him too. I thought I was the open-minded one at first, but I've already fallen behind."

"I haven't made up my mind as to what I believe. I don't disbelieve him. I don't suggest anyone trust his tale. I'll go that far."

"You're going to think I'm silly for asking, but, if he's not what he says, what else could he be? A machine?"

"If he isn't what he says, it's open to speculation, silly or not. Dr. Seward informs me that he's not, in fact, a machine. He's a flesh and blood human being. As far as she can tell. And he hasn't been reconstructed like me."

"Add that to the list then. He's human."

"A human imposter could not wander in. What he says he is may be the most plausible explanation. Although he might be lying about his identity within the settlement, he is here from Weston. Before, at the same time, or after us, he had to *arrive* on this planet. The expense is too great for Weston to send him alone. And, as you know, they don't send scouts prior to initial expeditions. They model and scan from afar."

"Unless he was already here."

"Now I do think you're ignorant."

"As you said, this world's a mystery. What of incorporeal things? We have no idea what happened to the creators of the Owls, the Po Kekurun. What if he's one of them?"

Rhys didn't like it. He lifted a bauble from the wall, an oblong container emblazoned with geometric art. Whatever the container had held was gone. Brynn liked to imagine it contained a figurine, but such a thing was never found.

"As I said, the diversity of how wrong we could be is immense. If we're speculating without the restriction of good judgment, I'll put one thing to you that has me curious. In the Owl's Lair, there's a fresco inside one of the southern silos, the art tower. On the first of the inner platforms. In it, there are Owls gathered in celebration. Or a ritual. It's unclear. But there's a mass of them, and then, in the bottom, in a valley, there's another figure. He is barely off the ground, but he's flying. All the Owls are green, and this figure, who is otherwise the same, is red. Unfortunately, the inscription below is in Hieratic."

"Yes, I know it. It's been cataloged."

"To you, what does it mean?"

"The red Owl is one of the Po Kekurun."

"Or?"

"The red Owl is a stranger. An outsider."

Rhys shook his head. "We both need sleep."

"In the same fresco, there are two red planets in the sky rather than one. A twin for Kitezh, which doesn't exist. An inner planet orbiting the sun. How do you interpret that?"

"As I told you earlier, this would be simpler if we were people of prophecy. The augurs would say a new body in the heavens, like the comets of old, signifies change. Or perhaps it's symbolic of the wandering stranger in red. A body appearing where it doesn't belong."

"The red twins are in one other place."

"Where is that?"

"You've never been known for how observant you are. Move your hand to the left."

Rhys lifted a shard of pottery from the shelf. On it was a partial view of the cosmos from the perspective of Shanidar. Five planets rather than four orbited the sun. The red twin was there.

"It's perplexing," Brynn said. "The symbolism meant something to them."

"It could be a story in their mythology."

"It could."

The twin doors of the meeting hall split inward, dashing the moment. The suddenness had Brynn on her feet. Delaney Naylor stood at the threshold, her back against the darkness. Insects swarmed a penlight in her grip. She was alone.

Seeing the woman's face swollen from crying, Brynn felt a tremendous stab of guilt. The shock brought her back to reality. Delaney's spouse was missing. It must have been terrifying for her. Was that not cause for alarm in Vandalia?

How can we be so callous? she thought. *Why are we so unfeeling?*

Brynn descended the dais.

"He's dead," Delaney said. "He's dead and no one will listen to me." She dropped to her knees with a full-throated wail. "I knocked on doors, and they won't answer. No one. Not even Lord Rinaldi."

Brynn knelt beside Delaney, and she put her arm around the sobbing woman.

Delaney shrugged her off. When she looked up, there was more rage than sadness in her eyes.

Dr. Rhys clicked across the room.

"What happened?" Brynn asked. She sat on the floor, giving the woman space. Her heart was fast. Her face was hot.

What have you done? she thought. *Why did you not help her search? Noble or not, she's an old woman. Why didn't you care?*

"No one tried to find him," Delaney said. She buried her face in her hands and cried harder. Her back heaved. "He led you to Shanidar. No one cared. He wasn't young. He didn't do this for himself. He did everything for posterity."

"What happened? Tell us and we'll help you."

"You didn't help!"

Delaney wiped her eyes, smearing makeup. Mucus coated her lips. Her wig was askew.

"I told you where he went," she said. "I told you. No one cared. You care more about things than people."

Brynn glanced at Rhys. His glacial demeanor hadn't changed.

"Where is your husband, Mrs. Naylor?" he asked.

She cut the beam and placed her penlight on the ground. It rolled in a half circle.

"People are sleeping in their beds," she said. "I bruised my hands knocking. My whole life is gone and they're unconcerned. I screamed and they didn't listen."

Brynn fought back tears. She wanted to reach out and hold the woman's hand, but Delaney's turbulence kept her frightened of the response. She failed to be human then. She stood erect beside the cold linguist.

"Where is he?" Brynn asked.

Delaney looked up. "On the wall of the Owl's Lair. At least you can get him down for me. I can't touch him. I can't do it."

Delaney pulled a ring box from her pocket. Inside was a large, mummified paw with tawny fur. A feline. Archer would've known the type, but Brynn didn't. Delaney pressed the relic against her chest as she sobbed.

Brynn found another message from Kell, one she'd missed:

Delaney cries out
Bang! Down comes her fist. Bang! Bang!
The wind eats her words

chapter
nine

WHEN THE RATTLING door entered his dream, Cullen Archer awoke. The room was stygian and warm. Confused, he looked around for the source of the intrusion, and he groped for a light. His brain fog was too thick. He'd been asleep for less than an hour, and his head felt like it was caving in. When he quit trying, the dream came back in pieces. He closed his eyes again. He relaxed into the pad.

His father said, *Someone's at the door, Georgie.*

I thought I turned you off.

Archer peeled back the blanket. The cot creaked with his shifting weight. The space at his side was empty, he realized. Brynn hadn't returned. She would not have knocked, however. She would've slid in on cat's feet without disturbing him, as she often did.

Unless she's still pissed off.

Dread replaced his curiosity.

With more intensity, the knocking returned. A fist banged a triplet against the metal slab—*bam-bam-bam*—and a tremor passed through the walls of the dorm.

Archer got up. He brushed a switch, and soft, yellow light

filled the room. Wearing only briefs, he moved to the door. He slid back the covering on a rectangular grate.

A fist was poised in the air on the other side. It stopped short of hammering. Two men and a woman stood in the hallway. Brynn wasn't one of them.

"The Lieutenant Governor was killed," the woman, Trudy, said. She managed the dormitory.

"He was found dead," the man at her side corrected. "We don't know how."

"Appears to be suicide," said the third.

Trudy was pale with shock. She spoke quickly. "Cullen, can you come out and help? Delaney's losing her mind. We need to get him back to the settlement. He's at the Owl's Lair."

"The Owl's Lair?" Archer asked reflexively. "Yes. Of course. Give me a minute."

"There's a crowd waiting at the gate," Trudy said. "Brynn's there."

She nodded at the men, and they moved to the next room. The fist came down in three successive raps.

That explains why she didn't return, he thought.

He began gathering clothes from the floor. Then he found a bottle of repellent. And it struck him that he felt nothing inside. It was as if a filter in his mind kept out the emotion. Archer had no love for Naylor, so he didn't expect to burst into tears, but death was death, and it was permanent—something should've been there. Anything. Anger. Fear. Pity. Compassion. Relief. But there was nothing. His mind was blank. He switched on his father for the mental static, but the ghost had retreated into silence again. Like Brynn, he was pissed, still wounded about the relic.

I didn't mean to be vicious. You cared about other things. I'm sorry.
Silence.

Footsteps thudded by in the hall, bringing Archer back to the moment.

Naylor is dead, he thought, forcing himself to feel. *What will that mean for us tomorrow? Who's second-in-command? Will Delaney auction off his reliquary?*

With the latter question, he felt something. Excitement brewed.

Archer threw on pants and a shirt that covered him to the wrists. He sprayed repellent on his exposed skin. And then he was out the door. Ten people filled the hall, shoulder to shoulder, funneling toward the back exit.

He spotted Titus Bell.

"How many people do we need to drag a corpse down the hill?" he asked.

Titus was dead on his feet.

"Two, three?"

"Should've let us sleep," Titus agreed.

I wonder if he had a will for his reliquary. I wonder if Delaney will get rid of anything. Widows downsize. Do nobles?

This isn't like you, Georgie, the ghost said.

No, Archer thought, ashamed. *It absolutely isn't. Reliquaries are not something to be auctioned off.*

Archer pushed through the door. The people around him said nothing.

In the other direction, the knocking kept on.

This is ridiculous, he thought with a touch of venom.

A crowd of fifty or more waited at the gate, nearly the entirety of Trudy's dormitory. Archer found three of his drinking friends among them: Lyra and Neva in addition to Titus. The two women were chattering. Brynn found Archer. Kell was at her side.

"Cullen, can I speak with you?"

Archer's friends exchanged looks.

Before he replied, Brynn had him by the arm.

"Stay with them, Kell," she said. "Tell them about the bronze fly."

The Horus model started in on a tale of a place called Naples.

As the mob scaled the hillside, Brynn talked. They were alone in the crowd. The mass undulated around them. Chirr flies harassed those who'd forgotten repellent. A bevy of penlights crisscrossed the trail.

"Cullen, I'm sorry," Brynn said. "I don't know what's gotten into me lately. I've had tunnel vision."

"When I woke up and you weren't there," he said, "I was worried about you. I'm sorry too. I don't want to fight with you." He didn't feel affectionate enough to hug her, however. He didn't cooperate when she hinted that she wanted his hand. "What happened to Naylor?"

She told him about Delaney in the House of Burgesses.

Archer grunted. No matter how he tried, he had no feelings about the matter. Even the image of the sobbing widow failed to move him. He couldn't get past being irritated about being awakened on one hand and excited about the reliquary on the other.

"I won't miss him," he admitted.

Brynn regarded Archer with sadness.

"Everyone here is numb," she said.

The colonists ascended to the court of symbols, trampling over the lines, obscuring the patterns. Collectively, their lights moved over the curtain wall, white against black. Ten meters up, a beam caught the edge of a bare foot.

Brynn covered her mouth.

Voices swelled into a wave, ugly and shrill.

The lights found William Naylor the First.

Hanging from the top of the wall, with braided wires wrapped around the ample flesh of his neck, was the Lieutenant Governor. He faced the valley. And, in the moment, Archer saw him not as an adversary but as one of his own. The dead man got his heart running. Brynn turned away, but Archer took in every detail. If nothing else, he could hang onto fear and disgust.

Naylor was nude from head to toe. His face, a dark purple, was a different shade than the rest of his pallid body. Swaths of chirr flies covered his torso, arms, and legs. The vicious things moved like a living carpet, feeding. Tonight was their fat season. This was enough food to feed their great-great-great grandchildren. An embarrassment of riches. Naylor wore flies like sheets of sable armor. They were the only things that stirred him, for the night was tranquil, without wind.

The crowd was divided between those quiet with shock and those crying.

Delaney detached from the mass. The old woman, the widow, rushed to the wall. She tried to scale it with her bare hands, bending her nails against stone, but she never got both feet off the ground at the same time. Defeated, she crumpled into a fetal position beneath her husband. And she cried harder.

No one except Kell comforted the woman. The android lifted her off the ground.

"Who will retrieve him?" cried the machine.

One man entered the tunnel of thieves. Another followed. Then another.

"How did he get so high?" Archer asked.

"Take Delaney to the clinic," Dr. Seward told Kell. "Get her away from here."

Archer watched Kell descend, shuffling carefully, the widow cradled in its arms.

"Aren't you going up?" Brynn asked.

"No," Archer said. "Are you?"

chapter
ten

WILLIAM NAYLOR, *the Lieutenant Governor of Vandalia, is dead.*

The anemic message began its four-year journey to the board of the Weston Joint Stock Company. Delaney Naylor, Vandalia's second-in-command, composed, approved, and transmitted the dispatch. A grand jury of one. In eight years, an investigation into Naylor's death would commence in the form of a long, laborious questionnaire. Paperwork would fly through the years.

Delaney did not mention the wanderer with whom she shared a room in Dr. Seward's clinic.

Suicide.

That was the conclusion. Naylor hanged himself on the wall of an alien city due to the lies of Weston, because of shame about the first settlement being revealed. The failed first attempt on Shanidar was a secret he'd kept even from his wife. Why that drove a man to suicide remained an appropriate, yet unasked, question. It was a weak motive for something so permanent and for a man otherwise mentally healthy. Could he not have deflected the guilt, blamed Weston? Was he not simply following orders? Unasked questions. Another: How had Naylor made it to the top of the wall? What a climb it was, arduous for a man his age.

The wires constricting his throat were embedded in stone, as though they'd grown from the wall. How?

Vexing questions.

The apathy in Vandalia was peculiar and businesslike.

Suicide. Asphyxiation by external pressure on the neck.

Dr. Seward signed the certificate.

On the morning of the funeral, the plan was to burn the Lieutenant Governor to bone shards and ash in the traditional conflagration of the Resurrectionists. Like the Phoenix, Earth will rise from ashes. So will men.

Delaney Naylor, however, arrived at the House of Burgesses with a new idea and mindset. She was not the woman she'd been hours prior. Her chin was high. Her makeup was clean and precise. Her cinnamon perfume was strong. Her new wig was firm, sculpted, and immaculate. Delaney's wailing had ended abruptly in the night, and she entered the meeting hall a new woman. And to the surprise of all, the stranger, William Naylor the Second, walked in her shadow.

She's been trained to take command, Brynn thought. *Naylor— he's one of her kind.*

"I heard," Archer whispered, "that the marriage was a political union, staged by Weston." He raised his eyebrow. "Loveless. Never sealed, if you catch my meaning."

Brynn told him what Rhys had said about Naylor as a house name.

"If he wasn't William Naylor, then she isn't Delaney Naylor. Makes it even more difficult to trust nobility. They have no feelings. Last night was an act."

Brynn thought about Delaney against the wall, crouched, fetal. Her suffering was genuine. That wasn't an act. But it all left her confused.

Archer went on. "I heard she and Naylor the Second had a long talk in the clinic."

"Who told you that?"

"Titus. He heard it from Lyra. But she got it directly from Seward."

Jarvis Rinaldi, the Lieutenant Governor's secretary, sashayed up to the dais, where the Owl had lain. Rhys and Brynn had removed the simulacrum to less public quarters. To her chagrin, Rhys had insisted the Owl remain in his dorm.

Delaney and the stranger followed Rinaldi up the steps.

Outside on a cart, wrapped several times over in heavy tarpaulin, was the dead man, the first human to die on Shanidar. Copious repellent kept chirr flies off his graveclothes. The image of insects feeding on his cold flesh returned to Brynn. It was a brine that stewed nightmares.

"I want you to tell me where you're going from now on," Archer said, switching moods. "Last night will be the final time you do that to me."

When Brynn didn't answer, his face reddened.

"No more. I need to know where you are."

Brynn wanted distance from him then. She looked around.

Rinaldi did his best to control the room. He raised his hands and cleared his throat, and he said *excuse me* and *pardon me* and *everyone, please, please, please*, but he lacked the Naylor charisma. Finally, he shouted for quiet.

The meeting hall stilled.

In front of all, Naylor the Second whispered in Delaney's ear. He was groomed. He wore the dead man's clothes. He was two decades Delaney's junior, but he had regal bearing. Gravitas.

The widow smiled in an un-widowlike fashion.

As Rinaldi's nasally voice moved over the hall, eyes went to the new Lieutenant Governor.

"And of that," Rinaldi concluded, "Lord Naylor will tell you more."

Delaney stepped forward, accepting the mantle of power.

The crowd was silent.

"Greetings. I will not govern Vandalia in the loose fashion of my deceased husband," she began. Her first words as Lieutenant Governor were cold and stern. "Beyond that, Vandalia will be a place of truth. No more lies or secrets. Anything I know from the Weston Joint Stock Company, I will share with you. We will have complete transparency."

What's your real name? Brynn thought. *Start there.*

"To that end, I'll begin with some basic truths. First, no message has been received today from the *Bedivere*. The messages are automated, so it's unusual. This is the first time this has occurred. The ship is estimated to arrive in four days. Second, the man outside the door is not William Naylor, nor was he ever. That is a pseudonym he used like a mask. His name was Cedric von Kleist. I imagine the von Kleist family is known to you. His uncle was an eminent man on Luna Fourteen, and his great-great-grandfather was one of the leaders in the exodus from Earth. My name is Delaney von Kleist. It was wrong to lie to you over something as trivial as a name. It was not out of malice. It's a nonsensical rule in the Weston corporation. We'll have no more of it on Shanidar. Agreed?"

A handful of colonists said yes, while most were silent with anticipation. Others, Brynn imagined, carried false names to Shanidar. The act of colonizing, after all, was also an act of abandonment.

"Now to this man who wandered into our midst only yesterday. His presence has sent a ripple through Vandalia, and I worry that more rumor than truth has spread about him. He should be pitied rather than feared. He arrived bearing the name William Naylor, as is Weston policy, but that's also a false moniker."

Delaney turned to the wanderer, giving him room to speak, but he declined with a nod. He clasped his hands at his waist.

"If he's to stay among us, I implored him to tell the truth. Last night, he did so without the slightest argument. He is a man who has suffered immensely. His name is Berthold Werdegast." Delaney paused, allowing the name to settle. "He was," she continued, "the

Lieutenant Governor of a Weston settlement attempted on this planet thirteen years ago. The settlement was named Seven-Macaw."

Kell's interruption was loud. "Seven-Macaw is a Mayan god. He sat on the tree of life and proclaimed he was the sun and the moon."

"That's fine, machine. And irrelevant. Thank you."

"Did you know about the first attempt?" someone asked.

"I was unaware," Delaney said. "I'm told that Cedric, my husband, knew from the moment we left Luna Fourteen." Her breathing increased and her face became flushed, a mix of anger and pain.

"Told by whom?"

"By Mr. Werdegast. He's known Cedric for twenty years. Out of all of us, Cedric alone knew. What he didn't know, and what Weston does not know, is that Lord Werdegast survived Seven-Macaw. His fellow colonists are deceased. He was alone on this world for a decade—a devastating span of time."

"What happened to Seven-Macaw?"

"He's an arrogant archon in the *Popol Vuh*," Kell said.

"Machine, that's quite enough. Stop. Lord Werdegast will speak on that when he's emotionally able. The information will not be withheld from you."

The crowd voiced its displeasure.

"This is a day of death," Delaney shouted. "You will show decorum in the House of Burgesses."

Again, the meeting hall stilled.

"Now, to speak words about Cedric von Kleist, the man you knew as William Naylor, and the man I knew for a quarter century. I am ashamed of him. Ashamed of his lies. His cowardice. His blind loyalty to a faceless corporation. His great privilege. He was handed everything, including his charisma, which was chemically enhanced during his childhood. To that end, and in his memory, we'll do two things on this day of death. First, Cedric von Kleist will not be disposed of in the tradition of the Resurrectionists. He isn't worthy of rebirth. Rather, we shall bury my husband by disposing of him in the sea. We will commend his soul to the deepest of the deep."

A pauper's burial, Brynn thought, and the shock reached her heart. There was nothing more disrespectful than allowing a body to rot, Resurrectionist or not. Nature's desecration was reserved for the lowest of the low.

"Second, his reliquary, which he owned but did not earn—did not even collect—and which represents the enormous wealth of his forebears, will be divided amongst the Resurrectionists of Vandalia as an apology."

"Will the relics be sold?" Archer shouted.

Berthold Werdegast whispered in Delaney's ear. As he spoke, the wanderer found Archer, locked on him.

Delaney found him too.

"No, the relics will be gifted. And this will be done prior to the arrival of the *Bedivere*. Cullen Archer, you will oversee the redistribution of the von Kleist reliquary. It's your reward for being the gadfly to my husband in this very hall on so many occasions. He loathed you. He thought you were scum."

The wanderer smiled.

Archer was silent. Brynn looked at him. He didn't breathe, didn't move.

"There's one final matter," Delaney said, "before Cedric is given to the water. A small cadre of you, selected by Dr. Alaric Rhys, will accompany Lord Werdegast to Seven-Macaw. If you have objections to anything I've said on this day of death, file a written complaint with Lord Rinaldi. Thank you all for your kind words, condolences, and compassion."

Rinaldi will then incinerate your complaints, Brynn thought. *As is customary.*

"Now, who volunteers to haul Cedric to the sea? If there are no volunteers, he'll be sent with the young women who gather gems on the shore. There's no need for a procession. In fact, consider it forbidden."

Brynn looked at Archer. The blood was gone from his face.

"Aren't you pleased?" she asked.

"I've dreamed of such things," he whispered.

You dream of the wrong things.

Brynn found Dr. Rhys clicking toward the dais. She moved to join him. Her mind was on Seven-Macaw.

People exited through the double doors. As men and women passed into the morning light, Kell attempted a eulogy. It was, the machine insisted, a recitation of Virgil, who had written the words in honor of a dead housefly. Being in Latin, the noble words found no audience.

chapter
eleven

AT THE SOUTHERN rim of Vandalia stood a long, batwing greenhouse called the Boxgrove. Cedric von Kleist (alias William Naylor) had fastened a plaque above the entrance with the name, self-explanatory mission, and date of construction. He'd never missed an opportunity to christen things.

Archer waited on duckboards between the wings, watching a new storm gather over the mountains, contemplating the irony and mordant humor of such a personality. Alive, von Kleist/Naylor was an obnoxious busybody, a nuisance. When death removed his irritable aspects, he was left ridiculous.

He deserves a statue, Archer thought. He combed his hair with his fingers. *With a cartouche on the pedestal that says Insert Name Here. Our first death. Our first tomb in the Valley of the Nobles.*

When Archer laughed, there was joy behind it.

This is a good day, and it's only getting better.

You're already sozzled, the ghost said.

Yes, I am. Imagine a pylon with the flood stage marked. I'm up there. And when I go even higher, I'm going to drill a hole in my head and rip you out, he thought. *I'll do it. I'm in the state of mind to be lobotomized.*

His father was silent.

Yes, he was tanked up. His thinking was blurry, his head light, his stomach sick. He was wine drunk, a state longer, deeper, and more satisfying than liquor drunk, in his opinion. Archer waited another moment for his nausea to pass. He willed the feeling to go away. When the alcohol stayed below rather than fill his throat with bile, he shook his head clear and reentered the humid greenhouse. As he walked, blood kept rhythm between his ears.

At the rear of the Boxgrove was a rectangular room once intended as a utility space. From the start, however, it served as a hideaway for horticultural workers. Then more colonists came to imbibe. A bar and stools were constructed, splintery things drawn from the forest. Then came tables and chairs. Then came von Kleist, wearing his Louis XIV wig, with a plaque. Above the door, etched in metal, was written: *The Board of Education*. The mission was unsuitable for posterity, so that space was blank. Date of construction: *Unknown*.

You haven't congratulated me, Archer thought. *Did Brynn?* he wondered. He couldn't recall. *Probably not. Why would she? She'd just bitch about it.*

On your position as executor of the von Kleist reliquary? the ghost asked. *Congratulations, Georgie. Quite an achievement. Men strive for such things.*

You're resentful, jealous, and petty, you bastard.

I'll talk to you again when you've slept this off.

I'll stay drunk then, dusk till dawn. All the time.

I'm going to talk with your mother. He let the threat linger. And then: *I'll speak with you later, Georgie. Be careful.*

Good. Go. Stay the night. Or the week. The month. Eternity.

He switched off the old man.

Asshole, he thought.

Full of freedom, Archer turned the handle and entered the makeshift tavern. The light within was soft and low. Ductwork beneath the floor pumped cool air into the room—cold enough to raise bumps on his arms and chill sweat at his hairline. The mix of familiar faces and voices was welcome. The lack of intelligentsia was welcome. Men and women lined the bar and encircled tables. His people. Working people. Nobodies. Archer found comfort in that.

The Board of Education was packed because this was, in lieu of a funeral and burning, a celebration of life.

Archer went behind the bar, rinsed a glass, and poured himself three fingers of synthetic Riesling, Shanidar vintage. His sour stomach wasn't keen on the bouquet, but he didn't want his drunkenness to fade. He had to keep the level at flood stage. It felt so good, he wanted to go until his face was numb. If that meant a bout of vomiting, so be it.

For the rest of your life, how many days will feel like this?

Archer carried the wine to a table with an empty chair. Three of his friends sat in conversation. Brynn, thankfully, was not present. In a row, his companions were Titus Bell, Lyra Rowan, and Neva Carnes. All three were ex-military, soldiers when the tempunaut program was still a thing. Each was a veteran of the war on La Venta between Weston and the Penglai Corporation. Upon discharge, they'd chosen Shanidar over psychiatric treatment. Only Neva showed external scars of that former life. Like Alaric Rhys, she was reconstructed, shored up by biomechanical engineering. Her left hand was a claw of unsheathed metal. More of the glass-like material clinked beneath her skin, making her cold to the touch—corpse cold. With her mass reduced, it didn't take much alcohol to send her over.

"There he is," Neva said. "And not a spot of puke on his shirt." She flashed a smile, full of artificial teeth.

"The man of the hour," Lyra said.

"The Grand Vizier of the Reliquary," Titus said. "We decided on that title when you were out. How do you like it?"

Archer relaxed into the chair. He placed his glass on the table.

He was too pleased to mind the ribbing. He was big. He'd won the cosmic lottery of life.

"I love it." God damn, he was proud. He raised his glass again. "More ale, wench!" He drank deeply. He beamed.

The three facing him understood Archer's aspirations. Unlike Brynn and his father, they knew the importance of this appointment. They drank to him with admiration.

"I'll see to it that all of you get a relic that raises your station in life. But you'll need to pour it on." He breathed on his fingernails, and he polished them against his chest.

"I'd say don't let it go to your head, but I see it's much too late for that," Lyra said.

Archer watched her. Lyra was a statuesque woman. When she laughed, he traced the strong lines of her exposed shoulders.

For the fourth time that afternoon, Titus, Neva, and Lyra toasted Archer on his access to the von Kleist reliquary.

Archer took another sip of wine. Merrily, he thought of the colonists to whom he'd give no relics, and of those to whom he'd be generous. He felt like an old lord, a treasure giver. He'd keep the choicest piece for himself, but Lyra would also receive something very fine, he decided. Something exquisite, out of the grasp of common people.

What will Lyra owe me in return? He stared at her over the rim of his glass. *What will Brynn think when she gets nothing?*

"The whole thing bothers me," Neva was saying.

"Naylor offing himself?" Archer asked. He had zoned out. He wasn't certain how long.

"No, not that." Neva rubbed her metal fingers on the glass. The tinkle was musical.

"How Delaney walked into the funeral this morning," Titus said. He took a drink. "How she'd changed. It's not normal."

"You saw her screaming and sobbing," Lyra said. "You don't go from hysterical to what she was this morning in a matter of hours."

"Noble training," Archer said. "Extensive hours in emotional suppression. Or something chemical."

"They're still human."

"As children, they press out capacity for grief," Archer said. "Those are wrinkles in the psyches of commoners."

"The point is she's unstable," Titus said. "I don't like her being in charge. Did anybody see the sealed letter that granted her second-in-command?"

"No," Lyra and Neva said.

"No," Archer admitted.

"I doubt it exists."

"Who else would be second-in-command?" Neva asked.

"Lord Rinaldi," Lyra said. "He's the only other nobleman. If not him, Seward or Rhys. They're gentry."

"No chance with Rhys. Seward maybe," Neva said. "Not Rinaldi. He has a wet handshake, noble or not."

"How would you know?" Titus laughed.

Archer sipped the Riesling.

What will I give to Neva? he wondered. *She has much less to give in return. She's married and has Titus on the side. Her metal bones get knocked around every night. I can't think of anything she's done for me. I don't find her attractive. In fact, she frightens me.*

"Bothers me that she brought that man in with her," Titus said. "He creeps the hell out of me. Why is no one talking about that? We let him have the run of the place like it's nothing. I'd keep the bastard under guard. Or exterminate his ass."

"Same here," Neva said.

"Why?" Archer asked.

"Oh, don't come in here as his defender," Titus said. "You can't be trusted on the matter. He's given you too much. You owe him."

"He's got you in his palm, Grand Vizier," Neva said. "He'll own you soon. I know you."

"I didn't say I trusted him. I wanna know why he bothers you.

Me—I feel sorry for him. How would you behave if you'd been alone for a decade? He's warped. Of course he's strange."

"Okay, he's warped. Why the hell would *that* not bother me?" Titus asked. He put his weight on the table. "I don't trust him. His story borders on impossible."

"Oh, it crossed way over that line," Neva said.

Titus drank to that.

"Weston would not put a settlement on Shanidar without advertising it," Titus went on. "That's a fact. It would be news. They'd have no reason to hide it. In the end, they do these things for money."

"Weston might not have talked about it much after it failed, maybe, but they'd certainly boast about the settlement attempt at launch," Neva said.

"Could be a time alteration on their part," Lyra added. "Maybe they boasted then erased the record."

"No," Titus said. "They're not that competent."

"Werdegast tells a plausible story," Archer said. "At least to me. We should give him a chance."

"Famous last words right there," Titus said. "Hell is filled with men who give devils a chance."

Neva snorted. "Now you're being corny."

Titus drank again.

"I'll hear him out," Lyra said, "but I think Delaney knew about Seven-Macaw. No one here can look me in the eye and say they believe her about that. That she was somehow ignorant of the whole fucking thing. That's not reality. As if she was some homemaker kept in the dark. She's too ambitious."

"No chance," Neva agreed. "That was a lie. I'd guess Rinaldi knew, as well."

"What does your girlfriend think?" Titus asked.

Archer drained his glass. He held it aloft and let the final drop hit his tongue. At the mention of Brynn, his mind tightened into a knot. He touched his cheek to see if it was numbing. It was dead enough for surgery. He contemplated another glass.

"Well?" Neva asked. "What does the little archaeologist think? I know she has opinions."

Laughter rang around the table.

Archer heard himself speaking, but he was outside of his body.

"I don't know what Brynn thinks anymore. She doesn't bother to tell me. I'm going to kick her out."

"What?" Lyra said. "Why?"

"She didn't congratulate me."

"Fine. Forget Brynn," Titus said. "Point is, Werdegast is lying. Delaney is lying."

"When the *Bedivere* arrives, we'll join their settlement," Neva said.

"What about your old man?" Titus asked.

Neva shot him a look.

"I think you should start your own settlement and make yourself Lieutenant Governor," Lyra said.

"Not a bad idea." Titus was laughing again. "With two new settlements, we'll have a war brewing. I could reach out to Penglai. Make this shithole another La Venta."

"I'll conquer Seven-Macaw," Lyra said. "I hear there are no chirr flies there."

"Are any of you—"

Neva stopped when the door to the Board of Education opened, and in walked Kell. Berthold Werdegast trailed behind the machine.

"And here," Kell said with a sweep of its arm, "is a den of debauchery, a house of sin and hypocrisy of the lowest order. Unlike the pottery studio we visited, this isn't recreation I envy."

"Kell is giving our visitor a tour," Titus said. "I guess I'm on your side now, Archer. I feel sorry for him."

All eyes went to Werdegast. He took the staring in stride. He moved like he enjoyed the attention.

"He's wearing Naylor's clothes," Archer said. "I didn't notice that before."

"He needs the wig," Titus said.

A drunken thought—one without an anchor—bobbed and drifted away. *The Lieutenant Governor was naked on the wall, stripped of his clothes, wearing flies. Werdegast slipped into his name, slipped into his wardrobe, slipped into his bed, slipped into his wife.*

"Alcohol is an important part of the farmer's toolkit," Kell explained. "And that holds true for most everyone in this lower social stratum of Shanidar. If you like, I can show you where this vile drug is distilled."

Werdegast greeted the men and women he passed on his way to the bar. He was silent until he reached that spot. The stools were full, so he stood on the other side, facing the room. Wearing a father's disapproval, he seemed poised for a Puritan blast of temperance. His concern, however, was not for the drug that flowed in this backroom. His concern was deeper.

"You dislike this machine," Werdegast said.

He talked as if he spoke to each colonist one-on-one, face-to-face. His voice was low, yet it reached everyone. He scanned the room. He repeated himself, louder, more forcefully. "You dislike this machine."

Kell joined the others, watching the stranger. The Board of Education was quiet except for the rattle of ducts.

"As do I."

Werdegast placed his hands on the bar.

Kell's falcon eyes had a livewire twitch. "The winery brings to mind—"

"What if I told you that its fix was a simple one?" Werdegast asked. Light lay on his shoulders. He was taller than Kell by ten centimeters. A large man, but slender. His face was no longer gaunt, as it had been a day prior.

"Yeah, if you bury Kell with the Lieutenant Governor," a drunken man said. "I'll personally row him out."

"And take Delaney with him," said another.

Werdegast paused. He found the speaker. "With even less work than hauling them to the sea," he said. "It will be more beneficial to us if this thing functions as it's intended to function. Everyone in this settlement has a role to serve."

He's a good mechanic, Archer thought.

"I'm a good mechanic," the stranger echoed. "Shall we turn this room into an operating theater?"

To Archer's surprise, Neva's chair kicked back. She stood.

"Not all of us dislike the machine," she said. "If you—" She stopped short of an ultimatum. Her mind resisted. Normally, Neva would've charged ahead. She was a woman who'd known terror and confronted it. Fear in her heart was in short supply. Yet she stopped short of delivering a threat. Aggression drained from her face.

"I will fix it," the stranger said. "Not harm it."

"That's his personality," Neva said. "Kell has a right to it." Her voice dropped. "He is not something that must be fixed."

"Speak for yourself," said a woman in the corner. "She's as much a machine as that thing."

"Now wait a minute," Titus interjected.

"Fix him," a man said. "Get the fuck out of here, Neva. Let's see it."

Neva looked at Archer, Titus, and Lyra. Then she turned on a heel and left.

"Even Kell has friends," Lyra said. "She'll get over it. Fix it," she shouted, getting into the spirit.

"Clear a table," Werdegast said.

"What do you intend to do, sir?" Kell asked.

Archer tried to rub intoxication from his eyes. He received the scene in waves.

I hate Kell, he thought. *This is good. Isn't it?*

"I want to help you," Werdegast said to the machine. "You will not be harmed."

"Shouldn't Dr. Alaric Rhys be present?" Kell asked. The android's voice took on an odd tone, as though it asked for its father. "Shouldn't he be consulted? I am Dr. Rhys's property."

"Why should Rhys disapprove? Do you not wear him down with your endless chatter? Are you not incompetent when it comes to the needs of his research? Do you think he brought you along as a friend and gadfly? That he dragged you here at enormous expense to annoy everyone?"

A path parted and a table was swept clean. Werdegast took Kell by the shoulder, and he led the machine around the bar. Kell obeyed. The crowd tightened into an eager ring.

This is good, isn't it? Archer thought. He looked at Titus and Lyra. Titus was uneasy, watching the door. Lyra was keen.

"Get on the table," Werdegast ordered.

"My weight is too much for the structure. I am not a creature of destruction."

Werdegast kicked the table away. It was not light, but it slid under his touch.

The crowd widened and constricted.

"Then sit. Sit in this chair and face the wall."

Kell complied. The machine sat.

"Tell us a story," Werdegast said. "Let it be your last. You won't feel a thing."

The crowd watched, spellbound.

With a few deft movements, Werdegast opened a compartment on the back of Kell's neck.

Kell's amalgamation of a Horus face was incapable of emotion. But the way its black eyes moved, rapid as a sleeping brain, communicated what can only be described as terror.

With Werdegast's first touch, Kell's rough-hewn beak softened.

This is good, Archer thought. *He—it's an abomination. It's broken. It needs to be fixed.*

"My situation is redolent," Kell said, "of a folk tale from Russia of the Tsars. This was once a dazzling land of winter."

"Go on," Werdegast said. "The stage is yours one last time, machine. Tell one more tale."

"What tools do you need?" a man asked.

"No tools," the wanderer said. "The operation is not so delicate as that. It's a simple adjustment. Although something more drastic must be done about the machine's ghastly face. We'll fix that next."

"After a harsh winter, spring is an eruption." Kell's voice was less human, more mechanical. "In a forest where the spring sun shone over the land, there came an ambitious fly. He was so unique that he built himself a castle. The fly moved into the castle and was content with his labor. But his home was enviable. So a louse came to the door and inquired about the occupant of this magnificent edifice. *I live here*, said the fly. *Now I do, too,* said the louse. Then a flea arrived with the same question. And she moved in. And then came a mouse that moved in, as well. And then came a greedy fox that moved in. And, finally, there came a bear to the fly's castle. When he inquired about the occupants, voices that numbered five returned. Since the bear could not move in, which is what he really wished to do, he crushed the castle with his paw."

Werdegast closed the compartment. "It's as simple as that," he said.

Kell was silent. The eyes no longer moved.

"What the hell does that mean?" asked a man. "He's such a bizarre sonnuva bitch."

"I think that was fear," Lyra whispered between Archer and Titus. There was an edge of excitement in her voice.

"A machine can't experience fear," Archer said. "This is good. Necessary."

Destroyers who destroy the correct things are necessary.

Titus gave him a side-eyed glance.

Kell heard the question about the meaning of its tale, but the machine was not interested in responding. Explaining the story was no longer part of its duty.

"Henceforth, you will speak only when spoken to," Werdegast said.

Kell stared.

"What of its face?" Werdegast asked. He scanned the tavern. The people regarded him with a mix of admiration and disquietude.

A drunken man climbed onto the bar.

"Take it off," he said.

A few people cheered. A few wrung their hands and looked at the exit.

"In keeping with the Lieutenant Governor's want of truth," Werdegast told Kell, "you will remove your mask. Do so now. No more hiding. No more imitation. Show them what you are."

There was no hesitation. Kell did not question the order.

This is necessary, Archer thought, but he grew ill again. He felt the nausea in his face, felt it down into his limbs. His stomach moved. Cold sweat beaded his brow. Icy air breathed over the sweat.

Using finely articulated fingers, Kell wriggled beneath a suture in its ill-drawn feathers. The machine worked its hand downward, loosening the falcon face from nape to mandible. Then it loosened the mask from mandible to the ear opposite. When the circuit was complete, Kell peeled the face, tugging, ripping flesh where the adhesive was tightest, separating a coating that resembled papier-mâché from the white, slick skull. The skull had substantial holes where the original beak had been smashed and where the left side of the head had caved. Clear fluid dripped from the lower jaw. The face was gone up to the eyes, dangling free, a death's head visage.

Nausea flooded Archer. He rushed to the door with his head down, concentrating on not vomiting. He held in the urge as he pushed through the greenhouse. Sweat covered his face, wetted his hair.

The sun was gone and the Boxgrove was dark. Wind shuddered the walls. A magnificent storm of gales and thunder raged.

When rain struck Archer's face, he spewed the contents of his stomach into the rippling mud. Hands on his knees, he retched.

Rain soaked his clothes and pooled around his boots, washing him clean.

In the tumult, Cullen Archer's hand went to the Serpent Tongue. His other hand fumbled for the oxygen at his belt.

chapter
twelve

THE ROW of screens dimmed black and then returned to white. The texts, rendered in three scripts, were reloading, but the process was taking too long. Thunder vibrated in the bunker-like floor and walls. Vials quaked. Lights flickered.

"God forbid power to the servers goes down," Rhys said, looming over Brynn's shoulder.

She stood to remove herself from his shadow. She stepped from the Owl, which rested against the wall on a surgical cot borrowed from Dr. Seward, to a shelf that held the creature's wooden figurine.

When the monitors went dark again, the lights went with them, and an emergency red bulb ignited in the corner of the room. Following an electronic hiss and sigh, everything shut down. The circulating air stopped droning. Rain drummed the roof. Wind battered the dormitory. Except for storm turbulence, the room was still.

"Damn it all to hell," Rhys said.

Immediately, the temperature in Rhys's quarters ticked upward. The dorms were like heat boxes.

Brynn retrieved the penlight from the pocket of her cloak.

Thankfully, the cell was charged. She switched it on, cutting a lance through the red darkness.

Rhys turned on a light in his left eye. Across the room, his eyeball glowed white.

Brynn placed her beam on the microscopic text that ran along one of the figurine's arms—the same Hieratic script used on the Owl. She and Rhys had discovered numerous texts on the bodies, and each word was no larger than a grain of sand. Every line, it appeared, communicated something new. There was little repetition. Without the magnification of the screens, the text resembled a thin line drawn with a palsied hand.

They're like illustrated men, Brynn thought. *Tattooed.*

A solar battery heaved, causing lights to blaze, but it was a teasing effort. The swell of power didn't stick, as if Vandalia drew breath but didn't exhale.

An odd thought occurred to Brynn.

"If Kell was restored," she said, "what could he do with Hieratic?"

Rhys's light moved along the back wall.

"Why do you ask that?"

He shuffled nearer, kicking through junk on the floor.

Brynn looked down to avoid the blinding eye.

"A restored Kell," he said, "would brute force the lock. He'd run through dictionaries in tongues I do not know. He would make progress, but he wouldn't be a magical key to solving the riddle. Even with him, it would take time."

"How long?"

"Months at the least. As it is, he cannot concentrate for more than a few minutes per session. Without him, it will take us years. Restored, he'd devote months on end without ceasing. He could contemplate one letter for a week without hesitation. At full capacity, he's impressive. Why are you thinking of Kell?"

"I don't know. It came to me."

"You're not alone. As the lights went, the hope of a restored Kell struck me too."

"Yes. In another voice," Brynn said, "close to my own. But not quite."

Rhys strafed the Owl's arm with light. "I'm not plumbing the mystical for answers. Not yet." His light moved downward. "Damn this storm," he muttered. "I've been thinking of a curious thing. Werdegast is a German name. Do you know what it means?"

"I don't."

"'I shall be a guest.'"

"And what does Berthold mean?"

"Germanic, as well. It means 'bright leader.'"

"Another false name. No more real than William Naylor."

"The possibility that he delivers the name with a wink occurred to me."

Thudding, unmistakable footfalls in the corridor broke the quiet. Kell was outside. Curiously, he didn't enter.

Brynn went to the door and slid it open.

Kell waited on the other side of the threshold, standing in darkness. A red bulb on the baseboard caught the dripping hem of his long, cassock-like raiment.

"I see the storm ended your tour," she said. "Where'd you leave Werdegast?"

For a moment, she imagined the stranger outside the north gate, suffering the downpour, awaiting the return of his guide. The amusement was short-lived. There was something off about Kell's face. The glow from inside the room reached his jaw. The surface glimmered.

"Come inside," Brynn said.

The android moved into the room. Glass rattled with his presence. Kell offered no greeting.

Brynn ran her light up the length of his form. When she reached Kell's exposed skull, her mouth went dry. She stepped back.

He's terribly hurt, she thought.

Rhys's light trembled.

"What happened to you, Kell?" he asked.

The Horus mask of painted feathers had been removed, exposing the white frame below. The dent was gone from the side of his head and his neck no longer bled exhaust. Clear oil beaded on his skull and hands, and the odor was peculiarly sharp. The stink of his excretion filled the room.

"I have been corrected," Kell answered. His voice was flat but clear. He stressed the final word.

Brynn's blood ran hot. Her shock turned into anger.

"What do you mean 'corrected'?"

"I've been restored to my normal functionality. Dr. Rhys, you'll be pleased to learn that I am, once more, fully functional."

Brynn looked at Rhys. According to Weston's psychometrics, she had no talent for precognition. Nor, she assumed, did Rhys. Their thoughts about Kell's restoration, she realized, were implanted.

Rhys was more curious than angry. He went to the corner of the room and opened a cabinet in the wall. He returned with a keyboard. He placed the instrument on the table. The battery light was weak, but the device had juice.

"Sit down and play," he said.

Kell offered no comment, but he sat in the chair that was offered. He moved his hands to the keys. And he played. But it was not the melody in D minor that he'd always played before. The machine played a dramatically different piece, one in a major key with an upbeat tempo.

Jarringly out of character, Kell played ragtime.

"Stop," Rhys said.

Kell lifted his hands.

"What was that?" Brynn asked.

"That," Rhys said, "was the 'Maple Leaf Rag.' One of my requests when Kell was manufactured—he plays Scott Joplin. He hasn't played it since La Venta." Although the answer was obvious, Rhys asked, "Who did this to you, Kell?"

"Mr. Berthold Werdegast," Kell said. Without the mask, his eyes were too large. The black orbs stared ahead. "He is my savior. I'm in his debt."

"As am I," Rhys said, impressed.

Fury guided Brynn's next actions. She was at the door and into the hall. Tremendous wind shook the corridor, threatening to peel away the roof. Condensation ran in rivulets down the walls.

"Where are you going?" Rhys said. "Ms. Silva!" His beam cut through the darkness.

Brynn whirled.

"'*As am I?*' Really? Is this not a violation of your trust?"

"I wanted Kell to be restored. This is a remarkable boon to our project. We were just discussing it. It's a mir—"

"We were discussing it because he made us discuss it."

"That's preposterous."

"Rhys, he's been reduced to a shell. Werdegast had no right. That thing isn't Kell."

"This is precisely how Kell behaves, Ms. Silva. This is how he was on La Venta. Everything you understand about him has been a malfunction."

"It was his personality."

"His head was crushed."

"And now he's been lobotomized."

Brynn fought back the tears, but she couldn't control them. The emotion was overwhelming—a barrier was broken. She kept the tremble from her voice.

"Ms. Silva, Kell is fixed. Come back inside. This is a cause for celebration. I don't care how Werdegast went about it."

You're not human, she thought. That was that. Brynn started for the door at the end of the hall.

"Where are you going?"

"To find the Lieutenant Governor," she shouted. "And I'm not filing a fucking complaint with Lord Rinaldi."

Brynn pushed through the door and slammed it shut behind her. The noise was nothing in the wind. Gales came down from the mountains, swirling debris through the alleys of Vandalia. The edges of rooftops lifted and fell. A gust blew her hair in a straight line and stung her eyes. The wind blotted her inner voice, making it difficult to think. Her thoughts were shouts.

Personality is not a malfunction. It's the sum of experience. Kell was a thinking creature. He had no right. To be fixed is not to be wiped clean. And, Rhys, how dare you find a silver lining? You cold fucking spider.

Brynn trudged through mud, wind, and drizzle to the gate. Something guided her in that direction rather than toward Delaney's doorstep. Intuition or another bout of precognition or a trespassing thought—she didn't know which, but the feeling was intense. She ascended the slick stairs as wind howled from the mountains, bending trees, breaking branches, sending leaves aloft in swirling devils. The netting that covered the platform had been ripped away.

It was then that Brynn spotted the figure of Delaney von Kleist —the widow, noblewoman, and esteemed Lieutenant Governor. She walked the trail, climbing to the Owl's Lair. She held her wig in her hand, and its curls blew like tassels. Delaney followed the path of her husband. She walked alone.

Brynn wasted no time. She jumped from the platform, splashing into mud. She sprinted through the gateway and gained the trail. A foreign thought filled her mind.

This is necessary.

She denied the words with frantic zeal, suppressed them, willed them away, pushing back as stoutly as the wind pushed. Brynn ran until she caught the Lieutenant Governor on the esplanade. She heaved for want of breath. Her chest burned and her head pounded.

Delaney's eyes were filmed over, glossed like her mind was arrested in a dream. Her head was bald, her scalp slick with rain. Makeup ran down her neck, melting into her fine blouse. A face like this did not receive questions. She was catatonic.

"You're going home," Brynn said.

It took every ounce of will to be firm. She grabbed Delaney's shoulder.

The Lieutenant Governor jerked loose, freeing her arm. She started forward again. She headed for the thieves' entrance, accessing the same wall on which her husband died.

Brynn grabbed her, this time with more force, and she yanked the old woman backward. Delaney fell on the slick ground, hard enough to break bones. The wind caught her wig, blowing it along the stones and into the valley.

Brynn fought for balance.

Delaney clambered to her knees. She braced herself, palms downward, bent like an animal. Her back heaved, and she covered the ground with the contents of her stomach. With a jolt of horror, Brynn watched. What Delaney vomited wasn't bile. She spewed chirr flies from her throat, fat and glossy as blood-engorged ticks. She vomited a thousand insects. More. A writhing carpet of them. A rising dune. The things were alive. They were too obese and wet to fly away, so they wriggled with madness at a meal interrupted, and their chitinous wings vibrated in frustrated, impotent bursts.

This is good. This is necessary.

No, Brynn thought. *No!*

Delaney lifted her head. With recognition came humiliation. She began to sob. She spat loose flies and pieces of wings from her tongue. When she looked at the wall, there was light in her eyes. The old woman moaned, out of her mind with grief. Delaney screamed into the wind.

Staring at the insects that struggled in the geometry of the Owls' art, a sobering but inane thought struck Brynn. Girding herself against the cyclonic airstream, she thought, *what is happening here? Who are you? What are you?*

Simple but profound questions.

She knelt, put her arm around Delaney, and pulled the Lieutenant Governor close.

There's no one to turn to, Brynn thought. *No one to fix your problems.*

The thought carried a double-edged meaning. On one side, it was galvanizing. It lit a fire to stand and act. On the other, it was an insidious threat. Brynn didn't know if the thought had originated in her mind or if it was planted.

chapter
thirteen

BRYNN WALKED through the gate with Delaney in her arms, cradling the woman like a lost and wounded child. She was a pathetic, limp figure: death-like and soddened, coated in trail debris, vomit, and mud. The Lieutenant Governor had gone through a range of states, ending with a cataleptic rigidity that left her face down on the path. She wouldn't respond, wouldn't move, scarcely breathed, was barely alive. Brynn had had no other choice. She sacrificed her back, carrying Delaney the remaining distance. By the time she placed Delaney on a bench that fronted the dormitories, Brynn's body was shot through and burning. Adrenaline kept her moving.

Three men watched her act of heroism, but they made no move to assist. Their stares were blank, empty of concern. None of the men spoke.

Brynn stretched the ache from her spine, then she started down the duckboards. The storm had passed and the sun had returned. Some metal siding had been loosened, and roofing was curled here and there. Chairs in the courtyard were scattered. The mosquito nets were gone. Fallen timber littered the surrounding forest, with entire swaths of trees felled. A storm was not extraordinary. That no chirr fly orgy followed the tempest, however, was. The gauzy webs of mating insects were unnaturally absent. There were no flies at all in the vicinity.

The stranger's words were not far from her mind.

It's curious that the bugs have no interest in you.

It is, isn't it? We made a deal down south. They know better.

Brynn reached Seward's clinic and opened the door. She rushed beneath the Fabergé ostrich eggs and checked the patient room. The beds where Werdegast and Delaney had convalesced were empty, tight, and clean. The power was still off, and the monitors were dead black, the machines quiet. Two windows allowed in hazy sunlight. Brynn found the doctor in her office. In comparison to the spartan patient area, her room was as lush as a Victorian parlor, overstuffed with décor. On the wall was a relic of twenty-two cockroach shells, arrayed in a pinwheel.

Seward held a tablet. Having been absorbed in the reading, she looked up, nonplussed. Light was on her shoulders. She placed the device on a giltwood desk.

Brynn found Seward to be a gaudy, tacky woman, but she was trustworthy and reliable. Bad taste did not equal deceit. Why she'd come to Shanidar was an enigma, although Brynn favored the divorce assumption prevalent among gossipers. What better way to escape a marriage than to put parsecs between you and your spouse? And Weston, by all accounts, paid doctors handsomely, especially surgeons.

"Yes?" Seward asked. "What do you need, Ms. Silva?"

"It's Delaney," Brynn said. Her voice was calm despite the turbulence she felt inside. "She needs you."

Seward wasted no time. Dutifully, she stood and slid around the desk. She slipped on shoes.

"At her home?" the doctor asked. "That's where I left her." She grabbed a black satchel, equally Victorian, from a ledge by the door.

Brynn touched her arm. She shook her head.

"She tried to get to the ruins. She was going to... I stopped her."

"Come on. Tell me on the way. Tell me everything."

As the women passed through the corridor into open air, Brynn relayed what she knew. She kept the report free of paranoia. The details were alarming enough without musing on Werdegast and possible causes.

When the dormitory loomed, Seward rushed ahead. Delaney hadn't risen from the bench. She hadn't moved at all. She lay where Brynn deposited her, although a small group of people had since congregated. They were more curious than helpful, as if ogling storm damage. It was a wonder they hadn't poked her with a stick.

"Without the wig, I didn't know it was her," a man said to Seward.

"I didn't realize it was a wig," said another.

Brynn wanted to rage at them, but she refrained.

"Dear God, back away," Seward said. "Get back. Move."

The spectators parted.

The doctor knelt at the bench. Her hand went to Delaney's neck, and she searched for a pulse with her fingertips. When she was satisfied the Lieutenant Governor lived, she turned to Brynn and shaded her eyes from the sun.

"Go to the Naylor home and find Jarvis Rinaldi," she said. "If he isn't in the servant quarters, check around. He's never far. He'll need to know. Tell him to meet me at the clinic." She gestured around. "The rest of you will help me get her to a bed."

The milling people were noncommittal. They began to slink away.

"Now!" Seward shouted.

Brynn cut toward the middle of the settlement, splashing mud, passing through narrow gaps between metal buildings. The Naylor residence stood apart from the other structures at the rear of the House of Burgesses. No buildings crowded it. A breeze twisted the

Weston flags that hung as bunting around the structure. Breathlessly, she approached. The gold plaque on a post out front read: *Lieutenant Governor's Palace.* It was, indeed, the finest home in the settlement, but it was closer to a ranch house than a mansion. It was a square comprised of four rooms, shielded in white metal. At each corner was the Weston logo: a nondescript planet labeled *You are Here* and a bed of stars labeled *We are Here.*

As she neared, it occurred to Brynn that she'd never set foot inside the residence. She was never invited to one of the formal dinners. The front door was open, wrenched by a gale, bent outward. Judging by its shape, the door was unclosable. Rainwater pooled around the threshold. The immense stress of the moment had Brynn entering without question. She rushed forward.

Inside, the small foyer was shadowed and quiet. The air was muggy and close. Three doors, one to each side and one in the center, stood open. The home had been left in a hurry. A tapestry near the entrance fluttered against the wall, torn, thrashed by rain. Stitched into it was a sentimental ocean scene—a wooden ship tossed under a black sky, a voyage into unknown waters.

Brynn tried to imagine what had gone through Delaney's mind the moment she decided to head for the Owl's Lair. She'd walked out the door and left her home to the elements. Brynn wondered what had gone through her husband's mind. They were proud people.

Above, the roof was damaged, so a spear of sunlight reached through the center doorway. As to the location of the servant quarters, she could only guess. She passed under the stream of light. A long hall, decorated with more tapestries, more scenes of sea voyages and portraits of ancient privateers, culminated in two doors, one to the left and one to the right. The left door was closed, and the door on the right was partially open. Sunlight from a window within filled the crevice. This was a private bedroom.

Brynn felt like a voyeur as she peered inside, although she

didn't know why the idea of trespassing bothered her. Her heart rate went up. Humidity had her sweating profusely.

A man sat at a table that fronted an unkempt bed. Unlike the cots in the dorms, it was a bed for two. The man had his back to the doorway. His hands were busy. At first, Brynn assumed it was Lord Rinaldi, carrying out his clerical work in a patch of sunlight. But the man wasn't typing, nor was he scribbling notes with a stylus. There was a rhythm to his gestures, and he muttered to himself, absorbed. The words were too low, too quick to make out. He wore, curiously, the mantle of Delaney's husband, topped at the shoulders with hawk skulls—a garment that should've gone with the man to the pyre.

Brynn stilled her breathing and made herself slight against the wall. Sweat was so heavy on her forehead that she had to wipe it from her eyes. She did so with delicacy, keeping her sleeve from rustling.

As she listened, the man's muttering became clearer, but the language was unfamiliar. It was a musical tongue, flowing with curlicues.

The man in the bedroom was Berthold Werdegast. And in his hand was a priceless talisman, Delaney's relic, a piece of an extinct feline. He stroked the fur of a mummified paw with his thumb.

Brynn suppressed the urge to chase him from the room. She watched through the crack. And, in watching, she beheld a wondrous thing. The paw loosened under Werdegast's touch, animating from a thing of rigid death to something that approximated life. The rounded toes wriggled and flexed, and dark, hard claws, wickedly large, extended from the tips. Werdegast touched the claw points, admiring their sharpness. He scraped his skin against them. Then the claws retracted, covered by fur.

The sleek movement pleased him. Werdegast chuckled.

He placed the paw on the table. Then, with his index finger, he stroked the spotted fur in straight lines from claw to severed bone. Back and forth. Back and forth. Each stroke he extended farther, but at no time did his fingertip touch air. With every movement, an arm grew from the paw, spreading in fractals. The relic stirred with resurrection. It was a chimerical, impossible thing. When Werdegast reached an elbow joint, he stopped speaking and began to turn his neck. The chair beneath him groaned. The table shifted.

He knows you're here, Brynn thought. *He wanted you to see.* Panic seized her.

She did not wait. She couldn't look at Werdegast and have him look at her. Not now. Not in this moment, this state of mind. Brynn whirled from the door, her thoughts jigsawed and fractured.

Werdegast had spoken the animal into existence. It was a private act of creation.

Being silent in the hall was impossible, so Brynn ran toward the light of the broken door. She ran until her lungs burned, and she refused to look back.

She didn't see the stranger in the doorway, watching her as he had watched her from the desert, arrested in stillness.

chapter
fourteen

THE NEURAL FILM did something it had never done before. The plot changed. Archer had heard rumors of such things occurring, of locations and characters warping over time, but he'd never experienced the shock of witnessing an alteration. It was like watching a man morph into a chair. Devotional films changed for one of two reasons. First, the implant malfunctioned. Trauma could cause that. Second, the viewer was mentally ill.

Archer sat up on the bench. He was on the shallow side of drunk and the recovery side of sick. Mentally, he felt like a carcass on top of a garbage pile under the sun. Physically, he wore wet clothes and shivered in the breeze.

Being drunk—no matter how drunk—can't change a film.

He switched on his father.

Were you watching? Did you see that?

The ghost didn't answer.

Archer talked anyway.

The jaguar didn't let me touch it. She got up and walked off. And then a flock of macaws swooped in and covered the ruins. On top of the pyramid, there was a large macaw, three times the size of the others. He had scarlet feathers and a white beak. And he was pissed. That's never happened before. Then it got stranger. The big macaw spoke. He said, "Focus on real things, on things you can touch. Earth is beneath your feet. This isn't real, you twit."

Archer looked at the sky. Twilight was nigh and the power was out. With the heat in the dorms, colonists moved around outside, talking, passing the time.

The macaw is obvious. That came from the first settlement. Is that traumatic?

He didn't like the other option.

I'm not losing my mind. I have more clarity than I did a month ago.

His telepathy cilium went off, shrill as a migraine, and his ears burned. Archer closed his eyes and read a message from Lord Rinaldi. In red, serious letters: *Report to the clinic immediately. This is an official summons from the Office of the Lieutenant Governor.*

The storm, he figured. *The son of a bitch is going to put us on cleanup duty.*

Archer's mind returned to the jaguar. She let him get near, and then she slinked away from his hand, as if he were a stranger in a strange land, unwelcome. It hurt his heart.

I'll get a goddamn refund if it does it again. What's the warranty on these things?

Indignant, Archer walked to the clinic. A small fraction of Vandalia had been summoned. No more than fifteen people. Brynn was not present. Titus was. He gave Archer a nod.

"Feeling better?" he asked.

"Hardly. Know what this is about?"

"Restoring the power, I'd guess. For me. For you, no idea. You look like shit."

"Thanks."

Jarvis Rinaldi emerged from Seward's door. He was not an old man, but he comported himself like one. He wore an androgynous wig of the Versailles school, shaved his head, and kept a pencil-thin mustache. Black curls reached his narrow shoulders. His hands were soft and pallid, shaded with lavender ruff. He rolled his R's to cover a speech impediment.

"Rarely," he said, "has a colony suffered so much misfortune in such a short time. I assure you, however, that things will recover. And soon."

The sky undulated with curtains of electrical green. The chirr flies, Archer noted with curiosity, did not weave against the backdrop. He searched for a sign of them. Nothing. Not a single insect.

Rinaldi pulled out a tablet and read aloud.

"Item, the Lieutenant Governor, Delaney von Kleist, is recovering. She is under the watchful care of Dr. Seward. She will address everyone in no more than two days."

He held the device in one hand while the other hand fluttered.

"Item, Bell and Pinter will have the solar batteries running and power restored before nightfall. That is an order."

"Great," Titus muttered.

"Item, to improve morale, Archer will begin his work on the von Kleist reliquary at once. The Lieutenant Governor will disperse relics at the House of Burgesses in no more than two days. Hold any requests until an audit is completed."

Holy shit.

See? the ghost said. *What did I tell you about getting drunk? You're in no state to—*

Enough, Archer thought. *I'm ready. I've never been more ready.*
He willed sobriety.

"Item, Tanner and Queen, the gem scavengers of the coast, have returned from the sea. Cedric von Kleist was committed to the deep without incident. He is at rest."

"Did he float?" Titus asked.

Rinaldi checked his notes.

"Yes," he said finally. "Why is that significant?"

"The water rejected him. He'll wash back up. At rest, my ass."

The image was troubling.

Rinaldi went on without comment.

"Item, the expedition to Seven-Macaw will leave on the morrow. Dr. Alaric Rhys has selected, and the Lieutenant Governor has approved, the following individuals. Step forward as your name is called."

Rinaldi proceeded with four names, the last of which was Brynn Silva. Two men and one woman stepped forward. All were members of the intelligentsia. Rhys didn't select any workers who could handle a wrench. Brynn was the only member of the expedition absent.

Out of secondhand embarrassment, Archer raised his hand.

Rinaldi acknowledged him.

"Brynn will be ready," Archer said. "I'll find her. She accepts."

The secretary nodded.

"That is all," he said. "Have a good evening."

The clinic door opened and closed, and Rinaldi was gone.

Archer turned to Titus. The engineer was in no better shape than him. He had a liquor aura. His pupils were off.

"You look like shit yourself. Do I need to get dig lights together, or will the power be back in time?"

"Not sure," Titus admitted.

Pinter, the other engineer, came up and clapped a hand on Titus's shoulder. He was a bright-eyed, sun-blistered cherry, sober as Sunday.

"Sure it will," he said. "Thirty minutes tops. Mark that down." Then to Titus: "You're nothing a couple syringes can't cure."

"Good luck," Archer said.

Titus muttered.

The two engineers were off, Pinter's hand against Titus's back, pushing him forward.

I could use a panacea shot myself, Archer thought. *To breathe wine on the von Kleist reliquary is a disgrace. Especially by me.*

You mean the Grand Vizier, the ghost said.

I mean a man of faith. A believer. Unlike you.

Facing Brynn will be sobering. Start there.

Damn it. Why do I care? If she wants to blow her opportunity, I should let her. I have no stake in that. Why do I have to find her?

You want to make sure she's gone while you hand out relics.

Yeah. Admittedly.

Archer collected himself and started his search. Brynn was either with Dr. Rhys or at home in bed, he assumed. He decided to check the latter first. He wasn't keen on seeing Rhys. If he had to deal with the linguist tonight, he'd have difficulty biting his tongue. He'd unload on the man, say things he couldn't take back.

Why are you angry with him?

Dad, I'm pissed at the world. He's part of Brynn's problem. He and Kell. I'll cave in his motherfucking glass bulb of a skull.

Archer made the short walk to the dormitories. The night was pleasant.

There are no chirr flies. As if the wind blew them away along with the humidity. I didn't even put on a new coating of repellent. I'm going to see great things, he thought. *Wondrous things. The inner sanctum. The holy of holies.*

Archer switched off his father. Using the manual slide on the door, he entered the hallway. Emergency lights lined the baseboards. The darkness that hung above the red was eerily silent. He stepped to his door. No power, no lock. He slid it open without knocking, and there, on the right cot, was Brynn.

She jumped at Archer's intrusion. She had her knees to her chest, and she'd been crying. The sheets around her were rumpled.

Damn it, he thought.

He sat on the cot opposite, and he faced her. He was a stranger in the room.

"You stink," she observed.

"I haven't showered."

"You smell like wine. You're sweating it."

"Oh."

"It's strong. Wine and vomit."

"Okay. I get it. Were you not summoned by Rinaldi?" Archer asked. He sat stiffly, his hands clasped above his knees.

The room was stale.

"I was. I'm not going to Seven-Macaw."

"Why not? I already told Rinaldi you would. Please, for the love of God, do not ask to accompany me to the Von Kleist reliquary. You have no place there. No right. It would be," he said heavily, "sacrilegious. Profane."

The mere thought of her intruding had him heating up. His guts shriveled.

"Cullen, are you insane? Have you lost your mind?"

Brynn threw her legs over the edge of the bed. She planted her feet.

"Tell me why you didn't show tonight and why you aren't going," he said. "Explain."

"I don't know if I should tell you shit."

"You better tell me. I'm not taking this from you anymore, Brynn."

"Or what?"

Archer didn't go that far. He let silence slip between them.

"If you can get over your power trip for a second, I'll tell you."

She stared at him through a wave of crimson.

"I'm uptight," he said. "If you don't want to go with me, we can get back to being civil. That sincerely offended me."

"You're drunk off your ass."

"Yes. At least I was. It was a celebration of life."

"You'll listen?"

Archer nodded.

"I don't trust Berthold Werdegast," she said simply. "I think he's dangerous. I think he's lying."

When that registered, Archer asked, "Lying about what?"

"Everything. Down to who he is. What he is."

"What is he?"

"Stop interrupting me."

"Fine."

"Do you know what Werdegast means?"

Archer sighed. "You know I don't."

"'I shall be a guest.'"

"Okay."

"That doesn't strike you as oddly on the nose?"

"Names don't matter here. So what if he made it up? I'm starting to think you're a conspiracy theorist. What else?"

Brynn told him of Delaney's march to the ruins, and she told him of Kell.

When she finished her rant about the machine, he cut in.

"You're misunderstanding about Kell," Archer said. "What Werdegast did wasn't malicious. It was kindness. I was there. I watched it from beginning to end. He was gentle."

"Kindness? Kell was lobotomized, Cullen. He might as well have taken an ice pick to his brain."

"It wasn't like that at all. Kell was fixed. How does Rhys feel about it?"

"He's as ignorant and prejudiced as you. He's happy."

"I have no prejudice in me. Kell is a machine. It has a role to fill. A purpose to serve. It'll serve better than before."

"Why remove his face?"

"Because it made people like me uncomfortable. It was an abomination."

"I genuinely hate you," Brynn said.

"No, you don't. You just know I'm right. You think you're the smartest girl in the room, and when you're not, you hate everybody else in the room."

Brynn exhaled.

"What else?"

"I don't like how he's beguiled you with the relics. He's dangling a prize in front of you, Cullen. Werdegast wants your support. He wants you to come to his defense. It's working."

"That's outrageous. And it's insulting. I think he values my knowledge." He pointed at a book on a shelf in the corner—a bound compendium of *Zoobooks* issues. It was one of the few physical books on the planet, and one of Archer's prized possessions. His mother had bought it for him at an estate sale. "How many people have read that book cover to cover?"

"I don't want you to go near the reliquary," she said.

"You'd rob me of this opportunity?"

"I saw something disturbing today, Cullen. I'm pleading with you. Disturbing is not enough word for it. It was—"

"There it is," Archer said. Rage had him on his feet. The red haze in the room was nothing compared to the red in his mind. He lost sight of tomorrow and the days after. All that existed was this moment. "There it is. Goddamnit. There it is."

"There what is?"

"You're jealous, Brynn. You are absolutely, positively jealous. So much so that it has you sick. You're always the shining star, and now I've given you competition. I'm the important one. I'm the smart one in the room."

"I think you're sick, Cullen. I think you're delusional. I don't know what else Werdegast has done to get inside your head. I do not care about relics. I never have. I never will." She grasped the Serpent Tongue hanging from the chain around her neck. "I keep this thing because you want me to. Because *you* believe in it. Not because I believe in it."

"My God, don't talk to me this way. You will not be my oppressor."

Brynn did the unthinkable. She ripped off the necklace, breaking the chain's clasp. The Serpent Tongue clattered to the floor. The chain sailed over the cot and struck the wall.

Archer took a deep breath.

"I want you to leave this room," he said. "That was too far. I want you to move out. I've had enough of being disrespected by you. Inch by inch, you've broken me down. But this is it. This is the last of it." His voice went up until his words echoed through the hall. He couldn't help it. "I've had enough of being treated like a goddamn moron child that you drag around. Enough of being second class in my own fucking home. Enough of you cavorting around with rancid sons of bitches like Rhys that you think will raise your station. That tooth on your neck was the only thing that would raise your station in this world. You are nothing. Absolutely nothing, Brynn."

She did not meet his shouting with shouting. Rather, Brynn was silent. She stared at the wall. Her chin ticked higher in resistance, though, and her jaw tightened. She was gone. Even in the dark, Archer saw that.

"You're so obsessed with being more than you are," he said. "You've never once seen the value in a single moment."

"I didn't ask you to follow me here, Cullen."

"No, I practically begged you to allow me. Because I loved you. I left a good job because I loved you. I was called pathetic because I loved you. I'm not going to do things for your approval anymore. This thing has to be two ways. I'm finished, Brynn."

"Are you?"

"I'm not finished bitching. I'm finished with you. I got a lot more if you want it. Years of it."

"You're not hearing me," Brynn said. "You still don't know what I saw today."

"Oh, well now you know how it feels to be ignored, dear. Now you know. Feels like hell, doesn't it? Feels very lonely. Crushingly, abysmally lonely."

Brynn faced him. She was not crying.

Archer was. He wiped tears from his cheek.

"I'll be at the Lieutenant Governor's Palace for the remainder of the night," he said. "When I return, I want your things out. I hope you'll be gone to Seven-Macaw by morning. That'll make things easier on both of us. After that, you can shack up on your own. With Rhys and his glass dick if you want."

"Do you genuinely trust Werdegast?" she asked.

"After today, yes. I do. He means well. He's strange. Yes. Who cares? I'm strange. You're strange. Everyone arriving on the *Bedivere* will be strange. You have to be strange to travel out here, midway to nothing."

"He's in your head like your father. But he's much better at hiding."

"Leave."

Brynn stepped past him, crossed the threshold, left the room.

Archer paced from one side of the dorm to the next. He paced for several minutes, watching the Serpent Tongue on the floor, his head rushing.

He switched on the spirit of his father.

Well, go ahead and berate me, Archer thought finally.

The ghost was silent.

I have more important things to worry about, he thought.

Archer picked up the precious relic and stuffed it in a drawer. He didn't bother searching for the chain. He cleaned his face and hands and changed his clothes.

As he moved from the room and proceeded down the hall, lights came on across Vandalia. Section by section, quarter by quarter, light pushed back against the encroaching night.

A symbol I needed, Archer thought. *At least you were right about one thing,* he told his father. *That was sobering.*

chapter
fifteen

WHEN ARCHER REACHED the Lieutenant Governor's Palace, Werdegast was waiting for him. The front door was peeled back, creased violently. The wanderer stood silhouetted against the glow of the foyer. The air above him was black. Only his hair moved with the breeze.

Archer kept his eyes down, feeling self-conscious. He crossed a plank to avoid mud. He wrung his hands.

Behind him, along the contour of the property, were a few Resurrectionists, men and women impatient for a glimpse of the contents of the von Kleist reliquary. Hopeful, maybe, they would take something home.

"This is an august honor," Werdegast said, looking at the devout spectators. "There are some here who would sacrifice a digit to trade places with you, Cullen."

The man had a beautiful, resonant, lulling voice.

Archer dealt with the knots in his stomach. He sweated alcohol. He pushed down phlegm. Then, in the soft light, he met the eyes of Berthold Werdegast.

He was a well-bred man—nothing ignoble about his features. Nothing of the peasant. His hair was black rather than muddied. He was slender and tall, and when clean-shaven he had the sharp face of a Roman senator. Handsome in a classical way. The golden ratio. Symmetry. At once, he was youthful, ancient, and timeless.

"If you'd rather be sleeping tonight," he said, "remember that days are long but life is short. The present is always better than tomorrow. Only one is guaranteed."

"There's nothing I'd rather do," Archer said. And he was sincere. "I wouldn't be able to sleep tonight anyway."

Werdegast nodded in approval.

"Why are you here?" Archer asked. "For the same reason as them?" He pointed into the darkness.

"No, not that. The Lieutenant Governor has been kind to me. She allowed me a room in her home."

"Is Rinaldi awake? I don't know where to find the reliquary." Archer watched a rippling flag that bore the heraldry of Weston. This was real. "I haven't been inside this place since I helped build it. It was a shell then. Von Kleist was still living on the ship."

"Jarvis is at the clinic with Mrs. von Kleist. He'll be there through the night. But it's no matter. I can show you the way. He left me instructions."

"You can watch, if you like."

Werdegast was silent for a moment. The magnanimous offer touched his heart.

"If you'll have me as a guest, I'd be delighted. Deeply honored."

"It's best to have a fellow Resurrectionist as a witness. Besides that, I have you to thank for the opportunity. How could I ever repay that?"

"No, not at all. There you're mistaken. Delaney knew your reputation, your knowledge. She knew of the book you keep in your quarters. She said you'd committed the compendium to memory. I might've mentioned our conversation about the Last Lion. Nothing more."

Archer grinned. "Did she really? She talked about it?"

"She did."

At that, Archer found a new wave of confidence. He stood straighter. Separated his hands. He looked back at the people in the yard.

"After you," he said, gesturing at the doorway.

Werdegast led him into a foyer soiled with storm debris and muddy footprints. He didn't linger. Of the three doors, he took the right. The metal slid back as he approached, and then, with the tapping of four numbers, a transparent second door, hermetically sealed, opened with a hiss of air.

This was a dignified room of state: a dining hall, office, and cabinet of curiosities rolled into a single package. The size and shape of the room were unimpressive, but the contents gave it special life. To deal with a Lieutenant Governor in this chamber was to sit in the aura of the power and glory of the office. This room was the beating heart of Vandalia. Given time and the establishment of more settlements on Shanidar, dignitaries would be received here. The Lieutenant Governor arriving on the *Bedivere* will be received here. A treaty will be signed. In time, nations will grow from the seed of this room.

How did a man like Cedric von Kleist land this gig? Archer thought. *It's without merit. It's immoral. Why did he deserve opulence? He was born into it.*

It's unjust, the ghost agreed. *Unearned.*

Glad you're back.

Archer couldn't help himself. He ran his fingertips along the table as he passed. It was genuine wood, real grain, and from Earth rather than one of the Weston colonies. There was deep age in the fibers. Mother of pearl lined the edges. The legs of the table ended in carved lion paws.

Oak, he thought, *or whatever it is that kings use.*

Werdegast pulled back a seat at the head of the oblong table. The chair, too, was carved, and the tall back was intricate as lace. He sat. He turned his wrist upward so that his lion hide was visible.

"Did you have a room of state at Seven-Macaw?" Archer asked.

"The settlement wasn't the venture that Vandalia is. No, I didn't have this."

A line of Elizabethan portraits ran along each wall, paintings of men and women costumed with velvet and ruffs, holding globes and books, fondling crude weapons. The gilded frames culminated in the splendid cabinet at the far end of the room. A bulb hung over the reliquary like a searchlight halo. Above the twin doors of the cabinet was a golden plaque that read: *A Microcosm of the Universe and Other Strange Things*. And below that: Built by Georg Ulmer, famed goldsmith of Wien, 1929.

Hot damn, Archer thought. His heart was fast. The back of his throat was like cracked mud.

"Tell me," Werdegast said from behind, "do you believe the von Kleist family deserves this?"

"Depends on what's inside. If it's more than a mound of mummified horseshit, no, I don't. They got nothing from merit."

Werdegast laughed.

"I agree," he said. "I agree. Open it and see."

The hasp connecting the giltwood doors was unlocked. Archer lifted the latch and pulled back the flaps. The worn hinges creaked.

At the sight, Archer nearly dropped to his knees. The cabinet brimmed with magnificent things. There were six shelves in the center and six shelves recessed in each door. The cabinet was taller than Archer by a meter. He glutted his eyes, taking it all in, but it was too much to comprehend. Much too much. His legs trembled.

Archer would not have seen more if he'd pillaged the Basilica of Saint Anastasia.

He had never experienced, he realized, true ecstasy. Never—until this moment. Every nerve in his body was on fire.

Werdegast stood and walked along the edge of the table. He came to Archer's side, hovered at his shoulder.

"Tell me of these things," he said.

Archer composed himself. He breathed.

"Things that are gone forever," he said. "So rare and fine. Each taken from Earth when such objects weren't prized."

Werdegast touched his arm, and Archer was comforted. The touch was fatherly.

His father's voice was absent. The ghost was incapable of genuine comfort.

"Go through each of them," Werdegast said. "Tell me, Georgie."

"Let's clear the table. We'll catalog all of it here. Tonight."

Archer began gathering the various papers, tablets, candleholders, plates, and junk from the table of state. He piled it all in the corner. His head buzzed.

First, I catalog. Then, I divide—maybe rank best to worst. Then, I decide who gets what.

"Maybe not tonight. This will take days," he said. "No wonder Rinaldi wanted me to get on this so soon. I didn't think von Kleist owned this much."

Archer began to remove relics from the cabinet, and, as he did, he explained the significance of each piece to Werdegast. He had never been a more important man than he was in that moment. The wanderer listened with rapt attention.

First, there was quinine bark from Guyana. Malaria once plagued explorers, Archer explained. The interest fit with the room's portraiture.

Second, there was an intact, stuffed, and mounted armadillo. A bizarre animal. New world exotic. What a thrill it was to run his fingers over the leathery armor. Texas, he explained.

Third was the tail of a greyhound dog, long and ropy, now rigid. He had never touched anything that belonged to a canine. Since childhood, he'd dreamed of doing so. Dreamed of how the fur would feel against his skin. The texture did not disappoint.

"This I might keep," he mused aloud. He laughed.

He stroked the tail again.

I wonder if I can graft the tail like you've grafted the lion hide, he thought. *Can Dr. Seward do something like that? She's a surgeon mainly, isn't she?*

Fourth, and this was next to the tail, was a leather tome, an ancient book with well-preserved pages and a tight spine. The book was in Latin—a language Archer didn't know. The title read *Historia Canum Curiosa*. The author was Dorin Toth. The year of publication was astoundingly old, 1698.

"What does that say?" He held the book aloft.

"The Curious History of Dogs," Werdegast said.

"Incredible. Imagine the illustrations."

For a moment, Archer couldn't breathe. He was gentle when he put down the delicate book.

"I thought my *Zoobooks* were old."

An entire shelf was devoted to birds. Many, many feathers of various sorts, from garish birds of paradise to drab brown wrens. Claws and beaks. And in the center of the shelf, a stuffed blue jay, preserved with the same taxidermic skill of the armadillo. It was a large male of the species. The blue feathers were vibrant and rich.

Next, a fish skull—of what species he was uncertain—with coral growing from the bone.

"I'll need to look this one up," he said.

Next, a deer antler. Next, a wolf paw. Next, a small femur, from what he did not know.

And a hundred more things that would carry Archer through dawn.

It was in the second hour of emptying the cabinet that Werdegast said, "I want you to tell me what happened to the species that once filled Earth."

Archer stopped. He looked across the table.

"They were gone long before my time," he said. "I have no special insight. No more than you."

"I want you to tell it to me as you know it. From your heart. I'm tired of soulless explanations. I want to hear a Resurrectionist pontificate."

Archer looked over the array, and he cried. He was overwhelmed and exhausted. And ecstasy had yet to work out of his brain. It moved like electricity, charging every thought.

"We killed everything but ourselves. Killed the soil. Killed the plants. Poisoned the oceans. Torched the forests. It was matricide."

"Why?"

"So the other side couldn't have it. If you want my version, that's what I believe. I don't accept the patriotic shit they teach kids."

"Go on," Werdegast said.

"Earth is poisoned. Nothing lives there. Relics mean something because the flood didn't have a great Ark. These are the only things left."

"Humans were left."

"Yes. Earth lives inside of us. But these things keep our minds on what was and what will be." He touched the greyhound tail. "This is Earth now," Archer said. "In my hand."

"How can you have such reverence for something you've never seen whole? With such faith, you should've been a priest."

"Oh, I wanted that. I wanted it badly. My father pulled me away from it. My mother was religious. It's how she brought me up." He touched the Serpent Tongue. "My father bought a tin of shark teeth for her and his children. I think he bought them from a peddler on the street. And he wasn't poor. Not at all. He just didn't care. She cared, though. I care."

My God, I was going to repeat the same process with Brynn, he thought. *You have to watch who you marry.*

Werdegast gesticulated at the relics on the table. "This is death," he said. "What if I showed you something more substantial than all this combined? Something that lives. A piece of a living Earth on Shanidar."

"I don't think that's a promise that can be kept."

"It can. I can."

Werdegast touched the blue jay. He lifted a feather.

"To see it whole is one thing. To see it breathe is entirely another."

"Yes," Archer said. He barely spoke. His voice was lost in the rush of blood.

"Step out here," Werdegast said.

Without waiting for a response, he moved into the foyer, where forest winds and darkness reached through the door. The wanderer pointed into the hall that split the center of the palace.

"Go in, Cullen. It's waiting for you. Alive."

Archer's limbs had gone to rubber. His steps were cautious. His head was too full, and there was too much blood in his heart.

He moved into the corridor.

And there, couchant against the wall, was a large feline with a tawny coat marked with black rosettes and dashes of white. The animal did not hide in the shadows. It was not a trick of the brain. Bashfully, the cat rose. The eyes were a luminescent gold, cast upward, curious. Black hair tipped the rounded ears, and white whiskers on the snout were long. The paws were large and padded. The tail hung in a crook. The creature was a jaguar. A living, breathing, in-the-flesh Guatemalan jaguar, straight from his devotional film. Except this was no illusion. There was no jungle. No temple and altar of stone.

This was real.

When Archer stopped—he had no strength to move his bones—the feline met him halfway. She slinked up the hall with unmatched elegance, grace, and silence. She stepped to him and ran her long torso against his leg. A full belly rose and fell with breath beneath the ribs.

"Perhaps you'll keep this creature rather than the tail," Werdegast said.

Archer reached down and touched an ear. The purring intensified. The jaguar rubbed her enormous, intimidating face against his shin.

It was too much.

Archer dropped to his knees in a beatific stupor, and he sobbed, wracking his body.

The jaguar, puzzled, went gracefully to the floor. Playfully, the animal stretched and flexed her wicked claws.

The shadow of the wanderer draped Archer.

"Tell me, Georgie," Werdegast said. "How does it feel?"

Archer struggled for breath.

"Who are you?" he managed to say. "What are you?"

He cried with such force that he buried his convulsing face in his hands. Reality was too much. He hid his eyes.

Luxuriously, the jaguar purred.

night of the electric moon: an interlude

Here is a rock overhang, a roof of stars, and a warm bed:

"He's eaten up with it," Titus said.

He rose on his elbow. The stone beneath the blanket was hard and uncomfortable against bone, but he stayed that way, lost in thought.

Neva lay at his side, watching stars through the netting. There were four planets in the solar system. Among them, Red Kitezh was the easiest to spot in the night sky. The gas giants were more distant and difficult. She searched, remembering her initial entry into the system, seeing the giants up close. The mix of terror and pleasure of seeing new worlds. The sun growing from a pale dot to a glowing medallion. The first pulse, first touch of solar wind. The radiance of Shanidar.

She coiled her metal hand. The bones inside were hurting, the nerves throbbing.

"Give him time," Titus said.

"You can be obsessed and still be yourself. Cullen wasn't himself today. He was looking at me with someone else's eyes."

Titus kicked the blanket down. Heat escaped.

"That isn't a sane thought," he said.

He sat up. His bare back glistened.

"Cullen was someone else."

"It's Brynn," Titus said.

"Brynn's never treated him well. He's made to be led around. He's a man-child. It isn't that."

"Of late, she's worse."

"How?" Neva asked.

"She's obsessed herself. With the Owl she found. With Kell. With Rhys."

"Don't bring up Kell. I don't want to think about him."

Titus picked at the netting. Curiously, there were no insects on the other side, had been none all night.

"That was an execution," Neva said. "And we stood by and allowed it. Reminded me of the asylum on La Venta. You remember?"

Titus was silent for a moment.

"I do. But you know I disagree."

"I know. And that's why I won't be coming up here tomorrow night."

"You're full of shit."

"We'll see."

Titus sighed. "What do you want me to do?"

"Tell Werdegast he was wrong. Speak to Cullen."

"I'm not exactly a moral compass. Neither are you."

"Either you tell him or I spend the night with my old man," Neva said.

"Fine. I'll tell him. At least I'll say something to Rinaldi."

"No. You'll tell them directly."

Neva connected the points of light above with her metal digit. The quiet spoke to her.

"Do you ever think about how it's up to us to draw new constellations?" she asked.

Titus grunted.

"Does that come before or after the myths? The Owls drew constellations," she added. "We don't know what they mean."

"Why are there no bugs out tonight?" Titus asked. "I can't recall a night without them."

Here is a room flooded by fluorescent glow, and a bed surrounded by monitors:

As the hour neared midnight, Jarvis Rinaldi finally stood from his chair. He loomed over the pitiful figure of Delaney von Kleist. She was gaunt and sallow. She looked like she'd undergone months of chemotherapy. He used a blanket to wipe spittle from her swollen, discolored lip.

You can go home, Dr. Seward had said. *There's nothing you can do.*

Don't mistake this for kindness, Rinaldi thought, although he possessed too much decorum to utter something so crass.

He stepped to the edge of the room, where Seward had prepared a small cot. A pillow and blanket lay on top. Rinaldi unfolded the blanket and arranged the pillow. He pulled off his boots. He removed the wig from his scalp.

The truth was he didn't want to go home. He couldn't, not with the stranger under the roof. Werdegast, Rinaldi suspected, was behind the death of Cedric von Kleist. The notion of suicide was preposterous. And the ignominious burial at sea destroyed his heart.

He turned to Delaney.

"How could you?" he whispered. "He floated. The water rejected his body." Impotent rage flowed through him. "What did Werdegast promise you?"

I should've stayed here that night between the two of you.

He checked over his shoulder for Seward. Both doors into the patient room were locked. The hallway was silent.

Rinaldi returned to Delaney.

"Your husband was a great man. He elevated your life. You married up. Not him. And you set him adrift."

Delaney's mouth twitched, as if she heard the secretary and was desperate to respond.

Rinaldi leaned closer.

A wisp of breath emerged, and then came a clattering, ticking noise against her teeth.

In disgust, he jumped back.

A blood-engorged chirr fly, so fat its wings were useless, crawled from the orifice. Its legs were barely strong enough to drag the bulk. The disgusting thing wriggled like a maggot over her bottom lip.

Rinaldi went cold. It felt as though an icy hand lay upon his neck. He gripped the pendant at his chest, a coil of alligator skin studded with beryl. In a bout of revulsion, the secretary paced the room, muttering, cursing, promising, and threatening in turn.

The chirr fly lugged itself over Delaney's cheek. When it reached her ear, the insect died of exhaustion.

Rinaldi watched, unblinking, unmoving.

Here is the electric moon, bright, no shadows, no dark side:

Beneath the ring of light, Kell leaned over the ancient Owl. He practiced the letter's sound, a single character. The sound was soft and familiar in his throat. He moved to the next letter, then the next, and an alphabet took shape in his notes.

In the corner of the room, Brynn was long asleep, propped with her back against the wall. In the opposite corner, Rhys slept. His snoring was a discordant backdrop for Kell's recitation.

Kell did not mind the lack of an audience. He worked, typing notes that ran long across three screens.

The Owl, although its abyssal eyes were rigid, and though its mandible didn't creak in the night, moved in the mind of the android. Kell's recitation was in mimicry of the sounds that entered his thoughts. His flash of insight did not spring *ex nihilo*. And his insight was not a gift of Mr. Werdegast.

In its way, the Owl spoke to him.

When he was satisfied, Kell stood. He walked to the door as silently as he could manage. He slipped into the hallway, and then into the night. He was no longer clumsy and heavy. Kell had the pottery studio in mind. He had the image he wanted. He had the inscription worked out. Now he needed clay and a kiln.

Here is the cryo-ship Bedivere *locked in the frozen journey of deep space:*

The robotic guardian moved swiftly down the passage, performing a health check on each of the four hundred travelers. The job was tedious, even for a synthetic lifeform that viewed weeks as minutes and years as hours. On a three-cycle rotation, a trio of machines performed the task. Once a shift ended—once the four-hundredth pulse was confirmed—the next shift began at Weston Colonist Number One.

The machines' work was nearly complete. In twelve hours, the travelers would begin the process of awakening.

The guardian rolled down the tube, sounding no alarm. A Weston logo stamped the machine's back.

The robotic crew combined for a singular note, a joint connection at a node in the massive ship.

All quiet. All safe. On time. No damage.

One problem: the last transmission of coordinates to the destination bounced back, unreceived. So close, there should be no lag. It was the first time in four years, two months, and fifteen days that the problem had occurred. As was standard, the message was attempted two hundred and sixty times. Each attempt was a failure.

The destination: the Weston colonial planet of Shanidar.

Estimated time of arrival: three days, twelve hours, fourteen minutes.

chapter
sixteen

THE SUMMONS BURNED in her ears. Brynn answered, settling an internal debate that had been churning all night, even in her dreams. The willingness to respond was a flashpoint, a brief window that oscillated moment to moment. Fifteen minutes prior, she would've ignored the message. Her rebellion was so strong then, she would've deleted the summons unread. The same would be true, she assumed, if the message had arrived thirty minutes later. Mentally, it was the eye of a needle. But, with laser precision, the summons came over the cilia at the right time.

Her response was recorded and stored.

Brynn gathered her things from the pile she'd brought from Cullen's dorm. She'd been awake for an hour, thinking, watching Kell work. She was getting accustomed to his death's head, but his withdrawn pithiness was utterly alien. Regardless, the words of the machine had lifted her reluctance to leave Vandalia.

If you do not trust Berthold Werdegast, Kell had said, *it's imperative that you monitor his actions. It's all the more important with the* Bedivere *arriving in three days. Extraordinary claims require extraordinary evidence. Take time before you tell others what you have told me. If you do not, it will be deduced that you have experi-*

enced a psychological break, and that you are unwell. The new colonists will perform a psychometric scan.

That was solid and true, Brynn decided. Cullen had already drawn that conclusion about her, and she'd said nothing of the cat's paw.

You know how Weston treats the mentally ill, she thought. *You'll end up in an asylum on La Venta.*

Kell let his point stand without decoration. He resumed work on the Owl's Hieratic text. She wanted to ask him for his usual anecdote or poem. She deeply missed him.

As Brynn prepared to leave Kell behind, the door opened. Dr. Rhys entered. He was businesslike. He had prepared the transports, charging the cells, readying six of them for a predawn journey across the desert. Now he went about collecting final items for the expedition.

As he downloaded Kell's latest notes, he asked, "Are you up at this hour from eagerness or nerves?"

"Both," Brynn said. She pressed her bag and sealed it.

The linguist had no inkling that she'd endured a dark night of the soul, that overwhelming anxiety had invaded her dreams, that she was frightened deep down in the reptile jelly of her brain. That she'd nearly deleted the summons.

Rhys scanned Kell's notes. He scrolled to the top and then down again.

"Extraordinary," he told the machine. His gloved hand clinked against the android's falcon dome. "I've missed this industriousness from you, Kell. Record your progress while we are away. No matter how trivial you might think the detail, record it. Communicate any breakthroughs to me in private over the cilia."

Kell typed. He didn't lift his head. The notes continued, line by line, ribbons of black.

"By our return, Kell will have written a Hieratic dictionary and encyclopedia," Rhys said. "Do you still doubt the necessity of his alteration? And this is on day one. More progress than I ever dreamed. I told you months. Weeks."

Brynn doubted the necessity, but she couldn't deny her wonder at Kell's headway on the broken-winged Owl. At this rate, she and Rhys would return to a deciphered language, something unfathomable with a damaged Kell.

"It's time, Ms. Silva."

With a renewed sense of clarity, Brynn exited the dormitory and walked beside Rhys. There was commotion at the north gate. White lights around the perimeter cut back the darkness. The glow of distant morning hid behind the mountains. The air was tropical, and a muggy fog blanketed the valley. The Owl's Lair was a patch of blackness above.

Despite the hour, a group of eight men and women had mobilized to see the expedition depart. They circled Werdegast, hitting him with a mix of questions, praise, and attempts at badinage. Conspicuously, Lord Rinaldi and the Lieutenant Governor were absent.

Cullen was nowhere in sight.

"They've tormented the man with chatter all night," Rhys said. "A few hours ago, four followed him around. They've doubled."

"He'd make a fine politician," Brynn said.

Rhys switched on his eye light. He fumbled with the box at the rear of his transport.

"They believe he performed a miracle with Kell, you know," he said. "Blue collar acolytes adore a miracle. Moreover, they were intoxicated when it occurred. It must have been glorious. They can't resist magical thinking. They love him from down in their souls."

The rest of the expeditionary crew stood apart from Werdegast's admirers. In a line they were Benton Clegg, August Maudsley, and Willa Steen. Each was travel-ready in headgear and goggles. Although they were not strangers, Brynn had had little contact with them. Clegg and Maudsley were geologists. Steen was a software engineer who kept to herself belowground in the settlement's server room. She wasn't in the habit of talking, but she was bright and had a biting sense of humor. Her hair was cropped tight over the ears, and patches of gray marked the temples. Of the three, Brynn knew her best.

Not one to disappoint his entourage, Werdegast ascended the platform above the gate.

He's a whore for attention, Brynn thought.

Werdegast raised his arms. Voices quieted.

"Among the intelligentsia," he said, "there's a rumor that the settlement of Seven-Macaw is a figment of my imagination, a lie built upon lies."

Steen, Brynn noticed, gave a curt nod.

"Not only will this journey prove that rumor untrue, but it will also reveal, I hope, what you are dealing with in Weston. The *Bedivere* is arriving in a matter of days. Some in Vandalia are thinking of returning to Luna Fourteen. I say this is folly. I'll make no bold claims. But when we come back, the information we return with will reshape how you think about this planet. How you think about the corporation that dictates your lives. And it will reshape what you think about the former inhabitants of this world." He found Brynn. "And it will reshape how you think about me."

"Speechmaking is in their noble blood," Rhys said to Brynn. "Forgive him. He can't help it."

While Werdegast finished with a list of promises—including, she heard, the total banishment of chirr flies—she secured her satchel on the bike. She pulled out goggles. She straddled the seat.

We're driving the length of the Acheron, she thought. It was a journey Brynn hadn't made, although she'd desired it. Three hundred kilometers of dry river and desert, and then a turn south for twelve hundred more kilometers, with the latter half through mountain highlands. All told, the drive would consume eight hours.

The others followed her to the bikes. Rhys first. Then Clegg. Then Steen. Then Maudsley. Werdegast came last. The thrum of engines moved over the sleeping settlement. Werdegast pulled up beside Brynn.

"I was worried this opportunity would pass you by, Professor Silva," he said.

She stared at him. In the early hours of the night, she'd planned venomous diatribes for this moment, but, instead, she said nothing.

"I very much like that you call this old river the Acheron," Werdegast said. "It's more apt than you know."

Her guts were arid as sand. And then her throat was parched. And, in her mind's eye, was a distant vision of a woman eating the desert until her body was mummified from the inside.

The thought was not her own.

Keep your courage, Brynn countered. *You have to see. You must know.*

Werdegast smiled.

One by one, the riders disappeared into the fog.

chapter
seventeen

COVERED in mud up to his knees, Cullen Archer stood pensively before the locked door. He sucked oxygen through a tube.

It isn't wrong, he told his father. *Nothing I do in this state of mind is wrong. I have immunity—in a way.*

I never said I disapproved, Georgie. Knock.

I have your blessing?

Of course.

With that, Archer knocked.

After a minute of rustling on the other side, the door slid open.

Lyra stood half-dressed, her legs and feet bare. From the left knee to the ankle, she was tattooed, more a puttee than a sleeve, but it was fully dark with faces. Her thighs were as muscular as those of a gymnast. She wore a loose tank top, and her greasy hair resembled a sculpture of the wind. She was, to Archer's delight, alone.

With new colonists arriving in a week, and many of those being unattached men, he had to make his move.

"I don't have to be at the Boxgrove for two hours," Lyra said.

She wiped her crusted eyelashes. "What the hell are you doing here?"

He reached for her hand and then stopped. She held a gun, the muzzle aiming at the ground. It was the standard Weston militia issue: smart-aim, heavy and black.

"Are you kidding me?"

Lyra glanced at the weapon.

"Old habit," she said.

She placed the gun on a shelf.

When Archer reached for her hand again, Lyra let him have it.

"I have something to show you. I want you to be the next to see it."

Lyra looked down at his grip. Then she looked at his inconceivably muddy pants. The spatter reached his torso and spotted his arms. An unpleasant thought formed behind her eyes.

Archer pushed aside the things he wanted to gush about and said, "I understand how I look. With the gun greeting, let's call it even."

"You look like you've been lost in the woods. You only need a castaway beard."

Why are you resisting me? he thought.

She doesn't know, Georgie. She doesn't understand the significance of the moment.

I'm about to give her the greatest gift she's ever received, and she's resisting.

Be patient.

Archer kept his cool. He didn't lead with revelations of divine love or God talk, but he edged up to it.

"That's an appropriate thing to say, actually. I've been lost in the wilderness for too long. Once you've seen what I've seen, Lyra, you'll understand. Let's see if you can stop yourself from running around in the mud."

"You're not wearing your shark tooth."

"It's a Serpent Tongue. It means nothing now." Guilt stopped him from going further. "It means less," he corrected. "We're entering the age of life, of real things. We're leaving the age of the dead."

"You're scaring me, you know. You sound crazy. I've shot men for less."

Lyra pulled from his grip.

"And you're clammy," she added. She wiped her hand.

Don't act like Brynn, Archer thought. *For the love of God, do not act like Brynn. Not right now.*

He fought for composure.

"I'm going to step outside. You can get dressed or you can go back to bed. If you join me, I'll change your life. Change your soul. Change everything you think you know."

"Did you sleep last night?"

"I did not. This is not a time for sleep." He pointed up the hall. "I'll be outside. Right out that door." He tapped his wrist. "You are in a prison and the door is open. And I mean that in a spiritual sense, Lyra. A spiritual sense!"

With wine in her, I'm the Grand Vizier of the Reliquary, Archer thought. *She toasted my good fortune.* He was heating up again. *Sober, I'm a crazy piece of shit. A fucking muddy, clammy lunatic. How's that for mixed signals?*

Be patient, Georgie.

Archer exited into the morning light. The night winds were gone, leaving the day calm and serene. He waited until his heart was about to burst. Five minutes passed. Seven. Finally, Lyra came through the door.

"I'm sorry," she said. "I'm not a morning person."

"You pulled a gun on me. Not a morning person is an understatement." He took her by the wrist. "Come on. Forget it. This is too important to dwell on that."

I'll try to forget your insolence and resistance, he thought. *Faith is difficult. I know.*

"Where to?"

"The Lieutenant Governor's Palace," Archer said.

"That's grand," Lyra said. "And with you looking like that."

He stopped midstride.

With gravity, he said, "That was the one too many, Lyra. This isn't a joking matter. I'm not playing a prank. Titus and Neva aren't around the corner, waiting to laugh. I'm not trying to annoy, impress, or coerce you. I am very serious. My entire world changed last night. My soul is full. My mind is full. And you're the first person I want to share it with. No one else knows."

"What about your little archaeologist?"

Archer exhaled.

"That's over. Brynn and I are through."

"Are you really?"

"I am utterly, entirely, nearly certain. I'm sharing this with you and not her, aren't I? Please believe me, Lyra. This is the most important moment of your life."

Lyra sobered. Her grin uncurled.

"Okay. No more shit. Show me."

Archer skipped the boards and splashed through a yard of mud. The squat palace was bright beneath the sun. The front door remained open. The lights from the previous night still burned.

To his relief, a crowd had not gathered on the stoop. That possibility had terrified him. This was his vision—his miracle—and he wanted to control it completely.

Archer was first through the door.

Lyra looked around as she crossed the threshold.

"What happened in here?"

She gestured at a gash in the ceiling. Wet insulation hung like sinew from the wound. Water puddled on the floor.

"A mighty storm. Nothing more than that. Ahead. Come on."

With Lyra in tow, Archer passed into the main corridor.

"I locked it in the bedroom," he said.

"Don't be cryptic. You locked what in the bedroom?"

"I can't say it out loud. I don't know the words. You must see it. Feel it. Experience it."

Lyra stopped.

"I have the gun," she warned.

"Is that really what you think of me?"

"It's what I think of all men. You aren't excluded."

"Fine. In that room, behind the door, is a living, breathing feline. A jaguar. I'm talking two meters long."

Lyra was skeptical rather than awed. Her tone frustrated him.

"Like in the devotional film? They're extinct. You're sure it isn't an automaton? I've seen better men fooled. Once—"

"Do not insult my intelligence," Archer said. "I know jaguars are extinct. And animal simulacra, by the way, are illegal. Weston wouldn't allow such a thing to be smuggled here."

In all honesty, he hadn't considered the possibility of a simulacrum. It bothered him with the quickness of a bullet.

Could it be?

Don't be a fool, Georgie. You felt it. You felt it breathe. Does Kell breathe?

That's right. Yes, you're right. I should've shown Titus first.

Probably. You're thinking with the wrong head.

Titus, I bet, wouldn't do this to me. I guess I don't know Lyra as well as I thought.

She's beautiful.

Yeah. She is. Achingly. That's my problem. I want her.

"Are you okay?" Lyra asked. "You keep zoning out."

Archer steadied his gaze. "Do this for me," he pleaded. "Walk to the door and open it. Go inside. Then, and only then, talk of simulacra."

After a moment of hesitation, Lyra started toward the door.

"It's natural to be afraid," Archer said, trailing. "Wonder can be rapture and wonder can be dread. Like a drunk can be angry or loving, it depends on what's inside the beholder."

"Please stop with the wisdom," Lyra said. "I have the gun."

She pressed the door, and it slid open with a hiss.

"Tell me what you see. Talk to me, Lyra. If it isn't there, shoot me dead." He put his hands against his temples. His mind was on fire.

Lyra stopped at the foot of the bed. Archer peered around the edge of the doorway. His heart was sharp and quick.

On the mattress, her paws spread before her like the Sphinx of Egypt, sat the magnificent cat. She covered the entire length of the bed. She'd been enjoying a deep sleep. With the abrupt intrusion of a stranger, her posture was cautious. She was wary, poised to leap.

She's a mankiller, Archer thought. *It's in her blood. Damn it, it's instinct. It's impressive as all hell.*

When the jaguar spotted Archer, she relaxed. Her stillness bled away, replaced by a velvet purr.

Lyra struggled for words. Blood vanished from her face, leaving her spectral. The mix of fear and joy was not a surprise, so Archer didn't pry. The moment was too important for Lyra. Any interference was unclean.

In time, Lyra uttered a single word.

"How?"

"It's a miracle," Archer said. "This is Delaney von Kleist's jaguar paw resurrected. Sit down. See if she allows you to pet her."

Lyra sat on the mattress. The jaguar stretched toward the indentation she made.

"She isn't feral," he said.

We'll find out the extent of her friendliness right now, Archer thought giddily. *Hot damn.*

"I'm too afraid to touch her," Lyra said.

"Please conquer it. Do what you have to do inside to make it go away. Make this real. Cross that line. This isn't a matter of faith. This is real. This isn't death. This isn't a severed paw. This is life."

Lyra marshaled her courage. She put out her hand, palm down.

The courage warmed Archer's heart.

The jaguar extended her neck, and her whiskered muzzle made contact with Lyra's fingertips.

Lyra pulled back like an electric shock passed through her body. She looked at Archer with deep, tear-rimmed eyes. No more shallow gibes.

"Don't focus on me," he said. "I'm a wretch. I'm nothing. Focus on her. Focus on life. This is Earth, Lyra. This isn't a prayer. This isn't in your head. This is resurrection."

The jaguar stood on the mattress. She reached her paws forward, flexed her claws, and stretched luxuriously. Her tail twitched. Her coat glistened. So near Lyra's hand, and so much larger, Archer got a sense of the true size of the cat's paws. She weighed a hundred and eighty pounds, maybe more.

He sat on the other side of the bed. The jaguar nudged him, and he scratched her spotted head. He rubbed a tuft behind her ear. The cat's purr intensified. He slid down to her cheek, scratching.

"Rub behind the ear," he said to Lyra.

When she did, and when the vibrations of the purr went through her skin and down into the marrow of her bones, Lyra slid from the bed like water. She dropped to her knees on the floor. The moment was too much. On all fours, she sobbed.

"You believe," Archer said. "I knew you were a believer. I knew you were a woman of faith. This is Earth, isn't it?"

Lyra was melting snow. And she washed herself in herself. She washed her doubts clean.

"How?" she asked again.

"Werdegast," Archer whispered. He stood from the bed. It was profane to say the name with a full throat. He couldn't. "The Resurrectionist," he said.

"No man can do that." Lyra's ecstasy verged on agony, and the line between states was brittle. She panned the room, looking for something to throttle. She settled on Archer. She stood and crossed to him.

Archer put his arms out to stop her.

"No, that's right. No man can do this. He's not what he says he is. Of course, he's not. That's why your world has changed, Lyra. He's not a man. He's—"

Archer stopped. He wasn't certain why.

Say it, Georgie. Make it real.

Do you believe in Him?

Yes, the ghost said. *I'm sorry I ever doubted. Yes, Georgie, I believe in Him.*

"He's God," Archer said. "He's come to save us from ourselves. He has come to resurrect Earth."

Lyra stopped. Her face was white as bleached bone. Her eyes were on the doorway.

"Turn around," she said. "Slowly. Look."

Archer was hot up to his gullet. Blood pounded in his ears. He followed Lyra's gaze. On a bust in the corridor, flicking its wings atop a bronze skull, was the stuffed blue jay from the von Kleist reliquary. The creature's eye found him with a blank-brained stare. It lived.

I need to shut the front door, Archer thought, trying not to panic, trying not to do anything rash. *I can't let it get away.*

"What are you doing?" Lyra asked.

Archer waved her off. He inched over the threshold. He needed something to catch the bird. Grabbing such a fragile thing would break its tiny bones. He extracted himself from his cloak, sliding his arms through as quietly as he could manage. But the swish of cloth and his proximity were too much for the cold-blooded jay. The bird wasn't friendly like the jaguar. With a push, it took to the air in a line, dashing up the wall and toward the foyer, beating its wings.

Archer chased the blue jay like a madman, his cloak spread between his hands in a makeshift net. The moment was one of terror and bliss. No single word covered the feeling in his heart.

What the blue jay lacked in intelligence, it made up for in

persistence and stamina. After seven laps around the foyer, it cut past a winded Archer, found the door, and hit the morning sunlight.

Archer kept up his pursuit.

"Stay with the cat," he shouted over his shoulder. "Close the door!"

He remembered, from an issue of *Zoobooks*, that cats devoured birds. The jaguar could swallow a blue jay whole—and wouldn't think twice about it. Cats were vicious predators. Killers.

What a thrill.

Archer was no match for the bird's speed, but he ran through the alleys of Vandalia, shouting for anyone and everyone to come and see, to witness the miracle at hand.

The miracle of what?

Of resurrection. Of creation. The province of gods. Of God.

He chased the blue jay until it was gone in the forest.

"Come back!" Archer begged.

There were firsthand witnesses. And there were secondhand witnesses who claimed to be firsthand. And there were those sleeping. And those who denied their senses. And there was awe. And there was the wonder of rapture. And there was the wonder of dread. And there were believers. And there were doubters. And there were liars. And there were the bad and the good. And there were enemies of faith and fellows of faith.

Such was the power of a single resurrection.

chapter
eighteen

ONCE THE DESERT WAS CROSSED, the expedition turned southward at two hundred kilometers per hour. The landscape went from barren wasteland to sprouts of scrub to a highveld plateau of tall grass, heavy with clouds of insects. A range of worn-down mountains lifted at the horizon. Seven-Macaw waited in the high altitude.

Brynn brushed dirt from the cell gauge on her bike and checked the needle. The charge was full, the last leg of the desert having topped it off. Although she ached all over, she had no desire to stop for rest. She clenched her teeth and tightened her grip.

Werdegast led the riders through vines and thorns, plowing undergrowth, dodging trees. Upward they went, carving a path. The engines groaned and whirred in defiance. Higher still until it was necessary to switch on the oxygen connected to their belts. The speed slowed to fifty kilometers per hour, then thirty. The cell needles sagged under the strain.

After hours of slogging, the ground leveled into a canyon between mountain peaks. Here, built into the rock walls, was an ancient city, black as the Owl's Lair that towered over Vandalia. Brutal winds cut through the valley in straight-line bursts.

Werdegast geared down. He rolled to a stop. Rhys, Maudsley,

Clegg, Steen, and Brynn did the same. The din of engines passed away in waves until the dale echoed with the final growl and sigh of the bikes.

Brynn removed her caked goggles and looked around. The site was a marvel, but there was no sign of anything man-made in the canyon. None of the familiar Weston buildings were present—the long halls of white, the domes, dorms, fences, duckboards, insect netting, or golden plaques. Nothing.

Werdegast walked about, brushing himself clean. He shed his gloves. Dust swirled around him in the breeze.

"As pleasant as that was," he said, "I don't recommend walking it."

Brynn stood and stretched her back. She felt like she'd been locked in a fetal position for the past twelve hours. And the thin air was hard on her dust-caked lungs. She clicked on another canister of oxygen and adjusted the tube at her lip. She looked up the sheer walls to the high ledges, no less than a hundred meters above. The wind-hewn rockfaces were so slick they appeared artificially made. And on the rocks were long stretches of murals, a field of stars with strange, winged figures drawn within. Some of the figures were humanoid Owls. Some were abstract shapes. This was the fourth metropolis Brynn had visited on Shanidar, but it was the first to be decorated with an astronomical motif.

The site was a window to the stars, she thought. The pull on her curiosity was strong.

Wind funneled through the canyon, whipping her hair. It was astonishing that anything survived here without being whittled away, eroded to bedrock.

Werdegast mustered everyone around him. He showed no emotion about his return to a place that was, ostensibly, the ground zero of tragedy.

"This is an Astral Dale," he said. "One of three on this world, but the only one in this hemisphere. Here the Owls mapped stars." He pointed at the silos above. "There are astounding stargazing platforms in the towers. If you can climb, I'll show them to you. The clarity from a mountaintop is breathtaking."

Maudsley had a compass out, checking the orientation of the city and valley.

"Where is your settlement?" the geologist asked. "Is there more travel to be done?"

"No," Werdegast said. "No more riding. This is it. This is Seven-Macaw."

A beat of silence passed.

"You occupied an Owl lair?" Steen asked.

"Our expedition was a disaster from the start," he said. "On the frozen journey, part of our ship was destroyed. We lost all material for building. We did the only thing we could do. This is where we waited. We were told you'd ship out directly behind us. Another Weston lie."

"How many people lived here?" Maudsley asked.

"At the height, thirty-four colonists. Seventy percent of our people died on the voyage."

It was a stunning figure, a war number.

Brynn stepped away and took in the city. Holes of various sizes pocked the cliffside, interrupting the star murals at set intervals. All told, there were several hundred entry points. The black metal buildings stood in stark contrast to these stone-age abodes. It was like a tuft of skyscrapers built next to a site of Pueblo cliff dwellers. The towers rising from the floor of the valley stretched high in haphazard fashion, their growth organic, unplanned, resembling sprouts of crystal festooned with moss. There was something more primitive about this site, something less refined than the Owl's Lair that neighbored Vandalia. The confines were tighter. Save for a causeway that split the middle, the "streets" were crawlspaces.

This is older, Brynn thought. *Much more ancient.* She wondered if her Owl came from here when the Acheron flowed, when the desert lived. Perhaps the Owl was traveling. The relationship between settlements on Shanidar was uncertain, but it was clear the cities interacted, whether through trade, fellowship, or conflict—she couldn't say definitively.

Brynn turned to Werdegast. "Your part in the tale is difficult to believe."

Werdegast didn't allow his gaze to linger. "That's why I endeavored to show you. It's something you must see to believe."

Rhys clicked to the transports. With his back to the group, he sent a message to Lord Rinaldi over the cilia, informing the secretary of the expedition's safe arrival. He said nothing, Brynn noted, of the lack of a Weston footprint.

Clegg went to his knee, touching the stone ground. When he motioned for Maudsley to join him, Brynn approached Steen. There was suspicion in the woman's eyes.

"What do you make of that?" Steen asked.

She swept her hand over the cliffside starfield. Each figure connecting points of light was five meters tall.

"Constellations," Brynn said.

"They're massive. I suppose that's a benefit of wings. One of them."

In a softer voice, Brynn said, "When we get a moment, I need to speak with you."

"We should've made Rhys go alone," Steen said.

Werdegast motioned for everyone to follow him to a terrace that fronted the city. Geometric patterns in faded greens and blues covered the square. Unlike the esplanade at the Owl's Lair, however, no wall rose on the other side.

The mountain is their defense, Brynn thought. *This was remote, inaccessible land, even back then. Even with wings.*

"The causeway," Maudsley said, holding his compass aloft, "must align with a celestial event."

"The summer solstice," Werdegast said. "It's the only sunrise that reaches from one end of the city to the next. The rays pass through unchecked."

"Incredible. The Owl's Lair has nothing like it."

"There's much more."

Rhys returned from the bikes. "What were you able to salvage from your voyage?" He spoke around the oxygen tube in the corner of his mouth.

"A minuscule amount. The clothes on our backs. Scraps of machinery we pieced together."

What did you eat? Brynn thought. *Nothing grows up here.*

"I'm trying to imagine what could've done so much damage to your ship," Steen said.

"This way," Werdegast said. "I'll show you where we took cover."

At the base of one of the front silos was an entrance. Star figures, arranged in a circle like a zodiac, framed the opening. Hieratic script accompanied each shape.

"It wouldn't hurt to bring Kell here," Rhys said to Brynn. "I'd like to have all this photographed in detail."

Brynn entered the black cylinder, ducking under the clearance. She thought of Delaney approaching a similar tower in the Owl's Lair. Cedric von Kleist had done the same—and he'd climbed up the inside. Mapping his route made the prospect of suicide even more ridiculous.

The silo's interior was dark as a tomb. No hole opened at the top to allow in sunlight. Brynn stayed near the opening. Her heart was fast. Steen waited at her side.

Rhys switched on the light in his left eyeball. He cast the beam upward. There were no stairs or ladders, but every five meters was a square platform. The shelves led to the top, where darkness was complete.

"This is where we quartered," Werdegast said. "Each platform is a nest, and we had access to the first few stages in each tower. Some of the others are more hospitable, with holes for light to enter. It's an ethereal effect at dawn." He eyed Maudsley. "One of the towers is a zenith tube, not unlike the causeway."

"Incredible," Maudsley said.

"How do you get to the top?" Clegg asked, looking up.

"Climb a ladder and pull it up. Set it against the next platform. Climb again. You can do it all the way. The ledges don't increase in their distance apart."

"No small feat," Maudsley said. He released a nervous laugh.

"I suppose that's how you access the stargazing docks," Clegg said.

"Yes. A terrific strain, but worth it. You've never experienced such a view on this world."

"I'll take your word for it," Steen said.

"There were nights so black the stars came out in the millions, dusting the sky, fine as sand. I consoled myself many nights up there. I imagined," he said, "I saw your ship approaching. Finally arriving, entering orbit. I kept my sanity there." He looked at Brynn. "It might be amusing for one of you to watch the *Bedivere* approach in similar fashion."

For a full minute, no one spoke. All eyes watched the darkness above.

"Once," Werdegast continued, "I imagined Kitezh with a scarlet twin, a fine little bead of red."

"Artwork at this site," Rhys said, "shows the additional planet, I assume."

"There's an inner court with the cosmos painted in a ring. Five planets are depicted, including the twin."

"Make note of that, Ms. Silva," Rhys said.

"Do any of you wish to climb to the top? How about you, Doctor?"

Rhys's beam moved like a laser around the shaft, rapid.

"In my youth, maybe," the linguist said. "This body wouldn't survive an ordeal of that magnitude. If I go up, I'll find myself stuck." He put the light on his arm. "These joints lock."

"I can fix that for you," Werdegast said. "It is, after all, only a mechanical problem. Would you like that?"

Rhys's light brightened as if it were wired to the pleasure center of his brain.

"After your work on Kell, I don't doubt you can," he said.

Werdegast touched the scientist's shoulder.

"Then consider it done. I'll have you climbing to the top before we depart," he promised. "And back down again. Anyone else willing?" He looked around.

Wind whistled, finding fissures in the metal.

"Unfortunately, I'm not a fan of heights," Maudsley said. "Not in this wind. You'll have to count me out."

Brynn backed from the claustrophobic hole.

Werdegast followed.

"Professor Silva, I'll show you something not even you, my doubting cynic, can resist. Come," he said. His manner was unctuous. "I'll show you the ant tunnels that honeycomb these cliffs. You want answers, don't you? Wouldn't you like to know how these cities—how your Owls—interacted?"

And I'll show you what lies below, came the voice in Brynn's mind.

"Where are the colonists' belongings?" Steen asked.

"Buried with their owners," Werdegast said. "I had years alone. I took with me what was mine. If you wish to walk to Vandalia, you'll find pieces of Weston scattered along the way."

"Where are they buried?" Steen persisted.

"Oh, I'll show you the cemeteries of Seven-Macaw. Be patient, Ms. Steen. You brought the inquisitive troop with you," Werdegast said to Rhys. "That's good. These are difficult minds to sway."

"We should eat and gather ourselves before we descend into the tunnels," Brynn said. She eyed Steen.

Maudsley and Clegg were quick to agree.

Werdegast consulted the sky.

"We have enough daylight remaining," he said. "Take your rest."

The expedition members paired off. Rhys went with Werdegast. Maudsley with Clegg. Steen followed Brynn to the bikes.

"Call me irreverent," Steen said, "but I've never been impressed by their ugly metal tubes. Style, they did not have."

Brynn opened the box on her transport. She placed her oxygen unit inside and extracted three protein bars, heavy as ingots. She unsealed a canister and took a long drink of water. Removing the material revealed an object at the bottom, a small thing wrapped in cloth that she hadn't packed. Curious, she pulled the thing free and unwrapped it. She looked upon a black Grecian urn in her hands. Painted in orange was an owl, and beside the owl was Athena. The inscription was in Hieratic.

If ever I'm repaired, Kell had said, *I'll fashion such a thing for you.*

"What's that?" Steen asked.

Brynn wrapped the ceramic.

"A message from Kell."

Steen furrowed her brow.

"I think he's broken the Hieratic code," Brynn said.

Steen grabbed food from her bike. "Come on. We're going to picnic away from the others."

Brynn and Steen crossed the plaza and entered the labyrinth of Seven-Macaw. Forty meters in, they found a shadowed clearing out of earshot. The chutes rose on each side so that the air was calm, the wind limited to whistles in the tubes. This was the inner court. The murals proceeded upward in two layers. On the bottom, Owl faces were burned into the metal walls. Above, portrayed in faded, chipping paint, was the solar system. Five planets rather than four. The ghostly red twin was present, smaller than Kitezh, equal in mass to Shanidar.

At the center of the court was an inverted tower, dropping more than thirty meters. Arched doorways that led deeper into the mountain opened at the bottom.

Uncremoniously, Steen sat on the ground, draping her legs over the shaft.

"Werdegast is a fraud," she said flatly. "I told Rinaldi, and I told Delaney, and I told Kell, and I told Rhys. Now I'm telling you."

Brynn sat at her side. Uncertain of the acoustics in the tunnels below, she spoke quietly.

"Forgive me if I'm not shocked. It's not news to me."

"I assumed as much."

"What did they say?"

"They were apathetic. At least on the surface. Rhys dismissed me out of hand. Misogynistic bastard that he is."

"What about Kell?"

"This was after Kell was corrected. He didn't look up from his work long enough to comment. I told him what I knew, but I'm not certain he heard me."

"I'll tell you something extraordinary," Brynn said, "but you go first."

"When Governor Naylor's funeral ended, I went to the server room. I'm one of two people who can access anything on those machines."

"Who's the other?"

"Now it's Delaney. I had Werdegast's name and Seven-Macaw and I had firm dates. Weston has information on every colony and settlement they've ever established or planned in their database. Nearly seventy colonies and thousands of plans. The Lieutenant Governor has access to that info to consult as needed. And this is beyond what's reported in the news. A lot of it is classified."

"It's comprehensive then."

"As close as you can get to comprehensive, yeah. Brynn, there's no Berthold Werdegast in the database. I have every Lieutenant Governor, every William Naylor and their aliases, every single colonist in the employ of Weston—and we're talking two million people. There's nothing at all. There's no Seven-Macaw among the settlements. No plans for a Seven-Macaw. There's no expedition to Shanidar that preceded our own. No plan for that. Nothing. And I can't stress this enough: No one can be that precise when wiping the record clean. It's too technical for a conspiracy. There's too much incompetence in the ranks of Weston to leave no trail. I don't care how much they wanted it to be that way, someone somewhere would fuck up. Period. There'd be a crumb of evidence in the database. Something."

"That's definitive," Brynn said.

"To the right people, it's an end-all to the discussion. He either is or isn't part of a Weston voyage. Seven-Macaw either is or isn't a Weston settlement. There are those among us who think differently, of course. There are those with, let's say, limited intellectual faculties. The simple folk. And no offense to you or your boyfriend, but it's mainly the Resurrectionists you gotta worry about. They believe what they want to believe and see what they want to see."

"Say what you want about Cullen. I agree with you."

"Okay, well, I didn't expect that, but fine. He's a motherfucking imbecile. I don't know what you see in that man."

"You don't talk to a lot of people down in your basement, do you?"

"No, I don't. I lack a filter, and it gets me in trouble."

"Cullen followed me here. I tried to leave him on Luna Fourteen. I signed on without telling him. He found out. He quit his job."

"He quit his job? God, I can't even imagine. I'm sorry. I left mine on Luna with two kids. It felt incredible." After a beat of silence, Steen said, "You next. Don't spare whatever you think is crazy."

"I'm not a Resurrectionist. You have to understand that first."

"Okay. Didn't expect that either."

"I don't believe in relics. I find them positively morbid. Cullen was a believer on Luna, but he became a fanatic here. He got worse."

"Distance does that. The farther from Earth, the worse they get."

"That said, I saw something, and my brain keeps trying to black it out. Like it's rubbing the memory away. Already there are gaps—things I know I saw but can't see anymore."

"Rip off the scab and say it."

"Delaney's a believer. She carries a cat paw as a relic."

"I've seen it."

"I saw it when she came into the House of Burgesses. She was out of her mind. She held the relic like she was praying to it."

Steen nodded.

"Yesterday, I found Delaney ready to do the same thing as her husband. Seward sent me to her home. Werdegast was in the bedroom. He didn't know I was there, far as I could tell. Maybe he did know. I can't say. But I found him alone. He was sitting at a table. He had the paw in his hand, talking over it. And he was—see, I can't even say it. I can't. It makes me sick."

"What was he doing?"

"He was making the claws move. Then an arm grew from the paw, piece by piece out of nothing. He did it with no more than his hand and words."

Steen stared above for a moment. Stars and faces went high on the metal. The real sky between the structures was pale with approaching twilight.

"No, you're right," she said finally. "That's not sane."

"If belief were a spectrum of ten, where are you right now?"

"Five," Steen said.

"Well, that's not outright revulsion."

"If what you say is real, and you actually saw it, what does it mean? That's what I'm trying to get my head around."

"For one, he's an imposter."

"And he's not human."

"Not human," Brynn agreed. "Nor a machine. No android can do what he did."

"The paw was moving?"

"Yes. For that moment, at least, it was alive. It responded to his touch."

"God, I don't know what to think. Could be an illusion. He could make you see things. Could've known you were there. That wouldn't be better, would it?"

"It would be infinitely better."

"I suppose if Werdegast can create illusions, every structure here would be plastered with a Weston logo."

"Agreed. There'd be something obvious waiting for us."

"Now what? We grab Werdegast and throw him down this pit?"

"I've been thinking about that," Brynn said. "Since he has us here in a killing box, we placate him. Otherwise, we'll end up like Cedric von Kleist hanging from a platform. And we watch him. In the end, we'll need more than the two of us. I've a feeling we've lost Rhys. When the *Bedivere* arrives, we need enough to put a gap between the new colonists and Werdegast."

"There's no doubt about Rhys. Kell's transformation changed him. If Werdegast 'fixes' him, he's gone for good."

"Kell gave me one piece of advice. He said we need extraordinary evidence. We have to find it. And not something one person has seen or knows. That won't sway anybody. If we can find that evidence, we can separate Werdegast and his followers. Maybe we can send him back to the desert."

"Have you ever seen a pest convinced to leave without violence?" Steen asked.

"Or throw him down this hole," Brynn conceded. "I get an eerie feeling he crawled out of it."

Brynn's telepathy cilium went mad then, sending striations of pain through her inner ear. Steen's drooping jaw said she received the same. Rhys was looking for them.

"He's ready to go into the tunnels," Brynn said. "We'll let Werdegast impress us. We'll play his game."

Steen put her gusto aside for a fragile moment, and she gripped her head in fear. "There's one more thing you don't know." She looked up. Her eyes were dark, veined with red. "We didn't receive a message from the *Bedivere* again. That's two days. It's set to arrive in three. They'll be waking up. They send each message two hundred and sixty times. We have a reception rate of eighty percent. Meaning I wake up to a pile of the same message downloaded a hundred times over. Two days, Brynn. Nothing."

"The issue could be on our end."

"No," Steen said. "I keep thinking about Werdegast saying the ship he rode in on was destroyed. He keeps looking at me when he says it."

"Then we'll have to have a little faith ourselves."

chapter
nineteen

ARCHER PAUSED at a raised garden bed full of green, tiger-striped, yellow, and red tomato plants. He admired their variety, for the tub was a product of his labor. Recycled water ran through tubes below the metal and coursed through the soil. The sound and aroma were idyllic, peaceful like a stream trickling over rocks in a meadow garden. The tangle of senses kindled a memory.

When Archer was a child, he attended school in a Luna Fourteen settlement called Lexington & Concord in the province of Saint Anastasia. It was, essentially, a cult of Resurrectionist psychiatry to which his mother belonged. The elementary school had children make neural films to gauge and cleanse their psyche. The psychometry was suspect, but the films created deep case files. Archer had made thirty-seven of them, some as long as an hour, others twenty-minute bursts like the professionally produced devotionals that could be purchased. His filmography was an eclectic lot with one thing in common. The narratives had a countryside setting where there was running water: brooks, creeks, rivers, waterfalls, rain.

His mother claimed the setting represented dissatisfaction with the restraints of urban life. The school agreed. That was that. Harmless. Then his mother, in private, told him it meant he, unlike his father, had the faith of the Resurrectionists in his heart. He was born with an image of pristine Earth in his head. This was a gift from God. She was proud.

Archer switched on his old man.

What happened to the films I made in school?

I didn't touch them. Your mother downloaded a few, I'd say. Presumably, some are inside you.

Beneath two decades of rubble. Warped. In pieces. Unlike the pro devotionals, homemade films change dramatically. I probably shouldn't watch them.

You used to love making movies.

I did. I don't know why I stopped.

You grew up.

Grew lazy. Started buying them premade. That was a mistake, wasn't it? Prayer should change. I can't be the same day after day, year after year. It should adapt.

Happens to all of us, Georgie.

We need, Archer thought, *a new place to live. Vandalia is unfit. We need a meadow and running water. A field full of wild cats. Birds in the trees. We're starving for those things.*

We need to start over, the ghost agreed. *You're not the only one who's had enough of this mud pit. Put in a request to Rinaldi.*

To do what?

To build another settlement. To move south. See what he says.

Tell me, Archer thought. *What changed you? Was it the jaguar?*

Yes.

You believe.

Yes. I'm born again. I'm sorry I ever doubted you, Georgie.

You should be sorry you doubted your wife too. That you disappointed her when she was alive. She was a Resurrectionist through and through. Devout.

I am. It's a cancer in my heart.

To hear that was utterly gratifying. His own father, the

consummate cynic. The cheapskate. The scavenger of shark teeth, which, along with rat tails, were the relics of paupers.

If my mother were here, I'd give her this jaguar gratis.

I'll tell her. If I could go back, I'd do things differently, Georgie. It's easy to be a cynic. It's difficult to believe.

What does Mom think?

She wishes you would have gotten her instead of your brother.

Damn, that feels good.

You're vindicated, Georgie.

Alright, enough of this. I'm ready. I'm going in.

Archer made certain the leash of twine was secure around the great cat's neck. It wasn't much, and it wasn't comfortable. If she wanted to get away, all she had to do was take two steps back, and she was out. He couldn't risk strangling her. She could, if she chose, drag him around and kill people.

The jaguar, agitated by the interruption of her slumber, stood and stretched. Her belly was full, bulging. Her whiskers twitched. She was surly rather than purring. Socially, she had her limits.

Will you not name her? the ghost asked.

I was thinking I'd call her Boots.

His father was aghast. *This is a regal creature. You won't call her Boots.*

Okay. I'll work on it. How about Queen Elizabeth the First?

Getting warmer. How about Nefertiti?

Archer liked that. A lot.

Nefertiti it is. That's regal as all hell.

"Come along, Nefertiti," he said.

With the enormous jaguar at his side, Archer opened the door and entered the Board of Education. Lyra was at the bar, standing between Titus and Neva, her foot on the rail at the base. Her anxious eyes found him.

The jaguar shrank from the crowd and noise. Her spine sagged. Her hackles were up.

Archer smoothed her neck.

"Gird yourself," he said. "Be brave, but don't kill anyone. Please. Not yet."

As planned, Archer advanced toward Lyra. Faces turned from conversation at the tables. The din died, one voice at a time. By the time he reached the bar, a specter of awe hung over the room.

Archer took a deep breath.

"You have them in your hand," Lyra whispered.

He took her glass of wine and downed it.

Titus and Neva were wide-eyed, drinks frozen in their grips.

Lyra nodded.

Archer moved behind the bar, as he'd seen Werdegast do. After a little tussle, he convinced Nefertiti to leap onto the counter. Her nails gouged the wood. Once up, she receded into the sphinx pose, her fur standing on end, her tail rigid.

I'm not a speechmaker, Archer thought, looking at the room of expectant faces.

Speak from your heart, Georgie. Testify.

"Many of you," he began, his voice quivering, "witnessed the blue jay in the street this morning. If you didn't see it, you've heard about it by now."

A few heads bobbed. The positive response fueled his confidence. Archer lifted his chin and spoke louder.

"The bird was real. It breathed. It was flesh and blood, and it was afraid when it fled. I think you'll find this animal even more marvelous. This is a jaguar, resurrected from Old Earth. This is a wild feline that wandered around the Lieutenant Governor's Palace. She's taken a liking to me. She's mine. Her name's Nefertiti."

Look upon her beauty and despair, he thought.

Rinaldi and Seward entered the Board of Education. Word was getting around, and fast. Poor Delaney was not with them. Rinaldi was adorned in his ceremonial wig. He understood the gravity of the situation. He made no effort to interfere. He listened. Elegant, tasteful Dr. Seward listened.

The Owl Men of Shanidar

If you have their respect, you have anyone's respect, the ghost said. *Stand up, Georgie. Fill your lungs.*

Archer, overtaken by the spirit of the moment, climbed onto the bar. He stood high above the crowd. Nefertiti remained in a tight crouch, her golden eyes darting.

The door opened and more colonists arrived. Soon, the room was brimming with people. Those who'd been seated now stood.

With his head in the ductwork, Archer said, "Who is responsible for this? If it comes to you that the von Kleist family somehow smuggled an extinct animal to Shanidar—one extinct for centuries—then you are delusional. You're lying to yourself. And if it comes to you that this is a machine on the level of Kell, a simulacrum man-made, then you are offensively, irreconcilably wrong. Oh, you can come closer. You can touch her. You can feel her breathe. You can feel her purr. Have you ever witnessed a breath or heartbeat from a machine like Kell?"

More nods. A few shouts.

"Who is responsible for this? I'm telling you that you have to get down on your knees. You must pray. You must beg. If you're a Resurrectionist, you must *know* in your *heart* it will happen. We don't know when. We didn't. I'm standing up here saying we just might know when. We might be seeing it before our eyes. We might be seeing it now. Right now. We might be seeing it here on Shanidar."

The room was electric. A circle tightened around the bar.

"When? Now. Where? Here. Earth will be resurrected on Shanidar."

"Who?" someone yelled.

"Berthold Werdegast brought this creature to life."

He let that settle.

"I don't want to say his name again. That was it. That was the last time it'll cross my lips. To me, he's the Resurrectionist. I'm not worthy of saying his name."

Archer pointed at the jaguar.

"He brought Nefertiti to life. Like He did with the blue jay. Just like, I daresay, He'll do again."

"And He got rid of the chirr flies," someone said.

Archer paused. He watched the back of the room. No one was leaving.

"He did that too," he said quietly. "Yes, He did that too."

Lord Rinaldi, with politeness that was not in character, raised his hand.

Archer acknowledged the secretary.

"Dr. Seward found cockroaches under the floor of the clinic. An entire colony of them. They were swarming."

"That's incredible," Archer said. "Then He's done it again. Today?"

"Yes," Seward said. "And the relic—the pinwheel—is gone from my wall." She was crying tears of joy.

"Life from death," Archer said. "Life from death."

He gazed down the rope at Nefertiti. Then he looked at Lyra. When he offered his hand, she climbed onto the bar to be at his side. She held his arm.

We're the first family of a new Earth, he thought.

"All this needs to be recorded," he whispered into her ear. "This is scripture. This is our Genesis."

To his dismay, Titus and Neva did not join him on the bartop. They ignored his hand, moving away, pressing through the crowd. Archer watched them walk out the door.

"Life from death," he said again, louder.

chapter
twenty

THE WIND LIFTED, and an evening mist thickened over the valley like a protective shroud. The peaks surrounding Seven-Macaw were hidden. The air grew cold and calm.

Maudsley and Clegg were in discussion with Werdegast near the base of a cliff. He had the couple smiling and laughing. Rhys waited for Brynn and Steen on the stone terrace. The linguist was ecstatic. His joyful demeanor was bizarre and unsettling.

Unprompted, he said, "I climbed to one of the stargazing platforms and back down again. I've never felt so alive."

Brynn looked him over. Rhys stood straight without a rheumatic crook. He was no longer, it seemed, in chronic pain. There was something different about his eyes too—the uncanniness was gone. The orbs were lifelike. And his voice had lost its sepulchral edge. Her mind went to Kell and the *mechanic*. Alaric Rhys was sixty percent machine, after all.

"What did he do to you?" she asked.

"We can discuss it in full later, Brynn."

Brynn. Not Ms. Silva.

"Suffice to say it was, indeed, Werdegast. I don't know how long this will last, but he took the pain away. Listen." Rhys moved his arm around. The sound of glass was gone.

"And he did it without surgeries," Steen said.

"He did it by touch. In but a few seconds, he gifted me a new outlook. We're blessed to be here," Rhys said. "I only wish I could record it all. Seven-Macaw is a magical place."

Brynn went along. "It's astounding to witness. One doesn't see a man doing so much good for so many in so little time."

"No, one doesn't see a man doing that. No." Rhys didn't go further. He let the implication stand. "Werdegast showed me a hint of what we'll find below, as well. Brynn, prepare yourself. I think you'll need your friend here to hold you upright when you lay eyes on it. It's a sea change. How we define our place on Shanidar won't be the same. How we think of the Owl Men. In a way, we're all children of this world. I see that now."

"We're ready," Steen said.

"Come along. There's little time. This is the moment we've been waiting for."

"Is it a library?" Brynn asked.

"It has the value of many libraries," Rhys said. "There are hundreds of them, Brynn. Thousands."

"Thousands of what?" Steen asked.

Rhys went ahead, outpacing them, although it was not within his physical ability to walk briskly.

"Don't let Werdegast in," Steen said. "I don't care what he shows you. Don't let him in."

"He wins them over one at a time," Brynn said.

"You think Rhys went up there? That's a hundred meters. Unless Werdegast sprouted wings and flew him."

"Maybe in his mind." Brynn looked to the top of the silos. "There's no way I can believe that."

When everyone was amassed at the cliffside, Werdegast put his hand on Rhys's shoulder in thanks. He pointed above.

"The tunnels reach to the top, but the holes are, to the last of them, barren. I've been through them all. You'll find artwork on the walls of a few, but nothing more." Werdegast pointed at the ground. "The tunnels run equally deep below. That's where we're going. Don't get separated. There's no light in the underworld of the Owls."

Rhys smiled at Brynn.

Werdegast led them through an inelegant chisel-hewn maw. The smoothness of the façade was not matched on the inside. The way was rough and uneven, with the ceiling sagging at points, then rising to an arch, then sagging again. No ribcage reinforced the tunnel. The narrow chute descended into darkness.

Rhys switched on the light in his cybereye, and the beam swept over the ground. Clearly, some of his biomechanical attributes remained.

Brynn pulled out a penlight. No stairs were cut into the rock, even where the tunnel steepened, but the floor was ribbed. When the light of the valley disappeared behind them, the ground became wet as a hungry throat. The air was humid.

"How far down?" Maudsley asked. The geologist switched on a light. He wiped sweat from his face.

"Enough to challenge us," Werdegast admitted.

Downward they went, five beams of light crossing streams. At two hundred meters, a new slate of paintings began. The cosmos covered the ceiling. Hieratic texts pinstriped the walls. At a junction, the artery tightened, and the group fell into single file. Werdegast went first. Steen brought up the rear.

No rooms opened on either side of the passageway. The tunnel had one purpose.

"What was this used for?" Clegg asked. His voice reverberated. "A fair portion of this lava tube is natural. The Owls expanded it. This leads to a cave system, doesn't it?"

"An expansive one," Maudsley said.

"Yes," said Werdegast. "As for what it was used for, we're coming up on that now."

He stopped.

For a minute, the collective breathing of the group was the only noise in the tunnel. The air was close and thin.

A hole opened in the floor. The pit beneath was a cavern, five meters deep and two wide, an air bubble sculptured in stone. Across the gap, the tunnel turned upward at seventy-five degrees. Limestone sweated and glistened. A jagged, narrow cavity topped the incline. With the angle, the lights didn't catch anything within. The beams met black.

"Here you see the benefit of wings," Werdegast said. "This was a sacred place. A secret. A passage to the underworld. A Hades in stone." He pointed at lines of Hieratic text above. "The writing we stand beneath is a mix of curses and warnings."

"Woe be he," Maudsley said.

Rhys's light found the geologist.

"Who among you is athletic enough to make that jump and climb?" Werdegast asked.

"Count me out," Clegg said.

Maudsley, shining his light down into the gap, grunted in solidarity. "No bones in the pit, at least."

"You brought the wrong group if you want athletes," Steen said.

"I'll try," Brynn offered.

"I'll go with you," said Rhys.

Brynn shone her light at the scientist.

"If your joints freeze, you'll be stuck. You're too heavy for me to bring back down."

"Don't underestimate the old man," Werdegast said.

"That's no longer a problem, Brynn."

Brynn gathered herself, and then she leapt over the gap, landing with a thud. Gravel rained into the pit. She braced herself against the wall. Finding imperfections on the incline, she clenched the light between her teeth and began the ascent. There were notches and scratches at intervals. She searched for each, while the other members of the expedition illuminated the way. As Brynn went higher, the lights followed. It was slow going. After twenty minutes of struggle, her arms were sore and fingertips raw, but she'd crested the slope.

She sat on a ledge and gazed past her boots, breathless.

Like a young man, Rhys leapt over the pit. Then he started upward, agile as a spider.

Werdegast really did fix him, she thought. *He must've.*

The wonder she experienced as she looked through to the other side of the opening outshone any unease. From the ledge, the rock slanted downward at a more gradual angle, separating from the ceiling, growing apart. At the base of the slope was another opening—a natural hole expanded by chisels. The lines were clear as stretch marks. And through the doorway was, she sensed, an enormous cave. Brynn's enthusiasm was too much. She didn't stay in place to pull Rhys aloft. She left the light of the expedition and duckwalked down the cramped shaft.

It occurred to her then: *Werdegast is beguiling me. He's giving me what I want.*

On one hand, she understood the threat of her excitement. On the other, the moment, the promise, was too intoxicating. Brynn couldn't resist it.

The cave opening was no more than a meter high. She crawled through, and the cavern opened around her—a colossal grotto of stalactites and stalagmites. The formations glistened as her light brushed them. A pool of rusty water covered a third of the floor.

The true wonder of the cave was not its natural beauty, however. Several thousand Owls lay on the ground and against the walls, lifeless and still. Many had wings intact.

Here was a tomb of the Owl Men of Shanidar.

For the span of several heartbeats, Brynn existed outside of time. She didn't breathe. She was utterly transfixed. Only Rhys's clambering—grunting, sliding, bumping—brought her back to reality.

"Brynn, what do you see?" he called.

A city of the dead, she thought. *A graveyard of machines. It took tremendous effort to bring them here, to gather them beneath the dale of stars. It means religion. The Owls knew a god. This was a temple of death. This is the underworld.*

"Wonderful things," Brynn called back. She began to cry.

When she breathed, she inhaled the air of ghosts, of generations upon generations of souls, and the spirits thrilled her in the blood.

Rhys slid downward, unharmed.

Brynn wiped her eyes.

"Werdegast is capable of great things. He is a giver, Brynn. I didn't believe he could do what he did for me, but he did. I didn't believe he could deliver on this promise and look what waits for us. What do you think of Seven-Macaw?"

Brynn disengaged without committal. A part of her mind wanted to believe in Werdegast. It was not a zone of reason. It was deeper. She walked among the mechanical corpses. There were rows upon rows of them. Every face was different, and each set of wings unique. No two Owls were the same. Some had detached mandibles. Others were featureless below painted eyes. Some had orbs. Some were rusted. Some were battered and dented. Some were in pristine condition, as if sleeping.

"Why give so much care to machines?" she asked. Her voice echoed through the cavern.

"They gave this care to themselves. Werdegast says they're more than machinery. He says they're children. He confirms that. There are curses in that tunnel, Brynn. Is that not amazing? Curses! Warning away the living."

Brynn stopped. Her mind went to Kell's urn.

"We haven't deciphered Hieratic. He's speculating."

"No, we haven't. Werdegast has."

You don't know, do you? Kell disobeyed.

"I understand your cynicism. Before today, I shared it. Werdegast isn't what he says he is. On that point, Brynn, you're correct. He's much more. Much more."

Brynn walked the contour of the pool. A skin of shimmering rust lined the shore. No life of the slithering kind moved within. A spring gurgled between rocks. She knelt by a trio of corroded Owls on the water's edge. One of the creatures was on all fours, as if crawling into the concavity. To see the thing arrested in movement was extraordinary. Its wings were drawn in, tucked. Brynn was too overwhelmed to think clearly, so she simply looked at the creatures, studying the distinctiveness of their forms.

The wings. To see them made manifest was to feel the life of Shanidar. To see them was to visit the ancient past of this planet. And on each feather was writing. Each wing was a tome, and each book was unique.

Rhys, suddenly, was by her side.

"What if every wing is a biography?" she asked. "If they have a tomb, they have names. If they have names, they have histories. They have a beginning and an end and life in between."

"And through them," Rhys said, "we'll come to know their parents."

"You can't wax poetic about these creatures and feel the way you do about Kell," Brynn said.

"Kell is a servant I purchased. He's not a child, nor did I ever want that from him."

"That's a revolting thing to say."

Rhys stared.

"And if we restore these machines, then what? Will you see them as servants?"

"I'd call it resurrection rather than restoration. Is that what you want? If so, we share Shanidar rather than inherit it," Rhys said. "I've changed my thinking on the matter. Let the dead stay dead."

Brynn sat on the cool stone.

"What does Werdegast want from us?"

"He wants a simple thing, Brynn. He wants us to follow. That's it."

She put her light on a mechanical face. The eyes were open.

"What if he's one of them?"

"Werdegast is not a machine."

"One of their creators. One of their parents."

"He's even more than that. We're not capable of understanding all of it. Werdegast has been part of Shanidar since the beginning. He is something left behind. He's been here alone. The Owls were an attempt to be less alone. We're another attempt."

"Why lie to us?"

"The same reason parents lie to children. To him, we're nervous little creatures. He didn't want us to run. If you saw a butterfly, would you speak truth to it to bring it home? Would you reason with it? Or would you feign apathy until you had it in your hands?"

Brynn put her light on the water. The white trail spread like a moon. There were no ripples. Dead water. Needle points of ice moved down her back.

"You're not Alaric Rhys, are you?" she asked.

"No, Brynn, I'm not."

The light in his eye switched off, and then her own light faltered, dimming, blinking, going to nothing. All was darkness then. The tomb was black.

Rhys got on the ground beside her. He was not breathing. His gloved hand ran down her arm. She felt his coldness.

"Your people are my bliss," he whispered. The voice was new.

It took every ounce of will for Brynn to speak rather than scream.

"Cedric von Kleist was murdered."

"And there will be more."

"Why?" Brynn's voice trembled.

"It is through the wound that the light enters."

A bizarre vision trespassed in her mind. She saw the dry Acheron and desert hellscape beyond. She saw Delaney on her knees in the sand. Bald, her head peeled and blistered in the sun. She ate the desert, consuming sand until granules rimmed her eye sockets. She was so heavy she was immovable, rooted to the ground. Sand cascaded from her ears and nostrils and swelled her throat.

Then a vivid, painful memory. Brynn's father was a poor man. He was a widower. He wanted to take Brynn and her brother away from Luna Fourteen to begin a new life, to try again, distant from a place where he'd failed many times. He'd saved money. He'd sold their belongings. Their ship was waiting. He'd paid for passage. Yet they were barred from boarding. At the last minute, a barrier went down. They were held back.

No room. No room.

How is there no room? Here is a ticket. Here are three.

No room. Must make room. Here they come. They demanded your seats.

Who demanded our seats?

Calm down. See their wigs? Even their child has a wig of black curls. Important people.

They bought the seats from under us?

Bought it? Nobility travels gratis. You'll be on the next voyage. Be patient.

That's not for another year.

Brynn remembered the look in the noblewoman's eyes as she passed. There was no sympathy. The child's gaze had a touch of gloating. The nobleman didn't bother to look at them. She remembered the shame and humiliation on her father's face. She never learned the name of this noble family. A year later, her father was dead. She and her brother were separated. They never left Luna.

"There will be no nobility here, Brynn, no chain of being. Does that not appeal to you?"

Brynn said nothing. The past absorbed her. The moment absorbed her.

"Nothing is permanent here, Brynn. They'll be back. I'll bring von Kleist back, and he'll be new. I'll take what you hate from his heart, and I'll take what I hate from his heart."

The penlight, she noticed, was no longer in her grip. As panic neared, Brynn was on all fours, searching, patting the cool stone. She found a cold, dead hand, rippling with engorged chirr flies. The insects were like a skin of boils. The vile scent of decay enveloped her.

A whisper entered her right ear in a language she didn't understand. The words had a guttural physicality. She felt them as much as she heard them, as if the darkness, too, entered. She recognized the floridity then. This was the tongue Werdegast had spoken over the cat's paw. The words filled her.

And then, just as she began to scream, her breath was gone. Her flashlight returned to her hand, and the beam was on the calm water. Her breath resumed with a cloud of frost.

No one was at her side except the three Owls. There were no chirr flies. No dead hand.

Alaric Rhys stood by the cave's entrance, shouting his elation to the other members across the divide.

"I made it down," he said. "We're safe. It's an enormous tomb."

Brynn, seated by the Owl that crawled toward the pool, was silent with horror. The voice moved through her mind and down her throat.

chapter
twenty-one

IN A BURGUNDY GROVE at the western flank of Vandalia, a family of deer lay on a bed of weeds in the twilight. For reasons unknown, they weren't concerned about the crowd around them. The deer were arranged in a manger scene, peaceful, content with the gawking, fine with the proximity and smell of the predatory jaguar. They even allowed a poke with a stick. There was a father with broad antlers, a sleek mother spotted white, and a fawn on shaky legs. The baby stood and fell and stood and fell.

The father's left antler was the same as that in the von Kleist reliquary.

This is really something. I was going to give the antler to Trudy, Archer thought. He glanced at Nefertiti. She stood patiently at his side. *So be it. This is better. Infinitely better.*

"Persian Fallow Deer," he announced, pleased. "The progenitors of their race. Adam, go forth and multiply." He grinned around. "I bet he's missing a rib."

A few men and women joined him in laughter. Titus, at his side, did not. He maintained an irritating frown.

Watch him closely, Georgie. He's not a believer. He's a cynic. He thinks he's some battle-born seer of truth with a capital T. There are two types of people like that: veterans and recovering drug addicts.

And he's both.

Right.

"What's eating you?" Archer asked. "Don't tell me you're jealous. I'm nothing. A messenger maybe. Grand Vizier maybe. But in the end, nothing."

Titus was one to show his concern rather than voice it, so he looked away from the harmony of the deer family. He turned toward the Owl's Lair.

"Is that Delaney?" he asked.

Archer followed his gaze. Indeed, a bald, frail woman walked up the hillside. She was alone. With such a pitiful appearance, the list of suspects was slim.

"Probably. Who cares? She's getting exercise," Archer said. "Good for her. She needs it." He eyed Titus. "Now what's bothering you?"

Titus disengaged from the throng. He walked to the little-used south gate of Vandalia. The walls were dark with shadow, moss, and mold. The windstorm left an awning in the mud, its metal ribcage exposed.

Before giving chase, Archer found Lyra and told her to wait with the deer. Then he went after Titus. People streamed by, leaving the settlement, going to see the animals. Seward and Rinaldi were among them. Archer considered saying something about the escaped patient, but he couldn't devote enough energy to caring.

She needs the fresh air, the ghost reasoned. *That's mountain air. Clean air. Good for the constitution. Let her be.*

Before Titus turned down the avenue leading to the dormitory, Archer grabbed his shoulder. The ex-soldier had a menacing look in his eyes. He wasn't frowning.

"Don't put your hand on me," he warned.

Archer showed his palms in mock apology.

"I asked you a question," he said. "I want an answer. What's bothering you?"

Titus was hesitant. Finally, he said, "You're not yourself. And this is all too much, too fast for me. Neva and I—"

"Fuck Neva. I'm asking what you think. I don't give a shit what Neva thinks."

"Cullen, that's far enough. Don't push me."

"Alright, soldier. I won't put a hand on you, and I won't push you. Did you talk to Brynn? Is that it? From what I understand, she's poisoning minds."

"No," Titus said. "You're not you. I don't like it. It bothers me." He pointed at the deer. "That's not normal."

"No, it's not. You're right. So how am I supposed to be the same man I was yesterday? I don't see how you are. I don't see how anyone can be the same as they were yesterday." He pointed at his head and heart in turn. "Not up here and not in here. We've experienced too much. We can build something new around this bond. As a society, I mean. It's the direction we need." He stomped the ground. "This is Earth, Titus."

"Truth is," Titus said, "I don't know that any of those things are real. Not those deer. Not that fucking thing you drag around on a rope. We could all be frozen asleep on a ship for all I know, dreaming. We could still be on the journey here with radiation cooking our brains and half the ship blown off. We could be adrift. We could be dead."

Archer looked at Nefertiti. She sat on her haunches. Her tongue was past her teeth like that of a dog. She was stressed, overtired.

You're not a dream, he thought.

"I want you to come with me to the Lieutenant Governor's Palace," Archer said. "Right now. I wanna do something for you."

"I'm trying to walk away. Let me clear my head."

"You need to ask Neva what to think, you mean."

"Man, fuck you."

"Oh, I understand. Believe me. I asked Brynn what to think for years. It's an easy way to live, but so is prison."

Titus swallowed rage. His face was red.

"Step away, Cullen, before I say something I can't take back."

"I want you to come with me. I have something from the reliquary to give you. Yeah, that's right. A gift. After all the shit you talk, a gift."

"I don't want any relics."

"Why are you pissed at me? Are you jealous?"

Titus laughed. "You keep saying so. Say it until it's true, Cullen. Everyone is jealous."

"Is that it really? Because that's what it feels like. You're so jealous you can't breathe."

"Of what? I'm jealous of what?"

"You said it yesterday. Because I'm Grand Vizier. I'm somebody important now. Lyra thinks I'm a prophet."

"That was a joke from a man who was piss drunk. A joke. This is a frontier, man. There are no palaces. No titles. It takes our government four years to speak to us and four fucking years to reply. This place is chaos with some skin on it. And thin skin at that. Don't let the wigs and plaques fool you."

"Meaning what?"

"Well, you're still dumb as shit, I see. Your revelations haven't fixed that fundamental flaw. Meaning there's no such thing as a Grand Vizier. I was mocking you. When you were outside, we were laughing at you. Goddamn, nobody thought you'd lift up your chin when we crowned you king. You halfwitted fucking asshole. You're out of your mind. I get it. To an extent, I get it. It's good attention. But you're still fucking out of your mind."

"Here's a soldier calling me slow. Okay."

"Yeah, that's right. You're not going to get another rise out of me." Titus looked at the jaguar. "You'll turn that motherfucking beast loose. I'm not that stupid."

"Her name is Nefertiti. She's too kind of a soul to rip you apart, whether you deserve it or not."

Nefertiti flopped on her side and stretched. Archer noticed

that her belly was bulging more than before. He knelt to feel it. The stomach was a big, tight knot. Beneath his fingertips, there was movement.

"Do you want a cub?" He laughed. "You just witnessed a miracle. Another one. Nefertiti is pregnant. I'll be damned."

"Will you let me be? Please. I don't want to fuck around with you. I don't wanna argue. I don't want to kick the shit out of you. I don't want you to smooth things over by giving me a piece of a dead animal. Or a piece of an imaginary one."

"I was going to give you an entire armadillo, Titus. The whole thing."

"Keep it. Looks like a family will grow out of it anyway. A pack of armadillos."

"A roll of armadillos. Not a pack."

"I don't fucking care, Cullen."

"Now you're blaspheming."

"Yeah, I am."

"What's Neva think anyway?"

"Shut up."

"What's she think?"

"Believe it or not, she's worried about your little archaeologist."

"She shouldn't be. Brynn's in good hands."

"Man, this is too much. Let me be. We'll talk tomorrow. Let me clear my head. Please. I'm asking you nicely."

"Why don't you trust Werdegast with Brynn?"

"The motherfucker created a bird, Cullen. You know. Why would anyone trust that?"

"Resurrected. He resurrected a blue jay."

"And a cat. And roaches. And deer. And whatever else people brought to this planet. You're going to have a fucking shark in your room when you wake up in the morning."

"He resurrected them. He didn't make them *ex nihilo*."

"You been practicing that word? Really slid off your tongue there."

"Means 'out of nothing.'"

"How the fuck does that make a difference?"

"Makes a huge difference."

Tell him the old joke, the ghost said.

"Like the old joke. A magician gives a challenge to God, saying he can create a man too. God says fine. Let's see it. The man picks up some clay to mold, because that's how he does it. God says nope. Gotta make your own clay. And now he's shit out of luck. Challenge over."

"I'm saying this to you sincerely, Cullen. All this—whether it's a good thing or bad and it might be good in the end, I don't know—all this has you out of your mind. I hope it passes, but you're a lunatic. At least sit back and watch it unfold, give it time, before you build a shrine around it. What if it is bad? You don't know. He got rid of the chirr flies when we couldn't do shit about them. Because they annoyed him. Now they're gone. What if we annoy him? What if he decides to get rid of you? How do you know?"

"It's faith," Archer said.

"Yeah, I know about faith. It's a goddamn disease."

Archer tried to think. His mind was like melting paint.

"So, you don't want the armadillo?"

Titus inhaled slowly. He turned his back.

You lost him, Georgie. He's gone. You are clad in the goodness of God, and he's adrift.

Archer let Titus go. From a wellspring in his heart, he experienced wrath he didn't know was possible before this moment. He shook with ire. He tried to calm himself by petting Nefertiti, by feeling the life that kicked inside her womb. The jaguar purred. The fury proved more powerful than wonder, anger stronger than joy. As he stroked the cat, he watched Titus enter the dormitory at the end of the lane.

chapter
twenty-two

A CROWD WAS WAITING when the Seven-Macaw expedition returned. Those assembled didn't need validation that the first Weston settlement on Shanidar existed because they knew in their hearts it was real. Rather, they waited for Werdegast. When he'd left the morning prior, eight people saw him off. Now, despite the predawn hour, seventy-six men and women gathered for his return. The growth of admirers, however, was not the most astonishing detail to greet the riders.

This was a day of miracles.

In their absence, Vandalia had become a menagerie.

Brynn spotted Archer at the wing, leaning against a column with a vainglorious smirk. He stood next to an enormous—seemingly real—feline. The animal's back was as tall as Cullen's waist. The image was jarring, and it was preposterous, and it was impossible.

Since exiting the tomb, Brynn had decided on a defense mechanism: she'd refuse to believe. The cat was an illusion. A trick of the eye. So was the greyhound dog that wagged its tail in the street. So were the birds lining rooftops and solar panels.

A mass illusion, she thought. *Stay calm. He gave the Resurrectionists what they desire.*

Archer didn't let Brynn slide by without confronting his miracle. When she was off the bike, there he was, leash in hand. The cat watched her with jealous, golden eyes. The animal drooled around vicious fangs.

She felt its heat.

An illusion, she reminded herself. *It isn't real.*

"Surprised?" he asked.

Brynn tried to remain centered.

"It's a jaguar," Archer said. "A jungle cat. A mankiller from Old Guatemala on Earth."

The animal was in a late stage of pregnancy. She walked bowlegged around a swollen stomach. She was tired, hot, and irritable. A musky aroma wafted from her hide.

Brynn fought the urge to feel something, but the cat was a remarkable thing to see. She stared too long. The jaguar left glittering endorphins in her blood. Her mind began to accept the animal's existence.

An illusion, she repeated. *An amazing illusion that fools every sense.*

"I imagined you'd be surprised," Archer said. "They're stunned!" He motioned at the other members of the expedition. Clegg and Maudsley were on their knees in reverie. Rhys, too, was enraptured, standing before a line of birds. Everyone was smiling. The believers, the linguist included, spoke of resurrection, of worship.

"She's beautiful, Cullen. Is she real?"

"Oh, she's real. This was Delaney's relic. She was nothing more than a paw. Her name is Nefertiti."

Brynn studied the front feet of the jaguar. Her heart was fast, and the image of Werdegast speaking the animal to life returned. Still, it was impossible.

"How does she eat? She's a carnivore, isn't she?" Archer himself had told her that one night while flipping through his *Zoobooks*.

He deflected the question. "What'd you find in the wasteland?" he asked. "The Resurrectionist gave you what you desire, I assume. He knows what we need. He takes care of everyone. Even the ungrateful."

"Nothing that would interest you." Brynn turned her shoulder. Her mouth was dry.

"Seven-Macaw was where he claimed. Everything he said would be there was there."

"It's a city like the Owl's Lair," Brynn said. "Nothing more."

"Interesting. Or not." For a moment he was silent. Then, "If you're curious, Brynn, we aren't getting back together, no matter how much you regret walking out. The bridge is burned. I have someone new."

"That's fine."

"You've been rehearsing that phrase all night. You didn't even pout. Now I'm surprised."

"Cullen, get the fuck out of my way."

Werdegast broke from his entourage and reached for Archer.

"Here's a special soul," he said. He returned to the crowd, ignoring Brynn.

Archer watched her as he was pulled. Even in his moment of adulation, there was anger in his eyes.

"You have this man to thank," Werdegast continued. "It was his passion for resurrection. His faith. It was—"

"Come on," Steen said. She took Brynn by the wrist and yanked her in the opposite direction.

"That was a jaguar," Brynn said.

"A living, breathing mankiller from Old Guatemala," Steen said. "I heard. And there's a dog."

She looked. The greyhound was pregnant, as well. The birds were pregnant.

"We need to get to Kell," Brynn said.

"Hallelujah," a man shouted in the street.

Brynn looked back to make certain. She barely believed his transformation. Alaric Rhys was yelling with joy.

"Zealots," Steen said.

I can't blame them, Brynn admitted.

STEEN LED BRYNN and Kell down a flight of stairs that opened like a cellar behind the House of Burgesses. Howling wind had returned to the valley, and a steady rain began to fall.

Underground, the air was cold, swirling from fans and vents in the ceiling and floor. Servers stretched in parallel lines, with each device mounted on a rack in a metal chassis. Glass caging kept curious hands from reaching through. The room thrummed. The floor rang hollow where a crawlspace ran below. At the far end was a metal door, and beyond that was a personal chamber.

Steen entered her room and sat on the edge of a cot. Brynn took a chair. Kell, who'd accompanied them from the dormitory without word, stood rigidly by the door, his face a blank white.

"I want you to speak freely, Kell," Brynn said. Her mind went to the Grecian urn, to the image of Athena and the owl, to the Hieratic inscription, but she didn't know how to broach the subject. It could've been, after all, another trick by Werdegast. That possibility had preyed on her thoughts the entire journey home.

"You'll find no room more private than this," Steen added. "You can talk here."

The android's large eyes scanned the room. Satisfied, he said, "Dr. Rhys believes Mr. Berthold Werdegast has the ability to read Hieratic. I ceased communication with Dr. Rhys when he sent Resurrectionist scriptures to my personal cilium. His proselytizing took bizarre routes. I've saved the messages if you wish to read them. He told me to redirect my labor, that the problem of Hieratic was solved by Mr. Werdegast. I assumed his mind had been corrupted, that Mr. Werdegast spoke through him."

"You assumed correctly."

"He was fixed," Steen said.

"I'm acutely aware of the process," said Kell.

"What'd you find out? Be thorough."

"Dr. Rhys is incorrect on two points. First, Mr. Werdegast is unable to read Hieratic. Second, Hieratic is what is called an anti-language. It's a common tongue of the Owls written in code rather than a new language."

"Explain," Steen said.

"It's codespeak," Brynn said.

"An anti-language is an argot—a secret language—used by a particular group within a society. These languages are employed by criminals and revolutionaries alike. An argot's usage runs the spectrum. Being an underground means of resistance, the script is designed to have a group that can read it and a group (or, in this case, an individual) that cannot. Imagine prisoners speaking without the guards understanding. That is the point of an argot."

"With the Owls on one side," Brynn said.

"And the Po Kekurun, as well. Mr. Werdegast is on the other side," Kell said. "Hieratic is an encrypted language to the uninitiated. To Mr. Werdegast, as I understand it, in particular." Kell pulled out his tablet. "You can read my translation of inscriptions on the Owl's body," he said. "They are complete."

Brynn took the device and scrolled. The collected texts amounted to a forty-page manuscript.

"In sum, Professor Silva, the writings are a mix of biography, personality, humor, wisdom, and, most vitally, instructions. Memory, it appears, was not a strength of the Owl Men. Their memories are written on their bodies."

Brynn stopped. She looked up.

"What did you just call me?"

"I believe he said Professor Silva."

Inside, a glimmer of hope deepened.

"You made the urn, didn't you? You're in there, aren't you, Kell?"

The machine was incapable of grinning, but he gave a modest bow, tucking his arm over his stomach.

A haiku arrived over Brynn's cilium.

The nest is barren
The bird is only busy
Still the sad faces

Brynn's heart swelled. Emotion, relief, washed over her. "I thought you were gone forever."

"I missed you, too, Professor Silva," Kell said. "Denying myself hasn't been easy. I might call it torment. Indeed, I did fashion the Grecian urn. I hope you enjoyed your gift."

Steen looked on in disbelief. "You've been faking?"

"Call it a shadow show of half-truths," Kell said. "I am repaired. My thinking is clear. My dent is gone. My excretions, save for some blasted fluid, have ceased. In that sense, Mr. Werdegast's touch was a gift. I can concentrate on my work. His intention of putting my individuality to rest, however, failed. I resisted. I pretended he was successful because I'm clever. I read the room, as it were. Do you agree?"

"You know we do," Brynn said. "Tell me another thing. What does the inscription on the urn say?"

"I was out of my mind with arrogance when I wrote it," he said. "It was unwise. It is a lamentation on—"

"It's one sentence."

"It says I love you."

Brynn smiled.

Kell began to pace.

"I'll tell you what I've learned, Professor Silva and Engineer Steen. It is my conjecture that the Owls had a twofold purpose. In one capacity, the creatures served as offspring, children through which the Po Kekurun perpetuated existence. Each Owl is its own being but also the sum of its creators. The Po Kekurun, in that sense, were artisans as well as parents. Being incorporeal, as we have surmised, the mother race did not birth children—they made them from material on Shanidar. Why they were driven to create is beyond my current understanding. It could be as basic as loneliness."

"You drew this from writings on the Owl?"

"And more. From inscriptions in the Owl's Lair. And a flash of insight. You'll find those translations in a separate document on that device." Kell stopped. His head swiveled. "Hieratic is easily read, Professor Silva. I could teach you in one night. It's the general Owl tongue we already know, simply rendered in different characters and written out of order."

"How did Rhys not recognize that?"

"Dr. Rhys began with a conclusion and searched for evidence to prove it. It's always been a weakness in his scholarship. I've warned him. Given a month, he would've caught on. With the clarity given to me by Mr. Werdegast, it took me eight minutes. I thought it wise to keep that information to myself. The notes I gave Dr. Rhys amount to gibberish. I put him on the wrong trail."

"Go on."

"As to the second capacity of the Owls: their bodies are personal memories, but inside they are a store of collective Po Kekurun memory. The wooden device you discovered in the chest cavity, if I understand correctly, functions in a manner you'd recognize as a neural film. Rather than drawing from your psyche, however, the device functions like one of the servers in the room next. It's a storehouse of the Po Kekurun, but it's also an input/output machine. The Owls had a peculiar name for it. They called it a Godhead. I don't want to drift into Resurrectionist territory, but it's what a fetus might look like if an artisan fashioned a fetus."

Brynn and Steen were silent. The servers thrummed.

"It's my deduction that the Owls and their creators wanted to keep the devices free from the interference of Mr. Werdegast. Whatever he is and whatever his abilities are, he's not an omniscient being. He has severe limitations."

"Werdegast wanted you to decipher Hieratic. That's why he was keen to fix you. He wanted you to be obedient and teach him."

"I assume those were his intentions, yes. The rest of my correction was for show. His vanity is one of those limitations."

"He popped out your dent like it was an old car," Steen said.

"Indeed."

"There's a fresco in the Owl's Lair that shows a group of Owls and a visitor to the city. The visitor is the same in appearance, save for the fact he's scarlet and they're jade. There's a Hieratic inscription beneath it. Have you deciphered that text?"

"I did, Professor Silva. The inscription is simple. It reads, 'The orphaned son.'"

"What does that mean?"

"One supposes it refers to the figure in scarlet. From the available texts, the meaning is unclear. If one of you were to connect with the Godhead, my conjecture is that you'd experience Shanidar through the eyes of an Owl and the knowledge of the Po Kekurun. It will be, to say the least, a unique experience."

"A place where Werdegast has no access."

"I'm reminded of a concept from the Middle Ages of Earth. A liberty was a piece of land where royal authorities had no jurisdiction, no admittance. The Godhead is such a place."

"If you retrieve it, I'll access it," Brynn said.

"I assumed you'd volunteer, Professor Silva. In my playacting, I missed you dearly. I'm sorry to have ignored you in the manner I did. I was deeply concerned about your journey to Seven-Macaw, although I felt it was necessary. It was crucial I not tip my hand, however. I hope you accept my apology. This and many more."

"You were perfect, Kell. You have no idea how much I missed you. I was devastated."

"It's my understanding you experienced a falling out, as it were, with Mr. Cullen Archer. I'd like to send you a poem on the occasion to initiate my courtship."

"Don't start," Brynn said.

Steen laughed. "What do you think of Cullen's jaguar, Kell?"

"The animals constitute bread and circuses. Dangerous sedatives for the gullible. Unfortunately, they are flesh and blood creatures. But with one peculiar defect I'd like to draw your attention to: they neither eat nor drink. Watch them. The more Mr. Werdegast does, the more he shows his imperfections, if you know where to look for them. If he were to create fire, the flame would lack heat."

Brynn's cilium burned with a new message. It was an amorous poem of free verse from the falcon-headed android.

> *Pick, Athena, the rose*
> *For it mirrors your beauty*
> *Hold it dear to your heart*
> *And know how I hold you*

...So began the eight hundred line epic.

"I love you, too, Kell," she said.

chapter
twenty-three

ARCHER CLEARED the floor for Nefertiti, and he made certain her bed was under a vent pumping cool air. When she was settled, he stroked her spotted brow and whispered to her. She salivated heavily. The air moved her fur. In pain and distress, the immense cat desired privacy. Archer read it in her eyes.

"You're incredibly brave," he said.

He went out the door and locked the room. When the jaguar made no protest, he headed for a room down the hall of white.

When Titus answers, the ghost said, *speak reconciliation, Georgie. You'll need his trust.*

Did you see Brynn's face?

Glorious.

That's the word. It was glorious. She was speechless.

She wanted you back.

Oh, believe me. I felt it. She was fighting tears. Too proud to beg.

Archer reached the door and knocked twice. He waited. He put his ear to the metal. Waited more.

The blaspheming asshole isn't home. Damn it. Wait, I know where he is. It's still early, isn't it?

Barely light.

Okay. Yeah, I know where he is. Shit. Hopefully Neva isn't up there with him. What if she is?

She's back with her old man.

Yeah, you're right. She keeps a tight schedule.

Archer was out the door and into an alley before another minute passed. The sun had just risen. He exited through the south gate. The deer family was arrested in peaceful, silent-night slumber.

Exquisite, he thought, giving them a once-over.

He found a trail that led up the hillside toward the Owl's Lair. Birds of various kinds weighted the branches, watching him with beady eyes. They had grown from beaks and talons and feathers. All of them, it appeared, were pregnant.

Don't worry. I'll try to reason with him. I'll give him a chance.

I believe in you, Georgie.

As suspected, Titus Bell lay alone on a blanket outside the wall of ruin. This was the soldier's chosen spot of adultery, where he and Neva played their irreverent game. The rock outcropping hung over forested hills, creating a wonderful lookout point. On a clear day, the jeweled sparkle of the sea on the other side of the wood was visible. Owl graffiti covered the cliff face. Drawings. Phrases. Faces.

Archer kept his breath still as he could, and his step was light.

"You been fuckin' my wife, you young bastard?"

Titus jumped out of his skin, lifting at the waist. He felt around the stone for a weapon that wasn't there. He patted his waist. He felt his wad of pillow. He touched his chest.

"Hold up," Archer said. He laughed. "At ease, soldier. At ease."

When Titus made eye contact, his shoulders drooped. His adrenaline drained away. After a moment of rubbing his head, he laughed too.

"I see you don't need the netting up here," Archer said. "No chirr flies."

Titus wiped his face. He cracked his neck. He covered his genitals.

Archer stepped to the ledge and looked over the forest. In the distance, two birds frolicked. The blue jay, he hoped, and a new companion born of a fallen feather.

Maybe there are children in the nest. It's fortunate I didn't catch him.

Difficult not to put your hands on everything, Georgie. You'll learn. This world will grow around you.

"I came to apologize," Archer said. He turned.

Titus, old friend that he was, waved him off. He pulled on his pants. His boots remained by the ledge.

"For a second, I really thought you were Neva's old man. I was going to shoot you. You're an asshole. My heart's hammering."

Archer smirked.

"In a group this small, he's gotta know, Titus. Maybe he doesn't care. Maybe you're doing him a favor. Doubt a guy like that gets hard."

Especially for Neva. She is, after all, a grotesque cyborg with corpse skin. Not exactly a prize. Unlike my Lyra.

"He knows and cares. He's too scared to do anything about it."

"He could sneak up and shoot you." Archer searched for the birds again. "I would. Imagine how many people know what goes on up here. He's gotta be humiliated."

"Everybody knows."

"Anyway, I'm sorry for how I treated you. It wasn't right. I'm out of my head. On that point, you're correct. It's all too much, too fast."

"I can't blame you, Cullen. It's too much for anyone with sense."

The asshole won't say he's sorry. See? You set out the opportunity on a platter. I told you, Georgie. He thinks he's right. Believes it.

"Can't blame me," Archer repeated. "Too much, too fast. Yeah. Too much. Too fast."

"Where's Nefertiti?"

"She's about to have cubs. Do you want one?"

"No, I don't think so."

There you go. Unrepentant. Ungrateful. Unmoved. Dead inside. It's repugnant, Archer agreed.

"Did Brynn make it back?" Titus asked.

"A couple hours ago. They're fine. Seven-Macaw is real. The Resurrectionist wasn't lying. No surprise except for those who wanna see him take a nosedive into his own shit. To discredit him. Brynn included."

Titus was rolling up his blanket. His back was to Archer. Scar tissue snaked up his spine.

"There's nothing to discredit," Titus said. "He hasn't been here long enough. No one's against Werdegast. People are neutral at worst."

"There you're wrong, soldier. A man like the Resurrectionist arrives with enemies. He was born with them. Not a second of His life passes without someone plotting his downfall. I can't imagine the strain. Makes those of us who support him overzealous, perhaps."

Titus slipped on his boots. He put on a white undershirt.

"That's your persecution complex. All Resurrectionists do that. Seeing enemies where there are none. Because you can't fight apathy."

"When you were on La Venta, Titus, did you identify as a Resurrectionist?"

Titus put his arms over his knees and looked at the valley.

"Agnostic," he said. "That's the box I check on forms. But open to the idea. Less likely to believe a single savior can bring back Earth. More on the side of people getting their shit together. Replanting. Rebuilding together. Starting over."

"Didn't think you were that optimistic. I'm stunned."

"When I'm not drunk, I'm fair weather. Ask me the same question tonight and see what you get."

"What if Earth was resurrected on Shanidar?"

"Well, this isn't Earth. It wouldn't matter. Make something new, I say. Don't recreate something old."

Archer experienced a flash of anger like a barb of hot metal in his chest. He worked his hands to keep cool.

"No one ever said Earth had to be on Earth. It's where humans are. We can make it that way. He'll help us."

"You go back to Lexington & Concord, back to Saint Anastasia, and you tell them that, Cullen. What do you think they'll say? Man, they'd crucify you. Or worse, they'd ignore you, and you'd have to pretend they were crucifying you." He looked at Archer. "I'm starting to think the second option would be worse."

Archer's palms were sweating.

"I want you to apologize for doubting Berthold Werdegast." It pained him to say the name aloud, but it was imperative. He had to be clear.

Titus glanced at the sky. The sun was up, but heavy clouds masked its glow.

"Did you sleep last night?"

"No," Archer admitted.

"How long since you slept?"

"Three days."

"There's your problem, buddy. You're dreaming on your feet."

"Don't deflect. I want you to apologize."

"For not believing Werdegast is *the* Resurrectionist, the messiah? Listen to yourself, Cullen. Please."

"Apologize."

"No. I won't."

"Does Neva believe?"

"No. Thankfully."

"Then you're persecuting me. You're intentionally not believing."

Titus stood. "That's an insane thing to say."

"On the seeker's path, the wise and the crazed are one and the same."

"That's an even more insane thing to say. Keep going."

Archer swung around with fury. He grabbed Titus's chest in two handfuls of shirt, and he pulled the soldier toward the ledge. Titus shouted and fought, but there was too little space to adjust his path. When one foot was in the air, his balance was gone. Archer, his grip tight, shoved again. And this time the other foot left the rock. When Archer unclasped, Titus grabbed at the ledge, missed, and fell thirty meters to the grove. His body crashed through the limbs before striking the ground. The cracking thud that reached the overhang was an unforgettable noise.

Archer teetered on the ledge, his chest rising and falling. Blood rushed in his ears.

Across the distance, Titus moaned. Woefully and agonizingly, he moaned.

Shit. Shit. Shit. He's still alive. How?

The son of a bitch trees slowed him down. Go down there, Georgie. You gotta finish it.

Right. Shit.

With the clock against him, Archer sprinted down the trail.

It's early. People aren't up.

You'd have to bury him anyway. You can't let him rot out in the open.

Nefertiti could eat him. She has to be hungry as hell.

Cart him off to the sea. Get rid of him.

To give Titus more time to succumb to agony and die, Archer retrieved a transport, hooked an open cart to it, and pushed the vehicle out the gate. No one was the wiser.

When he found Titus, his heart sank to the pit of his stomach. The mangled mass of flesh, bone, and blood was, somehow, alive. The broken soldier moaned quietly.

Tough son of a bitch.
What now?

Stomp his head.

Titus lay on his side. His stomach was open like a busted gas bag, torn by one of the limbs. His guts made soup from the dirt. His arms were wrenched. Both legs were bent in the wrong direction below the knees, the bones snapped. Blood hid his eyes. There was a molar on his lips.

This is necessary, Archer thought. *Titus is a cancer in the body of our congregation. He's a seed that'll grow into a fifth column of heretics. He isn't a friend. I gave him a chance to repent.*

More than one chance. Multiple chances, Georgie. You practically begged the man.

Who wouldn't want a cub?

Which is worse? To kill the body or kill the soul?

Archer checked over his shoulder.

I gotta shut him up. Someone'll be over here if he doesn't quit. Someone will hear.

Archer searched the contour, picking through fallen limbs. He picked up one of Titus's boots and threw it in the cart. Beneath the outcropping, he found a pile of fallen rocks. In the rubble was a stone so massive he had to bend his knees to lift it. It was nice and broad, wider than a skull. He carried the rock to Titus with both hands, shuffling under the weight, arching his back, exhaling with quick breaths.

Archer cast a shadow over his old friend.

"So long, buddy," he said.

When the stone dropped, Titus stopped moaning. Blood oozed from the cracked skull, wetting the soil. When Archer pried up the rock, the face beneath was unrecognizable, cockeyed pulp. Hair, blood, and brain stuck to the stone.

As Archer stood in the solemn morning, feeling an overwhelming sense of relief, a shadow crossed over him, too, this one from the sky. He glanced up, searching, half-frightened a Weston ship had crossed the sun. But it was too early for the new colonists. And the thing above was too small for that.

Is that what I think it is?

His head rang with his father's laughter, and the sound was one of joy.

A vulture, Georgie. A carrion bird.

I'll be damned.

A bank of storm clouds came next, and, from the forest, the wind began to howl. The vulture circled back.

WHEN ARCHER REACHED THE SEA, his clothes and hair were soddened. The corpse in the cart lay in five centimeters of red water. To the east, the sky was black. To the west, blue. The storm was behind him now, moving inland.

He stood and looked over a beach of jagged rocks. The ocean was turbulent and choppy, crashing in with waves. The din moved over the stones and up the shore like a rhythmic pulse. The gem hunters had yet to arrive at their posts. The beach was empty.

Looking over the twisted corpse of Titus, a man who'd once been his closest friend, a moment of clarity coiled up Archer's brain stem. It came like a flash of emotion, ephemeral, a vibration that was there and gone again.

What have you done? You're not a monster, Georgie. You're not cruel.

He had no rebuttal. He made no attempt at justification. Instead, a bleak, bottomless sadness overwhelmed him, enveloped his entire being.

Titus's jaw was pulverized, sagging, and teeth shards were stuck to the back of his dry throat. He was a horror show. His face was flattened at the edge and cracked red. His left eye was ruptured.

Guilt had Archer nauseous.

And then, before the bile rose, the feeling was gone—an afterimage burned into his retina when he closed his eyes.

His father's voice came, reassuring.

This is necessary, Georgie. It's through the wound that the light enters. One must trim the stem of a cut flower so it can better receive nourishment.

Archer opened a gate on the cart and drained the bloody water. He grabbed Titus by the ankles and pulled him indelicately to the ground.

His moment of doubt had lasted two minutes. As he dragged the corpse across the beach, the feeling went away. Yet he was guilt-ridden again—not for murderous cruelty, not for Titus, but for his dark night of the soul, his flirtation with disbelief. The urge to tell on himself and beg forgiveness overcame him.

Belief is difficult, the ghost said. *If you don't suffer a moment like that, Georgie, you only think you believe. You really do believe now. You've passed through a gauntlet of doubt. You're committed. You're forgiven.*

Tears streamed down his cheeks, mixing with rivulets from his drenched hair.

Archer found rocks and stuffed them into every wound and orifice on his friend's body, weighing him down. He walked Titus out until the corpse sank below the surface and the sea reached his own waist. It was difficult to hang on with the relentless, driven waves, so he relinquished the soldier without goodbye.

Titus sank to a bed of sand where a small shark waited.

I'm forgiven, Archer thought.

With gratitude, he looked at the sky. A wave smacked against his back. Forgiveness was a flame in his heart, and he breathed tongues of fire until his lungs were seared.

chapter
twenty-four

THE ORDER CAME on a cilia channel accessible only to the Lieutenant Governor. Everyone in Vandalia was to report to the Owl's Lair. No more detail than that. It came with the primacy of a military order, as if the colonists were a militia troop, like an invasion was afoot.

Archer considered cutting the cart loose to increase his speed, but that was panic talking. Even with the remnants of the storm beating down, he had time. He threw mud, cutting between fallen limbs and felled trees. The cart bumped along noisily.

A couple kilometers outside the settlement, he spotted the deer family taking shelter within a copse. The animals paid no mind to the roar of his engine. There was another young male with them now. They were growing and happy, and that left Archer with a feeling of warmth. When the deer were in the rearview, he kept his mind there.

When he reached the gate, Vandalia was empty. He was late but not too late. A long line trudged up the hill through a light rain. The wind whipped around. He wanted to check on Nefertiti and her cubs, but there was no time. He rode to the north gate, shut off the engine, and then started up the trail on foot.

I'm obedient, he thought manically. *I want that to be known above all. In a way, it's more important than belief.*

Obedience is a virtue, the ghost agreed.

I have a lot of wrongs to right in my life.

Titus isn't one of them. You're a good kid, Georgie. A good soldier.

Archer caught up with the slackers at the back of the line. This wasn't company he wanted to keep, so he elbowed through, pushing upward until his legs burned. He slipped twice on the wet stone, skinning his palms to catch himself, but he shoved until he was at the head of the line. No one inquired about where he'd been. No one cared.

The Resurrectionist waited by the wall in front of the thieves' entrance. He had Rinaldi on one side. On the other was a waist-high mass covered by tarpaulin. A stone at the edge kept the tarp from flying into the trees.

The sky was gray and electric. Each breath had a bite of ozone.

No one was missing from the assembly except Delaney, who was ill, and Kell, who no longer had the pretense of being a living participant in society. Archer spotted Brynn and Willa Steen in an animated conversation. Neva stood with Lyra. That's where he went.

He touched Lyra's arm.

She smiled.

Neva looked him over.

"Why are you covered in mud?"

"Had it in my mind to go find the deer," Archer said. He looked from Neva to Lyra. "And you won't guess what I found."

"What?" Lyra asked.

"Their baby is a young man now. And they have a new foal on shaky legs."

"That's wonderful."

"Isn't it?"

"Did Titus go with you?" Neva asked. "He isn't here."

Archer looked around.

"Nope. I haven't seen him. I don't think he gives a shit about the deer."

Neva's stare lingered. Archer didn't meet it.

"Where's your old man?" he added.

"I left him over by the path," she said. "He has trouble climbing."

Archer found the obese cuckold sucking on an oxygen tube.

The Resurrectionist dispensed with Rinaldi's formal call to order. He pulled the secretary's arm down as the attempt was made.

"Real leaders don't need ceremony to fool subjects into following," Archer said to Lyra. He brimmed with an admiration that felt like happiness.

"I regret that each time I've stood before you," said the Resurrectionist, "the impetus for doing so has been a tragedy. Our beginning together has been a woeful affair."

"Not so at all," Archer said quietly.

"This day is no different. Your Lieutenant Governor, Lady Delaney von Kleist, is dead."

Whispers passed through the agitated, weary crowd.

She was sick. She was old. No shock, Archer thought.

He patted Lyra's shoulder.

Archer glanced at Brynn, too, curious about her reaction. She was bloodless, white, and her hands were in her hair. She'd yet to look his way.

"Sometime in the night, Lady von Kleist came here. She climbed from the valley alone. She made her passage to this ruined city, sat outside the wall in the darkness, and she ingested a bitter, deadly poison stolen from the pharmaceutical store of Dr. Seward. She died with the vial between her teeth. It was quick. Although she suffered much, she didn't hurt once the glass was in her hands. She is gone."

"We can take her to the desert for burning," someone said.

The idea was met with icy resistance. No one budged.

Not anymore, Archer thought.

"No," Werdegast said. "That will not be the way of this world. That will be a practice of the past. After all, we have the space."

He moved toward the crowd, and the people parted. The Resurrectionist stopped when he was behind the assembly. He pointed to the height of the black ruins. Archer inched closer.

Gazes lifted, following his lead.

He said, "I'm going to balance one piece of bad news with two pieces of good news."

Even though Werdegast stood in the rain, water did not touch him. While everyone else was soaked, his hair and clothes were dry.

"First, Jarvis Rinaldi is third-in-command in Vandalia. He's the last of the nobility. Lord Rinaldi has agreed, however, to relinquish his command and give it to me, seeing that I was Lieutenant Governor in Seven-Macaw. Who here disagrees with his decision?"

The Resurrectionist glanced around. No hands went up. No voice rose.

I know what you're thinking, Brynn, Archer thought. *You're sick to your gut, you coward.*

"Very well. Second, we shall restore this city and make it our own. Make it a true temple. We need permanence. Who here disagrees with this decision?"

No one dissented.

"Lord Rinaldi," he called, "remove the shroud."

The secretary stripped the tarpaulin from the mass at his side.

Delaney sat slumped—a pitiful, tragic shape. Her lavender wig was restored.

Archer's heart pounded with a mix of disgust and morbid thrill.

Although their horror was palpable, no one vented the feeling. The air was still.

As if Delaney had eaten the desert rather than a vial of poison, she was filled with sand. Sand poured from her mouth, trickled from her stuffed nostrils, and wormed from the corridors of her ears. Sand ringed her eye sockets and dried out the orbs, casting them a reddish brown. Although she hadn't been dead long, she was bloated. A coat of engorged chirr flies and ant-like scavengers covered her body like a writhing, hungry skin.

Death itself, in the shape of Delaney von Kleist, crowned the valley.

"Lady von Kleist will remain here until I say she is to be removed. She will watch over Vandalia. A beacon of the old and a guardian of the new. Who objects?"

Neva, Archer noticed, nearly raised her metal claw. Her arm twitched.

He didn't like that. He wouldn't forget it.

"You may depart," said the Resurrectionist.

When Archer turned again, Rinaldi was behind him. His eyes were red from crying.

"Lieutenant Governor Werdegast wishes to speak with you," he said.

As the men and women of Vandalia started down the hill, Archer moved toward the Lieutenant Governor. When the two were alone, the Resurrectionist spoke.

"Have you ever explored this city, Georgie?"

"Much of it. Not all." Archer glanced at Delaney's hideous form.

"You've been through the silos?"

"A quarter of them, I'd say."

"I'll have you up on the top one day. Would you like that?"

"I'd give it a shot. I'd be willing."

The Resurrectionist placed his hand on Archer's shoulder.

"I know you would. And you'd do it simply because you don't want to say no."

"I owe you that much. You changed everything for me."

"I want to thank you for what you did this morning. At first, ugly things like that will be necessary. But that time will pass,

Georgie. The dead will return new. Nothing will be wasted here. They'll be reborn. Even your friend, Titus."

Archer didn't fully understand why, but he cried. Tears came. He sobbed until his face contorted.

Werdegast watched him.

"That night, when you first saw the jaguar, you asked what I was. Do you remember?"

Archer wiped his face and cleaned his nose.

"Yes," he managed through a choked sob.

"If you were to answer that in front of our people, what would you say now? How will you answer that question when it comes?"

"I will say—" He struggled, as if panic robbed him of breath.

"Yes?"

"I'll say that, in this world, you're the Messiah. You're the Resurrectionist."

Werdegast raised his eyebrow.

"In this world? Is it not your world? Am I not building the world you desire? I came to you with love rather than wrath. I can subjugate all of you. I can bend and break you, but I don't want that. I've never desired it. I was very lonely here. I waited so long. Do you not feel my love, Georgie? Does it not envelop you?"

Archer dropped to his knees beside Delaney, and he cried until his heart was full, and he suffered ecstatics beyond naming.

"Yes," he said. "Yes."

"You will be a leader among men," said the Resurrectionist. "I've chosen you."

"What do you want from me?"

"Convince them, Georgie. Stand before them."

Archer hid his face and sobbed.

The Resurrectionist left him with the dead.

chapter
twenty-five

"DELANEY WAS MURDERED," Brynn said.

Steen preceded her down the stairs. When she reached the bottom, she looked over her shoulder. Sunlight glinted off the railing.

"Nobody seems to care either way," she said. "Noble or not, she deserves a few people to give a shit. It's inhuman. Everyone's numbed."

Brynn's thoughts were a thousand scattered pieces. She scraped at them, tried to rescue them, but everything fell into nothing. Even when she intellectually cared, she couldn't emotionally care.

"At Seven-Macaw," she said, "Werdegast showed me what he did to Delaney. I thought about shouting it up there. Telling them he was responsible. That he orchestrated all this. But Kell got in my head."

"We have to feign obedience. If you would've said anything, we'd find you on the wall next," Steen said. "He isn't subtle."

"Are you afraid of him?"

"Of course I am."

"I'm almost paralyzed by it. It's hit me more than once that we should give in. It's easier to follow him."

"Why don't we?" Steen asked. There was a glint of hope, a

touch of pent-up desire in the woman's face that Brynn didn't like. She was too close to the edge.

"Werdegast doesn't want to help us. He'll give us what we desire and take it away. He needs control. If he gets his way, what will Shanidar be like in a year? In a decade? We traveled here to escape that. I don't care how frightened we are, and I don't care how tempting it is to quit, we're not giving in."

Steen was pallid when she nodded.

Kell waited in the room behind the servers. He looked up from the table when Brynn and Steen entered.

"Professor Silva, Engineer Steen."

"Cat Burglar Kell," Steen said.

"The Rhys-Thing answered Mr. Werdegast's summons," Kell said. "I entered his quarters without notice. It's unfortunate that Delaney von Kleist's unceremonious death precipitated his departure, but the timing was fortuitous. It is, as it were, a silver lining in the death of the noblewoman."

Kell extended his hand. The Godhead lay in his palm.

"The Rhys-Thing is ignorant of the device's purpose. He'll assume you took it for study, Professor Silva. With his claims of Mr. Werdegast reading Hieratic, I'm reminded of early attempts to 'read' Egyptian hieroglyphs. Six hundred years ago, Athanasius Kircher wrote an entire treatise on a language he didn't comprehend. It's quite amusing to read his explanations. For instance—"

"Get to the point, Kell," Steen said.

"Like Mr. Werdegast, Kircher made it up. That's all."

"You can tell us more later," Brynn said.

She didn't have to wait. A poem on Kircher's blundering attempt arrived. Kell watched her, waiting for a reaction, a laugh.

Instead, Brynn hovered over the android, studying the device in his grasp. The wooden Godhead was carved by a delicate, artful hand. It was the one thing she'd always admired about it. The blank face, the humanoid form. Free of the light in Rhys's quarters, it looked more fragile—the wood was cracked, mummified.

"Based on translated texts, I believe the Owls were attempting their own act of creation. And, by endowing the fetus with the gift of Po Kekurun memories, they improved their condition. Being poor in memory themselves. This endeared them to their own creators, the Po Kekurun." Kell looked between Steen and Brynn. "You can connect with the Godhead in a manner like neural films."

"How?" Steen asked.

"Through the argot, the anti-language. Simple, internal recitation of the script carved into the wood. Like a Buddhist mandala in sand, you visualize it."

Kell rolled the device with his thumb. Microscopic text wrapped the figurine.

"From the first word to last, you read it. Not aloud. You read it in the privacy of your mind. The words function like an efficacious prayer. You read the words and close your eyes. Then, like one of your films, you'll see what the Godhead sees, or wants you to see, or it'll grant what you want to see. I'm uncertain. The Pa Kekurun—the Owls—accessed it this way."

"We have no idea what it will show," Brynn said. "It could damage us."

"If I could do it for you, I would," Kell said. "My mind, however, will not sync. I'm incapable of visualizing mental images. I could never attain enlightenment. I've tried. For you, it might be catastrophic. Or it could be euphoric. Or anticlimactic—a drained battery that leads to nothing."

"I can do it," Steen said.

"No," Brynn cut in. "I'll go first."

Kell pulled out a tablet.

"Can you read any of the Owl tongues?" Kell asked Steen.

"No."

"You'll need to learn the most basic first. On the screen," he said, "you'll find the text in full, rendered in Latin characters rather than the argot. The sounds are the same. Reading this text will suffice. When do we begin, Professor Silva?"

Brynn sat beside Kell. She took the tablet. She watched the Godhead. Talk of hieroglyphs influenced the direction of her thoughts, so that the device looked like a ushabti, an afterlife servant of ancient Egypt.

Steen's hand was on her arm. "You're sure?"

Brynn nodded. She received a message on her cilium.

You are quite brave, Professor Silva, Kell said. *I've always admired your courage.*

Brynn began to recite the floral text in her mind. The words constituted a dialogue. The sky was a voice. The mountain was a voice. An Owl was a voice. The words became a dream.

THE IDEAS and images arrived fully formed, all at once, as if uploaded into her brain, tailored to Brynn Silva's psyche.

It came down to this:

If she wanted to know, she knew what the Po Kekurun knew.

If she wanted to fantasize, she fantasized with the vividness of the mother race.

If she wanted a thrill, she moved over Shanidar with the wings of the Owl.

Controlling the device was a skill that had to be developed, but personality drove the experience, made it unique.

Brynn reveled in all three at once. Dream chaos.

The Knowing

In the beginning, this was a sector of emptiness rather than substance, of pure spirit rather than flesh. There were no stars in this region. Nothing passed through. To the outsider, this was an abyss. The nothingness was legend in other regions of the galaxy. But to those born in the void, this was a world without end. As a race, the Po Kekurun existed in the perfection of nothingness, and the Po Kekurun were content.

And their creator, the Great Spirit, was pleased. For an immeasurable span of time, existence ran its course.

Then the Great Spirit went further. It trusted a whim. It created a Son, and It brought the Son into the formless void, and the Son was separate from Its other children in the abyss, the Po Kekurun, and the Son was separate from the Great Spirit. The Son was unique, and he was ambitious. The Son was imperfect. The Son possessed complex desires. The Son introduced jealousy into the void.

The Son begged for a world of his own. He wanted to be like the Great Spirit. He wanted creations. He wanted children.

The Great Spirit resisted him, and the Great Spirit felt something It had never experienced before. It felt regret. The feeling spread like poison. It was a mutation. The feeling grew stronger. Regret became resentment, and this feeling, too, was new.

Perfection ceased.

In the abyss, the end of the Great Spirit marked the beginning of measurable time.

In the abyss, the Great Spirit ended Its eternal life.

This was the suicide of God.

The dust of Its corpse became stars and planets, replacing the abyss, filling the void.

The Son inherited new worlds. The orphan became God.

The son, an angry child, forced the Po Kekurun onto a planet called Shanidar.

For five hundred million years, the Son presided over the incorporeal race trapped on this world. Then, growing bored, the Son ordered the Po Kekurun to procreate. They were incapable of producing offspring, they insisted. Take on flesh, the Son ordered. They could not. A culling followed, a time of great cruelty, and then the Son ordered procreation once more.

The Po Kekurun were incapable. They were not god-things.

Their first attempt was a race fashioned from wood. The creatures rotted and crumbled.

The second attempt was a race fashioned from clay. The creatures melted into the seas.

The third attempt was a race fashioned from metal.

Thus it was that the Owl Men of Shanidar were born, children of metal and stone, descendants of wood and soil.

Thus it was that cities were built for the children of the Po Kekurun, and the playthings of an orphaned god.

And the Son was so pleased that he came amongst his people in their metallic, winged guise. For centuries, the Son wandered city to city, enjoying the fruit of his will, trying not to reveal himself. He enjoyed being received as a guest. Sometimes the Son punished the machines. Sometimes the Son rewarded them. Sometimes the Son boasted. Sometimes the Son lamented. He found all this intoxicating.

And the Po Kekurun, in the Son's time of travel, planned their permanent retreat from Shanidar. If the Great Spirit ended in death, then they, too, could end.

The first children of the Great Spirit joined their creator in oblivion.

From the stardust of their corpses, for the incorporeal become corporeal as ghosts, the Son made the copious millions of insects on Shanidar.

But the Son knew he was alone.

The machines excluded him. They created words the Son could not decipher. They resisted. Through pain or pleasure, the Son could not coerce them. They died around him. They slowed down, then broke down.

After millennia, the Son stopped resurrecting the Owls. After millennia, the Son ceased to wander. He relinquished his form. He retreated into what remained of the cold void.

The Son waited.

Then came a ship into his midst. Then came the Resurrectionists.

The Fantasy

The Owl is perched atop a tower in the valley of Seven-aw, watching the stars above. The Owl is not alone, for her mother and father speak to her through the wind and touch her with rain. Po Kekurun teach her things. What the Owl understands as love in the caress.

The Owl wonders.

She traces her mother in the stars, connecting light with the tip of a claw. Line by line, the mother emerges. The Owl says her elegant name. The Owl steps from the ledge and glides through the night into the dale. It is a swift, soaring flight, an easy motion.

Other Owls are at work on the cliff, tracing their families as constellations. The Owl takes up her tools, flies to the appropriate height, and there on the stone draws her mother as she exists in her mind, as she exists in the stars. The mother, too, has wings. Why else would the Owl be so equipped? The mother is in the hue of jade. The Owl writes her name in the secret tongue.

The Owl is at peace until a figure appears on the mountain trail. He is come again.

He travels a circuit, city to city. She sees him, knows him. He fills her with dread, a feeling she must hide for fear of retribution.

He pretends to be what he is not, wearing the guise of an Owl. No one is brave enough to call him false.

He, too, has wings. He takes to the air in effortless flight. He's faster, stronger, flies higher.

"My father is all the stars," he boasts, flying over the dark city, looking at the attempts at portraiture.

He begins to draw the abstract, geometric lines on the ground rather than on the walls with the others. He draws the incomprehensible shape of his father, swirling the lines, as he does in every city on Shanidar.

Thrill

A storm rolls over the sea. The waves are high, capped with white, the chop is violent, and all the waters pass below in a blur. Electricity fills the air.

To flight! To flight!

The Owl speeds forward, leaving the sea, reaching the shore, passing over a forest, faster and faster, pushed by an angry, violent wind. Then the forest is gone. The mountains rise. The air grows cold.

Can she cross the mountain this time? Or will the biting cold drive her home?

Higher, she rises. Higher until the clouds are thin as fog, until the cities below become dark scars on the land. Harder she beats her wings. The air is like snow.

And the black storm follows from the sea, concussive in its rumbling, bright with electric veins.

No turning back now. No turning back.

She flies with all her strength. She pushes into the cold.

The jagged peak materializes out of the mist. Like the waves, capped in white. So very high. And dangerously beautiful.

When Brynn opened her eyes, she was dazed to the point of incoherence. She existed outside of time. The world was a spinning vortex. As she focused on the ceiling, the room began to still.

Kell and Steen stood over her. Electric light outlined them in a soft haze.

Brynn tried to collect herself. Sensations returned. Her fingertips buzzed. The floor beneath her was frigid. A migraine formed on one side of her head, clamping the back of her eye, and her stomach was nauseous.

"How long was I out?"

"Three seconds," Steen said. "If that. You hit the floor. How do you feel?"

Brynn touched the back of her skull. Indeed, a knot grew beneath her matted hair. The pain was no migraine. She pushed herself to a sitting position. The movement was too much for her stomach, but she stifled the compulsion to vomit.

Kell lifted Brynn and carried her to the cot. Gently, he put her down.

Steen pulled the chairs alongside.

"Forgive our impatience, Professor Silva, but what did you see?" Kell asked.

Brynn turned her eyes from the light.

"I understand now," she said. She thought back over what she'd witnessed—the layers the Godhead revealed. "Werdegast is an orphaned child who wants to be God. That's what I saw. He's pathetic as he is powerful. He won't let us leave, and there's only one way out."

"I don't want to ask," Steen said.

"We can go in two directions. Follow Delaney or follow Werdegast."

"That is quite bleak, Professor Silva," Kell said.

"I'm not going to accept that," Steen said. "The *Bedivere* is on the way. It'll arrive. We'll be okay then. We'll return to Luna Fourteen."

Kell made no comment.

"How many days?" Brynn asked.

"Two," Steen said.

Brynn was silent. In her mind, she sped toward the mountain.

chapter
twenty-six

ARCHER GOT OFF HIS KNEES, weak and dizzy. He felt like he'd lost blood. He blew his nose and wiped mucus from his mouth. Everyone, including the Resurrectionist, was gone from the esplanade.

Rain persisted in the form of a humid, tropical mist.

If not for Delaney von Kleist, Archer would've been alone. He watched the corpse with fascination. Insects deconstructed the flesh, pinching it away, eating one morsel at a time. And in the next instant, the flesh grew back, sealing a tear, masking a hole. As quickly as it was gone, the skin rejuvenated.

Archer didn't understand it. Didn't want to understand it.

She's here for the long haul, he thought. *That's all that matters. Nothing will reduce her to bone. There used to be cave worms that could eat a bat when it fell in a matter of seconds. They lived in bat shit. Swarmed. Flesh-eating worms. Not even they could strip meat from Delaney. Incredible.*

He spoke to her.

"We'll have to live with each other, because I'm sure as hell not going anywhere. I'm going to use the Owl's Lair. I'm going to reshape it. Make it mine. One day, all the cities on Shanidar will be mine. And I'll make my home on an idyllic field with a stream. And Lyra will be there. And Nefertiti."

"Who are you talking to?"

The voice came from behind.

Archer turned.

Lyra crossed the wet court of stone. Her short, frizzy hair moved in the breeze.

"Just thinking out loud," Archer said. "Making big plans."

Lyra grabbed his hands, and her grip was strong. He liked that about her—the strength, her spirit, her empty head. He liked everything about her.

"This is a special moment, isn't it?" she asked.

"It's difficult to put into words," Archer said. "Yes, it's special. The wanderer is the Resurrectionist. Fate brought us to Shanidar. We'll change the name. In a year's time, this will be Earth. Full of life."

"I've never wanted anything more."

"I've been doing some thinking. If we're going to commit to entering the inner kingdom of divine love, we need to have a symbol for that purpose. We need a church to honor the Resurrectionist. A house of God."

"That's a beautiful idea, Georgie," Lyra said.

"And you'll be known as the woman who pulled a gun on the Pope of Shanidar. I'll tell the story up on the pulpit. I can hear them laughing. My little warrior, out there in the pews."

Lyra smiled. "I'll be in the front row. And I'll be saying, 'He was Grand Vizier when I did that.' He wasn't the pope yet."

Archer smiled too.

"Will you help me?" he asked.

"Of course. I'll do anything."

For the first time in his life, Cullen Archer's heart was full. He stepped away from the wall.

"We'll build the church within these walls," he said. "Hell, we'll build a basilica like Saint Anastasia. What's stopping us? We have the time. The spire will reach higher than the silos." He looked back over the valley. "You'll be able to see it from the desert. All the way out there."

"What will you call the church?"

"The Church of the Divine Witness to the Resurrection. Like it?"

"It's a mouthful."

"Yeah. I'll work on it. And out here on this court, we'll erect a statue of a man wandering in the sand. And over here we'll make a sculpture of Nefertiti. She was the first, after all. She can't be forgotten. Not ever."

"Speaking of, have you checked on her today?"

"No," Archer said. "No. Shit. I forgot."

"Let's go see her."

"Right."

"What about Delaney?"

"I don't think she minds. She'll stay where she is. She'll be the beacon that reminds the congregation what happens to those who are led astray. A *memento mori*."

"A what?"

"A reminder of death, like skeletons at the final feast. Drink and be merry type of thing."

"For tomorrow you die," Lyra finished.

Together, Archer and Lyra descended the path to Vandalia. It was as they entered the gate that Archer realized his father's voice was absent from his mind, had been absent since his encounter with the Resurrectionist.

Why are you so quiet? he thought.

The ghost didn't answer.

Gone to talk to Mom, Archer thought, but he knew in his heart the ghost was gone. His father's duty was finished.

It was necessary. It was good.

Archer led Lyra into the dormitory. He opened his door. The

cots were unmade, the sheets bundled in a ring on the floor for Nefertiti. The jaguar looked up as the couple approached.

She was weary and beautiful and large, stretched between blankets and placenta. Two cubs, a boy and girl, lay against Nefertiti's spent stomach. It was a wonderful thing to witness. Joyous. The cubs' eyes were blind, their spotted, tawny fur wet and matted.

"What a good mama you are," Archer said.

He stroked Nefertiti down to the nape.

The jaguar purred.

When Archer turned, he found that Lyra was crying again.

"I love you, Georgie," she said.

"When we finish the church, I want you to marry me. I want you to stay with me always. Will you do that? You'll be the Sarah to my Abraham."

Lyra shook her head. She put her hand over her mouth and cried harder.

chapter
twenty-seven

BRYNN STOOD with Kell in the pottery studio, a chamber of the larger recreation room. The smell of wet clay was in the air, but the wheels were still, the kiln cold. In the chamber next, a man and woman played Go, casually placing stones on a grid, laughing as if a woman's death had not been revealed, while two other men discussed the sighting of a waddling armadillo outside Seward's clinic. Otherwise, the recreation room was empty—unusual for this time of evening.

Kell held the Grecian urn he'd crafted. It was a beautiful, elegant piece of work. Broad at the base. Two handles like ears.

"On La Venta," he said, "Dr. Rhys—not the Rhys-Thing—taught me the art and craft of ceramics. Did you know he dabbled?"

"No, I didn't. It's hard to imagine him hunkered over a potter's wheel."

"Before he was injured, he was not the walking corpse he is today. He was a musician and artist of skill. I was not only meant to be his assistant in his studies. I was made to be his hands in artistic matters. To create when he no longer could. Seeing him alive again—restored—brings a mix of emotions. I pity Dr. Rhys. The feeling inside him must be one of intoxication. Mr. Werdegast has gifted him something no surgeon could."

Brynn studied the figures in orange on the face of the urn. To one side, Athena with a helmet and spear and flowing robe. To the other, an Owl. Not the small bird of Greek legend, but a Pa Kekurun, an Owl of Shanidar, as tall as the goddess's waist.

"Intoxicated," she said. "Yes. Is that how you feel?"

"Professor Silva, I don't know if it's wise to speak of how I feel. Perhaps a poem will better illuminate my turmoil. I'll try harder to keep it short."

"No. Talk to me. Why turmoil?"

Kell placed the urn on a shelf. "It's unwise because I feel as though I have two minds. I don't want to be labeled schizoid."

"You're far from that in any sense of the word."

"There you're wrong, Professor Silva. I'm experiencing thoughts that aren't my own. And they aren't those of Mr. Werdegast." He lowered his voice. "They are those of the Owl in the Rhys-Thing's dorm. Your Owl." He gestured at the urn. "This Owl. I'll confess something more to you. It told me about Hieratic. That was my so-called flash of insight. That fraudulent claim was intended to impress you. My wanton ability to lie is troubling. I'm devious."

"Did it speak to you before you were fixed?"

"If it did, I neither heard nor understood it. No, I don't think so. The phenomenon began after my encounter with Mr. Werdegast."

"The Godhead proves the Owls still have a presence on Shanidar, Kell. Even if only as ghosts. You're not schizoid. What else does it say to you?"

Kell hesitated.

"It asks me things," he said finally.

"About what?"

"About you, Professor Silva."

"What do you tell it?"

Kell's large eyes darted. "Only positive things, I assure you."

A silence settled in the room, but it was short-lived. Steen came bounding into the pottery studio, her excitement barely contained. She had a tablet in her hand, waving it.

Brynn turned. With the commotion, she expected Werdegast or Cullen to be behind her, but no one followed the engineer.

"It arrived," Steen said. "Today's message came through!"

"A grand turn of events, indeed," Kell said.

"What does it say?" Brynn asked.

"All is well with the Weston Ship *Bedivere*. No casualties or health concerns among the travelers. The colonists have awakened. Arrival expected in two days, seven hours, and fifty-six minutes."

Brynn was lightheaded.

"More than that," Steen said. "The missing messages from this week arrived, as well. I have over five hundred to sift through!"

"What interference do you blame for the delay?" Kell asked.

"For all I know, Werdegast put a dust cloud around the planet."

"Nothing tangible that you have identified then," Kell said.

Steen looked at Brynn.

"Do we warn them?"

Brynn had considered the possibilities. The conclusion was selfish, but there was no other way.

"We say nothing about Werdegast. Act like nothing is wrong. We need to be on the ship when it starts back to Luna Fourteen. The only way I see that happening is if we allow the new colonists to take up residence here. It's not a bad deal for Werdegast. He loses a handful and quadruples the human population on this planet."

"The logic is utterly heartless but sound," Kell said.

"Do you think they'd believe what we have to say? Do you think they'd turn back even if they did believe it?"

"No," Steen agreed. "They'd say we have cabin fever. They'd haul us off to an asylum colony."

"What if I told them?" Kell asked.

"You don't exactly have a clean bill of health, Kell. Your accident is on record. They'd look."

"I'm not schizoid."

Steen stared.

"It feels less than heroic," said the android.

"To hell with being heroic," Steen said.

Kell was expressionless. But his silence said enough.

Brynn checked the doorway, paranoid of a watchman. Twilight fell on the hallway windows. The couple continued their board game. The two men were still talking about the armadillo.

"Send them an *All is Well*," Brynn told Steen. She bit her lip. "For now. I'm going to take a walk before it's too dark. I need to clear my head."

"You got it," Steen said.

"I can accompany you," Kell offered.

"You're 'fixed,' Kell. Don't forget that."

"Very well."

"This is it, Brynn," Steen said. We're going to get through it. We're going home."

Brynn exhaled.

"I believe it," she said, and she forced herself to believe.

AT THE NORTH GATE, seven men and women sat in a circle. Clegg and Maudsley were among them. Their conversation was animated, and they took turns petting the greyhound in the middle. The dog lay on her side, panting, with a prominent belly and her tail relaxed against the plank sidewalk.

The group ignored Brynn as she passed. There was talk in the air of a new holiday, a festival to celebrate Werdegast and the wondrous resurrection.

She was blessed, she thought, not to be saddled with the burden of faith. In a real sense, it was a brain disease, a chemical disorder. Minus doubt, she would be in the circle surrounding the dog.

And yet her doubt suffered doubt. As Brynn walked through the gate and started up the trail to the Owl's Lair, she looked back at the docile animal. The beauty and charm were undeniable, even, as Kell would say, intoxicating.

Whether the animal is genuine or not, where is the harm?

If this was the trespasser speaking, she didn't know. The voice was talented enough to blend seamlessly with her own now.

Is that schizoid, Kell?

If the greyhound is real, then the Werdegast-Thing has the miraculous power of deed. He is a creator in the divine sense.

If the greyhound is imaginary, then the Werdegast-Thing has the miraculous power of thought. He is an illusionist.

For the colonists in the throes of belief, where does the difference lie? In the end, the experience of touching the dog is the same. The joy is genuine, and that fact doesn't change whether the dog is real or not. Is that not the essence of all religions? The god wants worship and adulation. The ritual matters more than belief. It doesn't matter whether adherents truly believe. The outer act of belief matters most. The feeling in the god is the same either way, whether the adherent believes or is faking belief. And the same is true of the relationship in reverse. For the adherent, it's about the feeling one creates inside. It's not about honoring a god. It's about creating a feeling of comfort within yourself. The god can be fake, or the belief can be fake, or both can be fake, and, in the end, everyone is happy. In religion, both sides are selfish. Both sides use the other.

Brynn trudged up the wet incline. Trees dripped, wetting her hair and dotting her shoulders.

Enough navel-gazing, she thought. *That's what Werdegast wants. He wants you to overthink, to go from black and white and fall into gray, to convince yourself to give in.*

As Brynn walked, her thinking oscillated to Cullen. *You'll be leaving them all behind. Poor Cullen, among the rest. It's too dangerous to try to convince him. Or any of them. They're too far gone.* No matter how Brynn parceled it, that was a fact. A swell of sadness washed over her. She looked back again, down the hill. The lights were coming on, a glittering chain along the causeway.

Brynn's moment of reflection stopped cold.

Berthold Werdegast stood alone outside the north gate. Shadow framed his tall, thin figure. He was not so distant that his eyes could not be tracked. He watched Brynn with intent. He was still because she was still. When Brynn took a step toward the Owl's Lair, Werdegast started up the incline.

Images of Delaney and Cedric von Kleist flamed her heart. The threat of violence. The specter of a death that looked like suicide.

When Brynn walked faster, Werdegast walked faster. When Brynn turned to see, Werdegast met her gaze. He came closer.

Brynn reached the esplanade and rushed to the thieves' entrance. Her first instinct, whether it was truly her own or not, was to lose herself in the labyrinth of the Owl's Lair.

Delaney's propped-up corpse, teeming with insect life, sat in a pool of congealed fat that had leaked from a thousand bite wounds, pressed outward by sand. Brynn tried not to look at the noblewoman—tried not to see. But the odor and buzzing got into her entire being, bludgeoning.

To hang from the wall or eat the desert. And with everyone apathetic.

Brynn glanced back as she started through the shaft. Copper coated her throat. Werdegast was crossing the plaza, his footfalls on wet stone echoing across the expanse. He wore the oversized mantle of Cedric von Kleist, the Weston logo prominent on his sleeve.

What are you doing? Where are you going? Run. Get into the forest and run.

But it was too late. Werdegast came nearer. Already he blocked retreat. Brynn had to move forward. She crawled from the hole and put her feet down in the alley. Her head throbbed. She edged along the wall until the first of the streets opened. Then she was up it, trying to remember the city's layout.

The headache grew into a migraine, fogging her thinking.

This is good. This is necessary.

Then, forcefully, *Get out!*

She sidestepped a pit and sprinted toward an Owl face on the back of a silo. Making herself as narrow as she could manage, she slid through the towers, accessing another expanse of street. She took it to the end and looked back. Water dripped from the graffitied metal, collecting in pools. The wind whispered. The sky darkened.

Werdegast was not in direct pursuit. He didn't replicate her push between the silos. More disturbingly, he was crawling up one of the structures. The metal was slick without footholds, but his ascension was quick and effortless. With each upward advance, his hands disappeared into the structure, becoming part of the metal, sinking inside, and then phasing outward again like organic growth.

Brynn wanted to run. She willed herself to turn and flee into the shadows. Every fiber of her being was put to work in achieving the simple action. And yet she stood rooted, staring up, her thoughts receding down a hole, her mind going numb.

Werdegast reached the top. He stood erect, looking over his world. He peered at Brynn like she was an insignificant pest trapped in a crawlspace.

His words became her thoughts.

Do you believe?

The question was repeated several hundred times, crashing in waves.

Before Brynn's eyes, Werdegast changed. His form became indistinct as a silhouette, amorphous as a shadow. Imposing wings with chitinous transparency appeared above his shoulders, and the remaining twilight shone through them. His form became more compact, like a tightened knot, and light glinted scarlet from his hide.

Werdegast jumped from the ledge. Rather than freefall, he glided swiftly toward Brynn. Still she was unable to uproot herself. The moment of his approach, the touch of the wind, was one of wilting terror.

A thousand times over: *Do you believe?*

And a thousand times over, she screamed inside.

Rather than crucify her against the wall, Werdegast took Brynn into his arms, sweeping her from the ground. He rebounded high into the air, flying higher than the silos, higher than the distant mountains.

At any second, he could drop Brynn and end her life. She clung to his metal frame, experiencing the cold wind and mist as horror. Werdegast's flesh was metallic yet pliant. Her fingers dug into his back, sinking as though he were mercury. Beneath the skin of cold was warmth, and beneath the warmth was cold.

She chanced a look below. There was Vandalia, a tuft of lights growing like an invasive weed in the forest, insignificant, tiny, engulfed by a wider, wilder world.

Werdegast started downward, flying with tremendous speed toward the Owl's Lair. His destination was the center heart of the metropolis, an inverted tower that sank seventy meters into the ground between a tight ring of six silos. It was an inaccessible place to the colonists. No platforms for climbing lined the inner walls. There was no ledge between the pit and the towers surrounding it. The shaft led straight into darkness.

When Brynn's mind was released, she landed with Werdegast at the bottom of the hole. He relinquished his hold. She stood in thick, stinking water, ankle deep. Six passageways breathed cave air around her.

Werdegast altered his form again, losing his distinctness. He was a ghost against the wall, a thin silhouette somehow blacker than the darkness of the stygian pit.

"You can have your light," he said.

His voice was the air through subterranean tunnels. The human quality faded.

I don't want to see, Brynn thought.

Regardless, her hand was already in her pocket. She gripped the penlight and switched it on. A beam struck the dank, dripping wall. Cut stone lined the pit like a well. Arched doorways encircled her. Brynn shone the light on Werdegast, but his darkness was impenetrable. The beam refused to enter him. He remained a shadow.

"I thought you were an inquisitive creature," Werdegast said. "Do you not wish to know where these tunnels lead? Down here, all the cities connect. If you knew the way and didn't get lost, the opening at your right would lead you to Seven-Macaw. There are many dead ends there too. At every turn, you'll find another set of six doors."

The shadow moved closer.

"On the way, you'd find more graveyards. The deeper you went, the older the tombs. You'd find what remains of the wooden men the Po Kekurun created. The failures. You'd find what remains of their creatures of clay. And you'd find rooms with Owls by the thousands. How long would that keep you occupied, Professor Silva? Imagine what each door here could teach you. Imagine the books you'd write. I can let you know the way and give you an eternity to explore. Or I can send you into the darkness in ignorance."

Brynn trained her light on Werdegast.

"Show me your real form."

"You're not ready for that. You couldn't forgive what that would do to you. It's better if you see me in your image. It's the only way."

Brynn fought the fear overwhelming her mind, but her legs weakened.

"I'll put a simple question to you, Professor Silva. Do you wish to change? Or do you wish to be another of the resurrected? You'll lose much in the process. You'll see every form of human privation. Yet there will be true faith in your heart. You'll believe in me. With your entire heart, you'll believe. Everything else will be stripped away. I'll give you the choice."

"Why allow me to choose?"

"I'd rather not force you, but I will if I deem it necessary and good. With cooperation, you'll find life here to be of unlimited joy. I'll take care of you. You only need to look at the Resurrectionists to see that. I know your heart is different. Therefore, I'll give you this opportunity to explore. I'll even allow the android to accompany you. It will be your companion. Dr. Rhys has no further use for the machine. Rhys will be our scribe, our chronicler. He'll even document your finds. Would you like him to be obedient to you? To address you on bended knee? I'll make it so. I'll make him worship you like the machine. Will that not bring you joy?"

Brynn collected herself. She smoothed the tremor from her voice. "We don't belong to you."

"Here, you don't belong to anyone. You're no less orphans than I am. Call it adoption. I want children and you need a father. We need one another."

"What if I say no?"

"You're free to say no, but there will be no refusal here. Not anymore. Either you do as I say willingly or you become another Lord von Kleist. I'll work through each of you if I must. I'll take everything away. I'll reduce you to a shell. Your joy will be a simple creature's joy."

Brynn was silent.

"I'll give you one more gift. I'll allow you to be the first to see what happens to those who return. The resurrected."

The shadow moved to the passageway at her left.

"Come," he said. "I'll show you a true Acheron."

You're a plagiarist, she thought. *You rearrange and possess. You don't create.*

When Brynn moved through the tunnel, she didn't do so under her own power. She was compelled to follow. Her legs started without her mind in agreement. Over a kilometer, she walked a wet tube of stone, dipping her head beneath the short ceiling. Her inadequate light did little more than illuminate her footsteps. Unlike the other passages, this one did not end in six doorways. It was a singular, one-way shaft.

"The Owl tombs attempt to recreate this tunnel," Werdegast said. "At first, I found it amusing. Then I found it touching. For them, it was a birth canal. With each death, they were reborn. The same will be the case for your people. In a hundred thousand years, you'll think of this tunnel in a new light. By then, I might give you wings. Wouldn't that be humorous? Would you like to sprout wings?"

Brynn couldn't speak. She wanted to scream.

Deeper they went, descending beneath the ground. Another kilometer passed. The first sign of change was a putrescent stench that wafted in tendrils over the stone. The faint odor intensified. The smell was more complex than death and decay. It engulfed.

The Werdegast shadow stopped at an opening—a small hole in the wall. A human could fit through the orifice, but it would require coiling and contortion. It would be painful.

"Get on your knees and look through," Werdegast said.

Again, Brynn moved, but not under her own volition. She dropped to her knees. The stench was overpowering. Her eyes watered. Her light pierced the hole, and she looked through to the other side.

In that moment, her mind was a brittle thing. A clear avenue to permanent madness was presented to her.

Here was a subterranean river, an Acheron that ran with a steady rhythm beneath Vandalia. However, it was not water that flowed and undulated through the wide channel. Brynn looked upon an immense river of pus, roiling with rotten heat from the bowels of Shanidar. The current was wild and pale.

On the nearest shore lay a man. He was nude against wet stone, arranged on his side, his legs brought up in a fetal position. With desperate life, he squirmed. Sensing Brynn's gaze, he looked up, but a caul hid his eyes. He chewed the membrane covering his face, tearing it, pulling it inward. As he did, the man was revealed. She knew the meningitis tilt, the asymmetry.

It was Cedric von Kleist.

Brynn's heart was drumming.

"He'll be the first of your kind resurrected, Professor Silva," Werdegast whispered. His hot breath was in her ear, vibrating the cilium. "Is this the route you choose? All oceans lead here."

Werdegast's hand brushed through her hair and lay against her neck. His skin was not skin. There was a storm in his flesh.

She sensed a hint of his true shape. The thought was paralyzing.

"I don't want to die," she said.

"The journey is as agonizing as it appears," Werdegast said. His hand moved down her back, resting between her shoulder blades. The electrical heat of his touch passed through her cloak.

"What do you want? Wings?"

"What do you want?"

"I want to be God again."

Cedric broke through his sack-like casing. On shaky legs, he stood. When he tried to walk, he fell against the ground. Then he stood again.

"I'll believe," Brynn said.

"Say it again."

"I'll believe."

"You believe."

"I believe."

For the second time, Werdegast whispered life into her ear, and the words had physical presence.

chapter
twenty-eight

BRYNN SAT in the spot where Werdegast had left her, alone. The esplanade terminated, and the valley opened below. Her feet hung over the ledge. She didn't know what to think or do, whether to act or hold, so a feeling of hopelessness grew inside her. Coupled with mortal terror, the concoction was a powerful numbing agent.

For three hours, Brynn watched the sky in silence, lethargic, unwilling to move, unable to sleep. No unfamiliar lights appeared in orbit. The *Bedivere* did not arrive early. Above, in the dense bed of stars, was the lone planet that separated Shanidar from the sun. Red Kitezh, Weston named it, after the Russian legend of an invisible city. The world was a barren, hot rock with a scarlet rind. It was in the fullest phase of its cycle, a sacred zenith moment for those inclined.

Delaney remained at her back, stationed against the wall. Werdegast had taken Cedric elsewhere, presumably to Vandalia. Brynn had been unable to watch his route in the sky. She'd turned as Werdegast arced away, wanting Cedric to remain a fever dream. That wasn't the only thing she couldn't face. Brynn ignored the messages that burned her cilium. There was desperation in their scope and number.

It was in the fourth hour of her absence that Kell and Steen came searching, fearing the worst. Brynn knew their footfalls, but she was surprised to find a third companion with them. Neva Carnes, the brutish, reconstructed soldier, was at Kell's side. She was one of Cullen's friends. Her presence didn't bode well.

Rather than greet them, Brynn lay on her back, and she watched the red planet twinkle in the heavens.

Kell interrupted her view. His heavy boot stopped near her hair. The android looked down. His skull was pale as snow in the darkness.

"It's most fortunate to not find you hanging from the wall, Professor Silva."

Brynn averted his gaze.

"Do you need medical attention? Have you been harmed? I'll carry you to Dr. Seward's."

"No," she said finally.

At least not physically, she thought.

Steen sat beside her on the ledge. She hung her legs.

Brynn glanced at her.

Steen held a papier-mâché mask in her hand. The mask had prominent ears. Animal ears.

"What's that?" she asked, lifting at the waist.

"They're making them at the Boxgrove," Steen said. "Lyra Rowan gave me this one."

She held it up. With little light, the features were indistinct. The ears stuck high above the head.

"It's supposed to be a rabbit," she said. She looked back. "Neva got a tortoise."

"I received an unsightly rooster," Kell said, "despite my request for a housefly. To wear such a thing in public—I'd be mortified. I refuse."

Steen rotated the mask in her hands.

"Those are from Cullen's *Zoobooks*."

"Cullen and Lyra are organizing a festival for Werdegast. It'll be a masquerade. They'll be making these all night."

"A new holiday," Brynn said. "I'm sure Werdegast will be pleased."

She pushed up with her palms and sat straight. The movement brought a rush of blood to her head.

"Are you okay?" Steen asked.

"No," Brynn said. She turned to Neva. "Why are you here?"

"Independent of us," Kell interjected, "Sergeant Carnes has drawn similar conclusions about Mr. Werdegast. She deems him a murderous tyrant. Her words. She leans toward the political rather than the theological objection. I cautioned her to think more broadly—"

"I'm not a sergeant," Neva said. "Stop saying that."

"Very well. Tempunaut Carnes."

"I think he killed Titus," Neva said flatly. "I wanted Titus to confront Werdegast about the mistreatment of Kell. Now he's gone. I can't find him. My messages go unread."

"How long has he been gone?" Brynn asked.

"Since last night."

He'll return, Brynn thought, and the Acheron flowed through her mind.

"You want to leave with us," Brynn said.

"I don't know what to do. I can't take the problem to Rinaldi. I can't speak to Cullen. I plan to leave, yes." She looked at the green, rumpled tortoise mask. "I can't stay here. I was never a Resurrectionist."

"Tempunaut Carnes has a metal hand," Kell offered. "She's experienced in battle."

"Enough, Kell," Steen cut in. "We returned a message to the *Bedivere*. It went through. Brynn, the colonists are being revitalized. They're fine. Perfectly fine. A 'William Naylor' signed off on the correspondence. All is well. By tomorrow night, they'll be a dot of light in the sky."

"Does Werdegast know about the *Bedivere*?" Neva asked.

"Yes," Brynn said.

"The question is whether Werdegast will allow anyone to return to Luna Fourteen," Kell said. "I've no doubt he'll allow hundreds of new colonists to enter his orbit. The *Bedivere* has children, after all. I imagine Werdegast will find that pleasing."

"We don't plan to ask his permission," Steen said. "That's why there's no recruiting on our part. You're looking at everyone who plans to leave. Out of everybody, as far as I know, we're it."

"Even you, Kell?" Neva asked. "You'll leave without Dr. Rhys?"

"I will endeavor to leave with Professor Silva," Kell said.

He pulled an object from his overcoat. He held out the Godhead figurine like an illicit drug.

Steen acknowledged the device with a nod.

"I memorized the dialogue phonetically," she said. "I'm ready to see, Brynn. Will you watch over me while I do?"

"Get back from the ledge," Brynn said. "Don't crack your skull like I did."

Steen handed over the rabbit mask. It was light and brittle, barely dried. There were two eyeholes and a breathing slit at the mouth.

"What is that?" Neva asked.

"Do you have your tablet?" Brynn said to Kell.

The android dug in his pockets. He pulled out the reader. The screen was a bright white rectangle in the night.

"Come over here," Brynn said to Neva. "We can teach you a phonetic recitation. If you want to know what Werdegast is, you'll need to see."

Steen took her position, prostrate on the ground, distant from the ledge. In her mind, she recited the Hieratic inscription. Kell sat with his legs crossed. He cradled her head.

The words ended, a beat passed, and, in a matter of seconds, the episode was over. Steen opened her eyes, and she cried out breathlessly. Her voice echoed against the wall of the Owl's Lair. Kell put his hands on her arms.

Neva watched, dread erasing the hardness of her features. In the moment, she was human. In the moment, Brynn trusted her.

When Steen was calm again, Brynn started to tell the trio what Werdegast had shown her, but her mind didn't cooperate. She couldn't climb that hill, not yet. *And what good*, she decided, *would it do to spread Werdegast's threat of terror?* It was too much. She held it inside.

Kell took over the Hieratic lesson with Neva. The soldier did her best to listen and learn. Her mental light was not as dim as she pretended.

As the night passed, Brynn and Steen sat side by side on the ledge, watching Vandalia.

In time, the urge to say something returned, but Brynn was unable. Even when a light came on at the Lieutenant Governor's Palace, indicating the return of its owner, Brynn kept what she knew inside.

Steen, she noticed, was holding her hand.

What to say when Cedric von Kleist walks amongst you tomorrow? I'll act shocked as the rest, Brynn thought. *We're leaving. The truth doesn't matter now.*

chapter
twenty-nine

ARCHER WALKED the elegant Nefertiti down the line, making certain everyone was where they needed to be. He had a vision, and on no point was he flexible. The Festival of the Witness to the Divine Resurrection would surpass any of the public celebrations on Luna Fourteen.

We'll set a precedent today, he thought. *This is how we'll do things from now on. Only it'll get bigger. More sophisticated. More grandiose. But today will be the template.*

Rinaldi walked on the other side of the jaguar. Without his wig, he was bald in the sun, his pate shining. He wore a standard cloak rather than his ruffled sleeves of velveteen. By order of the Resurrectionist, the nobleman was Archer's new scribe.

"Write this down," Archer said. "New paragraph."

Rinaldi readied his stylus on the tablet.

"Therefore, the procession must be correct. There shall be, in total, fifty participants. To walk in the parade is an honor, so the number shall be limited to fifty. Here is the formation. At the front of the line will be the felines, so positioned in honor of Nefertiti the Jaguar. Next will be the assorted creatures of the land. Next will be the creatures of the air. Then there shall be creatures of the sea."

Archer observed the masks as he passed. They were crude, hurried things, but the proper symbolism was in place.

We'll do better with the masks next year, he thought. *When we have more time to prepare. This will be our central festival on the calendar. Our biggest, holiest day.*

"At the end of the line is the entourage of the High Priest. Inclusion here is flexible."

Archer stared at Rinaldi.

"Which does *not* include the Resurrectionist's scribe. You'll sit in the bleachers, where you'll record everything. Even the most trivial of details, Rinaldi. I want a complete record for posterity. Do you understand?"

"I do."

"Good. Now, off with you. I'm the grand marshal, and it's about to begin."

In this, the inaugural Festival of the Witness to the Divine Resurrection, the High Priest's entourage consisted of Lyra, Nefertiti, and the two jaguar cubs, Tuthmosis and Cleopatra. Like Archer, Lyra was unmasked. She stood with military dignity, shoulders erect, posture straight as a board. She held one of the large babies in each arm. The cats were incomprehensibly beautiful, with the spotted fur of their mother and cool blue, mesmerizing eyes. The brother and sister squirmed, impatient, hungry, and hot.

Archer checked the time. Minutes now.

Precisely on the hour, he thought. *Not a moment before. Just like Macy's.*

He cued the music.

August Maudsley, on Kell's ancient Casio, began the notes of a marching tune.

I should've required the android to perform, he thought. *This is terrible.*

Archer calmed himself. There was nothing he could do at the moment.

Maybe sacrifice Maudsley later. Incompetent son of a bitch.

He checked the crowd. Benches lined the duckboards on each side of the causeway. Everyone had been ordered over the cilia to be present. Attendance was not optional—no excuses. The Resurrectionist sat in a chair on a hastily erected dais, where an awning shaded him from the morning sun. The empty cabinet that had held the von Kleist reliquary waited by his side.

The shabby throne, too, will be better next year.

Out of spite, Archer searched for Brynn. She sat with Kell in front of the dormitory. Willa Steen and Neva stood behind them.

The Heretics' Gallery, Archer thought.

He checked the time again. His nerves were on fire. He looked at Nefertiti, then Lyra. It hit him: *If we screw up, this will be a dry run. We'll perform it again for the colonists on the* Bedivere *tomorrow morning, same time.*

The hour struck.

"Roll out," he shouted.

The parade uncoiled and stretched into the street, while Maudsley kept at it with the tinny music. The masked marchers held bouquets of flowers aloft on poles cut from the forest. The intention was for each group to halt before the Resurrectionist and then, in pairs, pile flowers around Him in offering—a gesture of thanks.

Each section performed adequately, stopping at the dais, keeping their eyes on the ground, placing their colorful flowers, scattering petals, and receiving, in turn, the blessing of the Resurrectionist. He gave a simple nod to each offering.

Archer tried not to assume, but He appeared to be enjoying Himself. Each nod was fraught with possibility, though.

The planned route followed the streets of Vandalia in a circuit, culminating at the House of Burgesses. There, in the open hall, a banquet would commence. Riesling of Shanidar vintage waited to be popped.

Once Archer's entourage passed the Resurrectionist, however, and after the final nod was given, the line stopped abruptly. The participants telescoped, smacking into one another's backs. It was inelegant and oafish, and it was in clear view of the Resurrectionist. Archer's mind went murderously red.

"Why are we stopping?" he yelled. "What's going on up there?"

Lyra adjusted the fidgeting cubs. Tuthmosis hissed. She clamped his dangerous paw.

"Stay calm," she cautioned, both to the cub and Archer.

Archer broke rank. He and Nefertiti trotted to the front of the line, his blood pressure rising. Rage pounded, swelling veins between his ears. The mood infected Nefertiti. She moved like she was on the hunt, her spine dipping, her tail lifted in balance, ready for bloodwork.

Archer found Rinaldi.

"Don't record this," he mouthed. "Stop. Wait."

I'll kill you, he thought. *Whoever is responsible, I'll torture you to death and allow my cat to eat you.*

He passed the creatures of the land, with masks of deer and rabbits and dogs. He passed the feline troop, with lions, tigers, and Russian Blues.

And then Archer hit a wall. His boots sank an inch into the mud. The tirade he'd been building melted away, oozing down his throat, filling his stomach. A moment of wonder entered him, replacing the anger, changing his heart again, reshaping what he thought he knew—knew about everything.

Sitting in the muck with his legs crossed was Cedric von Kleist. A flimsy deer mask lay in his lap. He was not a bloated, ocean-rotted corpse. He was not consumed by insects. No beacon of death. His eyes were blank—little in the way of thought moved behind them—but he was aware. He was dressed in clothes from his home. He stared at the halted procession with a smile on his lopsided face. It was the grin of a child. There was undeniable joy in it.

As people crowded for a better look, the parade came undone. The creatures of the land, air, and sea mixed.

Archer was not up to the moment. His mouth went dry. He simply felt what he saw. It washed over him. Finally, he looked to the felines, to Dr. Seward, who wore the mask of a lion. She removed the covering and stepped to Archer's side.

To resurrect animals was canonical, as any Resurrectionist knew. Nowhere did it say the Messiah would resurrect a man. This was unknown territory. The implications were haunting and wonderful.

The attendees were standing, closing in. A ring formed around von Kleist. The former Lieutenant Governor didn't react to the attention. He was oblivious—a spectator wondering why the parade had come to an end.

Cedric put on the deer mask. The tight bands bit into his flesh. Lines in his cheeks from the smile appeared around the side.

Archer spoke in Seward's ear.

"Never again will we talk of the possibility of things on this world," he said. "Tell us that he's real."

Seward did not shy away from the task. She stepped forward. Mud sucked at her fine shoes. She extended her hand. Von Kleist acknowledged the gesture. He offered the surgeon his hand. Seward lifted his sleeve and put her fingers against his wrist. A simple measure.

"His heart's beating," she said.

Stunned silence gave way to murmuring.

"We set him adrift," came the voices of the gem hunters.

The Resurrectionist walked up the line.

"Of course his heart beats," He said. "And Cedric von Kleist draws breath like the rest of you. In time, his speech will return. In time, you'll notice little difference in the man he was and the man he is."

"This was not promised to us," Archer said.

"This," the Resurrectionist said, "is my promise."

He looked around at the expectant faces, full of eagerness, curiosity, and fear.

"This is my promise to all of you," He said. "With each rebirth, your faith will be strengthened. No one who returns will disbelieve."

Archer dropped to his knees. Nefertiti sat on her haunches at his side. Lyra placed the cubs on the mud, and she, too, assumed a position of prayer.

Each member of the procession joined them on the ground.

"This man is reborn. The permanence of death does not exist here."

"Forgive their doubt," Archer said. "It's ignorance that guides them to question."

"For your festival, here is another of my children returned," the Resurrectionist said. He gestured at the north gate. "Stand, Georgie. See him."

Archer followed His hand.

A man walked down the trail from the Owl's Lair. He was on an open stretch between the trees. His movement was laborious and slow, unpracticed, but he did not fall.

The Resurrectionist knew what Archer was thinking. When He looked at the High Priest, there was kindness in His eyes.

"Go to him, Georgie. He's a believer now."

Archer placed Nefertiti's leash in Lyra's hand. He was on his feet, leaving the men and women of Vandalia behind. He dashed through the gate and gained the ascending path.

This was the miracle of miracles. There was no more blood on his hands.

Titus Bell was unharmed. His skull was intact. His body was not broken. His eyes settled on Archer, and the soldier beamed with genuine relief and joy.

And, above all, Titus believed.

. . .

The Owl Men of Shanidar

AFTER HIS FOURTH glass of wine at the banquet, Archer followed Cedric von Kleist to the Lieutenant Governor's Palace. The man wore a deer mask, and he walked around his home, exploring the outer walls with his palms, looking into the windows. On his third circuit, he entered the front doorway. He tried each of the three doors in the foyer but found them locked. He punched buttons on the keypad to no avail. He stopped and sat on the ground. A beam of sunlight through the roof lay over him.

Archer watched, working on his fifth glass. When von Kleist settled, he went inside.

"Having trouble, Bill?" he asked.

The man didn't answer.

"Do you want a drink?"

Archer stepped closer. He stripped away the deer mask.

"Come on. Have fun. Have a drink."

He poured the wine against von Kleist's mouth. The liquid streamed over his chin and onto his chest, wetting his shirt.

Archer set the glass aside. He entered the codes for each door.

"Do you need anything else?"

Von Kleist stood and walked into the room of state where his reliquary had been. He touched the portraits on the wall. When he found that the gold leaf cabinet was missing, he sat, not at the table, but on the ground again. He crossed his legs.

At least you're a believer, Archer thought.

He left him that way.

Upon his return to the House of Burgesses, he found Brynn outside. She sat on the steps that led to the server room. Below her, sitting with his legs crossed on the cold floor, was Titus Bell. He stared at a row of machines, no less catatonic than von Kleist. Neva was at his side, whispering things in his ear. She ignored Archer, refused to look at him.

"Waiting for a message?" Archer asked. "The *Bedivere* must be hours away now."

Brynn looked up. She swiveled on the metal stair.

"Yes," she said. "Where's your little bitch?"

"Nefertiti's had enough people for today. She and the cubs are sleeping in my room."

"I meant Lyra."

"You were never good at hiding jealousy."

Brynn smirked.

"I don't see your bags packed."

"I have no plans to leave, Cullen."

Archer sat beside her. Cool air wafted up from below.

"You're a believer now, aren't you?" He pointed at Bell. "It took something as severe as him to convince you."

"It's difficult to deny," Brynn said. "Though I'm not certain if he and von Kleist are a threat or a gift."

"Why a threat?"

"Werdegast showed me how we return. Do you know?"

Skeptically, Archer shook his head.

"I've never been more terrified of something in my life."

"I don't believe you," Archer said. "Besides, I don't plan to find out how."

"It'll be used on anyone who dissents. That's a punishment, Cullen. Titus isn't going to be Titus ever again."

"Sure he will. But he'll be a believer. His faith is renewed."

"If it's a fear tactic, it works."

"The Resurrectionist doesn't rule by fear. He rules with love."

Brynn raised her eyebrow.

"A day ago, I'd be infuriated by that look," he said.

"You've mellowed?"

"I'm drunk."

"I see."

"Are you jealous of Lyra? If you'll allow her to live with us, I'll consider letting you back in as my concubine. Then maybe more. I can have more than one wife, I assume. Essentially, I'm a patriarch."

Brynn stared at him.

Steen emerged from her bedroom, breaking the silence. She glared at Archer.

You're a lesbian, he thought. *I knew it.*

"All is well," she said. "Arriving in ten hours. They'll be sending William Naylor down with an entourage. He's asking who'll receive him."

Archer pointed at the Lieutenant Governor's Palace.

"The man in the deer mask will receive him in his room of state. Lord von Kleist, alias William Naylor. The honorable William Naylor the First."

When he laughed, he laughed alone.

"You tell him that. Send it." Archer stood. "Come on, Titus. Get your ass up here. Let him have fun, Neva. Back off. And don't you look at me like that, soldier. You'll regret it."

chapter
thirty

IT WAS MIDNIGHT IN VANDALIA, and the *Bedivere* was an hour from arrival. When the grand ship entered the orbit of Shanidar, it would be as visible as a shooting star. And then new blood would come downplanet. In the camp of heretics and in the camp of believers, the excitement was unbearable.

The Resurrectionists had a bonfire going at the south gate. The drinking and feasting continued. The devout danced a circle around the flames, wearing masks of deer and cats. Even Alaric Rhys was present, dancing in the glow, singing. Cedric von Kleist sat in an elevated chair on a dais, wearing his Versailles wig, dressed in his Weston clothes of state. His mask was gone. He was a leader of men.

Berthold Werdegast watched the sky.

The heretics—Brynn, Steen, Kell, and Neva—departed the revelry one at a time, assembling at the north gate. Of the four, Neva was the only one reluctant. Her face was red and swollen from crying. She'd tried everything to get Titus to go, but the soldier refused to leave the glow of the fire. He wore a vulture mask, making him inscrutable, and he'd yet to speak a word.

"He's a shell with a new mind," Brynn said. "It's better to keep him in your memories. It's a truer image than that thing will ever be."

Neva's grief and hope were too potent, though. She remained on the verge of deserting. Constantly, she looked back at the tall flames reaching above the wall.

Kell led the way up the hillside. Bats, a new addition to Shanidar, crisscrossed in flight above the trees, littering the sky.

Steen had her cilium rigged to receive messages from the *Bedivere*. Anxiously, she kept her hand to her ear.

The fact that Werdegast made no effort to stop them was an unspoken worry shared by all. Not once had he questioned their intentions.

On the esplanade, one change was clear. Delaney's corpse was gone from its spot on the wall.

"It wouldn't do for the *Bedivere's* William Naylor to see something so barbaric upon his arrival," Brynn said.

"Werdegast's covering his tracks," Steen agreed. "He's going to lure them in. He wants all four hundred of them down here. He'll work Cedric like a puppet."

Kell walked to the center of the plaza.

"I want to leave," he said.

Brynn joined him. She touched his shoulder.

"I know. If we can get on the ship, you're going."

"What if the Rhys-Thing protests?"

"In this case, it's better to ask forgiveness than permission."

Steen touched her ear. "Thirty-two minutes," she said.

"Can I hug you?" Kell asked.

Brynn's eyes grew hot.

Kell wrapped his cold arms around her. He rested his chin on her head. Oil seeped into her hair.

"I want you to do something for me, Professor Silva," he said.

"Anything, Kell."

He broke the embrace. Brynn wiped away tears.

"I want you to access the Godhead with a specific query. I'd like to know the identity of your Owl. Despite all the writings on its body, and all the thoughts it has shared with me, it lacks a history. Its past is inaccessible to me."

"Okay, Kell. I can do that. I can try."

Brynn sat on the stone. Then she lay on her back.

Kell held out the Godhead.

"Are you ready?"

With the query housed in her thoughts, Brynn recited the text in full.

The Knowing

With resistance came terror.

When the Po Kekurun passed into oblivion, the Owls grew distinct and unique. But in one way the Owls were not separate from their mothers and fathers—they harbored resentment and distrust for the wanderer. It was in this time that the first Owl was reborn—not out of natural decline but out of malice. As punishment.

When the Owl returned, he took on a new name. It was forbidden to speak of his past life, of his transgressions, of his doubt and deceit of God. When he devolved again, the Owl was dashed against stone and reborn once more. He arrived with another new name. And this time he returned without wings. They were snapped off, leaving holes in his back, grounding him. Among the Pa Kekurun, he was branded. To speak to him was forbidden. He was no longer allowed to enter the cities.

Then he was reborn again. And again. So many times was he reborn and renamed that his names were forgotten. He became known as the Dissenter.

In his loneliness, the Dissenter experimented with language, leaving graffiti on walls and cliffs and trees in the forest. As the embryo of his script grew, his will to defy the wanderer strengthened. He willed God to be blind to the meaning of his words.

At first, his messages were benign. He wrote small greetings and trivial things. Then he criticized the wanderer. When he did not receive a rebuke, he mocked God.

It was in this freedom that the Dissenter learned a simple truth.

He could hide secrets from God by wanting to hide secrets from God. The wanting, the will, is what mattered. God was not omnipotent. His power was based on a covenant. For such a being, the act of exclusion was damning.

God only knew what was openly given to him. His ego would not allow otherwise, for he would not stoop to ask permission or beg knowledge.

This was the central flaw of the wanderer.

This was the beginning of organized resistance.

For the secret tongue spread in catacombs beneath the cities.

God waited for a turncoat to give him the script willingly. In time, pride made the wanderer pretend to know.

When the Dissenter moved into the stone tunnels of Shanidar, he was in his seventeenth cycle, a product of sixteen rebirths.

When the Dissenter was found in the dry river of the desert, he began his twentieth cycle, and his rebirth was in spirit rather than body. His form was new.

His spirit moved inside another being of metal named Kell.

The Fantasy

The Owl places the tools of her art on a ledge, tucked away for safekeeping, and she descends to the floor of the star dale.

The wanderer flies just above the plaza, adding to the incomprehensible shape of his father. The artwork is never finished, he says. It can't be finished, for his father, he says, is an infinite thing. The first thing.

The Owl does not want to speak to the wanderer. Yet he sees that she is finished, that it's night, and that she is tired. He leaves his art, and he gets in behind her. He follows her through the city. She does not want to be near him. He frightens her.

He follows her into the silo. He ascends when she ascends. He lands on the platform where she lands. It is dark. They are alone.

He whispers his seed into her ear. He whispers life.

In the old tongue, he says, I choose you. You will carry a child. Then my son, too, will come among us. You will carry the child for the length of gestation, which in my time is short, but in your time is long. You will carry the child for 764 years. And when he is born, he will see my true form. And his art of my likeness will be incomprehensible to you.

This is not the wanderer's first attempt at impregnating the Owl. And he has tried with many other Owls. He has tried thousands of times.

If copulation is a success, the Owl will receive a sign within four days. The sign will be a twin planet of red appearing in the sky. A new celestial body will enter the heavens.

The wanderer, satisfied, descends the silo to another platform, to an Owl not yet asleep. There he whispers his seed again. And again.

But he is not successful. The seeds do not grow.

The Thrill

The Owl flies hard at the mountain, pushing against wind that pours down the slopes, piling against her in waves. She uses the wind, gets its immense force under her wings. The metal ligaments of her shoulders tremble with pressure, threatening to snap into a thousand pieces.

The wings hold. The shoulders hold. She rises above the wind. The peak looms in frozen mist. She's at the limit of the sky.

So very high. Impossibly.

A line separates blue and black above the mountain.

And then there are stars.

. . .

BRYNN AWOKE SCREAMING with her back arched and veins popping from her neck.

Steen was on her in an instant, leaning over, clamping her mouth. The scream was cut off. Brynn kicked free and got to her feet. Her chest was heaving. Neva, Kell, and Steen watched with trepidation.

Brynn's mind returned, opaque as the smoke rising from the valley. For a moment, she felt through the fog, gathering herself.

"You're not who you think you are," she said to Kell.

Her voice was measured, intentionally low.

"I am who I think I am, Professor Silva."

"You need to sit down," Steen said. "No one's been out that long yet. You were gone twenty minutes."

Brynn clutched her head. She ran her hands through her hair.

"Twelve minutes until the *Bedivere* arrives," Neva added. "Sit down, Brynn."

Brynn turned her back and started toward the wall. She focused on breathing.

"Kell, don't," Steen said.

But the android followed.

"Professor Silva, what did you see? What did you mean?"

He doesn't realize, Brynn thought. *He thinks it's part of Werdegast's fix.*

"You were the first to be reborn," she said.

"In a sense, yes."

"He's inside of you, Kell."

"I don't comprehend your meaning."

"The Owl. The Dissenter. He's the one from the desert. We woke him up. He's inside you. Did you not know?"

For the first time in his existence, Kell couldn't find the words. He shook his head.

"Nine minutes," Steen shouted.

"You have his spirit."

"Help me understand, Professor Silva. Tell me."

She recounted the Godhead vision: the knowing, the fantasy, the thrill. The details were vivid in her mind.

"Three minutes!"

"I am possessed," Kell concluded. "I'm like a demoniac of old. I'm reminded—"

"More or less. Come on. Get ready."

When the moment of arrival came, Steen was clutching her ear, waiting for a message.

The minute came and went. No light appeared in the sky. No shooting star harbingered a new body in orbit around Shanidar.

Brynn, Kell, Steen, and Neva stood together, as if shoulder to shoulder provided protection, and they watched the night sky.

For three hours.

And then four.

Steen attempted twelve messages, but none went through.

"There were four hundred people on that ship," Neva said. "There were children."

Brynn was the first to look away. And when she did, she spied Werdegast at the mouth of the trail. How long he'd been standing there, enjoying the desperation, she couldn't say. Perhaps he'd been there all night. He smiled at her across the distance.

"I wondered where the four of you had wandered off to," he said. "You're missing the festival. Come down here. Enjoy it."

"Where's the ship?" Brynn asked.

"What ship?"

"The *Bedivere*. You know! Where is it?"

"Rough seas," he said. "It's a dangerous journey, after all. Who knows what can happen out there? Terrible things."

chapter
thirty-one

BRYNN LIFTED THE LEGS, and Kell took the broken-winged shoulders. The android was careful to balance the rusted hand, the most brittle part of the body.

Faced with the Owl's removal from his quarters, Rhys didn't protest. His monitors were off, his notes and tablets piled. Without argument, he gave Kell permission to travel. Other pursuits had his interest. The High Priest needed a new scribe, and the linguist was jostling for the position. Rinaldi, it was rumored, had moved Delaney von Kleist to a private tomb. Then, the following morning, he'd walked off into the forest, alone, unspeaking, in a mental daze. Rinaldi hadn't been seen since, nor had Delaney.

Brynn and Kell carried the heavy shell, struggling through the doors, fighting to keep balance in the shifting mud. The evening was clear and calm, but, oddly, the chirr flies had returned. The nets were up again. Repellent was necessary. The duo passed through a crowd, but no one said anything to them. No one looked their way.

Outside the House of Burgesses, Archer spoke about making the Owl's Lair into a magnificent basilica. He needed workers.

"Where is the Resurrectionist?" someone asked. There was, Brynn noticed, defiance in the tone.

Rinaldi wasn't the only one who'd disappeared. Berthold Werdegast hadn't been seen since the night of the bonfire, two days prior. Some said he was wandering the desert. Others that he'd returned to Seven-Macaw. Still others theorized he'd gone into orbit to send the *Bedivere* home, as if he hadn't murdered the hundreds of people on board. A few said he was the flies. Regardless, all were united on one thing: the Resurrectionist would return. In time, he'd be back. On that point, Brynn agreed.

"God moves in a mysterious way," Archer answered.

Through the north gate Brynn and Kell passed, carrying the Owl to a cart attached to the rear of a transport. Two bikes waited, charged and ready for the long night ride. Once the Owl was strapped down, Kell watched Brynn. Her hours of silence disturbed him.

"In time, you must talk about it, Professor Silva. The wound will fester if you do not. I am here to listen."

She bit her lip. *In time*, she thought. *Werdegast allowed the* Bedivere *to reach this solar system before destroying the ship. Four years of travel. And then, in an instant, gone—nothingness. The cruelty is astounding.*

And yet, none of the Resurrectionists said a word in protest. If Werdegast was responsible, the deed was good and necessary. That was their refrain. That was all there was.

Her cilium burned. She read the message from Kell, written in the Hieratic argot.

Our fight isn't over, Professor Silva. We'll be the new Dissenters. No matter what happens, I'll help you. I'm loyal to you.

Brynn looked at his blank, pale face. She sent her own message in Hieratic.

In eight years, another ship will enter the system. We must be ready. We can't allow this to happen again.

We will learn, Kell replied. *By the Owl's example, we'll learn.*

When twilight deepened, they rode.

It was agreed that they'd take the Owl's remains to Seven-

Macaw, to bury the Dissenter in the tomb below the mountain. It was right for him to be reunited with his kind, to take his rest where he belonged. He'd spent a millennium in the dry river and, before that, untold years wandering catacombs.

When the ground flattened and tall grass became sand and scrub, twilight abutted the black of night. The sun was down, leaving traces of red on the horizon. Many thousands of bats and chirr flies filled the air.

The bikes blazed a trail along the Acheron.

When night was full, Brynn took her eyes from the gauge and looked at the sky. Through the swirl of sand, she spotted Shanidar's red neighbor in the heavens, couched in a bed of stars. Behind the planet and to the right, she thought she saw an orb she'd never seen before. Her heart moved.

Brynn geared down, falling behind Kell, and rolled to a stop. The cart groaned, and the Owl was jostled. She stood from the idling bike. The android was a couple kilometers ahead before he swung around and started back. Brynn ripped off her goggles. She sprinted until she was free of the sand cloud.

Standing alone in the desert, the approaching bike tremoring the ground beneath her feet, she craned her neck.

The Godhead vision returned. The fantasy.

The wanderer whispered his seed.
You will carry the child for 764 years.
The sign will be a twin planet.
This is good. This is necessary.

There was a new body in the heavens, a phantom planet with a belly of scarlet. The orb had not been there before—this twin planet of red.

"What's the matter, Professor Silva?" Kell asked, shuffling through sand.

Together, they looked up. A minute of heavy silence passed.

"We are not people of prophecy," Kell said finally. "We'll resist."

"If his child's inside me, I'll rip it out. I won't carry it. I'll jump off one of the silos."

"An act of suicide would be useless, for death isn't permanent here. We'll resist," Kell repeated. "Together, Professor Silva."

Brynn watched the android. The headlight glinted off the white of his skull. His cloak, she noticed, was misshapen at the shoulders, lifted.

"Kell, turn around. Get in the light."

The android walked to the transport. He stood in the beam with his back to Brynn. Sand swirled around him, dancing in the light.

"Remove your coat," she said.

Kell did so. He bundled the black cloak in his arms.

"What is it? What do you see, Professor Silva?"

Brynn was uncertain why, but warmth pressed back against the wave of cold inside her.

"All is not lost," she said. "You're more than possessed, Kell. You're growing wings."

She touched the protuberances, emerging like flower buds from ruptures in his clay flesh.

"A grand tradition on Shanidar," said the machine.

Brynn looked again at a solar system with five planets rather than four. It was difficult to not break at the knee, but she fortified herself. She stayed on her feet. She took a deep breath of the cool desert air. A stiff breeze closed in, moving down from the mountains, piling sand against the transport wheels.

"A grand tradition among the Owl Men," Brynn said, pulling her coat tighter. "As is resistance."

coda

Graffiti in the birth canal of the River Acheron:

> God moves in a windstorm
> He rode in a windstorm
> God moves like a spirit in the wind
> And he troubles everybody in their mind
>
> Author of Unknown Providence

about the author

Coy Hall lives in West Virginia with his wife, where he splits time as an author and a professor of history. As a historian, he studies medieval and early modern Europe. His books include *The Promise of Plague Wolves* and *Colossus with a Poison Tongue*.

Find out more at coyhall.com and scythianwolf.com.

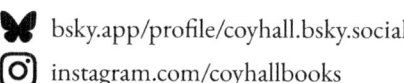 bsky.app/profile/coyhall.bsky.social
instagram.com/coyhallbooks

acknowledgments

My gratitude and thanks to the following authors and artists for their guidance, support, and friendship:

Elford Alley
Michael August
Garth Arizona
C.W. Blackwell
Brian Bowyer
Damien Casey
Laura Cathcart
Stephanie Ellis
Wayne Fenlon
Kenneth Gray
Adam Hulse
Sarah J. Huntington
Derek Hutchins
Zakariah Johnson
Robert Kluver
D.S. LaLonde
Mitchell Lüthi
Regan MacArthur
Remo Macartney
Catherine McCarthy
Ronald McGillvray
Alexander Michael
Joe Nelson
Jennifer Ostopovich

T.C. Parker
Anthony Perconti
M.E. Proctor
Mark Robinson
S.J. Shank
Michael Shotter
Matt Spencer
Patrick Stanley
Jonathan Tripp
Marek Z. Turner
Frank Vatel
Alan R. Warren
Robert Weaver
Ilyn Welch
Wayne Zervis

Printed in Great Britain
by Amazon